Even as he sang, Jon-Tom wondered just what it was he was conjuring. A small warship, perhaps, or even a craft like the merchant-magician's own, only larger and more powerful.

A great roaring sounded in his ears. He smiled to himself, expecting to see salamanders larger and stronger than the magician's own materialize out of the mist. Instead, out of the swirling storm of lavender and white emerged...a swirling storm. Of a sort.

It was round, and restrained by a large wire basket, and though he had never been to the part of the world from whence it came, he recognized it nonetheless. The four-thousand horsepower Pratt and Whitney stank of leaky gaskets and grungy oil. A sign, hand-lettered in red on wood buried beneath a thousand aging coats of yellow enamel was affixed with frayed electrical tape to the top of the cage.

MAMA LEROY'S EVERGLADES TOURS
SEE! SEE! SEE!
MAN-EATING GATORS! KILLER SNAKES!
GIANT LEECHES!
COFFEE AND SANDWICHES PROVIDED

Jon-Tom made a dive for the controls...

BOOKS BY ALAN DEAN FOSTER

The I Inside
Krull
The Man Who Used the Universe
Pale Rider
Shadowkeep
Starman
Cyber Way
Glory Lane
The Damned Trilogy
Flinx of the Commonwealth
Codgerspace
Midworld

THE SPELLSINGER SERIES:

Spellsinger*
The Hour of the Gate*
The Day of the Dissonance*
The Moment of the Magician*
The Paths of the Perambulator*
The Time of the Transference*
Son of Spellsinger*

*Published by
WARNER BOOKS

ALAN DEAN FOSTER

CHORUS SKATING

WARNER BOOKS

A Time Warner Company

WARNER BOOKS EDITION

Cover design by Don Puckey
Cover illustration by Tim Hildebrandt
Hand lettering by David Gatti

Warner Books, Inc.
1271 Avenue of the Americas
New York, NY 10020

A Time Warner Company

Printed in the United States of America

First Printing: October, 1994

10 9 8 7 6 5 4 3 2 1

For Vaughne Hansen,
Who works very hard to make the
work of others easier....
Including mine.
With thanks....

CHAPTER 1

IT STARTED IN L'BOR. OR PERHAPS IT WAS LYNCHBANY. IN any case the occurrence certainly was singular as opposed to simultaneous. Which is to say there was only one of whatever it was. It shifted from place to place, revealing itself with distinction and imprinting itself on the memories of all who encountered it. Trailing bemused contentment, it wandered aimlessly through the Bellwoods, leaving those whose path it momentarily crossed smiling to themselves without quite knowing why.

As benign phenomena don't have quite the same impact or occasion quite as much gossip as the kind that bring death and destruction, word of the manifestation traveled slowly at best. Since it caused no trouble, no one bothered to follow up tales of its appearance, to seek explanation or deeper meaning. At best it was a momentary source of curiosity and conversation to those who crossed its path—a brief diversion from the daily grind. Something to chat about when comfortably resnuggled back in one's house or cave or lair or den.

Flagyr the badger and his friend Invez the serval were neither working nor engaged in any sort of activity that might be called serious when they happened upon the phenomenon. Or rather, when it happened upon them.

In point of fact they were seated side by side upon a grassy shore bordering one of the most modest tributaries of the River Tailaroam, on a bright and altogether salubrious summer morning. Their fishing poles were cocked over the water in the time-honored fashion of fisherfolk everywhere. This undertaking they were pursuing with single-minded dedication and unusual forethought, which is to say that they actually had put bait on their lines.

Flagyr was leaning back against an obliging tree, the large, floppy-brimmed hat he favored on warm mornings tipped down to cover most of his face. He lay with paws folded across his chest and one leg over the other, his brown canvas shorts bunched up at the knee.

In an astonishing display of activity, Invez actually had one hand wrapped loosely around the shaft of his pole, easing it back and forth so that the line would bob in the placid water. One eye focused on the glassy surface while its companion slumbered.

This late in the morning few fish were jumping. Depending on one's point of view, this made it either the worst or best of times to be out fishing. The intent of such an expedition wasn't to actually catch fish. That was merely the time-honored excuse fisherfolk employed for going fishing. Contrary to what some might think, the process of fishing was not a means to an end. It *was* the end.

Save for the nearby canvas hamper which contained food and drink, they were quite alone. The serval took a lazy swat at a bee determined to mistake a tall, pointed ear for a place in which to set up housekeeping. Agitated, the insect fled, only to have its place in the aural spectrum taken by something which caused Invez to blink and sit up slightly.

"Hear that?"

The badger didn't bother to push back his hat and look up. "I hear it. Be something on the road."

Invez frowned, his long whiskers dipping. The road which roughly paralleled the course of the tributary lay some way back through the woods, and this new sound rather closer.

"I don't think so. There it is again!" He sat up straighter, forgetting his pole and allowing the end to dip into the stream. Both eyes were open now.

"Whatever it is, it's pretty," noted Flagyr, listening. His sole physical response was to shift his legs, crossing the left over the right. He hoped that was the sum of physical activity which would immediately be required of him, unless some fish was so impolite as to actually take his bait. "But back on the road, I think. Has to be."

"Some kind of music," Invez declared. "I don't recognize the instruments involved."

Forced to cogitate, the distracted badger let out a resigned sigh and for the first time concentrated on listening with something more than general indifference.

"Carillon flutes," he finally proclaimed. "With accompanying chimes. More than one instrument, certainly."

"Agreed." Invez was staring to his left. "But it doesn't look like any of those."

Beneath the cool shadow of the wide-brimmed hat, Flagyr frowned. "Look? You can see who is playing?"

"That's just it. I can't see who's playing. I can't see anyone at all."

"Then *what* are you seeing?"

"The music," Invez told him. "I've never actually seen music before."

"What *are* you talking about?" The badger struggled to sit up.

"Careful," Invez warned him. "It's very close now and you'll bump right into it."

"Urrr . . . bump into *what*?" The glare off the river caused the thoroughly irritated Flagyr to blink as his eyes sought to readjust.

"I told you: the music."

And just as Invez said, there it was. Flagyr found himself gaping at the glistening, translucent, slightly reflective armful of music. It hovered lazily in the warm air of morning not an arm's length from his face. Each time it resounded, flecks of golden iridescence exploded softly in midair, only to vanish as the music faded, like mist rising off a lake on a frosty morning. As the badger gawked, the pinkish cloud chimed several times in succession.

Invez was right. Not only was no performer present, neither was there any sign of an instrument. Instead, there was only the music itself, pure and shimmering, pealing insistently before their astonished faces. Whether it consisted of motes or notes, he couldn't truly tell.

Though they had no way of knowing it, the lyrical encounter had been repeated many times previously, in L'bor, Lynchbany, and elsewhere. Not everyone actually saw the music; some only heard it. But unlike many who had experienced the encounter before, the badger knew enough to propound a possible source.

"There's a wizard working around here somewhere," he declared decisively. Gently he reached toward the drifting notes.

Like glittering gnats they swirled ebulliently around his probing forefinger, singing softly. Then they backed off, the cloud cluster re-forming, to regard him with a querulous arpeggio.

The serval was on his feet, peering into the woods. "I don't see anyone."

"A practical joke," murmured Flagyr. "Perhaps a practice practical joke. Wizards!" he snorted, settling back down against his tree.

"It seems harmless enough." Invez took a couple of steps toward the notes, pausing when they swirled around him in an eager allegro. After a moment they darted away.

"The tempo and volume changes," he remarked, "but it's always the same tune. It's an odd sort of music. I don't recognize it. I wish I'd had some musical training."

"I've had a little." Flagyr did not look up.

Invez eyed his friend in surprise. "You never mentioned this."

"I'm not what you'd call a professional," the badger mumbled. "Not one, am I, to brag about something I'm not very good at." He gestured up at the soft singing. "I'd wager there's something wrong with that series of notes, and I don't mean from a musical standpoint."

"Wrong?" The serval's whiskers twitched.

The badger squinted up at the jittering notes. "It sounds unresolved, like something's missing. Both at the start and at the conclusion. It's not like a complete composition but more like a piece of one, cast off like a bad tooth." He shrugged. "But then, what do I know? Is there anything else?"

Invez peered up and down the stream. "These are the only notes I see."

"An unresolved, incomplete musical statement." Flagyr was quite sure of himself. "And too dissonant by half for my taste."

As if in response, the music concluded a complete and decidedly mournful restatement of its principal theme before it began to drift away, pacing itself to the flow of the stream. Invez followed until it vanished, still chiming softly to itself, into the woods.

"I had the distinct impression that it was looking for something," Flagyr added from somewhere beneath his hat.

Invez resumed his seat and fiddled with his pole. "What could that be? What would a piece of music be looking for?"

"How should I know?" The badger snuffled softly. "The rest of itself, I should imagine. If I were a part of a song or a symphony, I wouldn't want to go through the rest of eternity incomplete. I'd think that would invalidate my existence."

"Actually I never thought much about it," Invez murmured.

Flagyr tugged his hat fully down over his face, slid lower against the smooth-barked tree, and crossed his arms across his broad chest, wrinkling his brown vest. "I doubt anyone ever has. You're right about one thing, though."

"What's that?" The serval snuggled himself into the grass.

"The underlying melody was a nice one."

"I wonder," Invez mused. "If the tone had been more somber, would it have appeared darker? Does attitude affect the appearance of music?"

"What I think is that I've expended far too much thinking on it already." With that the badger rolled over and turned away from his loquacious friend. Invez started to comment further, hesitated, then shrugged and contented himself with concentrating on the tip of his pole.

By no means were that particular serval and that persnickety badger the only ones out fishing on that specific morning. A yawn and a stretch downstream, on the west bank of the larger concourse into which the tributary flowed, two friends of long standing were similarly engaged in the time-honored sport of killing time by attempting to catch fish.

One was human, tall and limber. He wore short pants and a favorite old shirt that was now badly weathered and torn. The long hair which fell to his shoulders was thinning conspicuously in front and his skin had been browned by long years of exposure to the sun. The wooden shaft of his fishing gear was firmly jammed into the earth and braced with several rocks, while the line drifted amiably downstream with the current.

He lay flat on his back, hands behind his head. The bank on which he reclined was sloped just enough toward the water to enable him to occasionally tilt his head up and study the moving stream.

On his left, exhibiting a degree of repose the most relaxed human could never have matched, was a very large otter. He was similarly attired save for the feathered cap that rested rakishly on his head. In his utter lack of activity he was being perfectly otterish, individuals of the species to which he belonged seeming to exist always in a state of either consummate immobility or uncontrolled frenzy.

At the moment the subatomic particles which comprised the essence of his form seemed to have ceased all movement. He was content to treat his pole and the water with equal disdain. Quicker than any fish, he could have acquired a full meal simply by leaping into the river and nosing about for ten minutes. But that would have been hunting as much as angling. In contrast, pole fishing required a degree of resignation and commitment.

Also, this way one didn't have to move very much.

"You know," Jon-Tom observed conversationally, as he crossed his bare legs, "I'm really proud of Buncan. Sure

Talea and I were mad at him for running off like that with your kids, but they got back alive and in one piece, and you have to admit he made his point. If he wants to be a spellsinger that badly, I'm sure he'll find some way to make a success of it."

Mudge glanced across at his friend, peering out from beneath the brim of his feathered cap. "Oi, 'ow's the little bugger doin' at Sorcerer's Vocational?"

"I'm afraid his grades aren't the best," Jon-Tom confessed, "but the instructors praise his enthusiasm. They still can't do anything about his voice, but his fingering just keeps getting better and better. Sadly, he also seems subject to the same difficulties that used to plague me. Which is to say that his musical inventions don't always result in what he's trying to magick."

With an agile digit the otter instigated a lazy exploration of one black nostril. "What do you mean, 'used to'?"

Jon-Tom ignored the obligatory dig. "How are Nocter and Squill doing? Buncan doesn't tell us a lot about his friends."

The otter chirped thoughtfully. "Doin' the opposite o' your boy, I fears. They sing like angels an' play like drunks. Seems we may be destined, mate, to 'ave sired a spellsingin' trio that can never split up. That is, unless me blessed offspring get a tickle up their butts an' decide to 'ave a go at somethin' else. You know 'ow 'ard it is for any otter to commit to anythin' for more than 'alf an 'our."

Jon-Tom was nodding at Mudge's line. "I think you may have a nibble there."

"Might I?" The otter considered his twitching pole. "Could be. Maybe I'll 'ave a go, if 'tis still there in a few minutes. Got to give the fish a sportin' chance, don't you know."

"I'll never understand why you just don't jump in and grab it."

"Like I said—wouldn't be sportin'." He leaned back, his spine as supple as a snake's, and contentedly regarded the cerulean sky. "At the moment I'd rather feed me soul than me belly."

Jon-Tom returned his attention to his own line. "I was thinking how fortunate we are in having understanding mates, who don't object when we want to get off by ourselves for a day or two."

The otter emitted a sardonic bark. "Understandin'? Mate, that's just so Weegee an' Talea can run off to town an' do wotever it is they do when we ain't around."

His companion grinned. "Actually, I think all females have secret access to an entirely separate universe, to which they commute freely when no males are about. Occasionally and by accident we get a brief glimpse of it. The consequent confusion gives rise to questions, but the replies always seem to consist of dress sizes or detailed descriptions of medical problems. Being both incomprehensible and boring, this inevitably results in the cessation of our inquiries by subtilely inducing in our unsuspecting minds a common medical condition best described as terminal bafflement."

"Funny—that's 'ow I've always thought of you, mate. Bobbin' through life in a sort o' drifting, permanent fog."

"An observation rendered inherently invalid by the limited mental powers of the individual making it."

"Oi! Did I ever claim to be otherwise? I ain't no bloomin' wizard nor spellsinger. All I ever wanted to be were a decent cutpurse an' thief who were good at 'is craft an' didn't 'urt 'is marks no more than were absolutely necessary." He jiggled the pole, the tip of which continued to dance.

"'Course, 'tis been some time since I engaged in any o' the controversial activities which define me chosen profession. Ain't fast enough anymore. I'd get caught too often to make a go of it. No, mate, this sedate family life suits me."

"Yeah, me too." Leaning back and resting his head on his arms, Jon-Tom stared at the water. "It's a good life."

Ten inconsequential minutes melted away, whereupon he looked to his left and inquired, "Does this mean that you're as bored as I am?"

"More so, mate. Infinitely more so." With a quick twist of his hips the otter sat up straight and gazed sharply at his friend. "Which ain't to say that I'm ready to take off with you on one o' your notoriously crack-brained an' life-threatenin' attempts to save the world. I got a family to look after now, I do."

"I wasn't *suggesting* anything," Jon-Tom demurred. "I was just saying that I was bored, and you agreed with me."

Mudge relaxed but remained wary. "That's right. Just bored. Not newly suicidal." Several more minutes went the way of their immediate predecessors. "You, uh, you ain't by chance been plannin' somethin', 'ave you?"

"Of course not."

"You're sure?"

"Certainly I'm sure."

"Glad to 'ear it." The otter resumed his resting position.

"You know," Jon-Tom avowed after more time had passed, "you're getting white around your muzzle."

The otter snorted at him even as he reached up reflexively to feel of his whiskery snout. "Wot d'you mean, white? Least I don't 'ave to worry about losing wot remainin' fur I've got."

Jon-Tom felt of his thinning forehead which, like a retreating glacier, had begun shrinking back several years ago. "What are you saying? Is it getting worse?"

"I don't figure it, mate. If it bothers you so much, why not just throw together a simple spellsong an' restore yourself to your favored condition o' juvenile hirsuteness?"

The spellsinger turned sullen. "Don't you think I've tried? There are plenty of songs that deal with hair, but neither traditional lyrics nor inventions of my own do any good. Receding hair seems to be one of the few things that's utterly resistant to sorcery. There's a lesson to be learned there, I'm sure, but for the life of me I can't figure out what it is.

"Though he decried the triviality of it, even Clothahump gave it a shot, and failed. It's a fine twist of fate in a cruel universe."

"One that don't trouble me," the otter remarked. "I'm quite

indifferent to such matters, I am." *White? His muzzle couldn't be turning* white!

"It's not like the old days," Jon-Tom sighed. "Responsibilities, respectability . . ."

"Watch your language, mate."

"Everything slows down . . . though there are days and nights when I feel as energetic as ever. It's all been traded for experience." He briefly considered time as a helix of semi-iridescent fish. "Anyway, life is peaceful and composed. No one's come galloping in search of Clothahump's help to assuage some great crisis or travail."

"Oi," agreed Mudge. "Life is rewardin' as it is. An' as for meself, I'm content, I am. Why, I wouldn't go off pursuin' some new trouble even if one 'opped up and bit me on the arse. I've already used up me nine lives, I 'ave."

"Those are cats. You're an otter."

"Don't interrupt, mate. Wot I'm sayin' is I ain't riskin' me life no more. Certainly not to 'elp bail you out o' difficulties an' situations you bloody well create for yourself."

"*You* bail *me* out? Now there's an amusing conceit. I can't remember how many times I've saved your fuzzy ass from your blind impetuousness, your rash decisions, and your reckless disregard for the safety of everyone and anyone unfortunate enough to be in your immediate vicinity. Not to mention your basic immorality and bad manners."

"Oi—there's a pungent observation," the otter retorted. "I suppose we ought always to 'ave relied instead on your never-fails precision spellsingin' to get us out o' the situations we kept findin' ourselves in?"

"It always did."

"More thanks to the goddess o' luck than the patron o' skill. You 'ave to confess the truth o' that, at least."

"I confess nothing of the sort. Maybe my spellsinging wasn't always perfect—"

"*Hah!*"

"—but it improved with time. I had to learn as I went

along. Out on the road there was no one to instruct me, including that stay-at-home Clothahump."

"One would think you'd 'ave got the point an' learned some sense." The otter's voice rose to a mocking squeal. "Stop the Plated Folk, destroy the evil magician, find the Per-ambulator! The danger these little jaunts brought to those around you didn't improve your judgment. You might as well 'ave been goin' shopping for a bushel o' bleedin' fish crack-ers!"

"Now there you're wrong," Jon-Tom insisted with becom-ing dignity. "I would never in my life eat a fish cracker."

" 'Umans 'ave no sense o' taste," Mudge grumbled. "Just like they 'ave no sense o' smell."

"And otters have no patience, or intellectual breadth. It's all physical with you."

Mudge smirked. "Now there I 'ave to admit you've got me, mate."

The spellsinger's expression turned weary. Any attempt to engage in an extended conversation with an otter was doomed to chaos. "Are you going to do anything with that poor fish on your line or are you just going to let it continue to writhe in torment?"

"Are you proposin' a choice?"

Exasperated, Jon-Tom reached over and grabbed the pole, but by then whatever had been on the hook had freed itself.

"You see? Otters never follow through to a conclusion anything they start. It's a good thing I was always around to look after you."

"Oi, an' 'ow many scars and bruises fewer would I be sportin' if you 'adn't 'looked after' me quite so closely?"

Jon-Tom busied himself rebaiting the pole. "You'd proba-bly be dead. Hung by the authorities, or run through by some outraged husband."

"Nah. They'd never have caught me." The otter snuggled back against the warm earth. Only after Jon-Tom had returned his pole did he comment casually, "Even if somethin' interestin' were to manifest itself, an' even if I were crazy enough to inquire after the details, I wouldn't dare bother even thinkin' about pursuin' the matter further."

"Why not?" Jon-Tom wondered aloud. "What are you afraid of? Nefarious sorcerers, degenerate dragons, the maleficent spirits of the Underworld?"

"You mean you don't know?" The otter turned to regard his friend. "You know wot kind o' temper Weegee 'as. If I were to so much as mention the possibility o' 'eadin' off for somewheres, she'd see me dismembered faster than any six-armed demon."

Jon-Tom shook his head sadly. "Is this the same Mudge I've known all these years? The Mudge I knew who was ready on a moment's notice to join in a fight or a quest."

"A brawl, aye. As for all those quests, I weren't never ready for none o' them. You just sort o' dragged me along before I knew wot were 'appenin' to me."

Jon-Tom ignored the comment as he continued wistfully. "That Mudge had a limitless capacity for living and loving, for experiencing new things and embarking on grand adventures. Whatever happened to him?"

" 'Ere now," protested the otter, sitting up again. "I 'aven't changed that much, I ain't. I'm just sayin' that a mate an' a 'ome an' a pair o' teenagers can wear anyone down. The more so if they're otters. You think Buncan wearies you? You ought to try dealin' with Nocter an' Squill for a two-month!" He fingered his fishing pole. "Not that it matters. As you say, there's nothin' wot needs doin'. We exist in a state o' contented bliss."

"Or enervation," Jon-Tom muttered.

"I don't know wot that means, but I think there's a lot o' it goin' around." His expression brightened. "With Weegee an' Talea off somewhere, we could go into Lynchbany an' break up a bar, or somethin'."

"A bar fight." Jon-Tom was saddened. "Mudge and Jon-Tom, the great adventurer and famed spellsinger, reduced to contemplating the entertainment value of an ordinary public tiff. We, who have explored much of the known world and a fair portion of the unknown, who have dealt with unimaginable dangers and overcome impossible obstacles, are we come to this? No thanks."

"Sorry. It were the best I could come up with on short notice, mate." Mudge was a bit taken aback by the emotional intensity of his friend's reaction. "Actually, I only thought o' it for you. I ain't sure 'ow much 'elp I'd be. Me back's been botherin' me for a bit now, an' when an otter's back is out, 'e's in serious 'urt, 'e is. See, we're *all* back."

Jon-Tom looked surprised. "You haven't said anything about your back before."

"Would you?"

"No. No, I suppose not. It's just that all this *quiet* is getting to me, what with Talea off with Weegee and the kids away at school. Even business is slow."

Mudge fumbled in his fishing kit for his glasses. "Did I ever read you that last letter, mate?"

Jon-Tom looked resigned. "You mean the one you carry around with you and drag out every chance you get? The one that tells how Nocter and Squill are constantly getting into fights, breaking things, fomenting trouble, and generally raising hell?"

The otter straightened his glasses. "Oi, that's the one. Great kids, eh?"

"Yes, they are," Jon-Tom admitted, squeezing out a smile.

"Something we agree on," a new voice interjected.

The two fishers sat up and turned sharply to their right.

"Talea?" Jon-Tom frowned. "I thought you and Weegee were off to shop in Lynchbany." She looked fantastic, he had to admit. Her figure had ripened eloquently from their first memorable encounter years ago, when she'd been inclined to cut his head off instead of accept compliments. Nothing like years of being on the run to get one in shape for a lifetime.

"Weegee and I are just now off to L'bor, dear, with several of the other ladies of the river. It's a journey of several days, not just an afternoon."

Jon-Tom smacked himself mentally. "That's right. You told me all about your plans last week. I'd just forgotten. I seem to forget a lot anymore."

She advanced to bestow an affectionate kiss on his forehead. "Don't be too hard on yourself, dear. You're a long way from the onset of senility."

"Thanks for the compliment," he replied dryly.

She turned to leave. "Please try to look after things, and stay out of the kitchen as much as possible. I've heard you verbally disparaging the dishes on more than one occasion, and you know how sensitive they are. Make sure any visitors use the cleaning spell at the door, and don't forget to put out the rat."

"I can take care of my own home," he assured her, a little stiffly.

"I know you can, dear, when you pay attention. But sometimes your mind wanders and you muddle your spells. Remember the last time the disposal had cavities and you backed up garbage all over the floor while trying to fill them?"

"So I forgot to include the incantation for calcium." He glared over at Mudge, who by dint of great effort was battling to suppress a smile.

Dutifully he wished his wife a good journey and they embraced. Only after she was well on her way did he carefully remove his line from the water, secure the hook, and proceed to chase the otter around the nearest tree. As always, he was unable to catch him. The passage of time had slowed the otter some, but it had been no kinder to his human companion.

CHAPTER 2

THERE WERE ONLY THREE SPRITES IN THE LIVING ROOM, BUT they were making the most of it. One transcribed ellipses atop the couch, another busied itself beneath the coffee table, while the third chose to dangle from the ceiling on suction-cup-shod feet.

Things were worse in the master bedroom, which found itself beset by a horde of tiny imps ranging in hue from a flat vinyl white to a chocolately beige. They were a blur of activity, at times appearing organized, at others chaotic. This resulted in a tendency to run into each other at high speed, with fractious and occasionally messy results. Many were the minuscle arguments over who had the right of way through the appropriate hermetic paths.

Angry and frustrated, Jon-Tom strode through the house trying to clean and keep order as best he could. He was in unusually bad temper and even the wondrous duar sounded off-key. His lyrics lacked inspiration and the result was a household more afflicted by the nether regions than usual. The bathroom was proving particularly difficult to exorcise, and when he broke an entire bottle of throat gargoyle he was forced to retire to his study and try to find some adequate disinfecting terminology. His failures pained his pride, and he was grateful there was no one around to witness his distress.

Gradually he managed to wrestle the tree house back into shape. Demons and imps hissed and expectorated and sputtered and (when no one was looking) spat fire at one another.

Only after Jon-Tom's music banished the last of them could he begin the tedious task of restoring the singed wallpaper.

Housework, he decided, was unexpectedly magic-intensive.

Loud clunks sounded from the vicinity of the laundry room. Sighing deeply, he headed in that direction while strumming a few uninspired bars on the duar. Almost immediately, a pale lavender sprite drifted out on membranous wins. Its features were petite and flat.

"Oh, Master," it piped, "the imps charged with the care of the dry cleaning have formed a ruckus."

"Why? All I asked was that they clean and de-spot half a dozen coats. A simple enough task."

"I know that, Master. Of course, if we sprites were in charge, things would be different."

"Sprites don't manipulate heat as well as imps. Get out of my way." He brushed the aggrieved sprite aside.

There were four of them—bloated of form, huge of mouth, warty of face. None stood taller than his waist. They were arguing vociferously. A pair of coats hung from a rack, neatly pressed and encased in a gellike substance that was neither plastic nor cellophane.

"What's the problem?"

Startled, the nearest imp belched, and Talea's good ruby dress vest popped out of its nose. The garment was only half clean, and a prominent spot was visible near the waistline. Sheepishly, the imp passed the vest to its companion, who expeditiously regurgitated a hangar while fumbling with the article of clothing.

"It's their fault," the hangar-puker insisted, gesturing at the pair seated across from him. "They're deliberately slowing things down."

"We're just being prudent," insisted one of the accused. "Too much heat will ruin the fabric. *Anybody* should know that."

"You can overpress." His sneering neighbor displayed chunky, flat molars in a wide, slightly sulfurous mouth.

Definitely need to put a deodorizing spell to work in here, Jon-Tom decided as he sniffed the air. "The parameters of the incantation demand that you work together. I want no more delays, and no more arguing." With that he turned and stalked out of the laundry room, ignoring the griping that filled the air behind him. Heat imps were notoriously contumacious . . . but they did excellent laundry.

Is it for this, he told himself, *that I have mastered the great powers and studied the old books? I am Jonathan Thomas Meriweather, the most proficient spellsinger this world or any other has ever seen! Twenty years I've toiled perfecting my skills and practicing my craft . . . the better to clean house and do laundry?*

He shook the duar and bellowed a challenge. All about the tree, throughout its dimensionally expanded rooms and nooks, demons and sprites and imps and spirits looked up out of things that were not eyes and listened through orifices that were not ears.

"Begone!" he cried. "I dismiss you all! I free you from your obligations. Leave this place, leave this home, and leave me!"

Something that was all long rubbery arms put aside a broom and hissed sibilantly. "About time! This is no work for an honest, self-respecting nightmare." Whereupon it promptly imploded and disappeared.

With moans and groans and hisses and howls and cries and sobs and wails of relief, they vanished: down drains, up chimneys, out windows, and through pores in the wood. One even used, somewhat disdainfully, the front door, but Jon-Tom chose not to chastise it for this breach of thaumaturgic protocol. He was too tired and too frustrated. Alone once more, he slumped into a partly dusted kitchen chair.

Well, perhaps not quite alone.

"Excuse me."

Jon-Tom wiped perspiration from his forehead. "What?"

"Excuse me, Master."

Turning, Jon-Tom found himself confronted by a four-foot-tall bright blue demon. It wore sandals of carved azurite and a dark turquoise vest. A most competent demon, he thought, for it was no easy task to weave turquoise. He slumped back in the chair.

"I thought I dismissed all of you. Well, what is it?"

A distinctly mournful cast colored the apparition's reply. "Master, don't you recognize me?"

Jon-Tom frowned uncertainly. "Recognize you? I see so many spirits and shades in my work."

"I'm Fugwheez, Master." Pointed, fringe-lined ears flicked rhythmically as the ugly yet homely face gazed anxiously at the man in the chair.

"Fugwheez? Sorry, doesn't ring any bells."

"You conjured me some four years ago, Master. To shellac the dining room table?" His manner was demonically earnest.

"Dining room table." A flicker of recognition creased Jon-Tom's face. "Oh, yeah, I remember. The job description was pretty specific. According to the info Clothahump gave me, you were the only one who could vomit varnish. Talea wasn't crazy about the idea at the time, but she was delighted with the results."

"Wives generally are not pleased with most anything demons can do," Fugwheez avowed. "How's the table holding up, by the way? I didn't come in through the dining room." He gestured apologetically at the kitchen door. "The linoleum has occupied all my time since coalescence."

"The table's fine. Shines like marble."

Fugwheez smiled, revealing contented fangs. "There, you see?"

Jon-Tom's brows contracted. "This is all very pleasant and domestic, but it doesn't explain why you're still here."

"Ordinarily we inhabitants of the Nether Regions resent being dragged out of a cold bath or away from our regular work to attend to the requests of mortal meddling mystics, but you struck me years ago as a pretty decent sort, for a mortal being. You're understanding instead of demanding, and willing to allow for cross-Aether mistakes. None of this 'Do that, I order you!' and 'Do this, I demand it!' rubbish.

"I found myself caught up in the general housecleaning crew you conjured, but it didn't bother me because I recalled your tolerance. We're not supposed to show sympathy for mortals—actually we're suppose to rend and cleave them if the opportunity presents itself—but you're different, and I hate to see you moping about like this. Extended moping's part of a Grump's job description, not yours, Master Meriweather."

"See me like what?" Jon-Tom didn't meet the demon's dark cobalt eyes.

"I think you know. Look at yourself, Master. Look at what you're doing with your life and your unique skills. Frittering away your talents on mundanities like housecleaning."

"Don't you think I'm aware of the irony?" Jon-Tom grumbled. "But what can I do about it?"

"You could start by first losing that apron," Fugwheez suggested. "It's unsuitable to your position."

Jon-Tom hesitated, knowing that he who takes advice from demons risks eternal damnation and destruction.

On the other hand, it was only an apron.

Rising, he untied it and laid it carefully aside.

"That's much better." Fugwheez looked satisfied. "Second, I think that your immortal soul may be in danger."

"I beg your pardon? Are you saying that I am being stalked by hostile forces? By some lingering ancient evil I may have accidentally offended in my travels? By some wicked and as yet unsuspected nefarious force?"

"No, no." The demon gestured soothingly, his long blue fingernails glistening wetly in the kitchen light. "Nothing like that."

"Oh," murmured Jon-Tom, sounding unaccountably disappointed.

"It's the torment you're inflicting on yourself that has me concerned. Can't you see your own unhappiness? If someone as inherently insensitive as a demon can sense it, surely you can't be oblivious to your own emotional condition."

"I know I'm not a bundle of good cheer here lately," Jon-Tom admitted. "I think it's because I'm not doing what I want. In fact, I'm not doing much of anything. But what can I do about it when there's nothing that needs doing? The world is at present an ordered and placid place. I can't invent a crisis."

The demon hopped up on the kitchen counter across from Jon-Tom and planted his hairy legs and backside on the edge of the tile. With extraordinary presumption for a conjured fiend, he put a comradely arm around the spellsinger's shoulders. Jon-Tom didn't shrug it off.

"You can get off this track and out of this rut if you want to, Master Meriweather." With his free hand he gestured at the kitchen. "Or are you going to spend the rest of your life attending to such as this? Spellsinging brooms and feather dusters?"

Jon-Tom scrutinized the grotesque but concerned face. "I've told you. There's nothing going on that requires my attention."

"A resourceful mortal has access to situations and circumstances that are denied even to such as myself," Fugwheez reminded him. "If you persist in rationalizing your present situation, you will indeed end up like the great mass of humans: content on the outside, desperate on the inside. I know. I've consumed quite a lot of human desperation." A long clawed finger tapped the center of Jon-Tom's chest. "It's usually a small knot right about here, though it varies in size from individual to individual. Nourishing but rather bland, not unlike enriched white bread. Don't you know that most men lead lives of quiet desperation?"

"That's from *Walden*, isn't it?"

The demon nodded. "Thoreau's quite popular in the Nether Regions. All that talk about civil disobedience, you know. Anarchy has a distinctive flavor."

"Why this unnatural concern for me?" Jon-Tom watched the blue demon intently.

"I told you: you're different. Also, we find your antics entertaining, and because of the nature of your work, it's likely that someday one of us will have the opportunity to disembowel and consume you. Nothing personal, I assure you. But sweet tastes better than bitter."

"So what this all comes down to is not altruism or concern for my welfare, but food?"

The demon replied innocently, "Doesn't everything?"

"I told you, I can't just go out and manufacture a crisis."

"Of course not. That's my job. But surely the great spellsinger Jonathan Thomas Meriweather can think of something more suitable to engage his talent than defrosting the freezer and fluffing the sheets on his bed." Fugwheez leaped ceilingward and hung dangling by one arm from the light fixture, looking like the ugliest and bluest of all apes.

"Maybe. . . ." Jon-Tom let his fingers drift across the duar's strings. The sound they produced in the kitchen was melancholy yet hopeful. "Maybe I haven't been trying hard enough. Maybe it's time I stopped waiting for something to happen and went looking for it."

"That's it!" Fugwheez cheered him on. "Be active, not reactive." He skittered across the ceiling, irritating the glowspells. "And the next time you need something varnished, don't hesitate to call on me. All I ask in return is that when you finally make a fatal slip, I get the first bite of your brains. I'm sure the flavor will be delicate and exceptionally sweet."

"If that circumstance arises, I'll try and make sure that you're first in line," Jon-Tom assured him dryly.

"Then I bid you a fond farewell, Master Meriweather." The fiend was becoming a blue vapor.

"Good-bye, Fugwheez. And . . . thank you."

"Don't mention it," the vapor told him. "Therapy's a hobby of mine. You'd be surprised how many demons and imps are deeply neurotic." With that he swirled in upon himself and, like a puff of smoke, vanished into the nearest light fixture. The air in the kitchen turned pale blue for just an

instant as the demon tested the protective parameters surrounding Jon-Tom. There sounded a mildly disappointed cry
of "Darn!" when these held firm, and then the interior illumination came back on clean and white. Fugwheez was gone.

And so was Jon-Tom—out the door, down the hall, and
through the main entrance to the tree. Duar bouncing gently
against his back, he strode determinedly away from his home
and toward the riverbank. Sunlight sparkled on his iridescent
vest. There was a spring to his step that had been missing for
some time, and it wasn't due to the presence in his boots of
coiled steel conjured by some mystic metallurgical spell.

"Mudge? Mudge, get up!" He pounded forcefully on the
door set flush with the smooth riverbank. When no reply was
forthcoming from within, he stepped back and began to sing.
Moments later he heard the internal latch click.

The door swung open and he stepped through, having to
bend low to clear the lintel. Designed to accommodate adult
otters, it was a good two feet lower than he would have found
comfortable.

The ceilings were higher, but he still had to walk bent over
as he made his way deeper into the riverbank, carefully
avoiding any fixtures attached to the ceiling. The light was
dim and he squinted as he advanced.

"Mudge? Mudge!" There was no sign of the otter in the
kitchen, with its little round windows that looked out over the
river and its rough-hewn, close-to-the-floor furniture. Nor
was the otter in the den, or the front hall.

Jon-Tom found him sprawled like a loosely scrawled letter
S in the middle of the rumpled master bed. The room showed
signs of Weegee's efficient touch as well as Mudge's more
anarchic tastes.

"Mudge, get up."

"Mphm, wot . . . ?" Blinking back sleep, the otter rolled
over, whiskers twitching. A hand-crocheted sleeping cap covered half his face. "Wot are you doin' 'ere, mate? I were
'avin' a sound sleep an' a loverly dream."

Jon-Tom made a face and indicated the single window

through which sunlight was pouring. "It's the middle of the day."

"Middle . . ." The otter squinted sleepily at a bedstand. "Wot time is it, exactly?"

"Seven-thirty. Get up."

"Seven-thirty! In the *mornin'*?" Grumbling, he sort of oozed out of the bed. "Wot is it with you 'umans an' your peculiar affection for sunlight?"

"Come on, move your tail," Jon-Tom demanded impatiently.

"All right, all right. Don't get your privates in an uproar." Mudge rubbed at his slightly bloodshot eyes as he straightened. "What's the bloody emergency?"

Jon-Tom didn't bother searching for a chair, knowing that none of the furniture in the riverside home was big enough to accommodate his lanky form. Instead, he sat down very carefully on the end of the bed. There was no frame, the mattress resting directly on a pad on the floor.

"Mudge, you're as bored as I am. You admitted as much yesterday."

The otter arched his back and stretched, which is to say he nearly stuck his head through his legs. It was an exhibition of spinal acrobatics few other creatures could have duplicated. Jon-Tom's back twitched in sympathy.

"You jostled me out o' a sound sleep to remind me o' that?"

"I was cleaning house this morning as per Talea's instructions and . . . look, Mudge." As he sidled closer on the bed, the otter eyed his friend warily. "We've been moping around doing nothing, or virtually nothing, for years. Then Buncan and Nocter and Squill ran off and had their little adventure."

"Little adventure?" Mudge barked sharply. "They ought to 'ave been dead 'alf a dozen times over, the bleedin' disrespectful rebellious adolescent little sods!"

"I know," Jon-Tom agreed soothingly, "but they accomplished what they set out to do and made it back in one piece. You heard their story. Didn't it excite you, make you want to get back out there and see what the distant corners of the world are made of?"

"They're made o' dirt, mate."

"You know what I mean."

"Oi, that I do." The otter yawned, showing sharp teeth, and lazily scratched his crotch. "I'm afraid I've become too good friends with me bed, 'ere. Besides, there ain't nothin' needin' your unsolicited attention. An' you know wot *I* mean."

"Maybe nothing major," Jon-Tom admitted, "but Clothahump is so busy, and he is getting on in years. It's possible he can't keep track of everything. There might be a problem or two he's overlooked."

"'Ow old is the 'ard-shelled old fossil fart these days anyway?" Mudge wondered aloud. "Three 'undred? Four 'undred? Not that you can tell any difference by lookin' at 'im. Turtles don't age much. Not only that, but 'is bloomin' back never seems to give 'im no trouble. It ain't fair."

"He has to lug that shell around all day," Jon-Tom reminded his friend. "That's not fair, either. I'm going to ask him to feel for anything that might be out of balance. I'm sick of sitting around, helping with the housework and spellsinging away common childhood diseases and household infestations. I'm tired of working parties and graduations. I want the old thrill back, Mudge!"

The otter looked thoughtful. "You mean the thrill of wonderin' whether we were goin' to be crushed like bugs or 'ave our throats slit or be ceremonially torn limb from limb? That sort o' thrill? I says, good luck to you in your reminiscin', mate."

"You don't mean that, Mudge. You're as bored as I am."

"Sure I am. I'm bleedin' bored out o' me wits, mate! But there's kinds o' excitement that don't require riskin' life an' limb to experience."

"Just a small thing, Mudge," Jon-Tom pleaded. "Something that wouldn't require much traveling, and no real danger. Just a little change of pace, of locale, of venue."

"Wot about Talea the thrice-beloved?"

"I'll leave her a note. She'll understand."

"Oh, sure she will. A note. I'll invent one for Weegee, too. ' 'Bye, darlin'. Gone off adventurin'. Back before the end o' next year. Don't wait up.' Oh, she'll love that, she will."

"She'll cope." Jon-Tom exuded false confidence. "They both will. It's not like we haven't gone off before."

"Think, mate. It's been a while. A goodly while. I think where that kind o' waitin' is concerned, our spouses might be out o' practice."

"I don't have any choice in this, Mudge," Jon-Tom explained earnestly. "It's too much part and partial of who I am. Of what I am. And you can't deny that you're having the same feelings." He rose from the low bed. "Come on."

"Come on?" The otter licked his lips. "Come on where, mate? 'Tis seven-thirty in the morn."

"Seven forty-two." Jon-Tom paused at the bedroom door. "To see Clothahump, of course. Surely there's something happening somewhere. Some lesser, casual causal catastrophe just waiting to be put right with a spellsong or two."

"Some tiny blade just waitin' to slip between me ribs," the otter groused. "I can see you ain't goin' to leave me be, so give me a minim to dress an' I'll sacrifice a perfectly good sleep-in to humor you." He shook a short finger at his much taller friend. "But I'm warnin' you, mate. I ain't skippin' away with some dumb smile on me face to watch you put life an' limb in mortal danger to satisfy some 'idden mindless cravin'. Especially not *me* life an' limb."

"Nothing dangerous, Mudge. I promise. I have a wife and child to think of, too."

"Oi. Now if you only 'ad a brain to go with 'em." The otter cursed volubly as he fought to step into a pair of recalcitrant shorts.

CHAPTER 3

THE GRAND OLD OAK STILL SQUATTED SERENE AND ETERNAL in the middle of the glade. Twisted and gnarled, prodigious roots spread out from the base of the thick trunk to plunge forcefully into the ground, as if seeking to grip the very center of the Earth. The tree appeared stolid and immovable, unaffected by time or the forces of nature.

Not unlike its occupant, Jon-Tom reflected as he and Mudge approached across the grass. Like his own home, the tree's interior was far more spacious than seemed possible, the result of a most excellent dimension-expanding spell the old wizard had perfected in his youth.

A terse cobblestone walkway led to the doorway. Jon-Tom halted before the entrance and reached for the button that protruded from the bark.

" 'Ang on a minim, mate." Mudge pointed. "Wot's that?"

"That's right—you haven't been here in a while, have you? It's a concept from my own world. I described it to Clothahump and I guess he was kind of taken with the notion. It's called a doorbell. More efficient than knocking. I wasn't sure he could make one function here." He jabbed the white button with a forefinger.

From deep within the tree a choir of trumpets blared sonorously, ringing out an impressive fanfare. Simultaneously, a septet of exquisite birds-of-paradise materialized to proclaim a greeting in what sounded to Jon-Tom's ears vaguely like avian Latin. As the resounding trumpets faded, the seven birds vanished, to be replaced by a pair of black bantam-sized storm clouds flanking the portal. Thunder pealed across the cobblestones as miniature lightning bolts struck and illuminated the nameplate fastened to the middle of the door.

The declaratory nimbuses mellowed and turned white, whereupon a petite rainbow no wider than Jon-Tom's waist arced from one puffy cloud to the other, forming a perfect fulgent archway over the door. As the last trumpet echoed from an unseen distance, the minuscule rainbow and tiny clouds shattered like soft glass, dusting the two visitors with a shower of pure color that adhered only to their memories.

"In retrospect," Jon-Tom murmured as the door swung inward to admit them, "I probably shouldn't have challenged him. I think he may have gone and overdone it a little."

A stocky figure clad in cloak and simple vestments stood just inside the entrance, gazing back at them. Jon-Tom sighed. Clothahump was not the easiest wizard to work for. The turtle went through famuli as fast as a pneumonic elephant went through nose drops.

The sloth before them blinked slow eyes and spoke carefully. "I am Ghorpul, Clothahump's famulus. I—"

"You don't have to go through the formalities, Ghorpul. I know who you are." Jon-Tom indicated his companion, who was eyeing the new assistant curiously. "This is my friend Mudge."

"Ghorpul," Mudge barked. "What kind of a name is *Ghorpul*?"

The sloth was slow, but not dense. "That's pretty funny, coming from someone named Mudge." He turned sideways in the hall and beckoned. "Enter, Master Jon-Tom. And," he added disapprovingly, "friend."

Clothahump was not to be found in any of his several studies, nor in the great library. When finally he arrived in the audience chamber, it was clear he had been napping.

"Jon-Tom, what are you doing here today?" He yawned, his beak stretching wide.

"Why not today, Master?"

"It's Crixxas."

"Who's ass?" quipped Mudge.

The wizard peered over his glasses at Jon-Tom's companion. "Ah, the otter," he murmured, as if that explained everything. Which it did. He returned his attention to the tall human.

"Crixxas is one of the more important wizardly holidays. A time for meditation on the great mysteries, for scrutiny of the Higher Plenum, for consideration of matters of time and space most profound. For unsullied cogitation and noble reflection." He gestured with a thick-fingered hand.

"Yet I see that you abjure all that in favor of traveling attire, on a morning when all responsible sorcerers and wizards and spellsingers should be devoting themselves to hermetic contemplation."

"My apologies, Master. I guess I didn't look at my calendar. I've been kind of preoccupied lately."

"So I've noticed." The turtle looked resigned. "Well, no matter. You are here. Sit and unburden yourselves." He glanced over at the sloth. "Ghorpul, go back to your cleaning."

"Yes, Master." The sloth shuffled off into the hallway.

Clothahump plumped himself down into a deeply concave chair, snugging his shell into the egg-shaped receptacle. "Slowest famulus I've ever had."

"I was meaning to ask you," said Jon-Tom, "why a sloth?"

"You know why, lad. He has an excellent memory, a real mind, and some notion of what honest study involves. This contrasts with the attitude of many previous assistants, who all too often seemed to have nothing between their ears except a lump of flavored sponge cake. Ghorpul's only drawback is that it takes him twice as long as it should to perform the simplest tasks." The wizard gazed longingly at the ceiling.

"Perhaps someday I'll finally find a famulus who combines speed and efficiency with intelligence. A brilliant otter, perhaps." He squinted appraisingly at Mudge, who was slumped in the chair he'd chosen, short legs spread wide, his stained vest hanging open and one finger up his nose.

"Then again," the wizard concluded thoughtfully, "perhaps not." He shifted his attention back to Jon-Tom. "Now that you have broken my concentration, what is it so urgent it makes you forget even Crixxas?"

Jon-Tom looked over at Mudge, who was ignoring him with practiced finesse. Finding no support from that quarter, he looked hopefully at the wizard.

"Really not much of anything, Master."

"Come come, lad. You can tell old Clothahump."

"I just did, sir. That *is* the problem. Nothing's the matter. Anywhere."

Clothahump looked dubious. "I fail to see why you should regard that as a disturbing state of affairs."

"Frankly, Clothahump, Mudge and I are bored."

"Ah!" The wizard's face lit with understanding. Which in Clothahump's case meant it actually took on a slight, pale evanescence. "Adventure self-denial. A not uncommon malady among individuals of your age and intellectual-emotional type. I, of course, am immune to such juvenile disorders. I presume you have given some thought to a possible course of treatment?"

Jon-Tom edged forward until he was sitting on the rim of his seat. "It doesn't have to be anything significant, Master. A small dilemma we could resolve. Something requiring the attention of a spellsinger. Nothing drastic, no real perils. Just a little spice."

Removing his glasses, Clothahump set to cleaning them with a soft cloth he extracted from one of the drawers built into his plastron. "I wish I could help you, lad, but insofar as I can tell, all is right with the world. There is a faint sense of occasional crises elsewhere, but you say you are averse to any serious commuting." He shrugged, his shell bobbing. "Now if you will excuse me, I desire to return to the profound mental state in which I had immersed myself prior to your unexpected and intrusive arrival. Remnants of a difficult conceptualization still cling to the heightened edge of my consciousness."

"Oi, let's leave 'im alone, mate." Mudge slid off his chair. "I'm ready to reacquaint meself with me bed, I am."

"But we agreed," Jon-Tom protested.

The otter walked over until he was staring straight into the seated human's face. "Look 'ere, mate, you've asked 'is sorcerership if there were any problems wot needed dealin' with and 'e's told you there ain't. So why don't you leave the both of us be and go back to your 'ousecleanin'?"

"No! There has to be *something*. Anything," he insisted, imploring the wizard.

"Welllll . . ." The turtle replaced his glasses on his beak. "There *is* one little thing. A genuine inconsequentiality."

"Anything," Jon-Tom reiterated.

Clothahump considered. "It involves music."

"There, you see?" the spellsinger informed a doubtful Mudge. "Something simple enough for me to deal with."

"Simple is as simple does," the otter muttered under his breath.

"I do not know if this is a matter fixable," Clothahump professed, "or if so, if it is even worth pondering over."

"Tell me," asked Jon-Tom eagerly.

The wizard composed himself. "It appears to involve a minor disturbance in the musical firmament. Nothing to titillate one, I'm afraid."

Jon-Tom slumped. "A musical disturbance? That's it?"

"I warned you."

"This disturbance. You're sure it's not destroying a village somewhere, or undermining the stability of a mountain, or driving to madness some ferocious being?"

"Afraid not."

"It hardly sounds worth wasting a spellsong on. A task for a minor adept, at most."

"Take it or leave it, lad."

Jon-Tom considered. "There's nothing else?" Clothahump

shook his head, whereupon his young partner looked resigned. "All right, then: Tell me about it."

"It's actually a bit more specific than just a disturbance. I've succeeded in isolating the condition, or rather, it appears to have isolated itself. As to an esthetic evaluation, that is beyond me. As you know, I have something of a tin ear. Or would, if I had ears." He chuckled at his own joke.

"That's our Clothahump," attested Mudge softly. "A regular barrel o' unrestrained mirth."

"Yes, well." Somewhat less than overwhelmed by companionable hilarity, the wizard regained his aplomb. "I suppose you should have a look at it."

"A look at it?" Jon-Tom's eyebrows lifted.

Rising from his chair, Clothahump beckoned for them to follow him deeper into the convoluted maze that was the tree's interior.

The subject of his terse discourse idled in an alcove hollowed out of an internal wall near the back of a workshop, soaking up numinous ambiance like a lizard on a hot rock. As the trio approached, the collage of scintillating motes oscillated, momentarily catching and throwing back the subdued light. It was a ghostly luminescence, Jon-Tom mused: a glimmering *not-there* existing at the outermost limits of visual perception, a faint phosphorescence that skated so lightly on the thin ice of one's corneas that the relevant rods and cones barely remarked on its presence.

Like the shadow of an aurora, it hovered before them. Then the motes seemed to twitch briefly and reposition themselves. As they did so, a musical tone sounded in the room. It was pleasant, plaintive, and fleeting.

"I can't see it very well," Jon-Tom declared, "but it's lovely. What is it?"

"Music, of course," said the wizard. "What did you think it was? An acoustical alignment. A harmonic convergence. A sonorous synchronicity."

"I don't follow. I heard the tone, but that doesn't tell me what it *is*."

"I've just told you, lad. It's music."

"I'll be recruited for a eunuch," Mudge exclaimed. "I've 'eard plenty o' music in me time, but I ain't never actually *seen* any before."

Jon-Tom regarded the wispy ovoid with great interest as it chimed afresh. "I didn't know you *could* see music."

"It's normally not this straightforward." Clothahump squinted through his glasses. "Usually conditions have to be exactly right. Even so, it's slippery stuff to try and get a visual fix on."

Taking a step forward, he extended a stubby hand. The mote-mass hesitated, then began to curl freely about his fingers, bathing them in halftones. They cast, Jon-Tom noted, no shadow.

"It appears to be a portion of a much larger musical thought," the wizard informed them. "I have done some research and find it to consist of a number of unvarying chords which are continuously re-forming themselves." He grunted. "Music is not an area in which I chose to specialize."

Jon-Tom moved forward. "May I?"

"By all means." The wizard stepped aside.

The motes drifted clear of Clothahump's fingers and cautiously swarmed Jon-Tom's extended hand. There was no feeling of physical contact, no tactile sensation whatsoever. Only a suggestion of a warm tingle whenever the notes periodically aligned themselves and sang out. Sometimes the tempo varied, sometimes the volume, but the basic underlying chords were always the same.

The spellsinger was quietly awed. "I've felt music before, but never quite this literally."

The motes left his hand and drifted off, hovering halfway between human and turtle. They continued to resonate, a distinctly mournful sound.

"Where did you find it?"

"Find it? I am not in the habit of seeking out stray music, lad. It found me. I woke up two days ago to Ghorpul's subdued shouting. This had somehow floated into the atrium study and was toying with a set of decorative chimes Padula the Clotted Witchess had given me a hundred or so years ago. I had the distinct impression it was trying to make friends."

"Music has a way of getting in anyplace." Jon-Tom continued to be fascinated by the wandering motes.

Clothahump harrumphed meaningfully. "That may be, but I hold an intense distrust of invasive phenomena, no matter how sweet or sad they may sound. I had Ghorpul take a feather duster to it and together we tried to shoo it away, until it began to sound so plaintive I decided to ignore it for a while. It doesn't seem harmful, and it leaves my food alone. It just hovers in that alcove and watches, if music can be said to watch. Sometimes it resounds urgently, at other times querulously. I take from it a feeling of increasing desperation."

"You think somethin's wrong with it, guv?" Mudge squinted uncertainly at the motes.

"I believe it wants something," the wizard informed them. "Or perhaps it is simply lost."

"Lost chords." Jon-Tom looked pensive. "I've heard of lost chords, but I never encountered any before. I certainly never expected to *see* any. If it's lost, how can we help it? How do you ask questions of a piece of music?"

"I have not the slightest idea," replied Clothahump laconically, "nor does the question especially interest me. But it clearly is in need of assistance, which I have no inclination to provide. I just did not have the heart to kick the poor thing out. It seems such a lamentably *anxious* piece of music." He extended his fingers again and once more the motes swirled about them.

"It changes, though whether it is responding to one's mood or to some other, unknown influence I cannot say."

Swinging the duar around in front of him, Jon-Tom let his fingers toy with the strings. A different kind of music filled the room as he sang, "Are you lost?"

The motes reacted instantly. They whisked away from the wizard's fingers, structured themselves, and repeated the same bright sequence of notes sharply, three times in succession.

"I would interpret that as a positive response," commented Clothahump unnecessarily.

Jon-Tom nodded, pleased with himself. "But how does music get lost?"

"Maybe it lives in a certain instrument that's gone missin'?" Mudge suggested.

"Nothing so prosaic, I would think." The wizard studied the drifting nimbus. "More likely it is absent from its place in a much longer sequence of notes. It belongs to a much more extensive and complex piece, from which it has somehow unaccountably strayed."

Jon-Tom glanced sharply at the wizard. "I thought you had no interest in music."

Clothahump shrugged. "I did not mean to indicate that I am entirely ignorant on the subject." He gestured at the cloudy aurora. "Clearly it exists in a state of distress, unable to partake of the musical thought of which it is a part. In short, it is lost, and suffering from what we might call *musicus interruptus*."

"Oi," murmured Mudge, "I can sympathize with that, I can."

"What did it come here for?" Jon-Tom wondered. "What could it want from you? Help in finding the rest of itself?"

"A reasonable supposition. Since you have already demonstrated a certain skill at such inquiry, why not ask it yourself?"

"I will." Whereupon he sang out the query in straightforward terms.

Instantly the motes dashed toward the doorway, returned, and raced off again, pausing each time at the open portal. It repeated this half a dozen times, resounding emphatically on each occasion, until finally it halted: not back in its comforting alcove, but within the open doorway.

"I should think that obvious enough," the wizard remarked. "It wants you to follow."

"Bloody 'ell," Mudge mumbled. " 'Ere we go."

"*I* would not waste my time on something so trivial as a bundle of lost chords," Clothahump went on, "but if you and your musk-minded friend are as bored as you say, here is an opportunity to pursue a puzzle that seems devoid of poison, fang, or claw."

Jon-Tom wavered. "It doesn't seem very significant, does it? You'd think even Ghorpul could solve the conundrum."

"Yes, you would," agreed the wizard, "but he has tried and has had no luck. He cannot spellsing to it, as you can. Anyway, I need him here."

"Not exactly something on the scale of confronting the Plated Folk," Jon-Tom muttered. "On the other hand, I suppose it's better than nothing."

"You have said to me on more than one occasion that your life consists of following music," Clothahump reminded him. "Here is an opportunity to do so literally."

"How far do you think it will lead us?" Jon-Tom wondered.

The turtle gazed skyward. "Who can say? All I know is that you have embarked before in the company of far less pleasant guides."

What if he did decide to follow the music's lead? Jon-Tom mused. It could vanish at any time, dissipate into the woods or sink into the ground, leaving him and Mudge with time wasted and feeling very foolish. How could they explain that to Talea and Weegee? As he hesitated, the object of study darted into the hallway, returned to chime at them with distinct agitation, and dashed off again.

"Follow or stay," Clothahump directed him, "but make up your mind. My meditative conditioning continues to deteriorate."

Jon-Tom would have preferred a more forthright emergency, something he could really sink his spellsinging talents into. But there was only the cluster of lost chords, calling plaintively.

"Mudge?" he asked, putting off an actual decision.

The otter rolled his eyes. "I suppose it'll be good for a stroll at least as far as the Tailaroam. By then maybe you'll be fixed, guv, if not it. At least 'tis 'armless, unlike certain o' the other loony notions you've followed." He ambled out into the hallway and waved at the motes. They swarmed curiously around his hand before darting off in the direction of the main entrance to the tree.

"Righty-ho, then! Lead on, an' try to sound a bit more cheerful about things, wot?"

"Go on," Clothahump urged the chords. "These two will try to help you. They are nominally competent, and in any event I must remain here, sequestered in the corners of my mind."

The scintillating susurration seemed to understand, swirling energetically around Jon-Tom's face like so many positrons with delusions of grandeur, before rushing off down the hallway once more. His skin tingled as if it had been briefly basted with extract of joy.

"You've been accepted," the wizard observed with satisfaction.

"I'd better be. No one else is going to blindly follow a bunch of notes off into the woods."

"That's for sure," Mudge added sharply.

"Let's go." He started down the hall.

Mudge made a face. "I've 'eard this before, I 'ave. Right, then. Lead on. Wherever *on* 'appens to be."

They followed the mote-chords out of the tree, onto the grass, and southward into the Bellwoods, man and otter trailing a glittering cloud of miniature stars and planets, moons and comets, that together formed not a constellation but a distinct and increasingly cheerful fragment of a tune.

Clothahump watched them depart, grateful to see the last of them. With Ghorpul engaged in his duties, the wizard was finally able to retire once more to the special room of velvet darkness in which he chose to lose himself in contemplation of the unfathomable mysteries of the Universe.

Seating himself in the exact center of the spherical chamber (which required that he hover precisely three body lengths off the floor), he made use of a quantity of drifting powders and potions. Soon the surroundings were illuminated by a nebulous, chromatic blush, which under the wizard's sonorous, hypnotic urging began to take on substance and form.

It was the shape of another turtle: young, lithe (insofar as a turtle could be lithe), decidedly female, and soft of shell. It was a most impressive conjuration, though its inherent philosophical gravity might well constitute a matter for some debate. Proximate to the phantasm Clothahump floated, hands and legs folded in front of him, his largely inflexible face cast in a perhaps less than profound grin. . . .

As they followed the main north-south trailway away from the river and their homes, Jon-Tom was convinced he detected a decided bounce in Mudge's step and a glint in the otter's eye.

"Getting that old anticipation back?"

The otter peered up at him. "Excited? About the possibility o' dyin' in some 'orrible fashion, or violently sacrificin' some important body part I've grown especially fond of? Oh, I'm in a terrible hurry for that, I am!" Then he flashed that irresistible grin Jon-Tom had come to know so well.

"Actually, for the first time ever takin' off in your company, mate, I feel 'alfway relaxed. After all, 'ow much trouble can a bit o' bemused music get one into?" He nodded in the direction of the cloud of swirling chords which bobbed impatiently along not a dozen paces in front of them, chiming as they beckoned.

Swinging the duar around, Jon-Tom began experimenting idly with a favorite melody. The response of the mote-notes was immediate. They darted toward him, causing Mudge to duck sideways, and swarmed the magical instrument: spiraling around the double stems, forming vortexes beneath the resonating chamber, testing the extent of the interdimensional harmonic flux that burned and throbbed where the two sets of strings intersected.

Mudge relaxed and smiled. "I think you've made a friend, mate."

Jon-Tom's fingers moved easily through the gentle glowing warmth of the orphaned chords. "Music's always been my friend. Over the years I've grown with it and it with me." A determined look crossed his face. "Where spellsinging is concerned, I intend for this journey to differ from all that have preceded it."

Mudge started. " 'Ang on a minim there, Jon-Tom. We ain't likely to be requirin' much in the way o' spellsingin' on this trip."

"We don't know that," replied his tall companion cheerfully. "But if the occasion demands, I plan to take a clue from Buncan. Who says you can't learn from your kids?"

"How do you mean?" asked Mudge darkly.

"I mean that I'm not just going to sing the same old songs anymore. When possible I'm going to try and do as he did and devise my own lyrics to cope with any unexpected situations."

" 'Ere now, guv, I know it ain't for me to say, but if it were up to me, I'd rather you didn't do that, don'tcha know. You always seemed to 'ave enough troubles findin' quite the right old song to spellsing. I ain't sure brilliant improvisin' is exactly your line."

"Employing lyrics of my own invention will give me a lot more control over each spell. Besides, you have to admit I can't do worse than I've done with the standards."

To this the otter had to nod sagely. "You 'ave me there, mate."

"Have some confidence, Mudge. After all, I've been doing this for nearly twenty years now."

"That's wot worries me," the otter confessed, but under his breath.

"Your feather's wilted." Jon-Tom indicated the battered green felt cap and its decorative quill.

The otter touched a finger to the tip of the weathered chapeau. "Weegee keeps throwin' it away. I keep sneakin' out and recoverin' it from the garbage. 'Tis a game we play." To change the subject he gestured toward the river. "Wot do we do if our musical accompaniment decides to make a sharp left-'and turn? Sing up a spellsong for walkin' on water?"

Jon-Tom beamed indulgently. "We'll do what we've always done, Mudge. Handle each crisis as it develops. Buy me no trouble and I'll sing you no lies."

"I'm encouraged no end," the otter replied dryly.

Days succeeded one another in comparative tranquillity as they reached the junction with the Tailaroam itself and turned southwestward. Small sailing craft coursed rapidly toward the distant Glittergeist, while the crews of vessels bound in the opposite direction strained at their oars to make headway against the current, rowing upstream toward Pfeiffumunter and still more distant Polastrindu. From time to time human and otter would wave at them, and various members of the disparate crews would wave back, occasionally hesitating, to gesture and gape at the softly tinkling cloud which preceded the odd pair down the trail.

"Weegee won't believe me letter." Mudge amused himself by catching a small grasshopper and letting it go, then catching it again with a snatch of the fingers that was little more than a blur. "She'll think I've stumbled off to Lynchbany to carouse and drink."

"A not unnatural assumption," Jon-Tom deposed.

"Oi now, mate, that ain't bloomin' fair. You know I've outgrown that wastrel existence. I'm a respected, settled family type, I am."

"Most all the time," his friend agreed. "Don't worry about it. As long as Weegee knows you're with me, she'll know that I'll keep an eye on you. For what that's worth. In any case, she'll be more tolerant of your taking off than will Talea."

"Well, naturally." Mudge looked mildly surprised. "I'm an otter."

Far behind them now his tree home stood deserted and silent. The wooden walls of the study did not tremble to the vibrations of Jon-Tom's bardic modalities, nor the kitchen to the vibrant rustling of Talea's apron or cursing. The spell-soundproofed upstairs bedrooms were devoid of human presence, not to mention the raucous rapping of Buncan, Squill, and Nocter. Beds stood neatly made, closets dripped with clothing unworn, and the floors reposed somnolent and unscuffed, awaiting the return of the occupants.

The only movement was produced by the infrequent sprite or demonic appurtenance as it skittered along a crack in the floor or ceiling, brightly tinted and shy. Anxious to avoid Jon-Tom's artfully concealed thaumaturgic traps, they were careful to manufacture no mischief, though there was the occasional disputatious encounter with this or that wandering, pugnacious cricket.

In the soporific silence of the empty dining room, the air crackled brilliantly as if a thousand old newspapers were suddenly being indecently assaulted by an army of starving termites. The carbonated atmosphere fractured shrilly, admitting the edgy components of an ambulatory *something* which rapidly coalesced into a shape possessed of weight as well as form.

Little taller than Mudge, the attenuated creature wore a strap-and-pouch arrangement across its upper back, and little else. Its hard-shell exoderm shone in the sun, throwing off echoes of lapis and malachite. Stiff-jointed fingers manipulated the devices strapped to its underside while the breathing orifices on its middle wheezed rhythmically.

Firmly braced on multiple legs, it turned a slow circle while considering its immediate environs. Six finely filigreed metal shoes shod its feet, each covered in delicately worked and utterly incomprehensible script. Vast eyes scrutinized the table, chairs, china cabinet, and assorted wall decorations. Except for the soft whisper of its breathing, it made not a sound, though its multiple mouth parts were in constant motion. The cutting edges were stained purple, as though their owner had eaten nothing but grapes for a month.

Less than a thumbnail in width and the same color as the metal shoes, radiant in the afternoon light, a bright golden headband encircled the hairless skull. A rectangular box fashioned of complex but unthreatening polymers dangled from the four fingers of a left hand. Lights and contact points dimpled its surface. Set flush in its center was a transparent oval readout. It whined insistently.

When the creature touched the transparent facing with another finger, the whine went away. Golden eyes finished scanning the room, whereupon it moved on to the kitchen. Its search eventually encompassed every room in the tree. Only briefly distracted by intriguing objects irrelevant to its purpose, the visitor finally found itself in Jon-Tom's study.

There it paused to massage with two sets of fingers tiny whorls located just beneath the gold headband. While performing this task it emitted a strong, aromatic perfume and a distinct air of puzzlement, giving every indication of having overlooked something vital.

Issuing a decidedly discouraged whistle, it flicked several of the contact points on the polymer box. Once more the atmosphere in its immediate vicinity began to effervesce. Accompanied by the piquant tinkling sound of miniature glass chimes, the creature fragmented, the multiple shards of itself sliding into transient tracks in space-time, until all was once again *non compos corpus*.

The peculiar visitor had brought nothing, taken nothing, and left nothing behind, save perhaps a faint odor of broiled nutmeg.

CHAPTER **4**

DAYS LATER, JON-TOM AND MUDGE WERE BEGINNING TO wonder if the vagrant music was going to lead them straight on into the tide-tossed waters of the Glittergeist Sea, when the flickering chord-cloud made a sudden and demanding turn southward. The only problem with the abrupt change of direction was that it took the music straight across the Tailaroam, which by now had become a river both wide and deep.

While Mudge could have crossed it easily, carrying with him not only his own gear but Jon-Tom's as well, the river confronted the spellsinger with a serious challenge. Cupping hands to mouth, he shouted toward their ethereal guide.

"Are you sure this is the right way?"

The cluster of sounds darted back until it was hovering directly in front of his face, then shot out across the river a second time. It repeated the action three times, the last time pausing a quarter of the way across, bobbing up and down with obvious impatience.

"I can tow you part o' the way, mate, but not to the bank awaitin' opposite. Not with carryin' all the gear as well, especially that bleedin' precious duar o' yours."

"We'll look for an easier way across. Not that I couldn't manage it if I had to. I'm still a pretty good swimmer."

"For a rock," the otter agreed.

"Your tolerance level hasn't improved with age. Want to have a high-jumping contest?"

There being only the most limited development along the

rocky south shore of the Tailaroam, they finally located not a ferry, but a genet with a boat. He was willing to take them across for what Jon-Tom thought was a reasonable fee and what a gagging Mudge insisted was outrageously exorbitant. Once they had been safely and efficiently deposited on the other side, Jon-Tom went so far as to insist that the otter return the fee he had efficiently pickpocketed from the startled boatman.

"I don't understand you." Jon-Tom chastised his friend as they resumed their march along the far less traveled path south of the river. "We're not youngsters scrabbling for change anymore. We can afford to pay for honest service. What you were trying to pull back there can only get us in trouble."

Mudge was only mildly abashed. "Old 'abits die 'ard, guv. I 'ave this aversion to lettin' money, *any* amount o' money, out o' me 'ands."

"I understand, but it was *my* money." Jon-Tom shifted his light pack against his shoulders.

" 'Tis not the owner, but the principle o' the matter," the otter argued as they followed the insistent chords across the beach and into the trees that marked the southernmost march of the Bellwoods.

While remaining heavily forested, the terrain soon grew hilly and difficult, gradual ascents alternating with steep slopes and fiendishly slippery ravines. They were entering the eastern reaches of the Duggakurra Hills, a rarely visited region noted for irksome terrain and little else. Streams and rivulets seemed to flow between every rock and boulder, tumbling remorselessly down from the towering mountains that lay wreathed in cloud far to the east, cutting their way through the solid granite as they groped blindly coastward, with gravity their indifferent and easily distracted guide. The endlessly winding gullies and arroyos made for hard walking, and the travelers had to pause frequently to rest.

Whenever they stopped, the chords would gather anxiously

nearby, ringing insistently lest they linger too long. Too long for what? Jon-Tom found himself wondering at the urgency.

"Hey you up there! Take it easy." Sucking air as they crested yet another hill, Jon-Tom did not stop to wonder at the incongruity of attempting to hold intelligent converse with a musical sequence. "We're not the hikers we used to be. Besides, we can't travel as perfectly straight a course as a piece of music. We're not made of light, you know."

"Oi, music don't give us wings, ya blitherin' blast o' bastard brass!" Slumping onto a broad, polished boulder, Mudge rubbed at his ankles and winced. On a long journey, the otter's unflagging energy did not always compensate for his absurdly short legs. He would have found the going far easier on level ground.

Also, he was becoming bored. The music tolerated no deviation in its course, chiding them sonically whenever they tried to find an easier way around the next ravine in their path. It cajoled and pleaded, urged and admonished. All most melodically, of course.

"Where d'you think these twisted tones are takin' us, mate?"

"How should I know?" Jon-Tom flinched as his ankle voiced a complaint. Having resumed the march, they found themselves skittering down a rocky slope where evergreens gave way to tall, swooping sycamores, red cyanimores, and a diversity of othermores. Splashing through the cold, shallow stream at the bottom, they started grudgingly up the other side.

"Clothahump thinks that it's after something. Whatever that might be, it evidently needs the help of others to accomplish its goal."

"So why us?"

"Maybe it senses that I have sorcerous capabilities. Beyond that you'd have to ask Clothahump. Perhaps it has a problem resolving itself, musically speaking. Maybe it just wants some company. I've always wondered if music remains music when there's no one around to hear it."

"Oh, no!" As they reached the crest of the next ridge, Mudge drew back from his friend. "I know where that sort o' philosophical shatscat leads, and I ain't 'avin' none o' it!"

They started down the other side. To no one's surprise, its base formed in the bank of yet another stream, which, like the dozens already encountered and traversed, also had to be crossed. Just as the slope on its far side had to be climbed. Beyond there doubtless lay other ravines, other streams, other slopes.

Mudge was eager for any change in the terrain. A sheer cliff, an impassable chasm: anything, so long as it was different. While humans tended to find consistency in their surroundings reassuring, a lack of variety made otters irritable.

While the rocky forest was less than comforting, at least they hadn't encountered any threatening inhabitants. No posionous plants or befanged animals crossed their path. The temperature at night was brisk but tolerable, and the profusion of shade ensured cool if not exactly comfortable hiking during the day. As for the numerous streams, they offered barriers that were damp but not impassable, and their presence obviated the need to carry more than a few swallows of water.

Occasionally Jon-Tom looked longingly to the west. An uncertain number of leagues in that direction lay the Lake District and the comely cities of Wrounipai and Quasequa, places he and Mudge knew well. They would be remembered and welcomed there.

But the music continued to flow resolutely southward, into country arduous and unknown, and showed no sign of swerving to pass anywhere near those accommodating communities.

There'd better be something to all of this, he found himself thinking. If after having led them all this way the insistent chiming simply and suddenly faded away, not only was he going to be angry, unlike Mudge he wouldn't have anything to be angry at. Mudge, he knew, could always vent his anger on him.

More than he would have liked, he found himself thinking of his warm study and comfortable bed back in the familiar home tree. Of Talea's stimulating presence and noteworthy meals. Almost in spite of herself, she had turned out to be something of a gourmet cook. He mused affectionately on the arguments he and Buncan enjoyed on the days when his son was home from school, and on the little interruptions that spiced his daily routine. He even missed Clothahump's gruff admonitions and predictably constructive insults.

He blinked. All that lay many days' walk behind him. In its place he had to be content with a cloud of cryptic modalities, a brooding if not openly hostile landscape, and an otter who had made the art of complaint a daunting proportion of his life's work.

Also, his back hurt.

What was he doing out here, sleeping on unforgiving ground and eating trail food and forage? What had possessed him? His questing days lay properly in the past, not the present. He was an accomplished member of a highly respected profession, with a reputation that reached across the length and breadth of the Bellwoods. The novelty of traipsing about the unknown Duggakurra in the company of a garrulous otter and a fragment of enigmatic music was beginning to flag.

It would help if he had someone else to talk to.

As if reading his state of mind, the music drifted back to embrace him with its tinkling warmth, trying to cheer and invigorate him. The motes danced before his eyes, insistent and optimistic.

"Yes, yes, I'm coming," he muttered as he grabbed a branch and hauled himself over a difficult spot. How much farther, he wondered, to wherever it was they were going? What if this clutch of notes had no particular destination? It could lead them right around the world and back again. What if Clothahump was wrong and it constituted a complete musical thought that was simply toying with whoever was dumb enough to follow its lead? What if they were going nowhere in particular, down a path with no end on course to a nonexistent destination?

Such thoughts did nothing to lengthen his stride or boost his spirits and he did his best not to dwell on them. Mudge could be pessimistic enough for both of them.

If naught else, the following morning brought a break in the seemingly endless geologic sequence of hills and ravines. Instead of a steep slope, the travelers had to work their way down a short but dangerous cliff, into a ravine that boasted not only a stream but a boulder-spotted beach of substantial breadth. Shallower and wider than the gullies they had previously crossed, the stream spread out to form a pond big enough to swim in.

Rugose lily pads and other water plants adorned with yellow and lavender blossoms clustered near the natural dam at the far end, supplying more color than the travelers had seen in many days. Small amphibians peeped and sang from beneath this sheltering verdure, seeking the water insects that shot through the crystalline depths. While hardly a temperate paradise, it was positively idyllic compared to the terrain they had been struggling through.

There was no restraining Mudge. He was out of his clothes before Jon-Tom could reach the pebbly beach. Plunging into the pool, he burst from its center like a breaching dolphin, his dark brown fur shiny and slicked back as he turned a neat somersault in the still air. A broad smile crossed his face as he swam back to rejoin his friend.

" 'Tis at least ten body lengths deep, and as clear and clean as old hardshell's favorite crystal sphere. Come an' join me!"

Jon-Tom studied the mirrorlike surface. "I don't know . . ."

"Cor, come on, mate. I won't let you sink." Mudge whirled and dove, surfacing moments later in the middle of the pool. "There's eatin'-size fish in 'ere, too. Maybe freshwater mussels on the rocks. Let's idle a day an' I'll do some serious fishin'. We've earned it." He swatted at a querulous chord idling above his ears. "As for our guide, 'ere, it can bloody well wait till we've put some decent food in our bellies."

Mudge was right, Jon-Tom realized as he began peeling off his clothes. They deserved a rest. He found himself seeking a protruding rock from which to attempt a proper dive.

When half an hour later Jon-Tom finally emerged from the pool refreshed and rejuvenated, Mudge already had a fire going in a little alcove running water had hollowed out of the northern cliff face. With his short sword the otter was gutting the half dozen thick-bodied fish he'd caught without aid of bait or line. The passage of time might have slowed him on land, but in the water he was as quick and agile as ever.

Otter and man lay back on a pair of smooth granite slabs and let the sun dry them while the spitted fish hissed and sputtered over Mudge's excellent fire.

A nude Jon-Tom considered the blue sky, framed by the walls of the miniature canyon. "You know, I'd forgotten how good it could be just to get away. To see different country and smell different smells."

"Aye." Even Mudge's whiskers were relaxed. "An' if I ain't mistakin', there's a distinct absence o' naggin' in the air which adds decidedly to the general ambiance."

Jon-Tom turned to regard his friend. "Talea doesn't nag."

The otter made a sound halfway between a snort and a squeak. "This is ol' Mudge you're talkin' to 'ere, mate. Females, they metamorphose, they do. Only 'tis all backwards reversed. Matin' changes their body chemistry. See, they start out as butterflies, but after they've been coccooned for a while, they pop back out as caterpillars, all predictability and bristles."

"Not Talea." The spellsinger rolled his head back to gaze anew at the sky. "And while I'm not qualified to comment on otterish pairings, I'd say you're pretty lucky to have Weegee. In fact, if it wasn't for her, I'd say you'd probably be dead."

"Get away with you, guv." Mudge whistled softly. "Weegee, she's okay. Wot you're forgettin' is that we otters do everythin' at twice your speed an' with twice as much energy. That includes naggin'."

"At least these days you don't have the twins underfoot."

When no reply was forthcoming, Jon-Tom repeated what he thought was a noteworthy observation, then turned to his right . . . and froze.

Looking like a coiled brown snake, Mudge was half sitting up, his attention fixed on something farther up the ravine than their supper. Having spent enough time in the otter's company to trust his instincts, Jon-Tom silently swung around and did his best to act as if nothing were amiss.

"What is it?" he whispered with apparent indifference.

"Movement in the bushes." Casually, the otter rose and dusted himself off, shaking out his short tail as he ambled with disarming ease in the direction of the cook fire. Jon-Tom moved to follow, forcing himself to dress slowly. The music hovered nearby, humming to itself.

Mudge made a show of turning the fish as Jon-Tom bent to watch.

"Some local predator?" the spellsinger inquired of his companion.

"I don't think so." The otter didn't look up. "There's at least four or five of 'em, and their movements are too erratic."

"Okay." Jon-Tom hefted the duar and fingered a tune. "Think I'll have time enough to use this?"

"Depends." Mudge moved around to the other side of the fire, which not incidentally placed him within grabbing distance of his bow and arrows.

"On what?"

"On whether or not they decide just to rush us or to ask questions first."

"They might just be wary, but friendly." Jon-Tom made sure his sword was close at hand.

"Friendly types don't sneak this long. They step out in the open where you can see 'em and ask if they can share your muffins. This lot's 'ungry, all right, but I 'ave a feelin' it ain't for fish."

Almost before he could finish, the stalkers burst from concealment, brandishing an astonishing variety of weapons and emitting bloodcurdling howls from a medley of throats. With an eye toward keeping the pool behind them and the fire between themselves and their attackers, Mudge sprang to Jon-Tom's side.

Seeing that surprise was lost, the attackers paused to size up their prey. A raccoon armed with a short saber in one hand and a pommeled knife in the other stood beside a large ax-carrying red squirrel with a torn, ragged tail. Looming over both of them was a grizzled javelina whose coat had turned almost completely gray. One broken tusk sported a silver crown. He clutched a long spear.

Flanking him were a nunchuck-wielding numbat, a capuchin, an elderly mandrill, and an ocelot whose muzzle was as gray as the javelina's coat. The cat gripped a beautifully engraved double-handed sword wholly out of keeping with the ragged character of the band. Instead of holding the heavy weapon over his head, he was dragging it along the ground, dulling the blade and risking the point.

Growling and whistling and muttering to themselves, this motley-looking assortment of would-be assailants faced their potential victims and waited for one of their number bolder than the rest to make the first move.

"Right, then." Dragging the massive sword, the ocelot advanced past the capuchin. The cat seemed to be the leader, perhaps because of his impressive weapon. In contrast, his maroon shorts and multipocketed vest were pretty threadbare, the gold trim on the vest hanging loose in at least two places. Like his companions, he gave the appearance of having seen better days.

"Hand over all your valuables and perhaps we'll spare your lives!"

Brash as always, Mudge gestured with his bow and notched arrow. "Take a hike an' maybe we'll spare *yours*. This 'ere tall 'uman is Jon-Tom Meriweather, most noted and notable spellsinger in all the Warmlands. Be off while the offing is good, before 'e turns the lot o' you into dung beetles!"

"A spellsinger. You don't say." The capuchin eyed Jon-

Tom openly. He walked with a pronounced limp. "I, for one, am convinced there is no such thing."

"Be not so hasty." The mandrill stepped forward. He had tired eyes, Jon-Tom decided. The simian yawned, displaying impressive but yellow-stained canines. "It seems to me that I have heard of such."

"Ploo!" snapped the squirrel. "Where would you know of anything magical, Tabbil? You pay no attention to much of anything."

"And he cannot read," added the raccoon for good measure.

The mandrill wagged an admonishing finger at his teasers. "It is true I cannot, but at least I listen instead of talking all the time, and one who listens is known to have—"

"Shut up, the lot of you," growled the ocelot. Argumentative but unwilling to challenge the cat, the debaters lapsed into silence. "You're letting yourselves get distracted again. How many times do I have to warn you about that?" He turned back to Jon-Tom and Mudge, who by this time were more wary than fearful. "Come on, come on, hand over your valuables."

Emboldened, Mudge raised his small but powerful bow. "Not a chance, pointy-ears." To Jon-Tom he added, "Go on, guv. Show 'em wot you can do. Sing up an army o' blood-sippin' ghouls to suck the flesh from their bones!"

This energetic request did nothing to lessen the air of apprehension that was increasingly evident among their would-be assailants.

Jon-Tom fingered the duar. "I haven't really had time to compose anything appropriate."

"Right, right, that's wot you always say," Mudge whispered urgently through his whiskers. "I don't think you need to extend yourself, I don't. Take a good look at this lot. Don't exactly set one to quakin' with uncontrollable terror, do they? Give 'em a bit o' a fright an' I'll wager they'll break an' run."

"They'd better," Jon-Tom replied. "We're badly outnumbered, and I can't swing a sword like I used to."

"You never could swing a sword, mate. So I reckon you'd better sing." The otter kept his bow at the ready.

Jon-Tom hadn't been forced to use his talents in a defensive capacity in longer than memory served, but he still remembered how to coax some formidable sounds from the duar. His first attempt had an immediate effect on the lost chords, which trembled and shuddered as if in pain. Its reaction to Jon-Tom's efforts differed little from those of Mudge and numerous others.

There was no denying their effectiveness, however. Recognizing that there had been perhaps one or two occasions in the past when his spellsinging had gotten them into trouble, Jon-Tom endeavored to conjure up not a ravening horde to drive their attackers from the ravine, but instead nothing more elaborate than a single modestly intimidating specter he could control. Just enough to terrify the bandits into fleeing.

An outline began to take shape on the far side of the fire, between the bandits and their chosen victims. This was sufficient to convince all but the ocelot to take several prudent steps backward. Their leader defiantly held his ground.

"Trickery! All smoke and light, can't you see?" he shouted at his unnerved companions. "Any carnival conjurer could do as well."

"See, look and see there!" stammered the raccoon.

Something squat and solid was solidifying within the growling, swirling nimbus that emanated from the duar's lambent nexus. The attendant atmospheres began to dissipate, leaving behind . . . an owl. An owl neatly attired in a gray, freshly pressed, pin-striped suit. Matching tie, watch fob, and horn-rimmed glasses completed and complemented the overall presentation.

It wasn't even a very big owl. Even the squirrel was taller.

The ocelot nodded approvingly. "So I was wrong. Apparently there *are* such creatures as spellsingers, and you manifestly are one." He grinned, showing sharp teeth. "You're simply not *much* of a spellsinger." He beckoned to his followers. "See, there is nothing here to be afeared of! This apparition is not even armed."

"No, wait." The capuchin gestured frantically as his companions started forward. "Surely it is carrying something."

Reaching back with a prehensile wingtip, the owl had brought forth a slim briefcase fashioned of smooth black leather. It brandished this enigmatic device threateningly at the ocelot.

The cat laughed, a high-pitched cough. With a determined effort he raised the blade of the massive sword off the ground. "First I will dispatch this avian interloper." His eyes blazed across the fire. "Then I will cut off your legs. We've done fair by you and given several chances. Now let the blood flow!"

"Of course." Peering through thick glasses, the owl fumbled inside the briefcase. "But before we can move on to that, I am afraid you will first have to fill this out."

Eyeing the paper uncertainly, the ocelot hesitated. "Fill what out? What are you talking about?"

"Form XL-3867-B1," the owl explained apologetically. "Permitting random acts of assault and mayhem on the person of not more than six nor less than one innocent traveler. I assure you it includes the appropriate attempted robbery and looting subrider."

"I don't have to fill out anything except my purse," the spotted cat growled. "We don't need no stinking forms." With that he raised the sword high. "I will fill my bed with your feathers!"

Quickly the owl reached a second time into the briefcase. "In that case," it declared, waving this time a whole sheaf of clipped-together papers, "I am required to advise you to read these three official pamphlets warning you of the penalties incurrable for committing the aforementioned referenced assault and mayhem without filling out Form XL-3867-B1 beforehand. Should you fail to do so, your permit to wield mayhem-related weaponry will be automatically withdrawn, as per the proper and appropriate statutes."

Looking slightly dazed, the ocelot paused, the massive blade drooping slightly in his hands.

"Furthermore," the owl went on, dipping yet again into the bottomless briefcase, "there are a number of other relevant forms that really should be completed prior to initiating any inimical activities, in addition to papers for ethereally notifying next of kin on both sides, in the event any actual deaths should occur." He adjusted his glasses. "I would also highly recommend filling out a complete environmental impact statement, since there is a distinct possibility of polluting this pristine pond with blood and other bodily wastes. It will save you a lot of trouble later." Eyes narrowing, he squinted at the ocelot's companions-in-arms.

"Each of you, of course, should really fill out your own set of forms. It's only proper jurisprudicial procedure." He turned back to their leader. "You should also submit, in triplicate, Request Form 287-B and C, granting you exclusive rights to mug, assault, rob, and otherwise impose upon these two travelers. Prior to swinging that weapon, of course."

By this time the ocelot's eyes had completely glazed over. Swaying slightly, unable either to raise the deadly sword or flee, he stood motionless while the owl rambled on, until the benumbed carnivore had vanished completely beneath a suffocating and steadily mounting pile of white paper, with a few yellow and pink forms tossed in for color.

". . . Batch Form four hundred and twelve," the owl droned on, "which simply *must* be turned in within twenty-four hours of rendering a victim into more than eleven pieces, but not less than three. Unless attached addenda ten and twelve have been filed beforehand, in which case . . ."

From within the burgeoning mountain of forms a faint, desperate voice could be heard crying for help. Or perhaps begging for mercy: The words were so thickly muffled that Jon-Tom couldn't be sure.

Led by the old mandrill, the rest of the bandits rushed forward to attack the pile. But the paper piled up faster than they could hack it away, a veritable torrent of forms, requisition sheets, and contracts, until the entire band found themselves overwhelmed and enveloped.

The avalanche spread out in high, curling waves, swamping the fire and sending the travelers' supper crashing to the ground. For an instant it blazed higher, until the flames were snuffed out by a squall of blank permits. Ever curious, Mudge darted forward and snatched one from the pile.

"It says we're suspected o' attemptin' to establish a restaurant without applyin' for a license." He threw Jon-Tom a warning look. "Maybe 'tis time to call a bit o' a halt to the music-mongerin', mate."

"I've already stopped." Jon-Tom found himself retreating toward the pool as the first hundred blank forms crept toward his feet. They could no longer see the owl, but they could sure hear him. His ominous bureaucratic drone continued to echo from the canyon walls.

Racing forward, Mudge snatched up the rest of their gear and threw it at Jon-Tom, who caught it reflexively. Then the otter was tugging on his friend's arm.

"Come on, mate!"

"W-what?" Jon-Tom mumbled. His eyes were beginning to glaze over as well.

So Mudge bit him.

"*Ow!*" Jon-Tom responded with dazed anger, which the otter ignored. "What'd you do that for?"

"It was gettin' to you to. Bleedin' insidious, it is." He was half leading, half dragging his friend along the beach toward the far end of the pool. Bemused but glad to be on their way again, the orphaned cloud of music preceded them. "Fortunately, I ain't smart enough to be susceptible."

With the nimble otter leading the way and selecting the easiest path, they scrambled out of the ravine. Jon-Tom boosted his short-legged friend over the long drops, while Mudge ascended narrow chimneys inaccessible to Jon-Tom, tossing down their rope to help the human up to the next ledge. With fear and apprehension motivating them, they soon found themselves standing on level ground above the canyon.

Looking back, they could see that it continued to fill up with a heaving sea of foamlike forms and informative pamphlets. The paper was already lapping at the rim of the ravine and clutching at the roots of terrified trees. From somewhere far below, the submerged owl continued to call forth additional flurries.

Of the bandits who had threatened them there was neither sight nor sound. They had vanished in a quicksand of newsprint and twenty-pound rag bond.

Moments later Jon-Tom thought he could hear the owl conclude, its voice terrifying in its ordinariness.

"And that comprises the requirements for today. Tomorrow, of course, is another day." It chuckled meaningfully, humorlessly. "Another day, another form."

Mudge strained to see down into the canyon. "Crikey, mate, sometimes you don't fool around."

"I didn't mean for it to go this far. I just wanted to, well, dissuade them."

The otter was shaking his head. "Wot a bleedin' 'orrible way to go, guv. 'Orrible. Formed to death. Meself, I'd far rather be cleanly run through." Shouldering his pack, he started after the drifting modality, which was once again urgently beckoning them southward.

Jon-Tom gazed a final moment at the canyon, stuffed to the rim with blank forms, before turning to follow. Though he had long since ceased singing, the image of that belching briefcase lingered in his mind, and he wanted to be completely sure it wasn't following before resuming their journey.

CHAPTER 5

DAYS PASSED WITHOUT ANY TROUBLE, THOUGH ANY FLASH of white caused both of them to glance nervously back the way they'd come. They remained alert, knowing that where one group of bandits was operating, there might well be others.

Making their way through the rugged terrain toughened old muscles, renewed long unused reactions. While they could not slough away the years, the constant exercise restored the spring to Mudge's step and caused the ring around Jon-Tom's middle to evaporate. Man and otter found themselves striding along a little easier, a little straighter.

When they eventually came up against the Barrier, they were far better prepared to deal with it than they would have been on the morning they'd left the Bellwoods.

For several days the hills had begun to flatten out, as though the air had been exhausted from an artificially inflated earth. Deciduous forest had given way to dense stands of cypress and yarra, teak and mahogany. Tanadria trees thickly wrapped in the frayed banners of doleful Socrus vines witnessed their passage in silence, like lost souls mummified in indigo. Webs spun by the lesser relatives of the Plated Folk linked branches together with gummy butt-spit.

A cloying dampness clung to everything. Even the ground had a spongy feel. Impassable bogs appeared with greater and greater frequency, forcing the travelers to pick their way carefully through the widening swamp as the guiding chords beckoned them impatiently onward.

Fortunately, there was one strip of reasonably dry, solid land that coiled more or less southward. Had it not been for that fortuitous pathway their progress would have slowed to a crawl. It was even conceivable they would have been forced to turn back. To encounter a bona fide gate in such surroundings was something of a shock.

Not that it was much of a gate. A single large, peeled pole lay balanced on two posts, blocking the trail. The left post boasted a crude pivot and counterweight, whereby a gatekeeper could raise the barrier to pass travelers beneath. Behind the pivot stood a pair of huts connected by an enclosed walkway. They had wooden walls and thatched roofs.

As man and otter considered the gate, a decidedly overweight ratal clad in light leather armor and carrying a two-pronged spear emerged from the larger of the two huts. A three-foot-tall shrew in baggy clothes scurried along in his wake. He wore a mean expression, which Jon-Tom was graciously prepared to credit to a natural shrewish squint over which its owner had no control. A small brown cap bobbed on his slightly pointed head.

"Halt where you stand!" Stopping behind the pivot post, the ratal jammed the butt of his spear into the ground and raised a heavy paw. Jon-Tom and Mudge obliged.

"Wot 'ave we 'ere, now?" The otter stared evenly at the gatekeepers.

"This be the Beconian Road Toll Gate, traveler! Those desirous of passing this way are assessed one gold piece per person." With a sweeping gesture the ratal indicated the surrounding inhospitable swamp. "As you can see and must by now know, there is no other suitable path."

Hands on his sides, Mudge took a step forward. "That's an outrageous fee, an' I ought to know, 'avin' overcharged plenty o' suck—travelers in my time." Even as he was replying, his sharp eyes were studying the twin huts, the nearby trees, the surrounding bogs. As near as he could tell, no army of associate gatekeepers lay waiting in ambush to add substance to the ratal's demand. The treetops were likewise devoid of possible assailants.

Which meant there really was only the ratal and shrew and their simple gate.

"On whose authority do you demand this payment?" Jon-Tom was likewise scrutinizing their immediate surroundings.

The ratal blinked, as though the answer were self-evident. "Why, on our own authority. We caused this gate to be built and we maintain it, as we do this portion of road."

"But it's a gate to nowhere," Jon-Tom pointed out, "across a road that exists only in name." The compacted cloud of music hovering near his shoulder drew the shrew's attention. Its sensitive ears twitched forward, listening. "Why should we pay you anything?"

"Why, for our time and efforts, of course," said the ratal. "One gold piece each, or you do not pass."

Jon-Tom considered. Like all his kind, the ratal looked sufficiently ferocious, but Jon-Tom overtopped him by a considerable margin. Once you got past the shrew's intimidating face, the rest of the rodent was decidedly unthreatening. He and Mudge had faced far worse many times over.

"Not to take another step if I was you, wouldn't I." The shrew gestured with a sword that was even shorter than the otter's.

"Why shouldn't I, guv?" Mudge inquired.

"Well." The shrew looked uncertain. "Put a lot of work into this gate, have we."

Jon-Tom examined the barrier. "Doesn't look like much to me. A pole, a couple of posts, some hardware."

"Ah, but there is much you are not seeing." The ratal smiled knowingly. "For example, there is the cleverly concealed trench whose bottom is lined with poison-tipped stakes."

Glancing reflexively at the ground, Jon-Tom thought he could make out where the surface had been disturbed and possibly camouflaged.

"Then there are the individual deep pits which are filled

with a carnivorous moss that grows in the hollows of certain swamp trees. It will grab you and suck you down to a horrid demise. Behind these lie a second concealed ditch, not as deep as the first but wide and difficult to cross. Lastly there is the hidden moat-pool stocked with Zazaipa fish, which we have collected at great risk to ourselves. Should you stumble in among them, they will strip the flesh from your bones before you can turn to swim clear." The ratal concluded with a grunt of satisfaction.

"Should you somehow manage to pass over and survive all that, which is very much doubtful, you would then have to deal with us." He gestured with the two-pronged spear. "While we may not possess the aspect of great warriors, should you somehow manage to get this far, I suspect you will at that point no longer be in sufficient condition to fight off a mewling cub."

As he studied the ground before them, Jon-Tom leaned over to whisper to his companion. "Your eyes are sharper than mine. What do you see?"

"There's no question the earth 'tween 'ere an' that bleedin' gate 'as been extensively worked. I can see signs o' the first trench and their moss-packed pits. Given that, there ain't no reason to doubt the presence o' their camouflaged fishbowl."

Jon-Tom grimly eyed the seemingly innocent trail ahead. "So that's it. Pay them their gold or they won't show you the way through."

"Aye. 'Tis an old racket. One I've practiced on occasion meself, in the old days. But it don't take an expert to sniff the flaw in this particular setup." With that he started confidently forward.

Startled, Jon-Tom reached to restrain the otter. But Mudge skipped effortlessly out of his friend's reach.

"Beware the trench filled with poisoned stakes!" the ratal called out warningly. "Beware the pits from which there be no escape!"

Turning sharply to his right, Mudge nonchalantly contin-ued on his way. Keeping a careful eye on the ground, he continued on until he'd reached the edge of the first bog. Turning there, he resumed his advance, occasionally making use of a sodden, half-submerged log, until he was past the gate, whereupon he angled back the way he'd started until he was standing a few yards from the ratal and shrew. They eyed him wordlessly as he ambled over to the pivot and calmly placed his weight against the post, crossing his arms over his chest.

"Far be it from me to tell anyone else their bloomin' business, but it strikes me as 'ow you two might do well to give a thought to considerin' another line o' work."

Without warning, the enraged ratal whirled to smack the shrew across its long, narrow muzzle. "You idiot! I told you this wouldn't work!"

The shrew held his ground, inclining his head to glare up at his enraged associate. "Don't at me yell! Your damned execution of the idea it was!"

This truth muted the ratal's fury. "I admit there were ramifications I failed to consider."

"I'm curious, I am," said Mudge as Jon-Tom, following in the otter's tracks, strode purposefully over to the bog's edge and around the far end of the barrier, retracing his friend's steps. "Are you makin' a livin' at this?"

Ignoring the shrew's offended chatter, the ratal turned tiredly to the otter. "We do on occasion encounter a traveler who is sufficiently uncertain or intimidated to pay up, though this usually requires some bargaining down of the fee. Sadly, most who pass this way are experienced travelers like yourselves, who soon note the slight flaw in our situation."

"Don't take much experience," commented Mudge. "Just someone with 'alf a spoonful o' brains."

The ratal glanced back at his associate. "Will you shut up?" Looking rebellious, the shrew subsided.

"What do you from me expect, Phembloch? I *am* a shrew."

Nodding, the ratal bestowed a newly resigned gaze on the approaching Jon-Tom. "Since we cannot extort any passage money from you, can we perhaps sell you some information?

Or have you come this way before?" Now that their scam had failed miserably, Phembloch was the soul of manners.

"No 'arm in confessin' that we're new to this country." Anxious as always to be on the way, a cluster of note-motes kept buzzing his face. The otter irritably waved them away. "We're followin' a tune, as it were, an' while 'tis heartily confident of itself, it ain't particularly free with detail."

"Ah!" The ratal smiled. "Then perhaps we can sell you something of value."

"Perhaps, guv. Though I 'ave me doubts you know anythin' worth two gold pieces."

The ratal made placating movements with his hands. "No no, we will be fair."

"You all right, Mudge?" asked Jon-Tom as he arrived to join them.

"Me? Why, we're gettin' along famously, mate."

The shrew eyed the human, who towered over him. His tone was apologetic. "Can't for trying blame us, can't you?"

Now that they were no longer threatening the travelers with extortion and various exotic varieties of agonizing death, Phembloch and the shrew, Tack, proved to be fairly congenial hosts. Disappearing into the lesser hut, Tack returned moments later with cups and a big pot of some aromatic, locally gathered tea that had been thickly sweetened with wild cane extract. This was complemented by a hand-carved tray of transparent mulwara wood piled high with small yellow and white cakes. The shrew offered them together with a degree of embarrassment.

"Actually, not much on extortion and slaughter am I." He looked suddenly wistful. "A grand and elegant bakery to open my dream is."

"Definitely in the wrong business." Mudge helped himself to a sweet, gooey cake.

Subsequent to some good-natured haggling, the travelers did agree to pay their hosts a small sum in return for information about the country which lay before them. Not that such information was vital, but Jon-Tom felt rather sorry for their inept, would-be extortionists. Mudge, of course, decried the notion. To the otter, giving away money that could otherwise be retained was worse than giving blood.

"You can always make more blood," he told his friend scornfully. "Gold's a tougher proposition."

"As always you're the soul of generosity, Mudge."

"Only when I'm the recipient, mate. Only when I'm the recipient."

"There's no one lives deeper in the swamps than Tack and I," the ratal was assuring them.

"Who'd want to?" Mudge groused quietly.

"That's a valid observation." Jon-Tom sipped his thick tea. "Why *do* you live way out here?" He suppressed a smile. "Surely not just to exploit the commercial potential."

Ratal and shrew exchanged a glance. "We somewhat wore out our welcome in the townships to the south and had to seek refuge as well as a fresh start. We are new at this enterprise and, as you have seen, less than proficient at it."

"Bloody right you are." Mudge put his plate aside and leaned forward. "Wot you 'ave to do is not so much develop these 'ere elaborate but useless traps as plant in travelers' minds the fear that—"

"Mudge!" Jon-Tom eyed the otter reprovingly.

"Sorry, mate." Mudge leaned back. "You know 'ow the old brain-pan works. Can't resist sharin' the experience o' a lifetime. Besides, it ain't like they're out to maim an' kill. An' they do keep the trail nice an' clean."

Tack abruptly jumped up, sloshing tea as he brushed frantically at the efflorescent motes which had snuck up to chime curiously around his tail.

"What manner of sorcery this is?"

"It's not really sorcery." Jon-Tom helped himself to another of the excellent cakes. "Just music."

"More than just that." Eyeing the drifting cloud of sound warily, the shrew resumed his seat. "I don't like apparitions. Control them you cannot, and they never pay."

"Apparitions rarely do," Jon-Tom agreed.

Mudge finally set his plate aside. "Time we were on our way. Wot's the lay o' the land we're about to pass through? Green fields and deep, clear streams, right?"

"Green, anyway," replied the ratal dryly. "What be your intended destination?"

"We don't really know, guv." The otter eyed the drifting nimbus of notes. "We're sort o' followin' the muse, you might say."

"It keeps fairly steady to a southerly heading." Jon-Tom tracked the glittering cloud as it shimmered and chimed. "It wants us to help it do something, but we've no idea what."

"Great strangeness," murmured the ratal. "And you say you've followed it all the way from the other side of the Tailaroam? I've heard of that land, but never have been there. Tell me: You do this for what end?"

Jon-Tom pondered. "To satisfy our own curiosity. To see what's so important to a piece of music."

"Now why would music the help of a person need?" Tack's gray brow furrowed.

"Actually, we haven't given it that much thought," Jon-Tom admitted. "It just feels right to me. In one sense I've already spent much of my life following music." He nodded in the direction of the cloud. "This is just the first time I've been able to do it literally."

The shrew was nodding vigorously. "Understand now I do. You both crazy are. It explains much."

"Be quiet, Tack." Phembloch shifted himself. "If you continue on the way you have been going, you will soon find yourselves in the Karrakas Delta. A land of shallow swamps, aimless rivers, and few inhabitants. An excellent place in which to lose oneself. Which is why Tack and I came here."

"What about this road?" Jon-Tom asked.

"Road?" The ratal chuckled, a deep, growling sound. "There is no road here. This is merely a high place in the swamp, a natural pathway. It splits and divides and disappears a hundred times long before the end of the delta is reached. Furthermore, the delta is full of dangers both foreign and exotic. You might do better to return now whence you came."

"There's no land we're not familiar with, guv," said Mudge pridefully. "Me warbling companion an' I 'ave seen much in our wanderin's. Not that I'm particularly lookin' forward to any difficult confrontations, but we'd be pretty 'ard to surprise, we would."

"If your luck is as strong as your confidence, you might survive," Phembloch conceded. "What will you do when you reach the head of the delta?"

Jon-Tom blinked. "What do you mean, the head of the delta?"

The ratal evinced surprise. "Why, the delta drains all the tributaries of the Karrakasan River, which eventually empties into the Farraglean Sea."

"A new ocean." Jon-Tom looked to Mudge. "I know only of the Glittergeist." The otter nodded, indicating that for him it was the same.

"I have heard of this Glittergeist," murmured Phembloch, "but having never visited it myself, I cannot say whether it is greater or less in extent than the Farraglean. I only know that the Farraglean cannot be seen across, nor crossed in a day. Being not fond of the sea myself, I've never had the desire or wish to explore its reaches.

"Consider yourselves fortunate enough to reach Mashupro Towne, which is the main port at the farthest tip of the delta. To do that will mean avoiding fearsome creatures and dangerous vegetation enough."

"Not to mention cheerfully extortionate locals," Mudge added pleasantly.

"That as well." Phembloch was not in the least offended. "Do you know of Mashupro?"

"Never heard of it," Jon-Tom admitted. "Never heard of anything in this part of the world."

"Not a big place, but unusual it is," said Tack. "Be there now we would, except—" He looked up at the ratal and quickly subsided.

"The delta is the abode of oddness," Phembloch continued. "A place of mystery and wonder."

"Stinks, too." Mudge wrinkled his nose.

"How do we get to this Mashupro?" asked Jon-Tom.

The ratal leaned back and considered. "It lies by the last of the land. When you can no longer walk southward but must start to swim, then you will be there."

"We have to follow the music."

"Then pray it leads you there." Tack sniffed. "Mashupro is the only town of any size within the delta. The only place of any sophistication. If you hope some portion of the Farraglean to cross, you must there transport find."

Phembloch was nodding assent. "Elsewhere within the delta you will find only tiny villages inhabited by ignorant, prejudiced, backward folk who make their living from the wetlands. They will be of no help to you and can on occasion prove dangerous."

Jon-Tom gave voice to a sudden idea. "Would you guide us to Mashupro? For a fee, of course."

The ratal didn't hesitate. "We cannot. We have raised up an enterprise here that needs attending to, as you have so straightforwardly pointed out. Nor are we in the guiding business. Besides which there are certain places within the delta, not to mention Mashupro, where our presence would be greeted with something other than unrestrained joy. Where it would, in point of fact, generate hysterical and entirely unwarranted hostility on the part of the inhabitants.

"No, it's best you make your own way. Follow your music, spellsinger, and hope it leads you in the right direction."

Jon-Tom eyed the drifting chords. "Well, does it sound like this Mashupro is out of your way?"

The drifting motes shifted, changing tempo and volume, leaving him wondering how to interpret the reaction. If it was any sort of reaction, he told himself.

"All the way from the Tailaroam." Phembloch was quietly astonished. "No, from beyond the Tailaroam. Simply to see where a bit of wandering music might lead you."

"Blimey, that's us," said Mudge sarcastically. "Puttin' our

lives on the line for no specific reason wotsoever. We've practically made a bleedin' career o' it."

Jon-Tom had to grin. "My short-furred friend is a natural pessimist."

"It comes from the company I keeps." Mudge sneered right back at him. "Wanderin' spellsingers ain't the most sensible o' travelin' companions."

"Are you truly a spellsinger?" Phembloch's tone was skeptical, but respectful.

"I am," Jon-Tom replied proudly.

"I would give a great deal to see such a wonder at work."

"Well, that's easy enough." He reached back for his duar.

The otter protested. "Oi, mate! Are we givin' out free samples now?"

"Just something simple." Feeling expansive, he strummed idly as he considered Phembloch. The lost chords compacted, as if the music were tensing up. "Consider it repayment for your delinquent hospitality."

The ratal rubbed his chin as he kept an eye on Mudge. "Your friend was about to suggest ways and means of improving our operation."

Jon-Tom demurred. "I won't aid you in extorting money from innocent, naive travelers."

"In the Karrakas are none such," Tack informed him. "If they either innocent or naive were, they wouldn't *be* in the Karrakas."

"Nevertheless." Jon-Tom was unyielding. "You'll have to think of something else."

Phembloch's thoughts were churning. "Perhaps if our gate was more impressive . . . not threatening, you understand. If it just had a little more presence, travelers might be inclined to support our efforts here out of the goodness of their hearts. We could also offer shelter and sustenance." He eyed his companion. "As you already know, Tack likes to cook."

"Now you've got the idea." Satisfied, Jon-Tom spent a moment formulating. Then he commenced to sing as well as play.

"Got those old Mashupro blues
Wore the souls out of my shoes
Looking for some place to rest
My tired bones.
This grand gate is not a test
But a place that's sure been blessed
Even though it's built of something less
Than stones."

From the start, Mudge kept his paws over his ears. The lost chords swirled about madly, like an overstressed typhoon. Tack winced, and even Phembloch looked as though he were wondering if his request had been a good idea.

A lustrous radiance cast shadows on the ratal's powerfully muzzled face. With a look of awe and then delight, he turned to watch the spellsong at work. So did Tack, though the shrew had to half close his more sensitive eyes in order to be able to look directly at the glow. Jon-Tom warbled on, pleased with his efforts, while Mudge hunted desperately for some thick moss with which to plug his ears.

So it was that when they finally took their leave of the two inherently inefficient, would-be con artists, they left behind them a gate that was rather more impressive than the pole and pivot arrangement they had originally encountered.

Arching over the narrow causeway of comparatively dry land, it plunged into the depths of the swamp on either side. The soaring, curved marble seemed to blaze from within. Leaves of gold fringed the multiple arches, which boasted mosaics fashioned from semiprecious stones. Red, blue, and yellow searchlights transfixed the air above the gate, in the center of which ten thousand twinkling glowbulbs spelled out the words REST STOP. Animated cherubs darted back and forth beneath the arch, beckoning visitors to ease their burden by pausing awhile. Flanking this were a pair of prominent, cone-crowned turrets. Over each hung a captive dark cloud from which flashed bolts of blue lightning.

The pole and pivot had been replaced with a translucent rail composed of strands of neon tubing. This burned so bright it was difficult to look at directly. The glow from the entire outrageous construct would be visible for miles in every direction, even at high noon.

Tack shaded his eyes as Jon-Tom concluded the spellsong. "Well, now. A gate that is."

"We are indebted for this wonder," added Phembloch. "Accept our deepest thanks."

"Oi, it 'tis incredibly vulgar, ain't it?" Mudge felt a certain pride in his friend's efforts as he eyed the flamboyant garishness.

Jon-Tom was less certain. "Maybe I overdid it a little."

"Wot, you, overdo a spell?" The otter was the very picture of mock outrage. "Not a chance, mate. Just to reassure you, you should know that it suits me taste perfectly."

"That bad, huh?"

"Better you turn back the way you've come." Phembloch couldn't resist offering one final bit of advice as the two travelers prepared to be on their way again.

Mudge glanced back over a shoulder. "Blimey, guv: If we tended to turn back the way we've come, we'd never 'ave gotten nowhere except where we'd already been." Ratal and shrew were left to mull this impenetrable profundity as man and otter strode off toward the southern horizon.

"Tell me truthfully, Mudge," Jon-Tom asked after they had left the gatekeepers far behind. "It's not that gaudy, is it?"

"Oh, 'tis unbelievably tawdry, mate. You can rest assured on that. A grand job, wholly in keepin' with your spellsingin' skills."

The glow from the ostentatious gate was still visible off to the north, rising above the treetops. "I tried to keep the lyrics simple. Not that it matters. Eventually the power of the spell will fade. Maybe by that time our erstwhile gatekeepers will have found gainful employment."

"Erstwhile? Wot the 'ell kind o' word is *erstwhile*?"

CHAPTER 6

THEY DEBATED JON-TOM'S CHOICE OF WORDS WHILE HACK-ing at the vegetation with their swords, for the path through the wetlands soon grew more difficult, and it quickly became an effort to keep to dry land. Phembloch and Tack had not been lying when they'd told them there were no readily rec-ognizable roads or trails through the thickening morass.

Mudge put as much energy into complaining as he did into chopping a path. The inimitable Mudge; Mudge the Clever, Mudge the Quick: playing gardener so that his simpleminded human friend could stumble along through dense swamp after a detached and maybe deranged bit of music! Oblivious to his thoughts the chordal concatenation thrummed contentedly nearby, vibrating the air. It was an attractive sound, and absolutely no help whatsoever in forging a path through the damp vegetation.

Jon-Tom knew every expression in his friend's consider-able arsenal and did his best to maintain his spirits. It wasn't easy to be cheerful, what with rivers of perspiration streaming down his front and back, soaking his clothes to his skin.

"Perk up, Mudge. Where's that irrepressible otter spirit?" He jabbed playfully at the other's tail with his own sap-smeared sword.

"Get away, ya bleatin' bloody enigma!" Mudge took a few swipes of his own at the hovering music, which at present was a faint pink blur against the greenery. It did not react as the blade passed through its wave-form substance, but when it resumed chiming it sounded decidedly melancholy.

"Don't be like that, Mudge. Think how much more of the world we're getting to see."

"Should've stayed home in me own bed," the otter grumbled as he peered up into the dense canopy. "If the rest o' the world is all green like this, I expect I could've kept to Weegee's garden an' been equally the wiser."

"What about your driving curiosity? I know you still have it." The spellsinger's sword sent chunks of obstructing verdure flying. "An incurious otter is a contradiction in terms."

"Oi, but a tired an' bored one is not." Mudge hitched up a fallen sleeve on his vest.

In the lead now, Jon-Tom looked back at his friend. "I think I know better than—"

He never finished the sentence. His next sword swipe caused him to overbalance and he went tumbling over a concealed ledge. Yelping and cursing all the way, he bounced down the slick slope. It was neither especially steep nor long, which was just as well, since he had to devote all his attention to making sure he didn't crush the precious duar beneath him or get tangled up with the sharp sword still clutched tightly in his right hand.

Reaching the bottom with everything precious still apparently intact, he rolled over one last time and bumped up against something soft that was not a representative of the plant kingdom. It let out a startled oath and sprang clear.

"Ho!" the voice yelled. "Brigands in the woods! On your guard, soldiers of Harakun!"

Jon-Tom struggled to process this unexpected information as he fought to get back on his feet. Unlike his dignity, the duar was intact.

Behind him he heard Mudge's familiar and more traditional otter war cry of "Watch your ass!" as a hazel-hued, green-capped blur sped past him. This was followed by the ring of metal on metal as the otter intercepted a thrust meant for his friend's left knee.

Blinking mud and swamp muck from his eyes while trying to wipe his face clean, Jon-Tom had just enough sense to parry the next blow himself, leaving Mudge to deal with fresh difficulties elsewhere. The blade that caromed off his own was as short as the otter's, a parody of a real sword.

His opponent was as wiry as Mudge and slightly shorter. Clad in gray leather armor striped and inlaid in blue, together with matching helmet, the creature darted about on shorter but equally quick feet. It had a longer muzzle, ears on the sides of its head, and a long, skinny tail that it used for balance as it darted nimbly from side to side. Light gray in color with six pale brown stripes across its back, it flashed small but wicked teeth at the much bigger human as it thrust and slashed with its weapon. Whiskers protruded not only from the muzzle but also above the eyes, as in many of the cats. But it was no cat, Jon-Tom was certain of that.

Three more scrambled to join the one doing battle with Jon-Tom, kicking dirt on their campfire and scattering gear in their haste to join the battle. Though outnumbered, Jon-Tom felt his greater size and strength coupled with Mudge's quickness served to equalize the confrontation.

Now that his companion was safely back on his feet and in fighting position once more, Mudge moved around in front of him. That way the otter could ward off any blows aimed at his friend's legs, while Jon-Tom could use his much greater reach and longer sword to keep their opponents at bay. In such close quarters there was no time to draw a bow or, for that matter, compose and play a suitable spellsong.

Repulsed, their assailants backed off, forming a semicircle with weapons at the ready. One looked longingly at the elegant halberds stacked neatly by the fire. Each blade was different, reflecting the work of some unknown but highly accomplished armorer.

"Banded mongoose." Jon-Tom watched the lethal quartet intently.

"Aye. One o' the few creatures that can give an otter a run for 'is money when it comes to speed an' agility. Watch yourself, mate. This ain't no sorry mob o' bandits. This lot 'as done some professional fightin' before, they 'ave."

For a while nothing was said as bright black eyes flicked from human to otter. The mongoose nearest the demolished campfire started edging his way toward the halberds. The intent was easy to figure. Unable to reach their opponents with their short swords, they would have to make use of the much longer, heavier weapons if they hoped to negate the human's impressive reach.

Clearly Jon-Tom and Mudge couldn't allow that.

The one who'd struck first at the spellsinger boasted three inlaid azure stripes on his helmet and shoulders, together with an embedded spiral shell motif. This was more in the way of insignia than any of the others displayed. He was clearly in charge.

"What are you afraid of?" he barked at his troops. "It's only one otter and a human!"

The soldier on the officer's left was watching Jon-Tom carefully. "Mighty *big* human."

"Let's everyone just calm down." Jon-Tom lowered the point of his sword. "We mean no one any harm. We're just travelers in a hard land, like yourselves."

"You attacked me," said the officer accusingly.

"I didn't attack anyone. I wasn't looking where I was going and I fell off that little ridge." Keeping his eyes on their assailants, he gestured up and back with his free hand. "It's the first ridge we've encountered in days, and I wasn't expecting it."

"Oi, you know 'ow clumsy 'umans are," Mudge added helpfully. "Not like me an' thee."

The officer looked uncertain, but dropped his own weapon slightly. "For such a short fall you made an awful great crash coming down into me."

Jon-Tom tapped the muddy but intact duar strapped to his back. "My instrument. I had to be careful of it." The mongoose strained to see. "I'm a musician by trade."

"Really?" The officer pushed back the brim of his leather helmet, which threatened to slip down over his eyes. "Your intent is not to kill and rob us?"

"Why would we want to do that, guv?" Mudge shook his head. "There's four o' you an' only the two o' us. Besides, everyone knows soldiers don't ever 'ave any money."

"The river-runner speaks truth there!" agreed one of the other soldiers heartily. The officer relaxed a little more.

A full head taller than any of his companions, the third member of the quartet ventured his own opinion. "It seems to have been an accident."

"Please accept my apology." Sheathing his sword, Jon-Tom extended a hand.

" 'Ere now, mate!" Mudge protested. " 'Twere an 'onest mistake. We don't 'ave to apologize for ... *umph!*" He bent double as a smiling Jon-Tom elbowed him gently but firmly in the solar plexus.

"Fair enough." The mongoose eyed the furless palm and took it in his own. The small, almost delicate-appearing fingers gripped like steel.

"It's funny," said Jon-Tom as he drew back his hand, "but we were thinking that *you* four might be bandits."

"Don't be ridiculous, mate." Mudge sucked air. "Look at 'em! Much too clean-cut to be proper robbers."

"We are soldiers of the Great and Noble Kingdom of Harakun!" The officer straightened visibly.

"Never 'eard o' it." Rubbing his chest, Mudge favored his traveling companion with a look more eloquent than any extended verbal commentary.

"It lies far from here, along the gentle eastern shore of the Farraglean," the officer added.

Jon-Tom brightened. "As a matter of fact, that's the direction we're headed. Not necessarily to your Harakun," he added quickly, "but the Farraglean. If you don't mind our presence, we'd be pleased to accompany you." He volunteered his most accommodating smile. "Since we've already made each other's acquaintance, all that's needed is to formalize it. I am called Jon-Tom, and this is my friend Mudge."

The mongoose smiled hesitantly. "I am Lieutenant Naike, and these are true soldiers of Harakun." He pointed them out as he named each one. "Heke, Pauko, and Karaukul. What you suggest has merit, for truly there is strength in numbers. But while I have no objection to your joining us for a portion of our homeward journey, we must first complete our mission. For that, alas, we must now travel in a different direction."

"Quite possibly to our deaths." The tall one called Karaukul wore a somber expression that seemed permanently etched into his face. A black streak that ran vertically down over his left eye only added to a naturally funereal air.

"Righty-ho," said Mudge briskly. "Well, nice chattin' with you lot." Sheathing his sword, he waved energetically in the direction of the hovering, slightly skittish cloud of music. "Come along then, mate, and leave us be on our way."

"Just a moment, Mudge."

The otter winced visibly. Those four simple words had nearly been the cause of his demise on more occasions than he cared to remember.

Jon-Tom eyed the officer sympathetically. "I don't understand."

"We are here because a great honor has been bestowed upon us."

"Uh-oh," mumbled Mudge. "Any time I 'ear 'honor' an' 'death' in the same frame o' reference I know we're goin' to 'ave problems reachin' any sort o' mutual understandin'."

Naike barely glanced in the otter's direction. "But our difficulties are no concern of yours. Though our initial encounter was somewhat acrimonious, it need not inhibit us now. In such a lonely place it's always good to hear the tales others have to tell." He gestured toward the remnants of the scattered campfire. "Please join us for a while. A pleasant exchange of conversation will be a good way to begin what might be our last day on earth."

"Oi, 'tis definitely time we were on our way," Mudge said quickly. "Clothahump would 'ave a fit, 'e would, if 'e thought we were malingerin', an' our trippin' tune is growin' impatient as ever." He pulled forcibly at Jon-Tom's sleeve.

Deeply intrigued by the mongoose, the spellsinger disengaged his companion. Mudge indulged in a heavy, deep sigh of resignation.

"What quest brings you so far from your homeland?"

The Lieutenant set himself to explain. "Again, it is no worry of yours, but since you ask, I can tell you that we four have been charged with restoring the Princess Aleaukauna ma ki Woluwariwari to the bosom of the distraught royal family from whence she has been disappeared."

"Princess?" A gamut of expression passed over Mudge's face in the blink of an eye. "Um, perhaps we might could spare a minim to listen to the details of your story. Be bloody impolite to rush off without at least grantin' 'em a listenin' to, don't you know." He folded his short legs under him as Pauko and Heke strove to restore the meal that had been so unexpectedly upset.

"First you must know that the Princess is somewhat headstrong."

"A characteristic common to many princesses, I believe," ventured Jon-Tom sympathetically.

"After what I am told was a protracted disagreement with her mother, the Queen, she chose to try and lose herself in the northern wilds. This protest caused no immediate alarm within Harakun because no one believed she could get very far, and that before she could place herself in danger, her anger would subside and she would return to the palace of her own accord." At this Karaukul muttered something under his breath and the Lieutenant frowned in his direction.

"Everyone was dreadfully wrong on both counts, and several court advisers lost various important parts of their anatomies as a result. Furthermore, the Princess has shown herself to be resourceful beyond imagining. Many were set on her trail, but as far as I know we are the only ones who have actually succeeded in locating her. There is great concern for her safety in Harakun."

"With good reason." Pauko didn't look up from his work.

Instead of chastising him for interrupting, Naike nodded in agreement.

"At what we believed at the time to be the limit of our wanderings," the officer went on, "we learned she had been seen in a coastal town south of here."

"Mashupro," Jon-Tom guessed.

Heke was surprised. "You know the place, then?"

"No. Never been there. That's to be our next destination."

"Ah." The soldier looked disappointed.

"It seems," Naike continued, "that the Princess's presence was noted by one Manzai. Although descriptions are imprecise, and were apt to be colored by everything from fear to admiration, this individual apparently enjoys a status somewhere between that of a brigand and a noble. He has carved his own little private fiefdom out of this detestable country, wherein he exercises absolute power.

"If what we learned is to be believed, it is he who has kidnapped our Princess."

"Oi!" Mudge was on familiar ground. "Ransom!"

"Apparently not." Naike's brow creased. "It is possible she was abducted for unmentionable activities, though there is no certainty of that. Our sources were somewhat obscure on the matter."

"Oh, them." Mudge leaned back against a mossy log.

Heke glared at the otter. "Do you disrespect our Princess?"

"Can't," Mudge responded nonchalantly. " 'Aven't met 'er yet."

The soldier hesitated, uncertain, and decided to return to his chores.

"We are sworn," the Lieutenant went on, "to bring back the Princess or perish in the attempt."

Mudge closed his eyes, pulled his feathered cap down over his face, and crossed his hands over his middle. "Oi, why ain't I surprised?"

"Then that is your honor," Jon-Tom commented thoughtfully. The chords tickled his right ear and he brushed away the impatient music.

"Yes."

"Actually," Karaukul muttered softly, "we were sort of volunteered." He did not sound especially ennobled.

"There was a lottery to decide which of us in the royal service would be so honored," the Lieutenant explained.

"I bet," Mudge murmured knowingly.

"We *will* rescue the Princess." But there was more determination and assurance in the Lieutenant's voice than in his face.

"This Manzai," said Jon-Tom. "Is he holed up in some kind of fort, or walled compound, or something?"

"We know nothing of his abode, or what may be his household strength. He is a shadowy figure in this part of the world, and we are far from Mashupro. The citizens of that worthy community prefer the coast to the pestilences and dangers of the interior, for which one cannot blame them." The Lieutenant stood tall. "We will press on, to glory or death."

"That's wot they always say." Mudge scrunched back against his log.

Unable to ignore the otter's gibes any longer, the indignant Naike glared in his direction. "At least our cause is noble. Something which, from the look and sound of you, is alien to your personality."

"They ain't very edible, are noble causes." Unperturbed, the otter peered out from beneath the brim of his cap. "I find 'em damn hard to digest, an' not particularly nutritious."

Naike let out a snort that was more of a squeak. "I would expect that from an otter, a tribe noted for its narcissism and laziness. I've yet to encounter one with half the fortitude and determination of a mongoose."

Eyes flashing, Mudge sat up quickly. "Is that so? That's interestin', comin' from someone with a striped behind. I'll 'ave you know that—"

"Not now, Mudge," said Jon-Tom irritably.

The officer was willing to drop it. "I do not have time to squander in frivolous argument."

"Princess, eh?" Mudge switched mental gears easily.

Visions of a lissome mongoose beauty swathed in silks and ever so grateful to her rescuers pirouetted through his brain. Because of their official position, the noble soldiers of Harakun would doubtless be constrained from accepting anything more than her formal thanks, while he would be under no such restrictions. Thrilled by her rescue and anxious, perhaps even desperate to show her gratitude to someone, the beauteous Aleaukauna would have no one to devote herself to but himself.

Under those conditions it would be highly impolite to do anything other than render what assistance he could.

"I expect it 'tis a bit o' a noble enterprise. Under such circumstances we'd be glad to 'elp out . . . in the background, o' course," he added hastily. "We wouldn't want to divert any o' the glory from those on whom it ought properly to fall."

Jon-Tom's brows rose. "That's what I was going to say. Mudge, this isn't like you."

The otter adopted a hurt mien. "Wot, can't me own noble instincts come to the fore every now an' again?"

"Sure. It's just that over the years I don't seem to recall ever encountering any."

"You always were a bit shortsighted, mate." Mudge indicated the rosy miasma drifting lazily behind his friend. "Wot about the bloomin' beatitudes?"

"You know," murmured Naike, "I was going to ask you about that."

"Yes, what sort of mischief is that?" Heke wanted to know.

Jon-Tom waved his fingers at the notes, which responded by chiming softly. "A lost piece of music. At least, that's what we think it is. For some reason it wants us to follow it."

"Not necessarily a noble quest," commented Naike speculatively, "but surely an unselfish one." He reached toward the cloud, which drew back from his fingers, ringing softly. The mongoose eyed Jon-Tom with new respect.

"Perhaps you are in truth what you say you are. A spellsinger, or any sort of sorcerer, would be a most useful ally. We are grateful for any assistance you can render us."

At last! Jon-Tom thought. Something to test their long-dormant abilities. Rescuing a kidnapped princess was a cause both difficult and worthy. It was more than he'd hoped for when they'd first set out to trail the beckoning music.

"We'll do what we can." Once more he extended a hand. The officer shook it, his own paw covered in short beige fuzz.

Behind them, the three soldiers were evaluating their new allies.

"You think the human's telling the truth?" Heke wondered aloud. "About being a magician, I mean?"

"I expect we'll find out." Pauko stirred the pot. "Most surely that's a strange instrument he carries."

"At least they can both fight," declared Karaukul. "Though in a tight place I don't think I'd want that otter guarding my back."

"They strike me as a little old for this," Heke observed.

Karaukul shrugged. "Ofttimes experience is a fair tradeoff for speed and strength, but that they have as well. Did you see how smoothly they fought together?"

Pauko squeaked softly. "I expect we'll find out more about that, too." He tasted of the stew and sighed. "I wish we had a little cumin, and some cardamom as well."

Karaukul passed him a small wooden cylinder. "Use some salt. And remember, if that doesn't do it, there's always more salt." Pauko essayed a friendly nip in his companion's direction.

Naike regarded the tall human. "For our mission to succeed we will need to employ stealth as well as daring. In that the aid of a spellsinger could prove more valuable than any sword."

"Like I said, I'll do what I can." Jon-Tom reached back for the duar. "If you're still unsure, I could give a little demonstra—" A hand forestalled him.

"That's all right, mate." Mudge had risen like lightning from his resting place. "I'm sure there'll be opportunity soon enough to show your skills."

"Yes, I suppose you're right." To the otter's great relief, his friend passed on the notion.

"How wondrous are the consequences of a chance meeting. As you've agreed to share our destiny, so too must you partake of our poor hospitality. Come and eat."

While they dined on Pauko's surprisingly adept stew, Jon-Tom regaled the soldiers with stories of his and Mudge's exploits. In return, the mongooses gave freely of what they had learned and experienced on the long, arduous journey in search of their Princess, as well as describing the beauties of their homeland.

CHAPTER 7

THE FOLLOWING MORNING THE RESCUE EXPEDITION, ITS number strengthened by two, broke camp and struck out in what the mongooses had been told by a nervous trapper was the approximate direction of Manzai's dwelling. Humming briskly, Mudge trailed along in the rear, working to convince himself that the potential rewards of this little digression would somehow far exceed the actual risks he might have to take.

He stuck protectively close to Jon-Tom. The soldiers thought the attention the otter paid to his friend's back admirable. What they didn't know was that Mudge chose to keep close because Jon-Tom's bulk would be first to catch any arrows or bolts or spears hurled from ambush.

Since they had no way of knowing when they might stumbled into their destination, or what might lie between it and them, no one spoke above a whisper. At that, there was little in the way of casual conversation. Every man, mongoose, and otter was concerned with what lay directly ahead as well as in the immediate vicinity. Any abrupt movement within the dense green morass through which they were advancing was looked upon with suspicion, any sudden sound a cause for caution.

It was while pondering the possible edibility of a bright green and black lizard that it suddenly struck Mudge with great force that something truly horrible had happened to him over the years. Something more devastating and awful than he ever could have imagined, worse even than having his fur start to fall out. It hit him like a physical shock, leaving him terrified and wondering how he was ever going to be able to handle it. The force of the realization threatened to strike him dumb.

In spite of his strenuous and ongoing attempts at prevention, despite his best efforts down through the years to see that it never happened, in spite of iron determination, it seemed that he had developed a conscience.

"Mudge, all of a sudden you look awful." There was real concern in Jon-Tom's voice. "Are you all right?"

The otter braced a palm against a tree. "I . . . I'll be okay, mate. I think." He smiled wanly. "Got a little dizzy for a minim, there. Somethin' I swallowed."

Don't give in, he urged himself. *You can fight this 'orrible development. 'Tain't irrevocable, it ain't.* Feeling better, he straightened and resumed walking. *Why, it weren't nothin' more than a crab clamped on a toe! Shake it off, fling it from you!*

But try as he would, it clung to him like a leech, bedeviling his thoughts and causing him to worry more about the Princess's fate than his own. It was a revolting development that left him nauseous and reeling, until he finally vowed to deal with the emergency at hand and take care of the other later, in more amenable surroundings.

"Seems to me," he propounded much later that day, after hours of trekking through trailless wilderness, "that we're a long ways from anyplace." Bent back by Karaukul, a branch whipped toward his face. He dodged it by the simple expedient of bending the upper half of his body sideways. "You bottle-brush tails sure you know where you're 'eadin'?"

Heke was closest. "We have been tracking the Princess Aleaukauna for months. Of all who were sent in search of her, only we have been able to follow her this far. Have some confidence, river-runner."

With his short sword Pauko was slashing methodically at the dank, clinging vegetation. "Are you in a rush, otter? Would you like to approach this Manzai's abode by the main path, where he is most likely to have posted any scouts and outriders?"

"D'you think I'm completely ignorant in these matters?"

"Of course not," put in Lieutenant Naike from up ahead. "Perhaps only a little out of practice."

The otter's gaze narrowed. "That comment wouldn't be a reference to me age, would it?"

"Keep your voice down." Jon-Tom bent slightly to clear an overhanging branch without having to push on it and rustle the leaves.

"Why? They bloody well like to talk so much, they can bleedin' sure listen to wot I 'ave to say."

"And I'm sure they will." His tall friend resorted to placating motions. "But not right now. I can see something that might be a structure up ahead."

That silenced the otter. A little ways on, the vegetation thinned slightly and he could see as clearly as the others.

Surrounded by flawlessly manicured grounds, the sprawling complex of single-storied buildings crowned a gentle bulge in the earth. There were flowers and rock gardens, bubbling fountains and diminutive waterfalls. Meticulously laid paths of colored pebbles and ground stone lay like flattened snakes amid the cube grass. The residence radiated a peace and contentment that seemed wholly out of keeping with Manzai's ferocious reputation.

Of course, he reminded himself, all the open space would also allow anyone inside the buildings a sweeping view in every direction.

Fanciful coils of purple topiary flanked a pair of entrances, while freshwater mother-of-pearl flashed from shuttered window screens. The many roofs were fashioned of sunheart tiles and were sharply peaked to cope with the tropical downpours the region doubtless experienced on a regular basis. There was nothing resembling a wall, a moat, or camouflaged barrier of any kind. Only the comparative absence of windows suggested even a slight concern for internal security.

To all outward intents and appearances a casual visitor

could step onto any of the various pathways and stroll right up to the main entrance before being challenged. Even then one would have to knock or ring a hidden bell, because there were no guards or other attendants visible, either.

The gentle slope of the hill masked the size of the complex. Covered hallways connected the numerous structures. Several of these were large, but hardly ostentatious. There were no elaborate woodcarvings, no flash use of gold or other precious metals. For a suspect warlord, Manzai presented a face to the world that could only be called subdued, if not positively serene.

Surely the pacific aspect of the domicile's exterior must belie the true nature of those who dwelled within, Jon-Tom told himself. Having expected to encounter spike-topped parapets and towers notched with arrow ports, he was more than a little taken aback.

From within the dense undergrowth they watched silently for an hour without observing a single guard or patrol.

"You sure we've got the right place?" he finally whispered to Lieutenant Naike.

"It fits all the descriptions that were given us." The mongoose's voice was a sibilant murmur. "Poisonous snakes frequently come cloaked in appealing colors." Jon-Tom could seen his lean muscles rippling beneath the soft fur. "Somewhere within, the Princess Aleaukauna is a prisoner. It matters not whether she wears chains of gold or brass."

"How to free her." Karaukul loomed over his companions, though he was still a good foot shorter than Jon-Tom. "I have to say, sir, that if this is truly a fortress, it is the most innocent in appearance I have ever seen."

"Indeed," the Lieutenant admitted. "Hard though I've searched, I have seen nothing to challenge an approach."

"That's when you 'ave to be ten times as bleedin' careful."

Everyone turned to look in Mudge's direction. "Innocence is the cleverest defense of all."

Heke frowned as he studied the complex. "What defense? I see no defense of any kind."

The otter barked softly. "Which is doubtless just wot those inside want any unannounced visitors who might be inclined toward a little mischief-makin' to think." He waved at the interlinked structures. "Why, this 'ole setup practically invites attack.

"Now, I'll wager you lot know your business, which means you know how to span a moat or ladder a wall, avoid a pit-drop or tunnel under a rampart. Specified solutions for specific fortifications. But this dump is slippery, it 'tis. Like a lass I once knew, you can't get a grip on 'er. No, no, me lads. The less danger you see, the more you 'ave to watch out for."

Naike turned a thoughtful gaze on Jon-Tom. "What think you, spellsinger?"

"I think that in matters like this," Jon-Tom replied readily, "it's a good idea to trust Mudge's instincts. He's been in more scrapes than any live person I know."

"Better always," the otter added, "to be cowardly and cautious and alive than brave an' bold an' dead."

"Honestly spoken," Pauko avowed.

Mudge squinted at the mongoose. "You can say that for seconds, dirt-digger. Ask yourself who your Princess would rather 'ave rescuin' 'er: a live coward or a dead 'ero."

"Then we must prove ourselves equally wily." Naike regarded the otter. "What would you suggest?"

Mudge was taken aback by the soldier's deference. "Wot, me? You want my advice? And 'ere I was thinkin' you were against consultin' with 'istorical relics like meself."

"Put a lid on it, Mudge," Jon-Tom instructed his companion.

"Now, mate, let me enjoy this a little, wot?"

"I have no time to waste on sarcasm." Naike turned away from the otter.

"Take 'er easy there, guv." Mudge hastened to make peace with the officer. "Now then—just because there ain't no fortifications visible on the outside don't mean the inside's all embossed wall coverin's an' thick-weave carpets. Since we don't 'ave a clue as to the true nature o' the interior, an' since your informants don't seem to 'ave been particularly 'elpful on that little matter, we need to lay our 'ands on someone who knows what we needs to know."

Heke glanced back toward the complex. "Abduct someone? But there are no guards patrolling whom we could take."

Mudge nodded agreeably. "Clever, wot? You can't extract information from nobody, can you?" He slapped at an overhanging vine. "But someone's got to keep this creepin' green gook at bay. That cube grass don't trim itself an' these branches don't die back out o' deference to the local aesthetics."

"Your meaning is clear." Naike contemplated their next move. "We must curb our impatience . . . and wait."

Jon-Tom shifted the bulk of the duar against his back. "It's taken you months to get this far. You can hold off a little longer."

The Lieutenant nodded in agreement. "Where would be a good spot to place ourselves, do you think?"

"As completely out o' sight o' the majority o' the buildings as possible," Mudge volunteered helpfully.

Slinking back into the swamp, they worked their way around to the north side of the complex as quietly as possible.

There they spent a fitful afternoon and night, sleeping in shifts so that there was always someone keeping an eye on the buildings. It was only after they had concluded a dry and (despite Pauko's best efforts) uninspiring breakfast that a wooden panel in the rear of the nearest structure slid aside and, for the first time, a figure showed itself. It wore a simple, embroidered cloak. Though it employed neither tools nor magic, it made rapid progress at trimming down the cube lawn and removing unsightly weeds.

"A goat," observed Karaukul.

"Why not a goat?" The Lieutenant pressed close to his fellow soldiers. "Who better to trim the grasses?"

"But why only one?" Jon-Tom wondered as he watched the ungulate operate.

"We only see one," Mudge responded. "For all we knows

there may be 'alf a dozen others workin' the far reaches o' the landscapin'. But one'll do us."

As they looked on, the quadrupedal groundskeeper stood carefully on its hind legs to reach the lower branches of a fruit tree. Resting its forelegs on the trunk, it carefully nipped off several suckers that were sprouting from the otherwise smooth-barked surface. Aberrations located higher up were doubtless the province of some other member of the groundskeeping staff: a giraffe, perhaps.

Its horns were in no way formidable, nor was it an especially robust physical specimen. Certainly the goat was no soldier.

"Let's take him." Heke started forward.

Naike put out a short, furry arm to restrain him. "Patience, good Heke. There are weeds over here as well. He will come closer. Better for us, if there are others nearby."

Jon-Tom admired the ungulate's skill with his teeth. "He's very good. I'd hire him myself. See? He keeps the cube grass at precisely the same height all the way around, regardless of whether it's growing on flat or sloping ground."

"That's it!" barked Mudge suddenly.

Naike turned to stare at him. "What's it?" But the otter had evaporated into the swamp.

Moments later he returned with a long, feathery branch tucked under one arm.

"What are you going to do with that?" Pauko looked bemused.

Mudge rolled his eyes heavenward. "Preserve me from the artless." He stepped forward. "Shut your cake-'oles and get ready."

Everyone tensed as the otter carefully eased the branch forward until it was sticking an entire body length beyond the otherwise neatly trimmed wall of greenery.

It was a while before the incongruous protrusion caught the attention of the busy gardener. First one eye, then the other inspected the innocuous frond, as if wondering how it could have been overlooked for so long. Then he started toward it.

. "Wait till 'e starts nibblin'," Mudge whispered tersely. "Then take 'im!" With quick little nods the mongooses silently dispersed. So did Jon-Tom, more slowly, as befitted his simian bulk.

Ever cautious, the gardener approached the fringes of the swamp's wild and undisciplined vegetation. A glance to the right and then to the left apparently satisfied him, whereupon he proceeded to take a sharp nip out of the base of the jutting stalk. Two or three such nips would be enough to bring the offending growth down.

It was interesting, he mused as he worked, how nearly several buds at the base of the branch resembled fingers.

He never had a chance to take the second nip. The quartet of mongooses pounced, allowing the shocked gardener time enough to utter no more than half a bleat before he found himself rolled up in several musky blankets. A strong cord quickly secured his jaws, preventing any further outbursts. Whisked into the depths of the swamp, the unfortunate ungulate could only gape in terror at his abductors.

"Are we being followed?" A worried Naike carried his portion of kidnapped goat by its left foreleg.

Looking back the way they'd come, Jon-Tom could make out only mist, gray-green verdure, and irritated insects.

"Let's get 'im to a place where 'e can safely scream 'is tail off." Mudge was breaking trail for the others.

Only when they were deep within the pathless morass did they undo the gardener's gag, leaving all four legs bound. His handsome cloak was now stained with moss and muck. As a helpful Jon-Tom reached to straighten the covering, its owner winced.

"Just try to relax. We don't want to hurt you."

"Which ain't to say that we won't," Mudge added sunnily.

"Please to explain yourselves," the goat moaned softly. "Please to tell this simple servant what you want of him." He focused on Jon-Tom. "What a very large human you are."

"Never mind that." The spellsinger tried to put a little steel into his tone without sounding overly intimidating. "We're not here to discuss me. You serve the warlord called Manzai?"

"Warlord?" The goat blinked. "Manzai? My master is but a simple country squire. Raising exotic fruits and vegetables is his passion. That and cataloging his many collections. Do not take it as an offense when I say to you that you have the wrong person." Almost apologetically he added, "Please to know me as Prought. May I know your honored names?"

"No!" declared Naike firmly.

"I thought as much. Please, sirs, if you will not untie me, at least lean me up against a tree or something. It is painful to raise my head from this position."

The Lieutenant considered the request briefly, seeking subterfuge and finding none. He nodded to his troops. Heke and Pauko wrestled the goat upright and left him propped against a nearby stump. His tail switched nervously back and forth.

"Please again to tell me what you wish from me, honored sirs."

"Polite little bugger, ain't 'e?" Mudge murmured. Then, more loudly, "We need some information, beet-browser."

For a second time the gardener appeared thoroughly baffled. "Information? Well, soon it will be the time to prepare the grounds for the summer fertilizing and weeding. I can also speak to—" Sudden realization struck home.

"Ah, now all is clear. You are brigands, come to rob or murder my master. Or assassins, hired by some misguided foe. The best advice I can give is for you to turn back the way you have come and depart with your skins intact. You will never reach the master's private chambers, for he is watched over constantly by devoted servitors and protectors."

"We ain't interested in disturbin' 'is beauty sleep," Mudge snapped.

"Your beloved master," Naike explained, "has stolen away our Princess, whom we are bound to return to her kingdom and family, or perish in the attempt."

The gardener pondered this solemn pronouncement before replying, quite unexpectedly, "Which princess?"

The four soldiers exchanged a glance. Jon-Tom and Mudge were no less bewildered.

Finally Pauko asked, "What do you mean, which princess?"

"Please to understand, honored sirs, that I pride myself in the precision of my speech. I mean just what I have said. Which princess?" He was straining to see behind Jon-Tom. "What an interesting instrument you have there. I play a little myself. Music is a refined pursuit which I find difficult to tally with your intentions."

"Never mind that." Naike jabbed at the goat throat with the tip of his sword. "Explain yourself!"

His left eye fixed on the blade, the trembling gardener tried to draw his head back into his neck. "Please to explain why, since you are going to kill me anyway, I should tell you anything?"

The sharp point dipped slightly, as did Naike's voice. "We've no interest in killing you or anyone else. We just want our Princess back."

"He will not give her up," the gardener told them. "He won't give up any of them."

"What you're telling us is that Manzai holds more than one princess captive," Jon-Tom stated flatly.

The goat blinked. "Why, certainly. Understand that while the fine details of my master's hobbies do not fall within my humble province, I am still conversant with most household matters."

"Hobbies," muttered Pauko.

"What does Manzai want with a 'collection' of princesses?" Naike inquired. Behind him Mudge let out a hoot of disbelief. He was ignored.

"Did I not mention that my master was an avid collector of many things? Some folk collect rare books or coinage, still others exotic shells. A few find contentment in the propagation of rare and beautiful flowers. In a sense Master Manzai may be counted among the latter." The gardener became thoughtful. "An expensive hobby, but, I am told, a satisfying one."

"Why you . . . !" Karaukul raised his sword.

The goat shrank back and closed his eyes. "Please to vent your anger on the source of your discontent and not on the mere dispenser of disconcerting tidings!"

"An exclusive pastime," declared Jon-Tom. "In fact, I really can't think of anyone else who collects princesses."

"We are only interested in one." The Lieutenant turned his attention back to the shivering goat. "You're very deferential. It's my experience that deferential, obsequious types generally know more than they volunteer. Now, among his 'collection' does your master count one of our tribe?"

"Ah, yes," the gardener answered readily. "A beauty of your kind who is known by the name Aleakuna."

"Aleaukauna," Naike corrected him. "Youngest daughter of our liege." Eyes flashing, he leaned forward. "In what part of the compound is she held?"

"I am not certain."

"Think hard." The Lieutenant prodded with the sword.

"A moment, please, to recall. My master treats his rarities with concern and even reverence. Each princess has her own quarters, with her own staff of servants. He is not an uncultured host."

"Oi, 'e's a real paragon, 'e is," Mudge snarled. "Quit stallin'."

"The Home has many turnings," the gardener insisted. "As it would please me to preserve my head, I am trying to remember exactly. It is a simple matter to enter, but most difficult to exit."

"We'll be the judges of that," Naike told him. "You just give us directions."

The goat nodded. "The large white building that lies immediately in front of the place where we encountered one another has a porch attached to its northern side. If you are successful in entering through that door, you will find yourselves facing a long hallway. It leads to another, larger structure with many rooms."

Mudge was nodding to himself. "Easier to guard a narrow corridor than 'alf a swamp."

"At the far end of this hallway there is a branching. Turn north once again and find a second corridor. This leads to a common dining area, which you must traverse. Beyond and to the south lies a gracious living area. Fortunately for you, the ones nearest the dining area serve as the present quarters of your princess."

"Is she in good health?" asked Heke anxiously.

"As I told you, my master takes only the best of care of his collection. With assurance I tell you that she is no doubt as healthy as she has ever been."

"Though not as happy, I'd wager," muttered Karaukul.

The goat shrugged. "Such matters are not for lowly ones like myself to speculate upon. I am only a humble trimmer of roses and digester of weeds." He looked up and idly rubbed a horn against the tree trunk. "If I have satisfied your curiosity, I would very much like to know what you intend to do with me, so that in any event I might have time to compose myself."

"Not a problem." Mudge fingered his short sword and eyed the goat's throat.

Naike stepped forward. "The prisoner has complied fully and willingly with our requests. A sense of honor demands that we spare his life."

"A sense o' 'onor'll get you killed every time," Mudge grumbled. "You want to untie 'im and let 'im get back to his grass grubbin'? O' course, 'e wouldn't 'appen to let it slip to a fellow garden type that the six o' us are caucusin' out 'ere, about to open up that complex like an echidna atop a rotten log?"

"Certainly we cannot do that." The Lieutenant considered the gardener. "In that respect we have a problem."

"Please to solve it in a fashion amenable to all?" offered the goat hopefully.

"Let me handle this." Unlimbering his duar, Jon-Tom stepped forward. Muttering under his breath, Mudge sidled out of the way. So did the goat, as much as he could with the tree behind him. The ominous shadow of the tall human blocked out the sun.

"The rest of you, plug your ears as thoroughly as you can."

"What for?" wondered Karaukul.

"You don't want to know, guv." Mudge was already hunting for suitable clumps of muffling moss. "I'd give 'im some space, too, if I were you."

For once the result was exactly as Jon-Tom intended. But then, between caring for Buncan and helping to raise Nocter and Squill, he'd had years in which to practice lullabies. He'd simply never had to spellsing one before.

He was half asleep himself when the goat finally keeled over.

"Gnnnncchh . . . baaa . . . gnnnchph . . . baaa . . ." The gardener snored softly to himself.

"That's that." Pleased with his effort, the spellsinger shook himself. Maybe he hadn't toppled any towering ramparts or outblazed an attacking dragon, but as Clothahump often said, any spell you could walk away from was a good one.

"Wot's that you say, mate?" Mudge leaned forward, straining to understand.

Jon-Tom impatiently plucked the packed moss from his friend's right ear. "I said, that's done. Taken care of." He nodded in the direction of their prisoner. The gardener lay on his right side by the base of the tree, wheezing contentedly. "I used a pretty heavy lullaby. He'll snooze for at least a day, probably two."

Obviously impressed, Naike stared at the goat. "You are a spellsinger true."

Jon-Tom shrugged modestly. "Listen, if you can get a pair of juvenile otters to go to sleep, you can put *anything* under."

"Actually, methinks it triggers the body's own defense mechanisms," Mudge hypothesized. "See, the best way to shut out me mate's caterwaulin' is to fall straightaway asleep."

"Thank you for that unsolicited encomium," Jon-Tom said dryly.

The otter grinned. "Don't mention it, mate."

"I try not to."

"We will wait until dark," Naike decided.

"Obviously." Mudge grew serious as he moved closer to Jon-Tom. "D'you think the grass-chomper was settin' us up, mate? Maybe 'e's gone an' given us directions to the 'ouse'old barracks instead o' the lady's quarters."

The spellsinger reflected. "I don't think so. Surely he realizes that any survivors would make it a point to come back here straightaway and slit his throat. His manner was subtle, not not duplicitous. I think he was too scared to think that far ahead."

Mudge nodded somberly. " 'Tis 'ard to be clever with a sword at your throat."

"We'll go carefully in any case." Naike turned to his troops.

"Righty-ho. Let's 'ave at the blighters, then." To everyone's surprise, it was Mudge who headed off first back the way they'd come.

CHAPTER 8

THEY WERE GRATEFUL FOR THE ABSENCE OF MUCH MOON AS they crept noiselessly across the grass and up onto the deserted porch. The highly polished wood was slick beneath feet and paws, and the simple door latch yielded silently to Mudge's experienced ministrations.

"This is too easy," Jon-Tom whispered as they tiptoed down the first hallway.

"Sometimes you think too much, mate." The otter trotted along at his left elbow. "Maybe this 'ere Manzai is convinced 'is reputation an' isolation give 'im security enough. 'E'd 'ear about any advancin' army in plenty o' time to prepare, an' small groups o' crazies like ourselves probably don't worry 'im none."

Thrown in with mongoose and otter, Jon-Tom felt as ungainly as a drunken elephant. Every squeak, every groan the floorboards made seemed to issue from under *his* feet.

"This way." Naike gestured for the others to follow his lead.

They soon found themselves in the common dining area the gardener had described. Paintings and drawings of surprising taste and sophistication lined the pastel walls. Entranced by an especially delicate watercolor showing a marshy landscape at dawn, Jon-Tom had to be nudged along by Mudge.

"For a kidnapping thug," Jon-Tom whispered as they entered the next corridor, "this Manzai has elevated taste."

" 'E's likely to elevate our gonads if you wake 'im up with your babblin'," Mudge reproached his companion.

As if to emphasize the warning, a heavy thud followed by a grunt came from the distant, dark end of the corridor. Something vast rose to block their path. It accomplished this through the simple means of occupying the entire hallway with its bulk.

At first Jon-Tom feared they had triggered some kind of automatic gate or portcullis. He was rapidly disabused of this notion when the outline took a step toward them. The hallway floor trembled slightly under its weight.

As starlight silhouetted the shape in silver, he saw that the metaphor he'd used earlier to describe his own progress had been inept. Or rather, inapt. Whatever else it might be, the elephant lurching toward them was not ungainly.

Caught napping at the far end of the corridor, it had taken a moment to rise to all fours. Impressive tusks had been filed down to sharp points tipped with steel. Custom-fitted leather chain mail protected skull and torso, while heavier leather leggings covered the pillarlike legs. Eyes sparkled while the sensitive trunk probed the air in the passageway.

"I don't recognize your shape or smell," it rumbled dangerously. "Intruders?"

"Watch out!" Heke blurted thoughtlessly. "He'll sound the alarm!"

The elephant generated a robust chuckle. "Why would I want to do that? If I give an alarm then I have to share you with others, when I'd much rather stomp you all flat by myself."

Only one guard to bypass. Of course, if that guard was a homicidal pachyderm, Jon-Tom realized, you might only need one.

"Back!" Naike yelled. He held his sword out in front of him, looking for a way past even as he retreated. There wasn't one. The elephant occupied the corridor completely, its hair brushing the walls on both sides.

Reaching out with the tip of its trunk, the guard tripped a

hidden lever. The imagined concealed door Jon-Tom had been worrying about all along finally made its debut, sliding down lubricated rollers to slam firmly shut . . . behind them.

When the gardener had spoken of the complex being easy to enter but difficult to escape, he had not been waxing philosophical. Now the reason for the compound's design became clear. Each of the corridors which connected the principal structures to one another was also a potential trap for the unwary, a restrictive and easily manipulated tunnel in which intruders could be isolated, trapped, and summarily dealt with without exposing the household staff or the elegant furnishings to any danger.

Still sampling the air, the elephant took another step toward them. Like Naike, Jon-Tom sought a way past. The mongooses and otter might be quick enough to dodge the probing trunk, but dashing between those massive legs was another proposition entirely. Anyone attempting it would get no second chance to correct a mistake in judgment. It was something to be tried only as a last resort.

Which, he mused as the prodigious guard backed them inexorably toward the unyielding barrier which had slammed down behind them, was a possibility they might have to consider all too soon.

"We're done!" moaned Pauko despondently.

Mudge had his bow out and took a careful shot, but the arrow failed to penetrate the leather armor.

"Don't make him mad," Heke urged the otter. Mudge turned a disbelieving eye on the mongoose nearest him.

"Don't make 'im mad? Why? So 'e won't kill us as much?" He looked fretfully at his old friend. "Much as it pains me to admit it, we've got only one 'ope." As he confessed this, he found himself wishing that he'd hung on to some of the sound-dampening moss he'd utilized back in the swamp.

Having decided that it was useless to try to parry trunk or tusk with a mere sword, Jon-Tom was already strumming vigorously on the duar. Built of laminated wood for added strength and inscribed with haughty admonitions, the unyielding gate loomed large behind them. He had no time to spend on becoming cleverness.

Mudge reminded him of this fact in his usual inimitable fashion. *"Sing something, stupid!"* the otter screamed even as he notched another futile arrow against his bowstring.

This time his feathered shaft pierced a delicate ear. Their tormentor responded with a startled wail of pain. "That hurt! Just for that I'm going to stomp your legs first and leave your heads for last!"

"We mean no one in this household any harm!" Naike explained desperately. "We wish only to recover our Princess."

The elephant trumpeted derisively. "Another party of princess rescuers! They come periodically. All end up as fodder for the swamp scavengers. As will you. Your puny weapons do not frighten me, nor do you look rich enough to buy me off. Not that you could anyway. Master Manzai takes care of his own, and I enjoy being part of his retinue." Lips flexed in a pachydermal grimace. "And every once in a while, I get to stomp bothersome intruders."

The trunk swiped suddenly, forcing Naike to jump backward. Anything slower than a mongoose would have been snatched up.

"Quick," complimented the elephant. "All of you look quick, except the human. It won't matter. You can't run around me, and if you try to run under me, I'll sit on you. They don't have time to scream when I sit on them."

Lyrics. He needed appropriate lyrics! Aware that he was fast running out of time, Jon-Tom strove furiously to think of something apropos.

Pertinent or not, he began to sing.

Mudge goggled at him. "Wot's *that*, mate? Wot nonsense are you blatherin'?" When the spellsinger ignored him, Mudge turned to the others. "Does any o' this make any sense to any o' you lot?"

A slack-jawed Pauko stared back at him. The mongoose's eyes were dimming.

The warm refulgence that issued from the duar's nexus expanded rapidly to fill the space between the rescuers and the guard. It impacted on the huge, flapping ears like blue fog, causing them to flick forward. An expression which could only be described as elemental goofiness took possession of the elephant's features.

Slumping, it tottered against the right-hand wall, which groaned but did not collapse beneath the weight. The flexible trunk bobbed loosely, like a fishing line cast in a millrace.

For good measure Jon-Tom invented two additional stanzas. Only when he'd concluded the last of them did he turn to congratulate his companion.

"Mudge, you're brilliant! It worked!"

"Duh, wot?" Whiskers drooping, upper body swaying, the otter gaped in dull-eyed bemusement up at his friend.

"I said that you're brilliant." His enthusiasm tempered by his friend's peculiar response, Jon-Tom leaned down and forward to study the otter's face. "Mudge, what's wrong with you?"

"Duh-eee? Nuttin's wrong wid me, mate." His bow dangled limply from one hand.

"Come on, all of you!" Jon-Tom indicated the dumb-dazzled guard. "Can't you see the spellsong worked? He's incapacitated, though I don't know for how long. Let's go." He stared at them. *"What's wrong with you all?"*

The mongooses were wandering about in a collective daze. Heke and Pauko were locked in an addlepated minuet, each attempting unsuccessfully to step past the other, only for the two of them to run repeatedly into each other every time they tried to pass. A befuddled Karaukul was engaged in an absorbed inspection of his own fingers, as if questioning not only their presence but their origin. Even Naike was bumping his head gently but repeatedly against the gate behind them, trying to batter his way through while doing little more than putting an unbecoming dent in the fur of his forehead.

It was left to an anxious Jon-Tom to cajole and shepherd them one at a time past the guard, who was now mumbling to himself as gelatinous drool dripped from his mouth.

Emerging into a spacious rotunda furnished for casual entertaining, the spellsinger searched until he found the hoped-for wall switch. Thrown, it dropped a duplicate of the first gate down between themselves and the befuddled elephant. Jon-Tom hoped the barriers were strong enough to keep their would-be executioner trapped in the now isolated corridor.

He didn't know how long the spell would last. When it wore off, the infuriated elephant was sure to rouse the entire household. Before that happened they had to find and free the Princess and return to the safety of the trackless swamp.

But first he had to round up the wandering mongooses and Mudge and devise an antidote to the previous spellsong. This wasted a fair amount of precious time, but he had no choice. Eventually, otter and soldiers found themselves restored.

"What sort of sly sorcery was that?" Naike felt of his forehead where he'd been bashing it against the first barrier. "What did you do to us?"

"I intended it only for the guard's benefit. It wasn't meant to affect you." He glanced guiltily in Mudge's direction. "Sometimes my spellsinging tends to be more omnidirectional than I'd like."

"Sometimes, 'ell." Alone among all of them, only the otter realized what had happened.

"It was a good idea."

"Your ideas are often good, mate. 'Tis your execution that's frequently found wantin'."

"I just did what you suggested."

The otter frowned uncertainly. "Wot *I* suggested?"

"You told me to sing something stupid."

Mudge pawed at his face with both hands even as he turned pleading eyes on the four soldiers. "See? See wot I've 'ad to cope with goin' on past these twenty years? Be grateful 'e didn't turn the lot o' us into newts. Or even oldts."

"It surely differs from any sorcery I have ever heard tell of," the Lieutenant admitted.

"But it is effective," added the dour Karaukul.

Jon-Tom was a bit miffed. "The important thing is that we're all all right and past the guard."

Heke glanced uneasily at the wooden gate. "For how long?"

"I don't know. Let's find your Princess and get out of here."

Naike had his nose high in the air, sniffing. "I believe I detect her scent in this very room, though it is heavily masked by that of many other individuals."

"Just as long as none o' it reeks o' elephant." Mudge was working the atmosphere with his own nostrils. Given such scent-sensitive companions Jon-Tom knew it would be futile to attempt any sniffing of his own.

They spread out to sample the air in the rotunda, gradually achieving a convergence of opinion which led them down another, narrower corridor. This time nothing materialized to challenge their presence. The passageway opened into a second rotunda that was a smaller but higher-ceilinged duplicate of the first.

As they neared the dimly lit chamber Naike bid them slow. A series of barred rooms radiated westward from the center of the domed room. Faint music could be heard emanating from several. Here even Jon-Tom could smell the perfume. On the far side of the rotunda still another corridor led off into darkness.

Seated at a table in the center of the room a pair of female raccoons jousted at what initially appeared to be a variant of chess but which, on closer inspection, revealed game pieces of quite different and obscene design. The intention of the game escaped him, nor did he choose to expend much curiosity on trying to puzzle it out.

The furnishings which surrounded them verged on the opulent. Fine silk cushions and overstuffed pillows lay scattered everywhere. Conspicuous luxury notwithstanding, the locks on the radiating doors were solid and heavy, as were the gilded bars on the small windows set into each door.

"Aleaukauna must be in one of those cells," Naike whispered.

"First on the left." Karaukul's nose was the most sensitive of the group. "There are many interesting smells. Some strange, yet—"

"Never mind them," snapped the Lieutenant laconically. "Aleaukauna is the only one who concerns us."

"What about the attendants?" Heke indicated the preoccupied raccoons.

"I could dazzle 'em with me charm," Mudge suggested blithely.

Jon-Tom was quick to respond. "Better we try something with a chance of working."

"Like another o' your site-specific spellsongs?" the otter shot back.

"It would seem the obvious choice." Naike missed the sarcasm completely. Or perhaps he was merely avoiding it. "Why not put them to sleep, as you did with the gardener?"

"I didn't have to worry about messing that spellsong up," Jon-Tom replied. "He was our captive. If I failed he wasn't going anywhere." He studied the two naturally masked females. "If I try it on this pair and it doesn't work but only alerts them to our presence, they could take off and wake the whole household."

"Then it would seem that more direct measures are called for." The Lieutenant removed a silken scarf from the pouch slung at his side. Holding an end in each hand, he twirled it twice. "Heke, you and Pauko take the one on the left. Karaukul, you come with me."

" 'Ere now, guv, wot about us?" Mudge wondered.

"Do as you see fit, but keep clear. This sort of activity falls comfortably within our province."

Before man or otter could say anything else, the four soldiers burst into the rotunda. Though not quite as agile as Mudge, they were even faster on their feet. By the time either of the two attendants had a chance to react to their presence, they found themselves stretched out on the floor, bound and gagged. Though they struggled furiously, they were no match for the four travel-toughened soldiers. Furious eyes gazed out at Naike from above silken gags.

Feeling clumsier than ever in the presence of so much speed and quickness, Jon-Tom kept well out of the way until the mongooses had concluded their business and plugged their ears. Only then did he croon the lullaby he'd used on the gardener. It worked equally well on the two attendants. Deep in sleep, they were propped up in their respective chairs by the soldiers. Anyone passing by who happened to look in on them would assume they had fallen asleep at their game.

Wasting no time in admiring their handiwork, Naike removed the ornamental key ring from the waistband of the eldest attendant and hurried to the first cell. The third key fit the lock precisely. There was no response from within as he pushed it aside. They crowded forward, Jon-Tom pulling the door shut soundlessly behind them.

Without question it was the most sumptuous prison he had ever seen. Thick draperies two stories high covered the vaulted windows at the far end of the chamber. A stained-glass skylight depicting streams and woodlands dominated the painted ceiling, allowing admittance to the light of the rising moon.

On their right squatted a massive yet elegant bathtub built up out of blocks of solid travertine and malachite. Gold fixtures in the shape of dolphins and seals gleamed from the far side. Where the material had been brought from and at what expense Jon-Tom could not imagine.

Thick cushions covered much of the floor, cresting like waves against a rocky shore wherever furniture rested. As they crept farther into the room, it grew progressively wider, as if they were advancing outward from the center of a pie.

Mudge was first to catch sight of the enormous bed, carved from wood as red as blood. It seemed to float gracefully above the richly carpeted floor, overtopped by a canopy of pink and green silk shot through with gold thread. Sitting up in it now and blinking sleepily at them was a lithe, supple gray-brown form. There was more concern than panic in her query.

"Who is it, who's there?"

At the sound of her voice the four soldiers rushed forward to prostrate themselves at the side and foot of the bed.

"Your most exalted and supreme Highness!" Naike's voice was constricted with emotion. "I am Lieutenant Naike of the Clan C'Huritoupa. These are my troops." He proceeded to name each of them before turning back to her. "All good and true soldiers of Harakun. We have dreamed of this moment for many months. Now we are here, and at your disposal. As are our allies and friends, the adventurer Mudge and the great spellsinger Jon-Tom." He was sufficiently emboldened by their accomplishment to meet her gaze directly.

"Your mother, the Queen, has all but despaired of your safe return. She misses you desperately, as do your sisters and brother."

The Princess nodded. She was wide awake now, and thinking hard. "That I regret, though not the confrontation which led to my present irksome situation. I take it you are here to effect my rescue?"

"No." Having had his long look at the royal self, Mudge was now anxiously watching the door. "We thought we might 'ave your company at a nice tea party, we did, and then be on our 'appy-go-lucky way."

"Be nice, Mudge." Jon-Tom chided his companion . "She's been under a lot of stress."

"Oi, I can see that from the 'orrific conditions to which she's been subjected." The otter kicked at a satin pillow stuffed with the finest down, his boot sinking into it up to the ankle.

Meanwhile she had slipped out of the bed and into a wrap that was like a snowstorm of pale blue chiffon. Jon-Tom observed that her shape was slightly slimmer, her coloring a shade lighter than that of the soldiers, though the dark bands on her lower body and tail were equally distinctive. Mudge was eyeing her afresh with something other than indifferent respect.

Same old Mudge. Jon-Tom smiled to himself. Otters never changed.

Aleaukauna rested a paw on Naike's shoulder. "You have come a long way to rescue me. I did not think I would *need* rescuing, but then I did not expect to have to deal with one as deceitful as my captor. Your reward shall be commensurate with your deeds." She bestowed an affectionate gaze upon the quartet of bright-eyed, eager soldiers. "But first there is much that needs be done."

"Truly yes." The Lieutenant nodded toward the door. "This place is defended from the inside out, making escape difficult."

"I have seen much of it," she told him. "Though my movements were controlled, my eyes were not. I think I can find us a safe way out."

Heke started for the portal. "Then let's be on our way, Your Highness, before the sleeping spell Jon-Tom laid on your guards wears off or another comes to check on you." Pausing at the doorway, he peered cautiously through the small barred window. "Still asleep," he informed his companions.

Eyes like polished onyx lit from within met Jon-Tom's own. It was a look of complete confidence and utter lack of inhibition. The combination rocked him.

"A real spellsinger," she murmured admiringly.

"Aye," declared Naike proudly. "And his brave companion."

Stepping forward, Mudge took the Princess's delicate hand and bestowed upon its back a whiskery kiss that Jon-Tom thought lingered long enough to exceed the bounds of propriety.

"Mudge . . ." he began warningly.

The otter glanced back reassuringly. "I know, mate, I know. We're only 'ere to 'elp with the rescue." Grinning ingratiatingly, he turned back to the Princess. "That don't mean we should overlook our bloomin' manners, it don't. I ain't never met a real princess before."

More amused than anything else, she regally withdrew her hand. "Evidently."

"You have to excuse my friend." Jon-Tom stepped up. "He's . . . not shy."

"Fortune favors the bold," she commented with a smile.

A frowning Naike interposed himself between Mudge and Aleaukauna. "The night wanes, and with it our margin of safety. If you truly know a circumspect path out of this place, Your Highness, we should pursue it as quickly as possible."

She nodded. Gathering her chiffon about her she started for the door, the Lieutenant hovering at her side.

"We'll have you back at the palace in a month's time."

"I know that you will, Lieutenant, bold and competent as you and your troops are. However, I cannot leave until certain obligations I have set upon myself are fulfilled."

Heke and Pauko exchanged a baffled look. Naike spoke uncertainly. "Your Highness, I'm afraid I don't understand. What obligations?"

"I am of royal blood. As such I have a duty not only to Harakun and to my family, but to others who share that status."

"Others?" Naike was trying to fight off the notion that was swelling in his mind.

They all fell within range of her sweetly imperious gaze, Mudge and Jon-Tom included. She had very long eyelashes, Jon-Tom noted.

"What I mean is that I could not in good conscience seek safety for myself if it meant abandoning my sisters to continued imprisonment."

"Why the 'ell not?" Mudge muttered under his breath. "Sounds like a reasonable course o' action to me."

From his position near the door Heke pleaded deferentially. "Your Highness, I am only a poor soldier, but it seems to me that we have no time here to spare on diversions, however noble the cause. Jon-Tom's spell could fail at any moment, or other guards could come and discover us. We need to be away from here, and quickly!"

Ignoring him, she indicated the ornate ring which jangled on Naike's wrist. "You have the keys to the other chambers. It will take only moments to free my sisters in isolation."

"Maybe," admitted Pauko, "but a larger party of escapees will be easier to detect."

"Already we are seven," she argued. "What matters a few more?"

"What indeed," Naike groused.

"Do I command you or not?" she snapped.

Placing his right arm across his chest, the Lieutenant bowed low. "We who serve are here to do your bidding, Highness."

"Speak for yourself, guv." Turning to leave, Mudge found himself held back by a heavy human hand.

"Mudge, we can't just abandon them now."

"Oi, can't we, then?" The otter eyed him coolly. "Just watch me."

"Going to find your own way out?" Jon-Tom inquired calmly.

At the door the otter paused with one hand on the handle. Then he turned and waved an angry finger at his friend. " 'Ere now, if I didn't think you'd get your bloody overbearin' self killed after all these years, I bloody well *would* take off on me own!"

"Of course you would." Jon-Tom suppressed a smile. "I know that I wouldn't have a chance out there without you to watch over me."

"Well, as long as you know that," said the otter huffily. He stepped aside to let Naike and the Princess pass.

The rotunda was still deserted save for the two somnolent attendants, who rested upright in their chairs like a pair of soft sculptures. Around them, the compound still slept. Of particular note, no outraged trumpeting reverberated from a distant, isolated corridor.

Still safe, Jon-Tom assured himself as he wondered how much longer the stupid spell (as it were) would hold.

The portal next to Aleaukauna's yielded to another of the ornate keys on Naike's ring. She pushed past him, whispering urgently into the moonlit interior. From out in the rotunda Jon-Tom could see that the chamber closely resembled the one that had been home and cell to the Princess.

"Umagi! It's Aleaukauna. Rouse yourself. From Harakun have come brave ones to free us!"

"Really?" The voice was quite deep, Jon-Tom thought, but still distinctively feminine. "It's about time. I wish I could speak as well for my own ineffectual followers."

There was a blur of activity within. Then the Princess and Naike stepped back, trailed by a massive shape draped in yellow and black suede.

Princess Umagi of Tuuro Exalted was a very graceful, very imposing, and very large mountain gorilla. Jon-Tom estimated her weight at between three hundred and four hundred pounds (it was hard to be any more precise because nearly everything was concealed beneath the flowing suede). Resting on massive feet and one set of knuckles, she used her other hand to brush back the tail of the black and silver scarf she had tied around her forehead. A matching, transparent veil masked her face.

Jon-Tom found himself thinking not about her, but about Manzai. Then he leaned over to whisper to Mudge.

"Well?"

"Well, wot, mate?"

"Aren't you going to be polite and kiss her hand?"

"Ain't sure I could lift it, mate. Why don't you give it a go?"

Jon-Tom straightened. "I'll stick with a simple hello, as always."

Princess Umagi hugged Aleaukauna, the mongoose all but vanishing within the expansive simian embrace. "The others?" the she-gorilla inquired.

Aleaukauna nodded emphatically. "Each in their turn. We'll leave no one here for our captor to toy with."

From the next cell they liberated Quiquell of Opan, a silky anteater fluid of form and tongue. That extraordinary organ bestowed a grateful lick upon each of the rescuers in turn, wrapping entirely around a startled Jon-Tom's face before the tip eventually touched him on the lips. It was, he reflected somewhat dazedly, a kiss of thanks like no other.

In contrast, her voice was whispery and barely audible—a reflection of the extremely narrow physiognomy from which it emerged.

"Half done," announced Aleaukauna briskly as they moved along.

Who next? Jon-Tom found himself wondering. Or rather, what next? One of the attendants let out a snuffle and he turned sharply in the sleeping raccoons' direction. How much longer could the rescuers count on passing unnoticed? It struck him that they were playing their luck for all it was worth.

From the next chamber they freed Seshenshe of Paressi Glissar, a lynx of fine form and grand manner. She was effusive in her thanks, giving Jon-Tom a nervous moment to admire the whitest, sharpest teeth he had ever seen so near to his own.

This won't be a problem, he tried to convince himself as Naike struggled with the lock to the next cell. *Everything's under control.*

Then the Lieutenant shoved aside the barrier to liberate the next princess, and the spellsinger's control went as shaky as his legs.

CHAPTER 9

ANSIBETTE OF BOROBOS HAD HAIR THE SHADE OF IMPERIAL topaz and eyes of translucent lapis. Six feet tall, she seemed formed from what at first glance appeared to be an unholy amalgam of taffy and marble. There was entirely too much of what she was to be restrained within a single epidermal envelope, yet somehow her body succeeded in sustaining this unprecedented feat of physiological legerdemain.

She was, if anything, more than human. Her natural grace left him feeling like a beached sturgeon.

Mudge eyed his friend appraisingly. "*Tch*—utter loss o' the critical faculties. Note the vacant expression, the slack jaw, the limp upper limbs." He jabbed his friend sharply in the ribs.

Jon-Tom blinked angrily. "What was that for?"

"Sorry, mate, but you were forgettin' to breathe." He rubbed his paws together. "One more to go an' then we're out o' this gilded cesspool. That is, if you can get your legs to work."

Princess Ansibette's voice was a duet for harp and celesta. "Oh, thank you, thank you all for your bravery and courage!" Like her royal sisters, she advanced to individually praise her rescuers. Unable to move, Jon-Tom awaited what was to come.

She took his hand and shook it firmly before moving on to likewise acknowledge Mudge and the others.

It broke the spell and enabled him to move, though his

head threatened to twist completely around atop his shoulders.

"She's just another damn spoiled royal," the otter reminded him. "One more we'll 'ave to baby-sit until we're clear o' this dump."

"Right." Jon-Tom managed to mumble. "Just another ex-prisoner. Or ex-collectible." It was easier to think about Manzai than about . . . than about . . .

He pressed on, resolutely struggling to keep his eyes to himself.

" 'Onestly." Mudge murmured his disapproval. " 'Umans!"

"One last chamber, and then all are freed and we can be off." Aleaukauna did her best to hurry Naike along.

Her urging was superfluous. Even as she spoke, the Lieutenant was turning the key in the lock. Awakened by all the activity, Pivver of Trenku-han was already dressed and waiting for them.

She was smaller than the princesses Ansibette and Umagi, but as tall as Aleaukauna. Perfectly groomed deep brown fur shone from beneath green and gold silks while alert eyes darted from one rescuer to the next. Legs and arms were as short as her tail, but her torso was sinuous and supple.

She was, in short, an otter, and it was Jon-Tom's turn to chortle.

As Aleaukauna started off, Naike was forced to restrain her.

"Your pardon, Highness, but we cannot flee that direction."

"why not?" Quiquell demanded to know.

"Because there's a temporarily loopy elephant blocking the way, and he's shut up behind doors we don't know how to open," Jon-Tom explained. "We'll have to find another way out."

"You were fortunate to get this far," Princess Pivver declared admiringly.

"Oi, fortunate's our middle names!" Mudge's whiskers quivered. The otter was the only creature Jon-Tom had ever met who could strut sitting down.

Pivver was lovely, he had to admit. For a member of the *Lutrinae*. As for Mudge, he was floating along a finger's width or so above the floor. His friend, Mudge. Mudge the Flagrant, Mudge the Lecherous, Mudge the . . .

You're worrying too much, Jon-Tom admonished himself. Pivver was a royal princess. No doubt she knew how to handle rogues, even one who had participated in her rescue and to whom she might feel she owed something. Not that it was any of his business.

This line of thought caused him to think of Talea, which made him more than a little uncomfortable every time Ansibette of Borobos crossed his line of vision.

"Then we must try to make our escape through the kitchens." Aleaukauna started off in the opposite direction, her short legs switching spryly back and forth. "They should be empty of servitors this time of night, and Manzai does not set a guard over his silverware and kettles."

Moonlight and the occasional flickering glowbulb lit their way, until they emerged into a room crowded with heavily lacquered tables and chairs. Passing silently past the empty seats, they pushed on into the kitchen itself. Sinks and soup vats glistened in the murky light.

It was Ansibette who, taking overmuch care in where she placed her feet, neglected to pay equal attention to the rest of herself and banged into a hanging copper strainer, setting it to jangling metallically. Knocked from its hook, it clattered to the hard floor, sounding in the shattered silence like a bolt of metallic lightning.

Everyone froze, eyes striving to pierce the darkness. Just as Jon-Tom was convinced everything was okay, a voice broke the silence.

"What's that? Who's there?"

The words were couched in sleepiness and possibly also a touch of alcohol. No one moved, no one breathed.

But the cursed figure refused to be put off by the unresponsive silence. Stumbling slightly and clutching a half-empty bottle in one hand, the ringtail rose up from behind a large, juice-streaked cutting block and gawked in their direction.

"I said, *who's there?*"

"Damnation!" Without hesitation Pivver headed straight for the slightly addled but now all too conscious servant. The bulky shadow of Umagi of Tuuro trailed behind.

A puzzled smile creased the face of the squinting ringtail. "Oh, it's you, Chamber Number One. And Number Two as well. Say, what are you doing out of your cells unescort—"

Realization struck before Pivver could.

"Help, help, escape, someone hel—"

Pivver hit him low while Umagi slapped an enormous paw over his mouth and snout. An instant later the four soldiers relieved the princesses of any further responsibility. They also relieved the hapless servant of his last breath.

Not quite in time, unfortunately.

From the far corners of the complex voices began to call: querulous, sleepy, uncertain, but very definitely awake.

"That's torn it," Mudge cursed.

"I'm sorry," mumbled a distraught Ansibette. "I was trying to be careful. Sometimes I just bump into things."

Jon-Tom was quick to comfort her. "Forget it. We've been incredibly lucky to make it this far without rousing someone." Even in the near darkness her eyes flashed azure.

"You're *very* understanding."

A tremor somewhere between eight and nine on the body's own seismic scale raced through him. This was a voice sweet enough, he realized, to candy a man's soul.

The all but forgotten cloud of chords chimed urgently at his shoulder, as if perceiving that something was amiss. He didn't need music to urge him on. As for Mudge, the otter looked drugged. Which he was, Jon-Tom knew. The drug's name was Pivver of Trenku.

She was either oblivious to his attentions or else aware and ignoring him as she plotted strategy with her fellow royals and the Lieutenant.

Aleaukauna and Seshenshe led the way down a side corridor as voices continued to grow louder all around them. The buzz of awakening servitors was nothing compared to the alarm they could expect when the body of the unlucky nocturnal imbiber was discovered. By that time they would do well to be far from the complex.

Aleaukauna indicated a bend in the corridor. "There should be a door here leading to a loading ramp."

"There'd better be." Pauko was puffing hard as he loped along.

They needn't have worried. As they rounded the corner, they were greeted by the sight of a large double doorway. This opened into a spacious chamber in which containers large and small were neatly sorted and stacked. At about the same time a muffled roar as of distant surf rose behind them.

"Someone's found the body," Heke announced.

"They sshouldn't ssusspect uss immediately." Seshenshe's long, tufted ears were turned in the direction of the distant confusion. "After all, we're ssuppossedly unarmed and locked up."

"That will gain us only a little more time. They'll find your two sleeping attendants soon enough." Naike was examining the doors. "Locked from the inside!"

"Tough to get out of," Karaukul murmured mournfully as he echoed the four-legged gardener.

Jon-Tom prepared to compose a lock-picking spell, but Mudge roused himself from his self-induced stupor long enough to give the heavy chain and padlock the professional once-over. As it developed, neither of their services were required.

"Pardon me." Trailing her fragile silk headband, princess Umagi lumbered daintily on all fours over to the doorway and gripped the restraining chain in both hands. At the same time a shout sounded in the corridor they had just vacated.

"There they are!"

" 'Ave at the rotters!" Drawing his bow and peering around the corner, Mudge put a feathered shaft in the neck of the first sentry to start toward them. This gave those coming up fast behind reason to hesitate.

The otter barked back at his companions. "No shilly-shal-lyin'! I can't 'old 'em 'ere for long!"

"Nice shot." Pivver had slipped up to stand just behind him.

He beamed irresistibly. "Want to see me stick the next one with one leg crossed?"

"Don't stand there gawking at me, you piss-eyed idiot! Pay attention to your work!"

Well, maybe he was resistible. Setting his jaw, he notched another arrow.

Expecting to encounter a brace of escaped princesses and finding themselves confronted instead by an arrow-shooting otter, a quartet of halberd-wielding mongooses, and an over-large human hefting a sword longer than any of them, the recently roused guards decided to restrain themselves until reinforcements could arrive. Which, Jon-Tom sensed as he readied himself, could be presently. He yelled back over a shoulder.

"Umagi . . . I mean, Your Highness! I don't advise hanging around here much longer!"

"Patience, man!" came the reply. It was followed a moment later by several deeply voiced but feminine profani-ties and then a metallic snapping sound as the chain restrict-ing their egress came apart in the princess's massive fists. "The way is clear!"

"Righty-ho, 'tis time to be off." Lowering his bow, Mudge put an arm around Pivver and hurried to join the others. She did not shake him off. Very tolerant she was, Jon-Tom reflected.

With the princesses leading the way, the fugitives piled out onto the wooden ramp and down to the narrow road that rapidly disappeared into the surrounding greenery. The moon had gone down and the sun was threatening to put in an appearance at any moment. Behind them, lights were coming on throughout the length and breadth of the complex.

"We must leave this road and try to conceal ourselves within the swamp," Naike told Jon-Tom.

The spellsinger shook his head. "There are too many of us and we'd make too much noise. Their Highnesses don't have proper clothing or footwear. And pursuers can track us by smell." He did not need to point out that the party of escapees reeked of expensive perfumes.

"Where does this road lead?" Naike inquired of their charges.

"there is no proper road." They had to strain to understand Quiquell's breathy reply. "but south lies mashupro."

"Then we have no choice. We must hope to outrun them."

For a time they jogged along in silence. Despite the muggy, cloying air, Jon-Tom was surprised at how good he felt. Better than he had in years, if the truth be known. With Pivver at his side, Mudge virtually flowed along nearby, his youthful enthusiasm restored along with his energy. For the moment, at least, the thought of being sliced and diced by Manzai's minions seemed to concern him not in the slightest.

Observing the two otters as they strode along chatting in tandem caused Jon-Tom's attention to shift involuntarily to the princess Ansibette. She ran easily, her long legs giving her an advantage over Umagi, Quiquell, and the others. They were also giving him fits.

"They're coming." Naike tried to decide whether to keep on running or counterattack, thereby hopefully giving the princesses some time in which to put more distance between themselves and their pursuers. He put the question to his troops.

"What about setting an ambush?" Heke suggested.

"If we do that, some will still get past us." The Lieutenant turned to query his charges. "How many servants and soldiers does this Manzai command?"

"We don't know," Pivver told him between breaths. "I can number at least a hundred from memory."

"And none of uss armed." Seshenshe was angry at herself.

"We sshould have taken weaponss before departing. Knivess from the kitchen, if nothing elsse."

"Belabor yourself not with recriminations," Naike told her. "We will do what we can." He slowed and the others with him. "Conceal yourselves as best you are able in these rushes."

Ansibette eyed the dense, mucky growth that lined the trail with obvious distaste. "It smells of something dead in there."

"That's the idea." The Lieutenant turned back toward the now distant complex. "The rest of us will confront them briefly and then retreat into the swamp, making as much noise as we can. Hopefully they will all follow us, leaving you time to flee in relative safety. If fortune smiles on us, we will lose them in the bogs while you find a helpful wagon driver or boatman." When Aleaukauna tried to speak, Naike forestalled her.

"No, Your Highness." Exhibiting uncharacteristic audacity, he reached out to tenderly brush her cheek. "We were prepared to sell our lives in your cause long before this."

"True soldiers of Harakun you are," she replied affectionately. "Noble and brave."

"And stupid," added Mudge. This time the Lieutenant overheard. He whirled sharply to confront the otter.

"You have a better idea?"

Mudge was not intimidated. "Look 'ere, guv. This Manzai bloke may be a bastard, but 'e's a smart bastard. You take off into the great green goo yonder an' 'e'll send pursuit after you, sure, but 'e's not goin' to assume you've abandoned the only road out o' 'ere. 'E'll send some to check on it, right enough. And they'll find our cache o' princesses." His whiskers twitched vigorously as he turned to face Jon-Tom.

"As for suggestions, it pains me to say this, mate, but your singin' is the nearest thing to a better idea I can think of."

"What, him?" Umagi's heavy brows lowered as she considered the tall human. "What can he do?"

" 'E's a spellsinger, 'e is. Through 'is music 'e commands vast if somewot fickle powers."

"This is so," put in Naike. "I myself have seen him at work." He looked up at Jon-Tom, who was already thoughtfully fingering the strings of the duar. "Use the sleeping spell, magician."

"Or the stupid one," added Heke hopefully.

Standing tall at the center of their concern, Jon-Tom plucked at the two sets of strings as he strode purposefully out into the center of the road. Nearby, the lost chords compacted into a concerned ball of light and sound.

"Actually, I think something stronger is in order."

"That's right, mate!" barked Mudge encouragingly. "Show 'em your power. Make 'em crawl whinin' an' whimperin' back to their beds!" To the princesses he added in a lower voice, "I suggest you each find yourselves a 'ollow or a stout tree to 'ide behind, I do."

Pivver glared at him. "Have you confidence in your friend's abilities or not?"

"Oh, I do, I do. But you 'ave to understand, I've also seen 'im work." Whereupon he began searching for a temporary refuge for himself.

A mob of angry, armed figures was advancing down the narrow dirt road toward the tired, sweaty refugees. The first suggestions of sunrise sparkled from the tips and edges of numerous weapons. There might be less than a hundred of them, Jon-Tom decided as he considered the unbroken wall of approaching mayhem. Still more than enough to overpower the little band of escapees.

Which meant it was all up to him. As usual.

It was a condition he was familiar with, though one he hadn't been forced to face for many years. Potential lyrics tumbled through his mind. In years past he would have sought to project overwhelming power, awesome strength. But that, he'd learned sometimes painfully, could be difficult or even impossible to control. Subtlety was the hallmark of the accomplished sorcerer. Select the magic to match the situation. "Waste not, want not" was a homily that applied as well to magic as to the rest of life.

It was also much safer.

As those behind him looked on (several from behind rocks or large trees), he began to sing. Not of fire and destruction, of chaos and cataclysm, but of better times and better climes. Of a more peaceful environment and genial surroundings. Sorcerially speaking, it was, given the danger bearing rapidly down on them, something of a departure. So much so that a baffled and worried Mudge rose from his hiding place.

"Oi, mate, wot the bloody 'ell are you posturin' on about? We need to be thinkin' life an' death 'ere, not meditation an' pretty posies!"

Ignoring him, Jon-Tom sang on.

"Another place, another time
a different day, a different clime
I'm so tired of trading blows
with enemies I don't even know
So shift us quick but shift us slow
Or I'll be forced to fight in mime."

At the appalling and sense-distorting mention of the word *mime* the hovering chord cloud began to tremble plangently. Simultaneously a sinister green mist began to issue from the glowing nexus at the heart of the duar.

"That's it, mate!" barked Mudge zealously. "Melt the flesh from their bones, suck the breath from their lungs! Fry 'em where they stand!"

Jon-Tom didn't have time to explain to his companion that he had something rather different in mind, though the precise structure and hue of the rising, swelling mist did worry him somewhat. It expanded until it had enveloped them all. The cool green fog tickled slightly. It was a sensation he had experienced once before—long, long ago, on a headland just outside San Francisco Bay.

For a horrible moment he saw the spellsong transporting the lot of them crossworld to that place, where the presence of an intelligent otter, four oversized mongoose soldiers, and half a dozen princesses of various species would be more than a little difficult to explain. They would make quite a sight materializing in Ghiradelli Square or at Fisherman's Wharf.

On the other hand, he reassured himself as he balladeered on, it *was* San Francisco he was thinking about.

Only when the mist was thick enough to obscure their surroundings utterly did he lower his voice and begin to seek an end to the music. Gradually the exhilarating vapor began to dissipate and he saw that the spellsong had indeed done its work. All those years of practice, those uncounted days of hard study under Clothahump's severe gaze and sage tutelage, those many long evenings spent reading and researching the ancient tomes, had finally paid off.

Physical transposition was among the most complex and difficult of all magics to master, and he had unarguably moved each and every one of the escapees: princesses, soldiers, Mudge, himself, even the lost music. Twisting itself into a microcosmic tornado of notes, it sang soft sibilant semihemiquavers of increasing harmonic confidence, perhaps sensing at last that it was in the presence of a master sorcerer and spellsinger.

There was just one problem. He'd only moved them half a mile down the road. They were still near enough to see the lights of Manzai's compound.

"Oh that's luverly, that is!" Mudge complained. With a resigned sigh he prepared to load his bow again.

"Well, I moved us, didn't I?" Jon-Tom frowned at the duar, fine-tuning one of the frets. "Must be a problem with the lyric-to-weight ratio. If there were fewer of us we'd probably have traveled farther. Remember, I'm used to working with just you and I."

"I do not undersstand," said Seshenshe. "What happened to uss?"

"Shifted us, 'e did, Your Softness," Mudge explained. " 'E just didn't shift us far enough for comfort."

A shout was heard from up the road. Momentarily taken

aback by the appearance of the billowing green cloud, their
tormentors had once again caught sight of the escapees and
resumed their pursuit.

"Oi, mate, you'd best sing it again. Maybe the spellsong
moves us slowly, but 'tis still faster than this lot can run."

"I don't know if that's such a good idea." Jon-Tom continued to fuss with the frets. Tuning an instrument that func-
tioned simultaneously in multiple dimensions was a task fit to
tax a Hendrix or Satriani. "As you pointed out, it didn't work
very well the last time."

"Oh, she worked all right, mate. She just didn't work
much. But a little magic's better than none. Try 'er again."

Not knowing what else to do and lacking time for languid
contemplation, Jon-Tom complied, varying the lyrics as
much as possible within the confines of the particular conjuration he was propounding. Only this time he kept right on
singing even after they'd rematerialized another half mile or
so down the road.

The green cloud re-formed and dissipated, dissipated and
re-formed. In that fashion they hopscotched in and out of
existence toward distant Mashupro, slowly but steadily out-
distancing their pursuers. Manzai's minions had only their
legs to convey them forward, while soldiers and princesses
alike traveled effortlessly on the wings of the spellsinger's
nimble fingers and off-key tenor.

A pity the kids weren't with them, Jon-Tom reflected even
as he sang on. They could have spelled him (so to speak).
And he would soon be in need of a break. Despite occasional
pauses for a quick swallow of water, hoarseness was beginning to creep into the back of his throat. If he gave out while
pursuit persisted, all would be lost. As if sensing his distress,
the chord cloud swirled anxiously around him, careful to
avoid the glowing duar but concerned for his condition.

"Be careful, spellsinger." Ansibette was shaking mud from
one foot. The last transposition had set them down dangerously close to a boggy sump.

"I'm doing the best I can!" Personally, he was grateful to

be surrounded by wetlands. In a drier land his throat would already have given out.

Out of breath, the coati scout staggered to a halt before his master. Glaring down at him, resplendent in shining armor, spiked club resting on his right shoulder, Manzai the grizzly growled threateningly from beneath his massive horned helmet.

"You mean to say they have not been overtaken *yet*?"

The coati fought for breath. "Master, each time we draw close, some magic lifts them up and sets them down farther from us."

"Magic?" Thick brows drew together. "What sort of magic?"

"I do not know, Master. A green sort."

"That's helpful," the grizzly muttered sardonically. Straightening, he considered the road ahead from his great height. "At least they haven't disappeared." He turned to a waiting attendant. "Bring forward my best runners. Helodiar, too, if he's recovered his wits." Dipping its head low to signify compliance, a brightly emblazoned antelope rushed to comply.

"We'll trample these intruders underfoot." Manzai returned his gaze to the road. "They have no conception of the fury of which a thwarted collector is capable!" He waved at the coati. "Rejoin your brethren and continue the pursuit!"

"At once, Master." Bowing obsequiously, the soldier spun and hurried on ahead, leaving his sovereign to follow at a more leisurely but resolute pace.

Already the main party of pursuers was near enough to make out the reflection cast by the intermittent green cloud. Manzai grinned mirthlessly. He would have Helodiar crush the interlopers one limb at a time while the princesses looked on. Even the inhabitants of a collection could use an occasional object lesson.

"See," he told the cougar marching at his side, "they are not so clever. Their own magic locates them for us."

"Soon we will be caught up with them, Master," the house officer agreed. "Your property will be recovered and your revenge assured."

"This is not a matter of revenge." Manzai patiently corrected his servitor. "It is a point of honor."

One moment they were striding determinedly along, and the next the tenuous dawn seemed to bloat and ripple. There was a loud popping sound and out of the unstable mist emerged a creature unlike anything Manzai had ever seen. His household guard bunched up in front of him.

"What manner of magic is this?"

Holding a small boxy device in one of four hands, the apparition calmly examined its surroundings. Its very posture was suggestive of bemusement and incertitude.

"Oh, dear. Missed again. Sometimes I feel blind as a larva feeling its way around an incubation chamber." He stared at Manzai out of unblinking compound eyes. "I beg your pardon, but I don't suppose you've happened to see—"

"Silence!" bellowed the grizzly. "You will address me in a tone of respect and by my proper title!"

"Sorry." The angular figure fiddled with the device it held. "Maybe another time. This is really very disconcerting."

The cougar leaned sideways to whisper to his master. "This must be another trick of the clever intruders, to confuse and delay us." He drew a needlelike rapier.

"No, let me." Shoving his gawking servants aside, Manzai let the huge spiked club fall meaningfully from his shoulder. Clutching it tight with both hands, he advanced on the strange creature.

"I know not what manner of sorcery you favor, but we shall see how well it copes with cold iron." He raised the intimidating weapon over his head.

Feathery antennae twitched as the stiff-bodied phantasm removed a small, flattened cylinder from a belt encircling the middle part of its body. "Locals can be so gauche."

As Manzai let out a roar that set the moss hanging from the branches of nearby trees to trembling, the creature pointed the cylinder and nudged a switch on its side. There was flash of light brighter than the midday sun at high summer and the self-anointed Lord of the Upper Karrakas vanished.

In the abrupt absence of their master, his loyal servitors considered the situation. Rapidly reaching a silent consensus, each and every one of them decided that they had left at least one important personal task undone back at the compound. As these tasks without exception did not seem to require the employment of weapons, these now superfluous devices were left behind in their owners' haste to return to enterprises previously abandoned.

Confronted with a cloud of settling dust, the solitary visitor glanced indifferently at the scattered clumps of abandoned armament. His upper body contorted in what might have been a shrug or a sigh. Or both.

"Nothing for it but to try again."

As he touched the contacts on the large box a shimmer of distortion enveloped him. For an instant the atmosphere around him turned the color and consistency of mercury.

Then, as before, he was elsewhere. Nor was he the only one.

On a cold peninsula that was very far indeed from the middle of the Karrakas Delta, space-time briefly warped silver. Siphoned back in on itself, it vanished like water down a drain, leaving behind a staggering Manzai. The grizzly's lower jaw dropped as he considered his new surroundings: snow-capped mountains, tundralike scrub, hassocks of grass rippling in a chill breeze. Clusters of small pink and yellow flowers carpeted the soil.

A fast-flowing river tumbled nearby, fringed by trees the like of which he'd never seen before. Blackberry bushes fought to fill the open gaps between rough-barked trunks. Small birds chirped overhead, singing nonsense rhymes to one another.

On the near bank of the river something grunted. Manzai tensed, raising his club, and then relaxed when he saw it was only one of his own tribe. The bear and its several companions wore no clothing and were down on all fours, but this was understandable since they were bathing and playing in the river. A shiver ran through him. The air was unbelievably crisp and cold.

As he moved toward them, grateful for a familiar face to talk to, he saw one of the adults swipe at something beneath the glassy surface. A large, strangely colored fish went flying, to land on the grassy bank. As a demonstration of manual dexterity it was most impressive, but hardly energy efficient. In vain he searched for signs of nets or poles.

Where was he, and where were his servants? What had happened to the impertinent creature he had been about to squash? Perhaps these primitive fisherfolk knew something. Raising a hand, he hailed them in what he hoped was an appropriate fashion.

Standing to sniff the air, the nearest looked straight at him and responded with an incomprehensible snort.

Incapable of speech, he realized in astonishment. They could not talk. It was not to be believed. While they accepted him as one of their own, they continued to ignore him in their single-minded devotion to the task at hand: that of swatting as many fish as possible out of the river. No matter what dialect he tried, he could not get them to do anything more than grunt.

Slumping down against a log, he tried to make some sense of the fate that had befallen him. He failed miserably.

The following morning found him still by the river, observing his idiot relations. A new problem had been added to his immediate environment, one he could neither order away or escape from. His stomach was growling continuously.

But there were no servants loitering anxiously nearby to fetch him plates of gourmet delights on gilded platters. Reaching a decision, he removed his cumbersome armor and waded resignedly into the river. There he commenced bashing away at the abundant fish with his club. They proved much too quick for him and easily avoided his blows.

By late afternoon he had abandoned the club in favor of trying to mimic the primitive technique utilized by the others, watching the shifting surface until a fish swam near and then swiping at it with one hand. The other bears treated him as one would an idiot cousin, giving him plenty of space in which to flail about futilely at the water.

By nightfall he had expended much of his remaining energy, to no avail. The few handfuls of blackberries he managed to gather before the sun went down did little to assuage his enormous hunger. Furious at the fate which had consigned him to his present situation, he strode imperiously over to where a pair of females were sleeping beneath several of the tall, straight-boled trees.

"Rouse yourselves, you morons!" He kicked at the nearest and was rewarded with a querulous grunt. "I know you can understand me, so enough of this pretending you cannot. I need something to eat, and you are going to provide it for me." Both females were awake now, watching him intently.

"And why do you remain on all fours like that? It's food I want, not sex." A deep, rumbling snarl, like the first awakenings of a long-dormant volcano come back to life, reverberated behind him.

Turning, he found himself staring into the face of an adult male who overtopped him by a full head. "And I don't want any trouble out of you, either! I've had enough of this nonsense. I can be generous to those who serve me, but if you persist in this absurd charade you'll force me to sterner measures."

With a roar that shook the branches the male charged the one who had invaded his territory and threatened his females. At the same time, they attacked the intruder from behind. A stunned Manzai fought back as best he could, but he'd left his club on the gravel bank. Despite his fighting prowess, he went down shrieking beneath their combined weight and unchecked primordial fury.

Right up until the end, his attackers uttered not a word between them.

CHAPTER 10

MUDGE HAD STOPPED LOOKING BACK OVER HIS SHOULDER. "Still no hint o' any pursuit, mate. Ain't seen sign o' the dirty buggers for more than an 'our." He shook his head in wonderment, grateful for the inexplicable reprieve. "Your little 'ops notwithstandin', I thought they'd be all over us by now, I did."

"Something happened to change Manzai's mind." Jon-Tom was cleaning the duar with a dry cloth.

"Maybe the bastard stepped on a snake," Mudge opined hopefully. "Or maybe 'is 'appy followers finally 'ad enough o' 'im an' told 'im where to get off."

Jon-Tom glanced over at his friend. "Never look a gift horse in the mouth, Mudge."

The otter squinted up at him. "Nobody's ever presented me with no 'orse, mate, an' no one's ever likely to. An' if they did, why the 'ell would I want to look 'im in the mouth? They like to natter on about nothings, 'orses do, an' the ones I've met tend to 'ave really bad breath."

"Yours isn't exactly scented," Jon-Tom replied.

"That's amusin', that is, comin' from a 'uman. You'll eat anythin', you lot will."

"if our pursuit has slackened, can't we rest awhile?" Quiquell slowed to take a seat on a fallen log by the side of the narrow road.

Naike was staring hard back the way they'd come. "Either we have somehow outdistanced them or they have truly abandoned the chase. A rest would do us all good. We should avail ourselves of the opportunity."

"I'm willing." Umagi took a decorous seat on a smooth-topped black rock.

"We're all exhaussted," Seshenshe exclaimed. The remaining princesses chorused their agreement.

Feeling a light touch on his shoulder, Jon-Tom turned to fall into a pair of bright blue eyes.

"You certainly are a spellsinger, sir."

He stood as tall as he could manage without actually rising on tiptoes and sucked in his stomach so hard Mudge expected to see his friend's intestines bulge clear out through his spine.

From her seat nearby a less awed Seshenshe spoke up before Jon-Tom could respond. "If you are ssuch a great sspellssinger, why can't you call up a royal carriage or two to carry uss from thiss place?"

"or six of them," whispered Quiquell. "with strong teams and knowledgeable drivers."

"For that matter," wondered Pivver, "why can't you just magic us home?"

Beset by a small but intense storm of querulous, demanding princesses, Jon-Tom found himself backed toward a tree. Mudge looked on with considerable amusement.

"Just a minute, just a minute. It's not that easy. Magic is not a precise science."

The otter chuckled. "Good thing ol' Clothybump ain't 'ere to 'ear you say that."

Jon-Tom glared at him before turning his attention back to the clamoring, insistent royals. "What I meant to say was that it's true I'm conversant with magic, but only certain kinds. Defensive sorcery is one example. Conjuring up transportation, especially the kind that involves other living creatures, is very complicated, and transposition infinitely more so. Do you think *I'd* be walking if I had an easy way out? You have to be careful with such things. There are real dangers involved." Choosing Umagi at random, he directed his explanation to her.

"Suppose I tried to sing you home, Princess, and sent you instead to Pivver's homeland?"

"Or," added Mudge dryly, " 'e might send your 'ead to Pivver's palace, your body to Aleaukauna's, an' your behind to—"

"I *beg* your pardon." The silk-swathed gorilla glared at the otter.

"No disrespect intended, Your Ladyhulk. As me warblin' companion can tell you, I'm a great respecter of behinds."

"I wouldn't take such a chance." Jon-Tom spread his hands helplessly. "The risks are too great."

"But did you not just advance us down this very road by means of your magic?" Ansibette reminded him.

"The spellsong I employed wasn't place-specific," he explained. "When you're not place-specific the magic has a lot more leeway. It has to do with fractal lines of force as they relate to spatial interstices."

Her perfect nose wrinkled up. "Sorcery is a very complicated business."

Mudge ventured some clarification. "Wot 'e's tryin' to tell you lot is that 'e might try to send a zucchini someplace and end up transposin' a tomato."

Pivver's whiskers twitched. "Why would anyone want to send a zucchini anyplace?"

"That'ss what I ssay!" added Seshenshe firmly. "And what iss a zucchini?"

"a fruit," explained Quiquell softly. "it's round and blue, with pink spots."

"No, no!" Umagi hastened to correct her. "It's long and purple and shiny."

"Are you sure?" Ansibette's confusion only deepened. "I thought—"

"Ladies, please!" Jon-Tom mopped perspiration from his forehead. "If I could send a zucchini or anything else to a specific destination, I'd gladly transpose us all right out of this swamp. But I'm afraid . . . I'm afraid I'm just not that good. We'll have to make our way to Mashupro as best we can."

"i understand." Under her breath Quiquell added, "blue."

"Purple!" Umagi glared at the anteater, who stuck out her tongue by way of response. Given the nature of its owner, it was a most impressive gesture.

"Well, what kind of a sspellssinger are you?" Crossing her arms over her furry chest, Seshenshe's face twisted into a ferocious pout. She was quickly joined in her frustration and outrage by her fellow royals.

Faced with this regal tumult, Jon-Tom didn't know what to say. This wasn't a problem, because Mudge always knew what to say.

"I'll tell you wot bleedin' kind 'e is!" The otter's uncharacteristic bellow was sufficiently violent to startle the complainers into silence. " 'E's the spellsinger who just saved all your 'igh 'an mighty backsides, that's who! Instead o' gripin' at 'im because 'e can't post you 'ome directly, you might consider thankin' 'im for savin' you from a lifetime o' servitude an' captivity!"

It was Umagi who finally broke the embarrassed silence which followed. "The river-runner is right. What has happened to our manners?" She daintily flicked the tailing end of her head scarf away from her face.

"Umagi remindss uss all of our sstation." As the one who had started the brouhaha, Seshenshe took it upon herself to make amends. This she did by walking up to Jon-Tom, drawing his head down toward her own, and planting a generous lynx lick square on his right cheek. She had a tongue like sandpaper, Jon-Tom noted.

Equally ashamed of their behavior, the rest of the former captives followed suit. He was unable to enjoy Ansibette's affectionate embrace because it followed immediately behind Umagi's. While offered with the best of intent, it left him feeling as if he'd just fallen from a twenty-foot cliff.

"If you can't provide proper transportation," Aleaukauna said when the apologies were concluded, "or send us straightaway home, can you at least provide us with adequate sleeping quarters?"

"And ssince there aren't enough of you to carry uss, perhapss alsso ssome more appropriate footwear." Seshenshe lifted one of her lightly sandaled feet.

"although," added Quiquell thoughtfully, "i suppose you could take turns."

With a sigh Mudge smiled over at the spellsinger. "Princesses 'ave notoriously short attention spans, mate."

Naike had been silent for some time. Now he turned from studying the road. "Argue if you must, but can we at least argue and move at the same time? Just because there is presently no pursuit does not mean it has been permanently terminated. Tomorrow may bring fresh resolve to Manzai's minions."

A good thing, Jon-Tom mused as he strode along, that there was no need at the moment to try to mask their location. The princesses seemed incapable of maintaining silence. Nor did their attire exactly blend into the sun-washed greenery of the delta.

To give himself a little peace he played light, inconsequential music on the duar. This time there was no magic in his playing—only beauty. The lost chords drifted nearby, sampling each melody with a ringing curiosity, sometimes chiming in with an attempt at counterpoint.

In the absence of any visible pursuit they made better progress than Jon-Tom expected. When Naike finally selected a campsite, Jon-Tom felt reasonably safe in attempting a homely fire spell. The soldiers carried fire-making gear in their packs, but given the saturated character of the vegetation it was felt that Jon-Tom might have better luck.

Freed of the need to supplicate the gods of friction, the soldiers and Mudge fanned out through the surrounding growth. One by one they returned with edibles: nuts and freshwater shellfish, berries and soft tubers, fish still freshly flapping, and fungi ready to fry.

An hour later Seshenshe studied the simple dish that was passed to her by the light of the blazing fire. "And what may I assk iss thiss?"

"Fish, m'lady." Pauko looked over innocently from his station by the cookware. "Is anything wrong with it?"

"Iss anything *wrong* with it?" The lynx waved a clawed paw at the platter. "Issn't it obviouss? There'ss no *ssauce.*"

"That's right." Umagi's lower lip curled clear up over her upper to touch the base of her nostrils. "No sauce."

"Abject apologies, Your Highnesses." Pauko's reply was tinged with a sarcasm that would have been absent under different circumstances. "But this was the best I could manage under the circumstances." He indicated his cookfire. "As you can see, the facilities are not of the best."

The Lieutenant supported his trooper. "There are conditions, ladies, under which gourmet cookery is not always possible."

"Nonssensse!" Seshenshe focused slitted eyes on Jon-Tom, who had already gobbled half his own portion. "Perhapss you cannot ssend uss home, but you did well to ssing up thiss fine fire. Can you not sspellssing ssome sspicess and proper utenssils as well?"

"Oh, right. And who'll carry them?" Heke muttered under his breath.

"One guess," Karaukul replied.

"Remind me again how we ended up on this mission?"

"We were volunteered, remember?" Karaukul smiled wanly in the flickering light. "It was that or lose certain vital body parts."

"Oh, yes," murmured his companion. "Now I recall. Glory or dismemberment."

"Have a thought for the other poor slob—other honored soldiers of Harakun, who have been sent to dangerous lands to seek the princess and who have found nothing but travail and death. It has been our good fortune to actually perform the rescue."

"Yes," replied Heke expressionlessly. "Aren't we lucky?"

"Six times over." Karaukul looked pained.

Rising from her seat, Seshenshe sauntered over to where

Jon-Tom was eating and with claws retracted ran her fingers lightly over his neck and shoulder.

"It'ss not too much to assk, iss it, sspellssinger?" she cooed. "Jusst a ssmall bottle of sslightly warmed cardonaisse ssauce?"

Frowning, he looked up from his meal. "I don't know. I've never tried to conjure a specific food before."

Aleaukauna was working her way less than enthusiastically through her own portion. Now she looked across the fire at where the lynx was plying the spellsinger. "If you're going to do that, I would rather see some keen spices. Maroon peppercorns and ground *wapani*." Her tongue wrapped around the top of her muzzle at the mere thought of it.

"I would like just a little black cream." Smiling tantalizingly, Ansibette leaned toward Jon-Tom, who for some reason found himself suddenly choking on a small, well-seared piece of fish.

Aleaukauna showed sharp teeth. "All in good time, but we should have *wapani* first."

"Black cream." Ansibette's perfect lips coiled sensuously around each syllable. Jon-Tom forced himself to swallow.

"Cardonaisse," hissed Seshenshe.

"Who is senior princess here?" Aleaukauna's onyx-black eyes glittered in the firelight.

"Senior princess?" Using a moistened hand, Pivver was delicately grooming fish grease from her whiskers. "Who made you senior here?"

"These soldiers are mine." The mongoose indicated the quartet of fighters, who, thus singled out, attempted forthwith to shrink back from the circle of illumination. "If not for me they would have been quite content to flee Manzai's abode in my company alone. It was at my insistence and mine alone that the rest of you secured your freedom."

"Perhaps their sense of honor is greater than you believe." Umagi had risen to place a friendly arm around Jon-Tom's shoulders. Her bulk was imposing. "This spellsinger and his friend owe allegiance to none here but themselves." Squeezing tenderly, she stared into his eyes, primate to primate. "*You* wouldn't have run off and abandoned us to Manzai's mercies, would you?"

"Uh, no, of course not. And by the way, you're hurting my shoulder."

"Sorry." Batting simian eyelashes, she released her grip.

Rising from her own seat, Ansibette undulated toward him. The resulting wave forms were of sufficient intensity to blur any male's vision. Or possibly melt lead. Pivver spoke up before Jon-Tom could be flattered into insensibility. "No one here can claim for themselves a title as encompassing as 'senior princess.' Some are older, some wiser, some stronger, others faster. Some come from larger, more powerful kingdoms, others from homes nearer our present locale. Only one among us is wise and experienced enough to decide such an important matter." Turning sharply, she stared straight at Jon-Tom. "The spellsinger!"

"Huh?" He looked up suddenly from the remnant of his meal, eyes wide and confused. Mudge, who had been eating nearby, hastened to slide as far as possible away from his companion.

"Yes!" Bending low, Ansibette formed her mouth into a perfect pout and smiled enticingly. "Who should be senior among us, Jon-Tom?"

"stop that," breathed Quiquell. "you are distracting him unfairly!"

Ansibette turned to blink innocently. "I? I would not demean myself."

"Sure you would," growled Umagi. That induced Ansibette to whirl on the genial gorilla.

Mudge considered whether to intervene or to allow his old friend to be sacrificed. The fuddled expression on the spellsinger's face, he decided, was simply too piteous to be ignored. Steeling himself, the otter stepped forward into the light and raised both hands. At least *he* was quick enough to dodge any claws that might happen to come his direction.

"Now listen 'ere, you graceless if exceptionally lovely lot!

There ain't no bloody 'senior princess.' In the sight o' danger an' desolation you're all equal. If you want to compare the sizes o' your respective kingdoms"—and he favored them individually with a leer so swift none had time to react to it— "ain't no one going to stop you. But if we're goin' to get out o' this place alive, we're damn well goin' to 'ave to depend on each other. So let's 'ave no more o' this nonsense, at least until we're in a right more comfortable situation than we are now."

With that he turned and stalked back to his seat, sat down on the fallen log, and resumed devouring the last of his dinner as noisily as possible.

"The otter is right." An abashed Aleaukauna surveyed her silent sisters. "Once again we have been shamed. Imagine trying to curry favor with such as the spellsinger, who clearly favors none among us above any other." Penetrating black eyes regarded him. "Is that not so?"

"Oh, sure, sure!" Jon-Tom fought manfully to avert his gaze from the fluid and all too proximate form of the princess Ansibette. "I'll do my best to help all of you equally."

"We should be devoting our efforts and thoughts to more important matters," Aleaukauna added.

"most certainly we should," murmured Quiquell.

"Then we are agreed." Fur quivering as she stretched, Seshenshe extended both arms out in front of her. Sharp claws caught the light of the fire. "For example, jusst look at my nailss! No paint, no insserts, no glitter outlining: nothing." She turned her paws over. "A dissgrace to my family and my kingdom."

"i know just how you feel." Quiquell had been cleaning her face with her tongue. Now she delicately traced her long, tapering snout with a heavy foreclaw. "i should have emblems and insignia painted all along here. i can't imagine what the supervisor designate of etiquette would say if he could see me like this."

"See *you*?" Pivver brushed hopelessly at her arms and waist. "My fur hasn't been properly groomed in days. Another week in this open swamp and I'll look more like a rag doll than a royal representative of great Trenku."

"I can sympathize." Ansibette fluffed her shoulder-length golden tresses. "This is all I have to worry about, and it gives me enough trouble." She gazed admiringly at Seshenshe. "I'd give anything if I had a thick natural pelt like you, or like Pivver."

"That's all right." The otter was understanding. "I'd give anything if I had your . . . your . . . Be glad you don't. Fur is no blessing in this humidity."

Aleaukauna had been thinking hard while listening to her sisters-in-distress. "We'd be better off if we spent our time dealing with instead of bemoaning our present situation. For example, do we not count a great spellsinger amongst our number?" Six equally intent feminine gazes turned to Jon-Tom, who once more found himself the center of dubious attention. "Surely one who can conjure so well could bring forth a few simple cosmetics."

Umagi snapped her fingers. "Yes! There wouldn't be any danger in that, Jon-Tom."

"do try, spellsinger!" requested Quiquell breathily.

"I don't know." He eyed them askance. "Mudge, what do you think?" He turned, frowning. "Mudge?"

"Said he was going fishing." Heke looked disgusted.

"In the middle of the night?"

"Hey, you ask him about it," barked the mongoose. "He's your friend."

"Well, what does Lieutenant Naike think? Surely he'll have an opinion on this."

"I suppose in a manner of speaking he does." Pauko looked up from where he was washing out a skillet. "However, he went with your friend."

"And you didn't go?" Jon-Tom said.

"You think we weren't *ordered* to stay here?" Karaukul replied ruefully.

Wordlessly, Jon-Tom picked up his duar from where he'd placed it carefully atop a relatively dry rock. He'd had about enough of the princesses and their individual concerns. "You want cosmetics? I'll give you cosmetics! Stand back."

They did so, looking on with a mixture of expectation and wonderment as he began to sing.

He had no trouble combining bits and pieces of old songs with new bridging lyrics. Half the old rock tunes he knew had at least something to do with personal appearance. The lost chords fluttered ecstatically about him as he sang.

"Ohhh, I got to look good for my bay-beee.
Got to look good for the ball.
Pretty 'em up, don't say may-beee
Color and glitz, one and all!
Glitter and paint and touch-up
Don't spare the glamour
Make sure they'll enamor
Anyone who chances to see
The best that each one can be!"

The duar actually vibrated as it responded to his wild playing. For the first time ever, a blast of multihued instead of monotonic light erupted from the interdimensional nexus, flaring in all directions to wrap about the squealing, screeching princesses like so many refulgent snakes. The soldiers dove for cover, the skillet Pauko had been cleaning clanging against the rocks as he flung it aside in his haste to conceal himself. Only the drifting chord cloud seemed enthused, serving up a soupçon of musical accompaniment to the dashing streams of light.

As he fought to hang on to his bucking, twitching instrument, Jon-Tom found himself wondering if perhaps he ought to have waited until he'd calmed down some. Too late now. He'd summoned the magic of the duar and it was out in full force, bright enough to conceal all but the outlines of the princesses from view.

Above the chiming of the chords and the flux of surging lights he heard Seshenshe's laughter.

"It tickless!"

"And it's cold!" added Aleaukauna from somewhere nearby.

Without pausing to see if he'd been successful he decided that this was one spellsong he'd better wrap up right quick. Concluding a last stanza with a few hasty, desultory words, he let his fingers rise from the duar's strings. The writhing shafts of color responded by bursting like so many party favors, cascading in a brief but intense shower of scintillating particulates to the ground. Melting into the damp soil, they caused the uneven surface of the dirt road to sparkle for just an instant like some sort of grandiose fairy freeway, a garish off ramp from the Yellow Brick Road.

As the colors dissipated, the princesses stood revealed in all their newly resplendent glory. Screeches and gasps were replaced by giggles and inadequately suppressed smiles.

"What are *you* laughing at?" Seshenshe grinned as she eyed Quiquell.

The anteater gestured with her tongue. "i'm not sure that purple and pink polka dots suit your fur. and wouldn't that ring look better in one of your ears than in your nose?"

The lynx's eyes crossed as she put both paws to her muzzle, from which now dangled a circlet of heavy-gauge twenty-four-carat gold wire. "No! Where did thiss come from? I don't wear anything like thiss!" She whirled on Jon-Tom.

"What's wrong with a nose ring?" Ansibette studied the lynx's new adornment speculatively. "I think it's kind of flattering."

"As flattering as your tattoo?" Umagi gestured at the blonde.

"Tattoo? What tatt . . . By my great-grandmother's uterus!" Clutching a handful of her flowing skirt, she began rubbing furiously at her right arm. "It doesn't come off! Doesn't it come off?"

Jon-Tom took a cautious step backward. Possibly she wouldn't have been quite as upset, he reflected, if the exorbitantly chromatic tattoo hadn't covered her entire body from forehead to toes. Personally he found the effect, as well as the actual artwork, quite elegant, though on closer inspection he did feel that there were one or two smaller drawings which could cause some offense. In particular there was one on her right shoulder running down into her cleavage which . . .

"Look what you've done!" she wailed at him. "How can I return to my family looking like . . . like a walking painting from the royal galleries? Especially *this* kind of painting!" She indicated the etching which began at her shoulder and ended in . . .

Jon-Tom stood his ground. "You all asked for a cosmetic makeover. This isn't exactly my area of specialization."

Umagi was rubbing furiously at the indelible body paint which had traced a complex geometric design over her entire massive body. Pivver now wore a mixture of gold-laced stripes and circles which seemed to be skin deep, while Aleaukauna's dark brown fur had suffered a radical body cut from crown to heel.

Overall, it could be said that the princesses were somewhat less than wholly pleased by the manner in which Jon-Tom had complied with their request. In fact, it would not be exaggerating their reaction to say that if it were possible to lynch someone with a glance, he would by then have been swinging from beneath a branch of the nearest tree.

To Jon-Tom's surprise it was Heke who came to his defense, pointing out calmly but firmly that the spellsinger had done no more than comply with their wishes, and if they hadn't badgered him into responding, they would not now be compelled to deal with their altered appearances. Which, he added, he personally could find nothing wrong with. While others might find a daub here and a razor cut there a touch extreme, he thought that on the whole they all looked most attractive.

This mollified them only slightly. They continued muttering dire imprecations while commiserating sorrowfully with one another.

"Look, I'm sorry," Jon-Tom told them, "but after all Mudge and I have gone through on our behalf, I thought your insistence on something so trivial was a bit out of line. I didn't intend for my response to your request to be so . . . emphatic.

"Besides which I kind of agree with Heke. I think you all look wonderful."

"Well . . ." Ansibette peered down at herself uncertainly. "Isn't it a bit . . . daring? I mean, can you see *all* of this?" So saying, she grabbed the scoop of her bodice and pulled it down to her waist, to reveal a great deal more of her remarkably elaborate tattoo.

Jon-Tom swallowed with difficulty. "Uh, yes, I can."

Moving much closer, she traced the scandalizing outline with the tip of one forefinger. "You really believe this is beautiful? You think this is attractive?"

He chose his words with great care. "Bearing in mind that it's difficult to improve on a blank canvas that's already perfection itself, then I'd have to say yes, I do."

Lips pursed thoughtfully, she pulled the bodice back up. "Maybe I've been too cloistered." Raising an arm, she examined the design which ran from shoulder to fingers. "It certainly is eye-catching."

"The soldier is right." Aleaukauna was running a finger along several spirals which had been neatly shaved into the fur of her chest. "We have no one to blame for our present appearance save ourselves. We asked for this."

"Maybe *you* did; I didn't. At leasst your fur will grow back." The lynx tugged on the rings which decorated various parts of her body.

Jon-Tom finally quieted them by reminding them that his spells had a habit of wearing off rapidly and that if this one lingered, he would decosmetize them one at a time until their individual appearance had been restored. Still muttering, each of them found a place to lie down. It was hardly surprising that no one asked him to conjure up a proper bed or even so much as a sleeping pad, fearful of what they might awaken atop.

Lieutenant Naike had sense enough to keep his reaction to himself when he and Mudge returned from their foraging. The otter was less restrained.

"Bugger me for a pie-eyed potu, mate! Wot the blazes did you *do* to 'em?"

Jon-Tom looked up irritably from where he lay beneath his

iridescent cape. "What makes you think I had anything to do with it?"

"Crikey, am I supposed to believe they did that to *themselves*?"

"Some of it's quite attractive," Jon-Tom argued back. "And keep your voice down."

"Attractive, is it?" The otter considered the recumbent, redecorated royals. "Well, perhaps it 'tis, in a barbaric sort o' fashion. Though I don't see a one who looks much like the scion o' some noble family." He chuckled. "Just *look* at wot you've done to 'em, mate!"

Keeping a grip on his temper, the spellsinger sat up. "So what are you saying? That you now find the princess Pivver, for example, unattractive just because she's undergone a little fur styling?"

"No, no. Did I say that?"

Jon-Tom rested his forehead against one palm. "They hounded me into it, Mudge. And you weren't exactly around to offer advice."

"Oi, wot could I 'ave done? I ain't no intermediary 'twixt sorcery and nobility." He was grinning broadly. "Though off wot I see 'ere, I don't think you'll 'ave to worry about bein' bothered by any more conjurin' requests anytime real soon."

"I was a little upset," his friend replied. "Still, I tried to choose my words carefully. But you know how music can get to me. I overdid things. Again." Behind him the cloud of ambulatory music hummed softly. "I told them that I'd try to repair matters."

The otter pursed his lips. "Can you?"

"I don't know. You know how it is with my spellsongs." He glanced past his friend. Huddled together for reassurance, the princesses sprawled on the far side of the fire, clustering close to the bulk of Umagi of Tuuro like buttercups in the shadow of a sheltering boulder.

"Watch your comments," he added as he laid back down and pulled his cape up around his neck.

CHAPTER 11

By midmorning of the following day the trees began to thin out. The travelers found themselves able to see across the marsh for quite some distance. In the absence of overbearing cypress and mahogany, they saw that sedges, reeds, and other grasses dominated the landscape, stretching southward toward the horizon.

"The Karrakas Delta." Lieutenant Naike wore an expression of satisfaction. "This is the way we came in." He looked back toward the tree line. "It will be harder out here in the open for anyone to sneak up on us."

"I think it's over this way, sir." Karaukul was pointing to his right.

"What's over that way?" Pivver asked as the princesses splashed along in the mongooses' wake. In addition to leaving behind the trees, they were also abandoning dry land. Mudge and Jon-Tom brought up the rear, still leery of possible pursuit. The otter was ever suspicious of good fortune.

Under Naike's direction the soldiers were energetically dismantling what appeared to be a grassy knoll. It wasn't long before the outlines of a shallow-draft, flat-bottomed boat became visible. Jon-Tom no longer had to wonder how the chosen of Harakun had made their way across the vast marshland.

As he watched, they quickly stepped the single square mast into a slot in the deck and secured it in place. There were bench seats fore and aft and oarlocks for four sweeps. A simple rudder hung from the stern.

"Surely you didn't navigate this bleedin' shingle all the

way from Harakun?" was Mudge's comment when the entire craft was finally fully revealed.

Naike gestured politely. "We purchased it in Mashupro, oceangoing vessels being useless in the marsh. It served us well enough."

"The four o' you, aye." The otter studied the simple vessel dubiously. "There's twelve o' us now."

Ansibette grasped the bow, teetering prettily on the spongy, unstable ground. "It will be awfully crowded."

"We shall manage." Back on at least partly familiar territory now, the Lieutenant oozed confidence. "It's a solid little craft, intended for ferrying cargo. Finding space for everyone will require some planning, but it will not sink under us."

"You only need to make room for ten, not twelve," Jon-Tom told him.

The Lieutenant and several of the princesses turned to him in surprise.

"You are not coming with uss?" murmured Seshenshe.

Jon-Tom gestured toward the chord cloud. It was drifting off to the southwest instead of the south, then racing back to spiral around him and chime insistently before repeating the motion. It was a pattern he and Mudge had come to know well.

"We follow the music," he explained.

"But you cannot do that." Naike was insistent.

"Can't we not, guv?" Mudge was testing the soil before him.

"How will you cross the marsh without a boat?" Several small amphibians had taken up residence in the craft's bow and Naike was gently returning them to the murky water.

Mudge put an arm around the spellsinger's waist. "Me mate 'ere an' I 'ave crossed country both wet and dry, country you lot can't begin to imagine. Country wot makes this 'ere bit o' bog look like the Polastrindu parade grounds on a celebration day. We'll arrange ourselves a raft or find another way through. We always do."

The Lieutenant walked over to them and lowered his voice, speaking now with the stealthiness so natural to his kind. "That is not what I mean. You cannot leave my soldiers and I to deal with these half dozen princesses. It would be difficult enough to cope with the presence and exigencies of Her Highness Aleaukauna. Add to her needs those of five equally demanding sisters and the situation becomes . . . how shall I say it . . . untenable."

"Oi, that's a bleedin' shame, that is," Mudge replied cheerfully. "Also one that ain't our responsibility. 'Tis a bit o' music we're followin', we are. Not a cloud o' bleedin' perfume." He waved at the softly ringing, faintly pink fog in question. It swirled lightly about his fingers before again darting insistently southwestward.

Naike straightened and his tone became formal. "I am an officer of Harakun, a soldier of the Imperial Guard. If need be, ten enemies would I face alone to defend my liege or any of her relations, or any of my troops. But there was nothing in my training or experience to prepare me for this."

" 'Ell," quipped Mudge, "there *ain't* no trainin' for somethin' like this. You'll bloody well 'ave to learn on the job, as it were. I 'opes you survive. Meself, I'd rather face the ten armed enemies."

The Lieutenant took a step forward and clutched Jon-Tom's shirt with both paws. His tone was pleading and his bright black eyes implored. To look at him, one would have thought him in imminent danger of undergoing the most profound sort of torture. Which was not far off the mark.

"Please, spellsinger Jon-Tom, traveler Mudge—do not leave us to chaperon these noble ladies alone."

Jon-Tom gently disengaged himself from the mongoose's grasp. "What makes you think Mudge and I would do any better?"

"You are clearly more experienced in the ways of the world, if not those of the court. And the princesses revere you as the wizard responsible for their rescue. If there is trouble, you can always threaten them with a spell, whereas I have in my arsenal of response only feeble words."

"On the contrary, Naike, they despise me as the wizard who's messed up their appearance."

"There is that," the Lieutenant conceded. "But that fades as they grow used to their new looks. Your presence would be desirable if only to give them others to talk with."

"You mean yell at, guv," put in Mudge.

Flicking water from her tail, Seshenshe came over to see what was causing the delay. Naike stepped aside.

"The spellsinger and his companion, m'lady, will not be making the journey with us to Mashupro."

The lynx's eyes widened as she regarded Jon-Tom. "What do you mean, you won't be coming with uss?"

"Yes, what's this all about?" Umagi ambled over through the reeds, muscles rippling beneath her shoulders.

Jon-Tom found himself facing a semicircle of princesses, all clamoring for his attention.

"i can't believe you intend abandoning us," whispered Quiquell.

"Yes." Ansibette pouted sumptuously. "Aren't you going to help us get out of this terrible place?"

"Ain't so terrible," Mudge grumbled. "Just a mite damp, is all."

"Our situation's not so simple." Jon-Tom struggled to hold on to what ground remained to him. "There are six of you. That means traveling to six different kingdoms that may lie great distances apart. My friend and I have business of our own to attend to, and loved ones awaiting our return. So much journeying would delay us unconscionably."

"Oi, you tell 'em, mate." Mudge made sure to keep Jon-Tom's bulk between himself and the angry princesses.

Aleaukauna pushed forward. "No *honorable* sorcerer would forsake a lady in such a place."

"And besides"—Pivver was fingering the whorls and chevrons shaved into her fur—"you owe us for what you've done to us."

"The cosmetic changes will fade, the piercings heal, the fur grow back," he reminded them.

"We've no guarantee of that," said Seshenshe softly. "Your continued pressence among uss iss the only reassurance we have of being returned to normal."

"Let us compromise." Everyone turned to Aleaukauna. She gestured in the direction of the boat, where the four other mongooses busied themselves readying it for travel while resolutely ignoring the noisy confrontation taking place behind them. "Accompany us only as far as Harakun, spellsinger. From there my family can provide individual escorts for each of my sisters, and you can resume your journey having detoured to only a single kingdom."

The princesses discussed the suggestion and found it acceptable. As for Jon-Tom, he wasn't quite ready to give in.

"How far is Harakun?"

"Not that far." Naike had bravely rejoined him.

Mudge squinted perceptively at the Lieutenant. "An' just 'ow far, guv, might 'not that far' be?"

The mongoose's long snout quivered. "You know, river-runner. Not that far."

The otter wasn't satisfied. "Is it only me, mate, or is there a gap in communications 'ere?"

Ansibette slipped between them. "Accompany us at least to this town of Mashupro, where we can secure transport across the Farraglean to the distant shores of our home. We can discuss this matter further once we've arrived there. If Lieutenant Naike is satisfied with the ship and crew we engage, then perhaps you and your friend can leave us there."

"I suppose we could do at least that much." Jon-Tom lost himself in her eyes, which, given the multitude of optional locations, was probably the least dangerous place for them to be. "We'd probably end up in Mashupro anyway."

Mudge gestured at the drifting, urgently chiming chords. "The music, mate. Wot about the music?"

"Music?" He blinked, breaking her stare, only to find himself encountering Naike's beseeching gaze. To protect himself, he concentrated on the Lieutenant. "This Mashupro—is it really the major port at the end of the delta?"

"Not only the major, but as far as we could determine it is the only one," Naike replied helpfully.

Nodding, Jon-Tom looked back down at Mudge. "The music can wait awhile."

A ripe stream of inventive invective flowed from the otter's lips. "Oi, but can we? A long journey in a small boat full to overflowin' with gabblin', spoiled females, each wantin' 'er own dollop o' personal attention. I didn't come all this way for that, mate. We owe these royal ramblers not a thing, nor their un'appy cavalry, either."

"Where's your spirit of gallantry, Mudge?"

"Wot, *that* old thing?" The otter uttered something choice. Ansibette blushed, while Quiquell inhaled sharply. Even Pivver's eyes dilated. "I believe I 'ad it exorcised a few years back."

"If the Lieutenant is right and the music leads us all the way down to the ocean, we'll have to find transportation in this Mashupro anyway. Unless you want me to try and spell-sing up a boat. Or have you forgotten what happened the last time I did that?"

Mudge hadn't. "You managed the boat, all right, but spent most o' the voyage stone drunk."*

"An experience I have no wish to repeat." The spellsinger was adamant. "I'd much rather try to hire a craft. Besides, for all we know, this kingdom of Harakun lies in the general direction the music is taking us."

"As always, you rationalize well, mate." The otter grimaced as he eyed the flat-bottomed boat. " 'Tis goin' to be one flavorful journey."

"I'm not unaware of the potential for discomfort," his friend assured him. "Our patience will be tested to the limit."

"Your patience, mate. Meself, I never 'ad any to test."

"I have confidence in you, Mudge." Pivver stepped forward and put a reassuring paw on the other otter's shoulder. Mudge's expression changed abruptly, and not necessarily for the better, Jon-Tom thought. But at least there were no more objections. He turned back to the others.

*See *The Day of the Dissonance.*

"It's settled. We'll accompany you as far as Mashupro, and then we'll see." He gestured in the direction of the swirling cloud of notes. "It all depends on whether we can stay with the music."

"Excellent!" exclaimed Aleaukauna.

"No one is going anywhere unless we can get this craft in the water." Naike nodded at the boat. "The tide is down and it's solidly beached."

When the four straining soldiers proved unable to move the craft, Mudge stripped down to his fur and plunged in, as did Jon-Tom. Pivver joined them soon after, daintily placing her discarded attire on one of the boat's bench seats.

After several moments of wrestling with the stern, she turned to Mudge, treading water effortlessly. "You know, it would probably be of greater benefit to the overall effort if you would put your hands on the wood and push instead of on me."

"Sorry, Your Highbornness. Just tryin' to find some better leverage."

"I'm sure you are." Her eyebrows rose. "However, in this instance that needs to be applied to the boat and not to my person."

"Sorry." Visibly miffed, he moved away from her. She strained against the sodden bulk a moment longer before her attitude softened slightly.

"We are going to be companions for some time. Given our circumstances, I see no need for you to refer to me as 'Highness' or by any other title. Informality being the order of the day, you may call me Lintania ler Culowyn aleyy Astrevian Pivver esTrenku."

"Formality strikes me as simpler." He spat out a mouthful of water plant. " 'Ow's about we say 'Pivver' an' leave it at that? Me name you already knows."

"Your name, yes, as well as that of your mate Weegee and your twinned offspring Nocter and Squill."

Mudge's gaze narrowed slightly as he strained to find footing in the mud. "Who told you that?"

"Why, your good friend the tall human."

" 'E would, the smiley son-of-a-simian." Raising his voice, the otter shouted toward the front of the boat. "Oi, mate! Put your great sloppy weight into it, will you?"

Jon-Tom called back from his place near the bow, "Just shut up and pull! We're doing all we can up here."

Their combined effort soon had the vessel back in the water. One by one, the other princesses were helped aboard. With each additional passenger the gunwales sank lower. But no waves disturbed the glassy surface of the somnolent marsh and Naike was reasonably confident that, short of a particularly violent storm, all would be able to stay high and dry.

Heke and Karaukul soon had the single lateen sail raised. Unfortunately, there was not even the suggestion of a breeze and the cloth triangle hung limp and useless against the mast. The brief discussion which ensued resulted in Mudge and Jon-Tom manning the tiller while the four soldiers resignedly settled themselves at the oars and began to row.

"Once we're out of these reeds and into a main channel, we'll pick up a current." The ever-optimistic Naike pulled hard on his sweep.

"In any event," added Karaukul as he strained on the starboard side, "it'll be easier than it was coming upstream."

"If you ignore the fact that we're riding much lower in the water." Heke grunted with each stroke.

To take his mind off the work at hand, Pauko had been watching the lost chords. The softly pulsing musical mist floated near the stern, occasionally darting off to the southwest, only to return when it was clear the boat would not be diverted from its current course.

"Your music sounds unhappy," he told the spellsinger.

"It sounds that way sometimes," Jon-Tom admitted.

"It'ss only a clusster of mussical notess." Intrigued, Seshenshe approached the cloud, experimentally waggling her fingers in its direction. "How can it ssound 'unhappy,' or, for that matter, anything elsse?"

"It's music," Jon-Tom reminded her. "Though a limited

number of notes are involved, its range of emotional expression is considerable."

"Then 'ow about you demonstrate by cheerin' it up, mate?" Mudge was watching Pivver carefully. "We could all use a bit o' upliftin', wot? But no magic," he added hastily.

"Yes, give us a song, spellsinger!" Umagi smiled encouragingly.

"Sure, why not?" Swinging the duar around, Jon-Tom considered the delta through whose vast, silent reaches they were drifting. "What should I sing about?"

"Some sort of river chantey would be in order, I should think." Aleaukauna picked at her fur.

"River chantey. A heavy metal river chantey. Neat idea." His fingers flashed across the strings.

The cloud sparkled and sang in counterpoint. When Jon-Tom essayed a certain chord, it rang particularly loud. Pleased, he began to improvise faster, accelerating the tempo until the duet was in full swing. The music that sang out across the reeds and water grass was not particularly profound, but it was certainly lively. And while it did nothing to advance their progress through means mystical or otherwise, the mongooses straining at the oars seemed to row a little easier.

Ever alert and always suspicious when things were quiet, Mudge would not allow himself to relax completely even though nothing larger than a newt appeared to contest their progress.

Once, off in the distance, they saw a flock of birds making their way to the northeast. Everyone aboard waved, hoping to attract the travelers' attention. Company and information both would have been welcomed, but either the fliers did not notice their presence or else chose to ignore it. The white wings vanished beyond a line of trees.

A newly depressing thought struck Mudge. Always unselfish in such matters, he hastened to share it with his companions.

"Sail an' oars notwithstandin', this tub is pretty much at the mercy o' the current. Wot 'appens if we enter a main channel and find ourselves poppin' out at the mouth o' the delta unable to tack sideways? We'll be at sea long before we can make it to this Mashupro." He scuffed the rough-hewn deck. "This wouldn't last ten minutes in the open ocean. One decent-sized wave'd swamp us."

"You court disaster unnecessarily, otter." Naike was pulling more easily at his oar now as his body settled into a recurring pattern of pushing and pulling. "My kind have an excellent sense of direction." He glanced briefly over his shoulder, eyeing the water ahead.

"All we have to do is find the main channel which we used to make our way up here. The mouth of the Karrakas is a maze of small straits, many of which run east to west instead of north and south. When the water starts to turn brackish, that is when we will use the sail to work our way eastward, to Mashupro. Coming in, we memorized our course most assiduously, lest we prove unable to find our way back out."

Heke smashed a blood-sucking fly against the deck. "Don't worry, otter. We don't want to spend any more time in this country than we have to." He sighed heavily. "I long for the cool breezes of Harakun."

"As do we all." The Lieutenant spoke feelingly.

An assortment of large, potentially dangerous denizens of the delta approached the boat on several occasions, most notably under cover of night. Each time they swam off without troubling its passengers. Perhaps the boat was too sturdy for any to attack. More likely it was the noise generated by the constantly chattering princesses.

Whatever the reason, the little craft proceeded southward unhindered and unchallenged.

Jon-Tom was handling the tiller, allowing Mudge to sit in the bow alongside the princess Pivver. Though too short to reach the water, the otters let their legs dangle over the side.

"I'd like to hear more of your wondrous adventures."

"Adventures? Wot adventures!" Mudge inhaled her musk discreetly. It stood out even in aroma-heavy country like the delta. "We've surely 'ad our share, that crazy 'uman an' I. I can't tell you 'ow many o' times I've 'ad to save 'is bald backside, 'ow many scrapes I've barely managed to pull 'im out of by the tips o' me whiskers. Why, if it weren't for me—"

She interrupted curiously. "Isn't he the spellsinger?"

"Oh, sure, 'e can do a few parlor tricks now an' again, but when the goin' gets truly tough, 'tis good ol' skill an' boldness that ends up savin' the day, as it were." He dropped his voice to a confidential whisper. "See, 'e's clever, Jonny-Tom is, but 'e ain't too bright. Sort o' instinctive-like rather than really intelligent. I don't make a point o' harpin' on 'im about it. As you may 'ave noticed, 'e's a bit o' sensitive."

"Perhaps a little," she admitted.

"Don't get me wrong," Mudge said quickly. "I like the silly sod. 'E's entertainin' enough, an' 'e builds a decent fire. A mite clumsy, though. You know 'ow 'umans are."

"The poor thing is so fortunate to have a friend like you."

"Oi, that 'e is, that 'e is. You should see 'im tryin' to swim. Why, many's the time I've 'ad to 'aul 'im out o' some gentle-flowin' river or stream an' push on 'is great 'airless chest until the water squeezed out o' 'is lungs like air from a bleedin' bellows. But wot can you expect from a creature wot flops about like a fish in sand an' calls it swimmin'?"

Leaning over, she pinched one of his whiskers and twirled it back and forth between thumb and forefinger. "It's not his fault. Our kind are so much more limber."

"Right! We 'ave—" He halted in midsentence, suddenly aware of what she was doing. Suddenly aware of a number of things.

"I want to know all about you." She was whispering into one ear. "I want to get to know you. Now then"—her alert brown eyes probed his own—"tell me about the places you've been and the marvels you've seen and the wondrous encounters you've had."

Mudge found himself damning his present location. There was about as much privacy to be had on the prow of the flat-boat as in Lynchbany's central square. Whiskers quivering, he leaned toward her.

"And your family," she added huskily, sharp teeth gleaming in the moonlight. "Tell me about your family."

Mudge stiffened slightly. " 'Tis just a family, like any other."

"Come now—you are too modest. I have brothers and sisters who are distinctively my own. Beyond that, I have not mated yet. It must be to a suitable noble, of course."

"O' course." Mudge gazed out across the moon-silvered wetlands. " 'Ad I run into you twenty years ago, I couldn't 'ave done nothin' anyways. 'Tis many things I've been, an' many things I am, but noble ain't one o' 'em."

Her lashes brushed the moist air. "Nobles are for mating, bold Mudge. Rogues are for practice. Now, tell me more about your family."

"You know wot a gamble globe is?"

She ruminated. "A spinning hollow sphere full of tiny numbered balls. Each time one falls through a hole in the side, its number is called out. Those with matching numbers or sequences of numbers may win money. Or so it goes in my country."

He nodded. "That's 'ow you make me feel, Princess."

"Like a gambler?" She frowned prettily.

"Cor, no! Like one o' those bleedin' balls, waitin' for its number to come up."

"I am sorry. I didn't mean to upset you."

"Oh, 'ell. You upset me every time I set me bloomin' eyes on you."

"Well, then." She massaged the back of his neck with strong fingers. "I'll try my best not to unnerve you as we talk."

"If that's your intent, then you're bloody failin', luv. No, don't stop. Might as well 'ave me body as confused an' unsettled as me brain."

He proceeded to regale her with reminiscences of his travels with the spellsinger Jon-Tom . . . with their respective contributions suitably skewed, and his own appropriately enhanced.

CHAPTER 12

THEY SOON FOUND THEMSELVES IN A MAIN CHANNEL AND proceeded southward at increased speed and in pleasant fashion. Only occasionally was it necessary for the soldiers to bend to the oars or to climb overboard to hack at the floating grasses and reeds which collected around the bow or tiller. Manzai the abductor had not troubled their thoughts for many days. For the princesses, the principal source of complaint continued to be their radically altered (not to say addled) appearance, which contrary to Jon-Tom's hopes had yet to begin to return to normal.

It was very early the next morning (much too early, Jon-Tom decided as he lifted his head from the pillow he'd made from his cloak) that Pauko let out a shout, followed immediately by words of warning.

"Rouse yourselves and to arms! Something comes!"

"Somethin' comes?" A sleepy Mudge fought to wake up. "Wot the bloody 'ell kind o' alarm is that, somethin' comes?"

"Explain yourself, Pauko!" Naike was already standing and gripping his sword. "What comes?"

"I . . . I don't know, sir. Something monstrous bright. It's heading straight for us, or else we're drifting down upon it."

By now the princesses were beginning to stir. They should be well rested, Jon-Tom mused, since none of them would stoop to taking a turn on watch. That plebeian duty was left to him, Mudge, and the mongooses.

Struggling to notch an arrow, the otter kept missing the bowstring due to lingering grogginess. As evidenced by the steady stream of curses he addressed to the bow, however, his mouth was already fully responsive and in excellent working order.

"Bloody bleedin' blinkin' string o' useless ratbag! Jon-Tommy, wot the 'ell's 'appenin'?"

"I'm trying to find out!" Stumbling forward, Jon-Tom dug sleep from his eyes.

A vast pale phosphorescence lay dead ahead, throbbing in the early morning darkness. What at first sight appeared to be a volute mass with two heads resolved itself into a pair of four-legged shapes as they drifted closer. There was no thought or hope of turning the boat: the flatbottom was no racing yacht, to be lithely pivoted on an imperceptible breeze.

Jon-Tom relaxed slightly when he saw that the creatures were harnessed in parallel. That implied domestication of some sort, which in turn suggested control. Whatever were bearing down upon them were no wild beasts of the marsh. Extraordinary they certainly were: He'd never before seen their like.

They came sloshing and sliding through the shallows, yoked to what at first sight appeared to be a luminescent white cloud. As the distance closed, they could see a third figure at the forefront of the singular vehicle.

"Someone rides upon it." Naike strained forward, his lean upper body and head streamlined as an arrow. "By my liege, the craft has wheels!"

"Wheels?" Karaukul's sight was not as sharp as that of the Lieutenant. "In the delta?"

"Are you daft as well as blind?" Mudge was wrestling with his shorts. "The wheels aren't turnin'. The 'ole 'alf-cocked contraption's ridin' on that cloud, or fog, or wotever 'tis."

By this time even Jon-Tom could see that the rims of the four wheels never touched the water. A powerful musk made him turn, to see Quiquell of Opan standing at his shoulder.

"what strange magic is this? i've never seen such a craft."

"None of us has," he told her. "I don't think it's a cloud.

The light's bad, but I still think I can make out some kind of transparent sack or envelope constraining the glow."

"Most wondrous." Aleaukauna joined them, while Pivver kept close to Mudge. Her nearness did not upset him.

As they looked on, the driver of the remarkable vehicle became very active, whistling and fighting with his reins in a desperate attempt to change course. Far from mounting some kind of attack, he was clearly doing his best to prevent a collision. His vehicle seemed little more maneuverable than the overladen flatbottom.

Seeing no weapons in evidence or anything else that could be construed as a threat, Naike gave the order to man the oars. The mongooses battled the current while the driver railed at his team, and with agonizing slowness the respective tracks of the two craft diverged.

When it became clear that the danger had been avoided, the Lieutenant yelled "Back oars!" and the winded soldiers changed position to bring them to a stop. Jon-Tom could now see that the peculiar floating wagon was being drawn by a pair of immense white salamanders. These were possessed of a natural phosphorescence which when observed from a distance could easily give the impression of a single sluggish, hulking monster.

Moonlight added to the effect, revealing that their flesh was semitransparent. Their vital organs could be seen within their bodies, quivering and pulsing, arteries and heart a distinct, dull maroon. Nearly blind, with tiny, rudimentary black eyes, they were dependent for direction on whomever held their reins.

As the travelers watched, the driver brought his team and vehicle to a halt. It floated alongside, sitting above the waterline and reeking like a bargeload of year-old eggs.

The golden emperor tamarin who occupied the driver's seat was slightly smaller than Mudge. What appeared to be an enormous walrus mustache was actually a natural feature of the species. Separating bright, intelligent eyes and tiny nose from a small mouth, the furry white crescent gave him the look of an aged munchkin. The effect was further enhanced by his embroidered and fringed vest, pants, and the gold-braided pillbox cap he wore cocked to one side. Jon-Tom thought he looked altogether too sophisticated and colorful for their drab surroundings.

Both delicate, long-fingered hands reached skyward as the terrified simian faced them. "I surrender; please don't hurt me! Take my stock if you will, but leave me in peace. I have a family, six little tamarins all my own, and—"

"Crikey, guv, quit your babblin'!" A disgusted Mudge set his bow aside. This long-haired nocturnal visitor was no threat, except perhaps to the olfactory nerves. His craft stunk prodigiously.

"What manner of transport is that?" Naike studied the floating wagon with undisguised interest.

"Manner?" The driver cautiously lowered his hands. With their enormous gaping mouths the two salamanders were cropping peacefully at the grass and reeds. "Do you mean my team?"

"No." Delicately holding his nose, Jon-Tom put a foot up on the gunwale. "They're obvious enough. What's less apparent is the means through which your wagon rides above the water."

"Oh, that. It rests upon a sack of swamp gas." He blinked wide eyes. "You don't intend to rob or kill me?"

"While I wouldn't discourage a little excitement," Mudge replied, "the sorry facts o' the matter are that at the moment we ain't interested even in a spot o' recreational maimin'."

"Swamp gas." Jon-Tom examined the luminous envelope. Watery ripples spread from its base. "I've never heard of it being utilized in this fashion. In fact, I've never heard of it being used in *any* fashion."

"It's quite buoyant." The relieved tamarin was eager to explain. "The trick is in the accumulating."

"Any drawbacks to its use?" Naike inquired professionally.

"Only a truly awful smell. But the benefits outweigh such a minor awkwardness."

Seshenshe held a hand tightly over her snout. "That iss only your opinion, traveler."

"I know." He whistled softly. "Traveling atop a cloud of stink and decay can be offputting to some customers. But it's the best way to cross flat, shallow waters. Once back on solid ground, I simply open the sack and let the gas disperse. Some of the smell lingers, but only for a little while."

"Who are you?" the Lieutenant demanded to know.

Putting his left hand to his chest, the driver bowed from the waist. His smile was barely visible beneath the prodigious mustache. Jon-Tom wondered at his age. The flamboyant facial decor made it hard to estimate.

"I am Silimbar the merchant."

"And what do you trade in?" Naike further inquired.

The tamarin blinked. With first dawn muting the ominous phosphorescent blush of the salamanders, their aspect began to change from frightening to inoffensive.

"Why, whatever's available. That's what a trader does."

"Does?" The Lieutenant frowned uncertainly.

"Takes advantage. I buy what I can and sell what I can. Can I interest you in anything?" His eyes fixed on the princesses, who now lined the flatbottom's railing with curiosity.

As the shifting chords hung nearby and sang objections to the interruption, Jon-Tom noted the wagon's triple axles and six brass-bound wooden wheels. Sturdily built, it obviously was designed to handle more difficult terrain than the delta presented.

An ever-suspicious Mudge crowded the rail. " 'Ere now, guv—'ow can we be sure that it 'tain't you wot's filled with swamp gas?"

"You are welcome to come and inspect my stock. Besides, there are many of you and I am alone." Something new had replaced the fear that had shone in his eyes when he'd first

drawn alongside their boat. Something Jon-Tom had seen frequently before . . . in Mudge's own expression.

Avarice.

"A trader!" Umagi clapped her huge hands together. "Do
you suppose he has any *real* cosmetics?"

"Lipsticks and rouges." A gleam was blossoming in Ansibette's beautiful blue eyes. "Eye shadow and blush."

"Fur groomers and moisturizers." Pivver's tone was appropriately reverent. "Combs and brushes."

Now the tamarin's grin was wide enough to see, even
beneath the overhang of his golden mustache. "Why, I carry
many such items, as a matter of course. Won't you come
aboard and tell me if you think any of them are up to your
exalted standards?"

There was a mass feminine rush to port. In vain, Naike
tried to stem the tide.

"Your Highnesses! I beg of you to use forethought and dis-
cretion. This is a laborious rescue we are engaged in, not a
shopping expedition."

He might as well have tried to channel a tidal wave, or
mute the thunder. Knowing better (after all, they had been
long-time married), Jon-Tom and Mudge hastened to get out
of the way. Both thought the Lieutenant did well to avoid
being knocked overboard.

The cushy capsule of swamp gas dimpled beneath their
feet as one by one the princesses climbed aboard the merchant's vehicle. Silimbar graciously descended from his seat
to lend each of them a hand, though he nearly balked when
confronted with Umagi's enveloping paw.

When the last had transferred from the flatbottom, he
showed them to his craft's copious interior. Left behind,
Naike fretted openly.

"Aw, let 'em enjoy themselves awhile." Luxuriating in the
space resulting from the princess's temporary absence, Heke
stretched his lean form out lengthwise on an empty bench and
sighed. "You can't do anything about it anyway, sir."

"Apparently not." Naike stared uneasily at the wagon.

Laugher and squeals of delight resounded from its well-lit interior. "I can't imagine what they'll offer in trade."

"For a presumed officer you miss a lot o' details." Mudge scuffed at the deck with one booted foot. "Each of 'em is wearin' at least a bit o' jewelry. I expect a ring 'ere, a bracelet there would buy a good deal o' face flack."

"You're right; I was not thinking."

Mudge gazed eastward. The rising sun outlined the taller reeds and occasional small tree, turning the water electric, gleaming off open, still patches that became like thin sheets of mica.

"Don't be too 'ard on yourself, guv. Takin' notice o' such things used to be in a way part o' me old profession."

Sitting on the deck, Pauko put his hands behind his head, closed his eyes, and let the new sun warm his face.

"Nice to have a little room for a while. Nice to smell nothing but mongoose. Well, mostly nothing but mongoose. No offense." He smiled apologetically over at Jon-Tom and Mudge.

"Forget it, guv." The otter jerked a thumb in the spellsinger's direction. "There's times when I think not 'avin' much o' a sense o' smell 'tis a blessin'. But not *many* times."

Jon-Tom was leaning over the side of the boat, left arm extended as he poked and prodded at the supportive sack of swamp gas. "I've never seen anything like this."

Mudge frowned. "Wot, like swamp gas?"

"No," replied his friend restively. "Like this envelope, or bag, or whatever it is. It feels like plastic, but I've never seen plastic here before. I can't imagine where it was manufactured or how this trader came by it."

"That's your answer right there, mate." As always, the otter was happy to explain. "Beyond this delta, beyond this 'ere Mashupro Town we're cruisin' toward, there's a bloody 'ole new ocean. Who knows wot marvels lie on its far side, where unfamiliar waves lap unknown shores?"

Jon-Tom glanced back. "Such eloquence is unlike you, Mudge."

The otter nodded. "Read that in a book, I did. Wouldn't want to disappoint you, mate."

"Over the years I've come to expect wonders rather than be surprised by them." Jon-Tom prodded the envelope again, his fingers sinking into the thin, flexible substance. "But plastic? Polyethylene? Pliable polymers?"

Mudge spat over the side. "Too much *pee*in' for me, mate. Don't strain your brain."

Naike's ears were cocked toward the odd wagon. "It sounds as if the ladies are enjoying themselves." He'd sheathed his weapon, as had his companions. The only sharp-edged device the tamarin had flaunted was an acute sense of business.

"I wonder," Jon-Tom mused aloud, "what customers this Silimbar was hoping to find in a place like this."

"Maybe 'e shaved a coin or two off the wrong bloke in Mashupro an' 'ad to leave in a 'urry." Mudge considered the wagon thoughtfully. " 'Avin' been compelled to vacate certain venues a mite precipitously in me own time, I could sympathize with that."

Whoops, squeals, and giggles continued to issue from the wagon's interior, indicating that the modest orgy of consumerism was continuing unabated. Radiating softly, the cluster of chords hovered near the top of the flatbottom's mast, away from the feminine cacophony.

Mudge shook his head slowly. " 'Ear that? The rowdy manifestations o' a disease for which there's no known cure."

"The supplicants are in their temple," Jon-Tom agreed. "It's not expected that we worship with them—only that we leave them to practice their rituals in peace."

"A female religion," the otter added.

"Why, Mudge—where I come from that might be considered a sexist remark."

"Sexist remark? Wot's that, mate? Some clever label somebody invented for coverin' up uncomfortable truths? Meself, I don't think 'tis broad enough. So to speak."

Dawn sifted steadily into morning, the temperature rising

in tandem with the sun. Humidity rose in invisible waves from the shallow marshland, until Jon-Tom felt as if he, his companions, and every other living thing were no more than individual ingredients in a vast, simmering soup.

Huddling as best they could in the shade of the luffing sail, the soldiers napped in the boat's stern. Having catnapped for an hour, Jon-Tom had resumed his examination of the trader's craft. Mudge had borrowed Heke's halberd and was probing the reeds and water plants for freshwater clams and crawfish.

Eventually the princesses began to file back aboard. With the aid of the tamarin's stock, they had made great strides in restoring themselves to their original appearance, though not all of the spellsinger's inadvertent handiwork was so easily overcome.

Aleaukauna was the last to return, accepting Lieutenant Naike's proferred hand gracefully. Grumbling softly, the soldiers roused themselves and made ready to get under way.

"A happy encounter for all concerned, it would seem." The Lieutenant was correctly formal with the merchant.

Eyes shining, Silimbar squatted in the driver's seat and nodded enthusiastically. "Yes indeedy." In the intensifying light of morning the ghostly phosphorescence of the swamp gas and the yoked salamanders was much reduced, lending to the entire outfit a sickly rather than threatening air.

"Now then. If you ladies are ready, I'll thank you all to come back aboard. I've made room and you'll be comfortable enough."

"It is kind of you to offer transportation," Ansibette told the tamarin, "but I think we should stay together on our boat, at least until we reach Mashupro." A small necklace of blue refracters now encircled her neck, Jon-Tom noticed, and in turn took up the creamy glow of her skin.

"It's not to Mashupro that I'm going. Or that you are going." The tamarin's voice had deepened. A sinister air seemed to rise about him: swamp gas of a different kind.

"You might as well be first." He extended a paw in Ansibette's direction.

She was puzzled rather than intimidated by the much smaller primate. "Why should any of us go with you?"

"Because of the terms of the IOUs that you signed, of course." Reaching behind his seat, he brought forth a sheaf of papers smeared with small print and fanned them in her direction. A sick feeling began to knot in the pit of Jon-Tom's belly, as if he'd inhaled a live minnow. Or too much swamp gas. A faint efflorescence not unlike that which clung to the slimy skin of the salamanders emanated from the ink-smeared seal affixed to the bottom of each paper.

It echoed the unwholesome light which was now burning in Silimbar's eyes.

"I am calling in the documents each of you signed. Now and here." With his free hand he beckoned again. "Some laws are universal." He rattled the sheets. "These are legal and binding in any land bordering the Farraglean."

"How can they be IOUss?" wondered Seshenshe. "We've already paid you, with our own gold and jewelss." The earrings in her high-tufted ears jingled musically. "We've kept only what wass necessary to meet minimum sstandardss of appearance."

"Oh, you may retain the rest of your artificial adornments. I have baubles enough. No, it is your actual selves I want. It is yourselves that I claim."

Pivver stepped angrily to the railing. "You've been sniffing gas from that bloated bag you ride upon. None of us is going anywhere with you."

"and i thought you were an honest merchant," a disappointed Quiquell whispered.

" 'Tis honest I am. Honest to a fault." Silimbar made a neat stack of the papers. "You should have read more closely what you signed. You are now indentured to me, all of you, for a period of not less than three nor more than ten years, your persons to be employed at my whim and direction."

Paw clasped tightly to his sword, a grim-faced Naike

pushed between the princesses. "Merchant, I suggest you be on your way."

"This Silimbar is not what he seems," Jon-Tom was murmuring.

"Oi, now there's a blindin' revelation." Mudge was bending to pick up his bow. "Wot gave 'im away to you, mate?"

Silimbar's entire form was now suffused with the unhealthy white glow. Like ghost tears it had leaked from his eyes to engulf his whole body, dripping like aerated latex from the tips of his fingers, from his ears, from his scimitar-like mustache.

Gesturing skyward with a shaky hand, he raised his true voice. "These are valid contracts. By all the instruments and magics included herein, by all the appendices and appurtenances, I call on them now!" A shaft of sickly white light rose from his hand to spiral into the sky.

Strong-willed as any mongoose, Aleaukauna wavered. Then she took a step forward. Naike hastened to interpose himself between her and the merchant's gaseous craft.

"No, Your Highness!" Her eyes, he saw, were glazing over. Glazing with a faint white phosphorescence.

"Don't . . . want. But . . . must." She started to push past him and he grabbed her by the left arm. Increasingly zombified, the other princesses began shuffling forward.

"Ansibette!" Moving to intercept the pride of Borobos, Jon-Tom was shocked to see refulgent white foam bubbling from her lips. Her eyes were already fogged, the bright blue masked by cataracts of pure phosphorescence.

Try as he would, he couldn't hold her. With unnatural strength born of a signed contract, she shoved past him.

Naike drew his sword. "Free them, or I'll cut you as cleanly as I'll shred those accursed papers!"

Silimbar glared imperiously down at the Lieutenant. "I warn you not to interfere. I have no quarrel with you; I wish only to claim that which is now rightfully due me."

As soon as the first of the princesses had boarded his craft, he gestured expansively. A wall of white mist coalesced between the wagon and the flatbottom. When Heke tried to jump through it, something unseen knocked him back and he fell hard to the bottom of the boat.

Karaukul stabbed at the cloying curtain. His blade passed through it cleanly, but when he tried to follow, he suffered the same fate as his companion. It was as if they were dueling with fog, Jon-Tom saw. There was more than the power of contract at work here, and it would take more than mere words to defeat it. Certainly more than sword or halberd.

"Do somethin', mate!" Mudge had a death grip on Pivver's right wrist as she dragged him toward the mist wall.

As he struggled with the duar, Jon-Tom reflected that he knew many songs that dealt with smoke and fog. He also knew he'd better get it right the first time. Quiquell had joined Aleaukauna aboard the wagon-mass and their sisters were not far behind. Hissing in harness, the salamanders were stirring as if they sensed that they were soon to be on their way.

"Let 'em go, ya bloody kidnapper!" Mudge barked at the top of his lungs. "You 'aven't the right!"

Trying to restrain Seshenshe, Pauko found himself hauled right over the railing. There was a loud splash as he landed tail-first in the water. Sputtering to the surface, he thrashed his way back to the boat.

"These give me all the right I need!" Roaring with laughter, Silimbar rattled the papers and their damning seals. "The right and the power!"

"Forgive me, Your Sleekness, this ain't wot you think!" So saying, Mudge threw his arms around Pivver's neck and tried to use his weight to hold her back. Empowered by the spell which now gripped her, she bore him easily as she stepped up onto the railing.

Edgy harmonies filled the air as Jon-Tom began to play. High up on the mast, the wandering chords tightened around the wood like bands of amethyst.

Silimbar's delight oozed from behind the pale glow of his mustache. "How charming! A musical send-off. Serenade them all you wish, minstrel. Neither plaintive threnody nor words of longing can alter the thrust of these contracts!"

"You know," Jon-Tom shouted up to the tamarin, "long ago, long before I took up the mantle of spellsinger, before I even came to this place, I was a pretty good student of law!" Some things from school, he mused seriously as he began to sing, stay with you always.

> "Don't speak to me of contracts!
> Don't talk to me of courts
> I'd rather that you freed them
> Than bury you with torts!
> I'm not afraid of paper
> I'm not afraid of seals
> If you don't cage your sorcery
> I'll squeeze it till it squeals!"

About to take Silimbar's hand, Ansibette hesitated. "Come, come! What uncertainty is this? You are bound and must comply!" The tamarin waved the sheaf of IOUs in her face as if they were the swinging pocket watch of some cheap hypnotist.

Lifting his voice, Jon-Tom sang as loud as he could. He ought to be able to break the spell. He *knew* he could. It was only based in simple IOUs. It wasn't as if he were confronting something truly formidable and inherently malign, such as the impenetrable, incomprehensible, soul-stifling contracts utilized by movie companies.

A pale lavender luminescence spilled from the duar and began to infuse the flatbottom with its glow. What was happening? It seemed irrelevant to the confrontation at hand. Not knowing what else to do, not imagining what else to do, he continued to sing of freedom and escape on behalf of the wavering princesses.

He heard Naike curse in wonder and Heke suck in his breath. Beneath their feet, the simple flatbottom was being transformed.

"That's it, mate, that's it!" Mudge urged his friend to greater efforts.

"Strong magic!" Resigned to the futility of his efforts, Naike was not even trying to hold Umagi back.

The hull of their craft did not change, but the railings vanished. Even as he sang, Jon-Tom wondered just what it was that he was conjuring. A small warship, perhaps, with which to overawe Silimbar. A sharp-prowed ram with which to break through his bulwark of sickly pale. Perhaps even a craft like the merchant's own, only larger and more powerful.

A great roaring sounded in his ears. He smiled to himself, expecting to see salamanders larger and stronger than Silimbar's own materialize out of the mist. Instead, out of the swirling storm of lavender and white emerged . . . a swirling storm. Of a sort.

It was round, and restrained by a large wire basket, and though he had never been to the part of the world from whence it came, he recognized it nonetheless. The four-thousand-horsepower Pratt and Whitney stank of leaky gaskets and gungy oil, but it drove the big props with angry energy. A sign, hand-lettered in red on wood buried beneath a thousand aging coats of yellow enamel the consistency of microwaved silly putty, was affixed with frayed electrical tape and rusting bolts to the top of the wire cage which contained the prop-storm.

MAMA LEROY'S EVERGLADES TOURS
HALF DAY $20
ALL DAY $35
SEE! SEE! SEE!
MAN-EATING GATORS! KILLER SNAKES!
GIANT LEECHES!
COFFEE AND SANDWICHES PROVIDED

Feeling the now shuddering deck start to shift beneath him, Jon-Tom made a dive for the controls attached to the six-foot-high pilot's chair and somehow got his hands on the control stick. Shocked out of their stupor, the princesses variously screamed, jumped for the boat, or covered their ears. Above the hiccuping thunder of the old aircraft engine, which even in neutral threatened to tear both itself and the boat apart, Silimbar could be heard raging.

With a blast of air that bent double the sawgrass and rushes around the boat, the transposed swamp buggy leaped forward, spinning in a tight circle. Utterly panicked, the heretofore docile salamanders reared and lurched. An outraged Silimbar was thrown from his seat, fighting to hang on to the all-important reins. The wagon and its cloud of supportive swamp gas pitched wildly in the swamp buggy's backwash as Jon-Tom struggled for control.

Umagi flopped down hard on her backside. It was worse for Naike, who was pinned between said simian buttocks of steel and the unyielding wooden deck. Restored to her senses, Pivver leaped for the flatbottom, landed aboard, and in the same motion rolled to her feet in a typical display of otterish agility. Aleaukauna nearly matched the feat, while the less agile Quiquell, Seshenshe, and Ansibette were variously dumped overboard or voluntarily leaped into the water.

Despite Jon-Tom's frantic efforts, the madly gyrating swamp buggy clipped the rear of the tamarin's craft. There was a soft ripping sound as the edge of the prop caught the back of the gas bag. Held under tremendous pressure, the suddenly freed swamp gas bolted for freedom with an explosive *whoosh!*

In accordance with the applicable laws of physics, this unexpected reaction provoked an equal and opposite reaction, propelling a bouncing mass of wagon, salamanders, and screeching Silimbar north by northwest at a velocity of approximately six agitated invectives per second. Jon-Tom was convinced he could still hear the merchant-magician howling in fury even after both he and his craft had gone skipping like a stone across the water and out of sight. What would happen when the formerly pressurized and now punc-

tured container of swamp gas finally exhausted itself, he
could only imagine. Most probably the whole outrageous
contraption would simply sink slowly and irrevocably into
the marsh muck.

Well, good, he thought.

Cloak flapping around him, he made sure the duar was
secured safely against his upper back as he dragged himself
into the pilot's chair. With his eyes still full of delta water and
sweat, he couldn't estimate the swamp buggy's speed, but he
knew it was considerable. Leaning on the stick and throttling
down the engine, he brought the craft back around in a tight
circle to where several sodden princesses anxiously treaded
water.

Mudge and Pivver promptly dove in to offer help, while
the soldiers divided their time between providing assistance
and gazing in a mixture of awe and terror at the deafening
tempest which seemed to be permanently affixed to the back
of the boat.

"Stuff that up your arse, ya rancid sack o' face fuzz!"
Mudge howled in the direction taken by the departed Silimbar. He knew the tamarin couldn't possibly hear him, but he
didn't care. "Try an' defeat a *real* sorcerer with a few bleedin' magicked scraps o' paper, will ya?" Turning to his friend,
he winked and added quietly, "Nice bit o' songsterin', mate. I
don't mind sayin' that for a minim there you 'ad me a mite
worried. This 'ere wonder boat were a stroke o' sheer
genius."

"Thanks." Jon-Tom was acutely conscious of the fact that
he had been trying to spellsing up something else entirely, but
under the circumstances he saw no need to elaborate.

"That's the way to break a contract fixed under false pre-
tensions," the otter rambled on. "That's the way to——" He let
out a yelping bark as his feet went out from under him, the
swamp buggy skewing wildly.

It took Jon-Tom a while to familiarize himself with the
craft's eccentricities. By no means could it be said that he
mastered it. Rather, there was achieved something of a man-

machine understanding. He didn't ask too much of the boat, and in return it no longer did its best to pitch him into the nearest clump of trees.

Only when he was positive that the threat presented by Silimbar had passed did he reach down to twist the key protruding from the ignition and switch the damn thing off. The bellowing motor coughed and quiesced, the props slowing to a halt as he beached the bow on a low hummock of reeds and spongy earth. A family of small, brightly colored flying lizards erupted from the grass and scattered across the water.

Standing in the pilot's chair and looking back over the top of the prop cage, it was clear to Jon-Tom that Silimbar was not now nor would be in the immediate future likely to present any sort of a threat. All that remained of his dire presence was a faint odor of rotten swamp gas, rapidly dissipating.

Those princesses who had ended up in the water were doing their best to dry themselves off. Several marveled at the clean, straight lines of the transformed flatbottom. Battered steel and aluminum had replaced the woodwork. Even the deck was smooth and cool underfoot. Mast and sail had vanished, while the wooden benches had been replaced by metal seats topped with thick cushions. These unfortunately reeked not of incense and perfume but of Tabasco and stale beer.

No one complained, however.

"What manner of marvels is this?" Umagi was doing her best to straighten her attire.

Jon-Tom had climbed down from the pilot's chair to inspect the smelly, exposed engine. "The words were my own, but I didn't have enough time to think of a tune. So I used one of Jimmy Buffett's."

"Buffett?" Mudge looked baffled. Then he smiled. "Oh, I gets it. As in givin' that rotter Silimbar a good buffetin'."

Jon-Tom blinked. "Actually that connection hadn't occurred to me, but as you know sometimes my spellsinging works better than I intend. Not to mention differently." He nodded at the engine. "Back where I come from, he does some very mild spellsinging of his own. This type of water craft hails from the region where he spends much of his time. Until now I've only seen them in pictures."

"Wot?" Mudge assumed a look of mock astonishment. "You mean you ain't experienced at drivin' one? Why, I never would o' guessed that, mate."

"I thought I did pretty good, under the circumstances. Save your sarcasm for Silimbar, if he comes back."

" 'E won't, mate. Not unless 'e's a better swimmer than I think 'e is."

"A craft most wondrous." Pivver was on hands and knees, examining the smooth metal floor of the swamp buggy. "Never have I seen its like."

"And it runss on thunder." Seshenshe was equally impressed.

"The spellsinger has caged a storm." Aleaukauna indicated the metal basket which protected the passengers from the propeller.

Ansibette wrinkled her perfect nose. "What is that strange odor?"

"Aviation fuel." Jon-Tom didn't try to explain. "Magic fluid."

Mudge flopped back on one of the old cushions, his feet dangling off the deck. "This'll carry us to Mashupro in double-quick time."

"*If* I can get it started again." Inspecting the hulking old aircraft engine, Jon-Tom prayed he wouldn't be required to perform any on-the-spot repairs. Mechanically, he was about as handy as a palsied sloth.

"It'ss so loud." The stink of diesel overwhelmed Seshenshe's sensitive nose. "Can't you make the sstorm work more quietly?"

"I'm afraid not," Jon-Tom told her. "A storm is a storm. I've only managed to, uh, tame this one enough to push us."

"Better us than our luck." Mudge was still grinning. "You don't mean to say you're in less than complete control o' this sled, mate?"

"How'd you like to try your hand at steering it? No," he

added quickly as the otter perked up, "forget I said that." There were simpler ways to commit suicide than by giving Mudge control of all that horsepower.

"Then if you know wot you're doin', mate, let's say farewell to this 'appy bit o' sodden real estate an' be on our way, wot?"

"Why not?" Ascending to the pilot's seat, Jon-Tom settled himself back against the old canvas cushion and peered down at Naike. As if sensing they were on the verge of making some real progress, the lost chords swirled enthusiastically about his head. "Continue due south?"

"For now." The Lieutenant remained wary. "We'll have to go carefully or we will miss the landmarks we noted on our way in."

"Right." Jon-Tom reached down for the key. "Everybody better take a seat or find something to hang on to."

"Oi, everybody! Grab 'old o' your tails!" Mudge tugged his feathered cap down tight over his ears.

"I've never seen metal like this." Karaukul was fingering one of the aluminum braces that supported his seat. "It would make good battle shields."

Holding his breath, Jon-Tom turned the ignition key. A dyspeptic groan rose from the bowels of the massive P&W. It coughed, belched black smoke, choked, coughed again, and rumbled to life. The propeller twitched, turned, and began to spin.

With the princesses squealing and screaming in delight, the swamp buggy took off southward. Caught by the wind, all the silk and satin aboard streamed sternward, giving the boat the look of a runaway boutique.

Heke chose the very prow of the craft to sit on, letting the brisk wind blow through his fur and ears. As the waters of the Karrakas slid beneath the vibrating hull, everyone aboard felt cleaner and more optimistic than they had in many days.

CHAPTER 13

AS WAS SO OFTEN THE CASE WITH JON-TOM'S SPELLSONGS, the confidence expressed in his efforts was premature. The swamp buggy ran for all the rest of that day and well into the following afternoon before it choked, sputtered, and died. They had covered miles enough to reduce the threat of Silimbar to a discomfiting memory but were still a long way from Mashupro. The marshland they found themselves drifting through was little different from that they had left behind.

"Bloody big place, this Karrakas." Mudge surveyed the endless stretches of reed and sawgrass thoughtfully.

"What'ss happened?" Seshenshe wondered.

"Yes, why have we stopped?" Umagi shifted from her seat near the back of the buggy. Relieved of her weight, the boat's hull slapped at the water.

Pivver gestured at the immobile propeller. "See, the captured storm has abated. Has the spell run down?"

Jon-Tom looked up from where he was bending over the engine and wiped grease from his fingers. "In a manner of speaking. We're out of gas."

"Gas." Aleaukauna's long, pointed muzzle gave a twitch. "You mean like swamp gas?"

"You're closer to the truth than you think, but what we really need is a special kind of liquid."

"Can you maybe sing some up?" Mudge eyed his friend questioningly.

"Don't know. I have a feeling that would take a pretty specific spellsong. It's not the sort of subject to inspire."

" 'Ows about the thought o' driftin' around 'ere for anoth-er six months?" the otter countered. "Ain't that adequate inspiration?"

"Perhaps something to eat first." Ansibette knelt to inspect their meager stores and Jon-Tom resolutely looked else-where. "I'm so hungry I could eat just about *anything*."

Mudge was preparing to comment as Jon-Tom hastily sug-gested that the two otters take a dive to see what edibles they could scrounge.

"A rest would do everyone good," declared Naike. "It's been a tense few days. I know that if we're going to have to row from here, I could use a break."

Jon-Tom was too tired from wrestling with the buggy and the cranky engine to argue. Naike was right. It would be nice simply to drift with the current till evening, eat a decently prepared meal, and get a good night's sleep. He could work on composing an appropriately fuelish spellsong and then try it out first thing in the morning.

As Mudge and Pivver brought up mussels, clams, crawfish, bubble crawlers, and other edibles, those on board did their best to unwind. Heke and Karaukul's curiosity drove them to prod and poke at the engine. Jon-Tom thought of warning them away from the silent mass of metal, then decided that since it was out of gas, there was little they could do to make trouble.

Evening was falling when the first sobs arose from Seshen-she: a plaintive, high-pitching yowling. One by one, the other princesses joined in as the buggy took on the atmosphere of a funeral barge.

"Now wot's all this?" Mudge moved to comfort Pivver, who did not push him away.

"Seshenshe's right." She rubbed at her muzzle. "You males have done so much to help us and we nearly went and threw it all away for reasons of avarice and vanity."

"we were desperate." Quiquell's crying consisted of terse little sniffs, her incredible tongue flicking in and out with each diminutive sob.

By way of contrast Umagi bawled thunderously, shedding

copious tears. "We were unable to resist his offerings. Fool-ishness and pride! He played to our weaknesses, inveigled us with magic words like *rouge* and *eye shadow*."

Ansibette wiped streaks from her face as Jon-Tom fought the urge to take her in his arms and reassure her. Clothahump had once told him that tears were a female's emotional warpaint. He was wary of sacrificing common sense on behalf of sympathy. The flat taste of dried fish in his mouth helped to steady him.

"Yes." Aleaukauna picked up the sorrowful refrain. "When we were presented with those damnable IOUs to sign, a part of me sensed what he was about. Then he smiled and said 'Buy one, get one free' and I was lost."

Seshenshe blew her nose, nodding knowingly. "And he ussed the most potent, most evil word of all." For just an instant, a hint of white glaze seemed to spread over her corneas, clouding not only vision but reason and common sense. "*Ssale.*"

Mudge clucked his tongue sardonically. "An obscenity of a four-letter word if ever there were one."

"I don't understand." Jon-Tom was honestly bemused. "You're all royalty. I'd wouldn't think you'd be affected by such terms."

Turning to face one another, the princesses exchanged a glance. It was Ansibette who spoke. "Poor spellsinger. You really *don't* understand."

"No, he doesn't." Resting her chin on one set of knuckles, a wistful Umagi gazed aft. "You know, I think if we had shown a little reticence, he would have gone for two for one."

A concerned Jon-Tom made a conscious effort to steer the conversation away from the incomprehensible. "Don't worry about the boat. I'll think of something to get us running again."

"Oi, that 'e will!" Mudge clapped his friend on the back. " 'E always thinks o' somethin'. That's usually the trouble."

Neither rest nor food nor sleep provided the inspiration Jon-Tom had hoped for. Morning brought light but not illumination. Nothing for it, he decided resignedly, but to try what little he'd been able to come up with.

Climbing up into the pilot's chair, he took a moment to make sure everything was ready: ignition key, throttle, control stick, duar. The few notes he drew from the venerable instrument floated out clear and pure on the humid morning air, pursued curiously by the cloud of lost chords. Then the luminescent mass of notes darted southwestward, returned to the buggy, and raced off again.

"Don't bother me now," he snapped at the cloud. "We have to see off these ladies. First we go to Mashupro, and only then to wherever you've been trying to lead us."

Unable to work "aviation fuel" into a proper lyric and unwilling to risk the possible consequences of referring simply to "gas," he instead sang a song of speed and propulsion, of rapid travel and calm voyage. Perhaps, he mused even as he improvised words and music, if he'd had any kind of background in country-western, coming up with a song about gasoline wouldn't have required such a musical stretch.

Below, the soldiers and princesses waited and watched. Mudge clung to his seat's struts with particular determination.

It was a most peculiar mist that emerged this time from the duar's nexus. Not that they weren't all outlandish to some degree, he knew as he sang. The billowing vapor was smaller in volume than he'd hoped for, and in hue an unpromising pale blue. Certainly it didn't look like any kind of fuel, nor did it boast the promising cylindrical silhouette of a fifty-five-gallon drum.

So startled was he by what finally coalesced out of the haze that he halted in midsong, something he rarely did. The cloud of chords went suddenly silent and darted forward to hide itself beneath the sharply angled prow of the swamp buggy.

"*What* is *that*?" Like her sister princesses, Ansibette gaped unashamedly at the manifestation.

"*I've* never seen anything like it," exclaimed a wide-eyed Umagi.

"Well, I have!" Naike's words were as unexpected as his reaction. Drawing his sword, he leaped forward.

"Wait a minim there, guv!" Mudge jumped in front of the determined Lieutenant.

The other soldiers had also drawn their weapons and stood poised to attack. "But it's one of the Plated Folk!" Heke insisted. "The loathsome, the ruthless, the dreaded Plated Folk."

Unimpressed, Mudge was studying the apparition carefully. "Nope, I don't 'appen to think it 'tis."

"Well, then, what is it?" While allowing himself to be restrained, Naike continued to eye the creature nervously. For its part it ignored them all as it calmly examined its surroundings.

"Look 'ere, guv. 'Ave you actually *seen* one o' the Plated Folk? 'Ave any o' you?"

The soldiers looked uncertainly at one another. It was left to Naike to respond.

"Well, no, not actually. Not in person. But we have all of us heard the tales and seen drawings."

"That so? As it 'appens, Jon-Tommy an' I 'ad the occasion many years ago to deal with more Plated Folk than you can think exist, an' dealt with 'em we did!" He indicated the creature standing before them. "This one's attired an' postured all wrong."

"So it's a fashion-conscious Plated One." Heke's eyes never left the visitor.

"Mudge is right," Jon-Tom avowed. "This being has one set of limbs too many. All Plated Folk have six, and this has eight. Nor is it one of the Weaver People."*

Cocking its head to peer up at him, the creature declared coolly, "You are observant. I am not one of these plated creatures, whatever they may be."

"Don't talk like 'em, neither." Mudge looked vindicated.

In lieu of further comment the visitor turned its attention to the device it held in two of its four hands, scrutinizing with great compound eyes the readouts plainly visible on one perfectly machined surface.

*See *The Hour of the Gate.*

"What are you?" Utterly baffled, Jon-Tom stared at the visitation. Surely his spellsinging hadn't called it up! "What are you doing here?"

"You think I like doing this?" It spoke without looking up at him. "Popping in and out of alternate realities like a blind nursemaid looking for the right brood tunnel? It's difficult, dangerous, time-consuming, and frustrating."

"Sounds like it." Mudge agreed without having the faintest idea what the creature was talking about. Behind him, Naike and the other soldiers were starting to relax. Their visitor sounded much less threatening than it looked.

"You may call me Cazpowarex. In deference to your simple minds I will answer to Caz."

Mudge bristled. "Who you callin' simple-minded, ya bleedin' oversized—"

"Mudge," Jon-Tom said warningly, "where's your sense of hospitality?"

"In the bloody 'ospital, in intensive care, mate." But the otter did not move to attack. How fortunate he was, he could not have imagined.

The one who called himself Caz considered the four mongoose soldiers, the covey of princesses, and in the forefront of the group, a single fuming otter. But his attention focused on Jon-Tom.

"You I know. You are human. These others are alien to me. As is this entire plenum." A raspy, chittering sound emerged from the breathing spicules which lined his thorax. "This is what happens when one goes mucking about with space-time."

"I was trying to conjure some aviation fuel." Jon-Tom couldn't think of anything else to say. "And instead, you showed up."

"Coincidence." The creature had a voice no less mellifluous than Ansibette's. Feathery antennae bobbed. "Aviation fuel? I wonder at your time-frame. Ah! Now I have it. Petroleum distillates which are burned to provide motive power?"

"That's it!" exclaimed Jon-Tom excitedly.

"Afraid I can't help you there. My kind did away with such wasteful practices centuries ago. As will your own."

Jon-Tom's fascinated gaze fixed on the complex backpack and side pouches the visitor wore. Wherever, whenever it came from, it was a place technologically more advanced than his own. He wished Clothahump were present, though he suspected that this was one confluence conflicted enough to baffle even that wise old turtle.

"You'd better be more respectful o' who you're talkin' to, guv."

The creature's head swiveled to face the otter. "Why?"

"Uh"—Mudge moved to slide slightly behind Naike—"me friend an' boon companion there just 'appens to be the greatest spellsinger who ever was."

Returning his attention to Jon-Tom, Caz inquired with open curiosity, "What, precisely, is a spellsinger?"

"I'll tell you wot 'e is." Mudge barked a reply before Jon-Tom could answer. " 'E's a bloomin' sorcerer! 'E makes magic, 'e does."

"There is no such thing as magic," the one called Caz declared conclusively.

"No such things as—" Ignoring Jon-Tom's frantic shushing motions the otter raced on. "Why, 'e can make things appear where none were afore! 'E can turn rocks to metal, an' alter the shape o' reality, and bring into existence anythin' you can dream of!" The otter's voice fell slightly. "That is, 'e can most o' the time. Sometimes," he concluded with an apologetic glance in his exasperated friend's direction, " 'e screws up."

"I believe I understand." The creature was less than impressed. "He is an engineer."

"No, no." Jon-Tom was finally able to get a word in. "I'm not an engineer, I'm a—" Mouth agape, he froze in midsentence.

An engineer had been what the wizard Clothahump had been seeking when he'd reached into Jon-Tom's world all those many years ago. Instead, he'd reeled in Jonathan Thomas Meriweather—amateur rock guitarist, law student, and part-time "sanitation engineer."

Now this. Where did reality end and coincidence begin? The same place, he decided, where science became magic and magic become science. *I live,* he decided, *in an interesting cosmos.*

Better just to play along.

"I, too, am searching for something." Demonstrating a double-jointedness not even the otters could match, Caz reached back with a lower arm to adjust several contact switches on his complex burden of electronics. "That I am here at all is thanks only to a project still in the experimental stage. If I were to suddenly explode in a million fragments before your eyes, I would not be surprised."

"I would be," commented Mudge. "Not necessarily disappointed, but surprised."

"For my initial experiment I have chosen to track something specific across space-time," the visitor went on. "It is proving more difficult than I envisioned, no doubt due to the largely insubstantial nature of my quarry. I had believed wave forms simpler to trail than particles. It seems that I may have been mistaken."

"What are you looking for?" Jon-Tom inquired, interested in spite of his own difficulties.

"That's the trouble: I'm pupaed if I can remember." Delicate antennae switched and bobbed in frustration. "Traveling between realities seems to affect the memory. The only thing I am certain of"—and he turned so sharply that Jon-Tom jerked back in his seat—"is that it has to do with *you.*"

"Righty-ho," barked Mudge. "Actually, we're just casual friends, him an' I. Not close a'tall. Nothin' much to do with one another, really." He stepped completely behind Naike.

"There is an energetic aura surrounding you," Caz went on. "Such auras attract."

"Is that what 'tis called?" Mudge pinched his nose. "Always tended to put me off, it did."

Imitating an all-too-human gesture, the creature shook its head from side to side. "Try as I will, I cannot recall the particulars of my quest. It is *most* frustrating. So I have resorted to tracking your very specific and bright aura in the hopes that it will lead me to that which I seek. Memory is a most pernicious thing."

"How long have you, um, been following us?" Jon-Tom asked.

"Too long. Until now you have always been a stride or two ahead of me. Speaking nonlinearly, of course. One rattles around the continuum like a larvae in a maturation chamber. And now that I have finally caught up with you, I cannot recall why it was necessary."

"Because 'e's a spellsinger an' maybe can 'elp you with 'is magickin'?" Mudge ventured cautiously.

"I tell you there is no such thing as magic! There is only physics, immutable regardless of how it is labeled."

Clothahump would understand that, Jon-Tom thought.

As Caz's tone turned doleful, Jon-Tom, having been on a quest or two himself in his time, felt suddenly sympathetic.

"This insertion has been a waste," the visitor was muttering aloud. "I am forced to return home to try and determine what it was I traveled here to find."

"Sounds like a good idea to me." Mudge was more than ready to be rid of their eccentric, not to mention incomprehensible, visitor.

"I really should make a note to carry with me. That would solve the problem. But the memory distortion which seems an unavoidable consequence of the transposition causes me to forget to do even that. I must find a way out of this conundrum!"

So saying, he fingered the controls on the backpack. The blue vapor reappeared and enveloped him. It was not unlike the mists which emerged from Jon-Tom's duar: slightly different in intensity, more structured in appearance.

When it dissipated, there was no sign that Caz had ever been there. Only his body odor lingered awhile, a faint scent of roses and lilac that stood out sharply amid the turgid stink of the marsh.

Though it looked no different from any other part of their craft, no one cared to step through the space formerly occupied by their visitor. Only Mudge went near, his black nose working overtime as it sampled the faintly singed air.

"Quaint little bugger. Polite enough, though."

"Where did it come from?" asked Seshenshe.

"Where did it go?" inquired Pivver.

"And what did it want?" wondered Aleaukauna.

"That thing on its back," Jon-Tom murmured. "Advanced science. Or magic. As the creature said, it's all in how you choose to define it. It certainly wasn't the product of Plated Folk technology. Wherever it came from lies far, far from this world. Probably in time as well as space."

Prosaic as always, Naike interrupted. "Speaking of time, we are not making any while we sit here gabbing. We are no longer in the main channel and the current here is slack. This craft is equipped with neither oars nor sail." As if to emphasize his impatience, the cloud of chords chimed away at the prow of the boat, a musical bowsprit.

Jon-Tom considered his duar. "I'm not sure I should try this again. I don't know if I called up that creature or if it simply materialized on its own, and I'd hate to conjure something worse. But if you're all against drifting awhile . . ."

The response was loud and earnest. Shrugging, he reprised the same melody and rhythm as best as he could recall it, not forgetting to modify the lyrics in what he hoped would be a more efficacious manner.

Encouragingly, the duar responded this time with light that was charcoal gray instead of blue, dull instead of intense. On the other hand, nothing much coalesced out of the consequent vapor. The engine gurgled thirstily a couple of times and then was silent.

As time wore on, so did Jon-Tom's voice. Not the most salubrious of singers when at his best, his increasingly haggard vocalizing was beginning to grate even on the most tolerant of the princesses. They began to whisper among themselves. Even Naike was prompted to inquire aloud if there was anything he could do to facilitate the process.

Jon-Tom took a break, to rest his larynx and fingers as well as the ears of his captive audience. "The magic doesn't work *every* time," he grumbled.

" 'Ere now, mate. Far be it from me to be overly encouragin', based on certain past experiences which shall remain unrecalled in this company, but maybe you're puttin' too much pressure on yourself. Instead o' strugglin' to come up with somethin' new, 'ow about tryin' the old method?" Mudge smiled encouragingly. "Use one o' the songs you know from your home world, like you used to."

"I can't think of any hard rock songs that deal with gasoline. Cars, sure, but not gas. And if I were to try 'Born to be Wild' or 'Turbo Lover' or even 'Little Deuce Coupe' and conjure up a car, it wouldn't do us much good out here."

"That's for sure," the otter agreed readily. "Wot's a car?"

Jon-Tom sighed wearily. "Never mind. There's got to be another way." He brightened. "Sure! That's it!"

"Righty-ho, mate, that's it. Wotever *it* is." Climbing down from the first step on the driver's chair and seeking what cover he could find, he retreated from his friend. Meanwhile, Jon-Tom raised his hands to the duar's strings and began to play. And to sing an old familiar song.

Whether it would be of any help to them remained to be seen.

A pale, silvery fog billowed from the duar. It curled around the silent engine like a great, ghostly anaconda, its tendrils probing the interior. The scarred, oil-stained metal sucked up the mist like a sponge. Encouraged, Jon-Tom played on. It was a relief to be able to fall back on well-known lyrics instead of having to concoct his own.

When the song reached its end and the last of the argent vapor had vanished into the machine, he swung his duar onto his back, took a deep breath, and tried the ignition.

A throaty snarl rose from the depths of the P&W as it sprang instantly to life. Soldiers and princesses cheered.

"See there?" Mudge gestured proudly at his companion. "Nothin' to it. Works every time, it does." He lowered his voice as he leaned toward Pivver. " 'Course, every once in a while I 'ave to tell 'im 'ow to go about it. 'E really would be lost without me."

The otter princess's expression was carefully neutral. "I have no doubt of that."

Mudge's whiskers twitched upward as he looked back at his friend. "Interestin' spellsong. Don't recall 'earin' 'im mention the magic word *gas*, though."

"Perhaps there are other magic words that mean the same thing?" Pivver speculated.

"I'd think that meself, except that 'e's always talkin' about the need to be specific in 'is spellsingin', and that if 'e ain't, 'tis impossible to predict wot might 'appen when—"

With a sharp *bang* from the engine, Jon-Tom was thrown back in his seat so abruptly that his desperate grab completely missed the control stick. Princesses and soldiers went flying. Only Umagi's quick thinking and great strength enabled her to grab the scion of Borobos before she went sailing overboard.

"Thank you," Ansibette told her rescuer.

"That's all right, dear. We primates must look out for one another."

Hard upon this rescue, a second blast erupted from the vicinity of the swamp buggy's engine, knocking both of them to the aluminum floor of the craft. This time Jon-Tom was nearly tossed from the boat and had to fight to hang on to his seat. Though slowed, his reflexes were still fast enough to save him from being thrown backward into the propeller, which was now spinning with the force of a small hurricane.

Balancing the precious duar, he fought to get a hand on the madly gyrating control stick. His fellow travelers clung to anything sturdy while the swamp buggy rocketed wildly across the marsh, scattering all manner of muck dwellers in a hundred directions. The princesses were wailing, the soldiers cursing, and Mudge complaining with an eloquence only he could muster as Jon-Tom fought to reestablish control while blue flames spewed from the buggy's exhaust pipes.

The otter's voice was barely audible above the blazing thunder. "Wot the bloody 'ell did you *sing* about, mate?"

Finally getting a hand on the stick, the spellsinger struggled to restrain the runaway craft. "Drag racing!" he shouted down at Mudge. "I was singing about drag racing!"

Flat on the deck, Seshenshe and Aleaukauna exchanged a confused glance. "Drag racing?" mumbled the mongoose. "What is this 'drag racing'?"

"Ssurely ssome ssort of powerful magic," replied Seshenshe. "Though, it would sseem, mosst difficult to masster."

"See the flames?" Both hands now wrapped securely around the stick, Jon-Tom was able to straighten the boat out. The Karrakas sped past, a blur on either side of the boat. "We're running on pure alcohol!"

Warm wind ripping at his ears, Mudge managed to stand in the middle of the violently rocking craft. "Wot! An' none for me to run on? Wot kind o' a spellsingin' friend are you?"

"This kind of alcohol you don't need!" Jon-Tom bellowed back. "Besides, you've always managed to run just fine on boasts and lies, and I know you're not running low on those!"

Once he had the swamp buggy back under control, he found time for other concerns. The first thing he did was direct everyone to move to the front of the craft to keep its nose down. Too much air under the bow at the speed they were going and there was a real danger that the swamp buggy might start to hydroplane. The last thing they wanted was to crash at their current speed.

Then he noticed Mudge and had to smile. Somehow hanging on to his hat, its long feather streaming straight back behind him, the otter was standing on the very prow of the buggy. Leaning forward and balancing himself into the wind, he looked for all the world like some crazed surfer hanging ten.

Yes, everything would be fine now, he told himself as they raced along at a velocity nothing short of preposterous. So long as they didn't blow up.

CHAPTER 14

Rising out of the water almost directly ahead, the low-lying island appeared at precisely the worst possible moment. Attending to a call of nature, Jon-Tom had allowed Mudge to take the stick and was unable to make it back up to the driver's chair in time to help avoid a collision.

As it was, he somehow managed to dodge around the big star-leaf trees which dominated the island vegetation. He was less successful in avoiding the profusion of smaller growths, a number of which, the travelers barely had time to note, were crowned with modest homes constructed of twigs, shells, and dried mud.

Peering curiously from the entrance of one tree house, an egret wearing a wafer-thin vest of yellow and chartreuse let out a startled screech and flapped frantically to gain altitude. Alerted, his terrified neighbors did their best to imitate him.

Traveling at close to forty miles per hour the swamp buggy hit the beach and skimmed straight across the island, smashing through small trees, bushes, gardens, houses, and everything else in its path. As the arboreal inhabitants scattered for their lives, those on board the boat ducked and covered their heads with their hands. Sand, branches, leaves, fruit, and the occasional household utensil ricocheted off princess and commoner with perfect equanimity.

Sliding back into the water on the far side of the abused islet, the swamp buggy's engine backfired impressively a couple of times before shutting down. Possibly for good, Jon-Tom worried as he uncovered his face and turned to inspect the frayed propeller. Burning smells rose from the blackened engine, but at least there was no fire.

Attire askew and with the assistance of Lieutenant Naike and his gallant trio, the dazed princesses were slowly picking themselves off the deck.

"What did we hit?" Seshenshe gingerly felt of her mouth. "I think I broke a tooth."

"an island. we hit an island." Quiquell was gasping softly. "i chipped a nail." As the claw in question was nearly four inches long, this minor catastrophe was not likely to physically inconvenience the Princess of Opan.

Mudge had adjusted his accoutrements and was standing close to his friend, peering over his shoulder as the spellsinger knelt to examine the engine. "Wot's our status, then, mate? Sorceral or otherwise."

"Where I come from, they call vehicles that run on alcohol 'funny cars.' Now I see why. We're out of fuel, Mudge."

"Crikey, that's no problem, then. Just resing the same tune you sang before."

"You know how I feel about repeating spellsongs. Though in this case I don't see that we have much choice." He squinted back at the inopportunely placed island. A clean swath was clearly visible right through the middle of the vegetation, as though a giant runaway lawn mower had viciously assaulted the unsuspecting verdure. "If we can get this going again, I'll just have to pay a little more attention to my driving."

Pivver plucked a whisker from her teeth. During the brief but madcap landward portion of their journey she had inadvertently bitten it off.

Jon-Tom brought his palm as close to the engine as he dared. Heat radiated powerfully from the overstressed metal. "Seems to be sound. We'll just let it cool down for a bit."

"While it's cooling down," a new voice said from behind him, "maybe you can decide what you're going to do about *us*."

Turning, man and otter looked on as a dozen or so feathered inhabitants of the island touched down gently on the starboard side of the swamp buggy, perching on the gunwale. The group consisted of males, females, and several two-foot-tall juveniles. Others were beginning to emerge from concealment in the surviving trees to inspect the damage the boat had wrought to their homes.

A four-foot-tall blue heron rested one wingtip on his hip while rubbing the lower portion of his long bill with the other. He wore a tattered but still serviceable decorative vest of some chiffonlike blue and green stripe. A pair of glasses perched precariously on his beak, halfway down its length.

Like the rest of his brethren, more than half his feathers had gone missing.

That last explosion from the engine, Jon-Tom told himself. That, and the violent effects of their props as the boat shot across the island. As he stared at the unfortunate heron, he fought to repress a smile.

Unsuccessful in a similar effort, Mudge found the sharp bill of an egret inches from his nose.

"What are you laughing at, water-rat?"

"N-nothing, guv." Stripping off his own clothing, the otter turned away from the battered bird. "Just thought I'd go for a quick swim." Diving over the side, he disappeared beneath the surface. An inordinate amount of bubbles rose from the place where he'd entered the water.

"Oh, the poor things!" Clasping her hands together, Aleaukauna looked properly empathetic.

"Indeed." Umagi adopted a look of dignified concern as she regarded the representatives of the devastated community.

All too soon, everyone's attention shifted to Jon-Tom.

"Hey, look, I'm sorry! It could've been worse. I might've lost control."

"Lost control? Lost control!" The blue heron glared through thick lenses at the spellsinger. "What do you call this? Look what you've done to our village! But at least that can be rebuilt. Look what you've done to *us*." He held up a half-denuded wing.

"More of us would have come to confront you with evidence of your perfidy, but the rest are in worse shape than those you see here. Without feathers we can't fly, without flying we can't fish, without fish we'll starve. What have you to say for yourselves?"

"Don't panic." Jon-Tom made soothing gestures. "I'm a sorcerer, a spellsinger. See?" He swung his duar around in front of him. The assembled villagers eyed the instrument dubiously. One juvenile swatted irritably at the chord cloud, which hung nearby, ringing curiously. "I'll put things right, you'll see."

"Is it your spellsinging that is responsible for our present unspeakable condition?" the heron inquired sharply. Its beak, Jon-Tom noted, was as sharp as an awl.

Having demonstrated uncharacteristic courtesy by relieving himself underwater of his irresistible urge to chortle maniacally, Mudge popped out among a cluster of reeds and swung lithely back aboard.

"Ah, don't sweat it, guv. Me mate'll fix things."

"And how, pray tell, do you intend to do that?" The egret's manner was slightly more curious and less testy than that of the heron. It held up a wing. "By gluing our feathers back on?"

Jon-Tom had to admit that he couldn't think of any old songs that dealt specifically with feathers. There were plenty of group allusions, from the Byrds to Hawkwind to the Eagles, but their songs tended to deal with subjects far less flighty than birds. As for original lyrics, he found the subject matter less than inspiring. He admitted as much to their indignant visitors.

"You knew enough to steal our feathers *away*." Devoid of his familiar pink plumage, the near-naked spoonbill perched on the stern looked like a sorry reject from a failed fried chicken franchise.

"I'll think of something, somehow," Jon-Tom insisted.

"You'd better!" Led by Aleaukauna, the princesses had assembled in a line facing him. Each of them generated a glare perfected through years of dealing with persistent courtiers. Collectively they made him feel about a quarter better than utterly worthless.

"I said I'd do something, and I will." *I just don't have the foggiest notion what that will be,* he admitted to himself.

It struck him that what had begun as a simple hike in the wake of some enigmatic music had ballooned out of all proportion to what he'd intended. Which was, he knew, exactly what he should have expected based on previous journeys. He sighed resignedly.

"If everyone will just leave me alone for a minute I'll try to satisfy *everybody*!" The unexpected outburst silenced his audience . . . for about ten seconds, after which time the princesses resumed excoriating him and the birds redoubled their complaints.

"Feathers first, I suppose. Give me some room, will you?" Still murmuring, the princesses retreated toward the bow, forcing the soldiers to make room where there was little to spare. The villagers watched with wary interest.

A gleam appeared in Jon-Tom's eye. "I'll fix things, but I want something in return."

The heron blinked. "We owe you nothing, bringer of despair."

"Nothing," chorused a pair of smaller female herons from nearby. "It's you who owe us."

"Nevertheless, that's the deal."

Mudge was slipping into his shorts when this declaration left him wide-eyed with mock wonderment. "Well wot do you know! Maybe all those years spent in me company 'as done you some good after all, mate. That's the first sensible thing I've 'eard you say since we started out on this bloody stroll."

"You shut up!" yelled Jon-Tom. "You've been no help in this at all."

"Oi, right, right!" Miffed, the otter turned his back on his friend. "Next you'll be blamin' your inept drivin' on me as well."

"I didn't say that," Jon-Tom protested. "Did I say that?"

"Please!" The heron spread his wings. "We have no choice. What is it you want?"

"Nothing for myself. But we're trying to help these princesses return to their homes, and we need help."

"Princesses?" The heron squinted, perhaps a little dazzled by the profusion of gold and chiffon gathered near the prow of the boat. "They don't look much like princesses to me. No feathers."

"That's all right," responded Seshenshe. "You have no manners." A couple of soldiers chuckled appreciatively.

Jon-Tom hurried on. "I've been told there's one decent-sized town at the bottom of the Karrakas, a place called Mashupro. I *think* I'm going the right way to get there, but there aren't a lot of landmarks around here. The services of a knowledgeable guide would be very useful."

"I know Mashupro. Sometimes we trade fish and crafts there." Turning his head and long bill, the heron called out, "Felgrin!"

A slightly smaller heron poked its head out of a nearby hummock. Flying awkwardly due to the absence of many feathers, it limped over to land on the side of the swamp buggy.

"The vandals won't help us unless someone agrees to guide them to Mashupro," the blue heron informed the newcomer.

The other avian nodded, his long beak bobbing. "No problem. I'll take them there, *if* I can get some feathers back."

The nominal leader of the deplumed community turned back to the tall human. "You heard him. Get on with it."

"I'll do what I can." Jon-Tom turned to advise his fellow travelers to keep clear, only to find that they had already taken precautions. By now they knew him well enough to need no urging.

Only mildly piqued, he contemplated potential lyrics. *Better tread carefully here,* he warned himself. Jeans and high-tops were not what was wanting.

When eventually he started to sing, it began to rain. Sheer

coincidence, he assured himself. In no way could his inventive lyrics about the beauty of birds on the wing be responsible for the sudden shower. Thunder rolled softly across the marsh, thunder that crackled intermittently, as if quilted.

The shower grew soft, and then it turned white. It was raining feathers. He smiled to himself as he played on. Exactly the result he'd hoped for, even if the methodology was a bit odd. The feathers continued to fall. Lots of feathers.

Tons of feathers.

They blanketed the marsh. Lilies disappeared beneath bushels of feathers. The princesses struggled to keep from being buried. Under Naike's direction, the soldiers worked frantically to keep the boat shoveled out. Mudge tried to lambaste his friend but could do no more than spit out the feathers that filled his mouth every time he parted his lips.

Jon-Tom could hardly sing for the seeping feathers. It was definitely time to abort the spellsong. One thing he made certain of as he concluded was not to sing anything even vaguely incendiary.

Wind seemed a more useful device, and that was a subject for which he had an ample supply of songs, old and new. The stiff breeze that arose in response to his demand banished the plumed hills and dales, the feathery valleys and mountains, sending the great soft mass scudding off to the north where it could do no harm.

Not every feather was whisked away. True to the spell and to his hopes, he saw that those which had come in contact with the pitifully denuded inhabitants of the island had adhered. Their soft, colorful coats had been fully restored.

"This is no kind of sorcery I am familiar with." The heron was preening his bright new plumage. "But I am willing to accept it."

One of the egrets reached up with a prehensile foot and plucked at a long tail feather. "Ouch! They're real enough, Singwit!"

The village leader was appeased. Feeling expansive and

not a little cocky, Jon-Tom was willing to toss in an extra or two.

"Now that I've fixed you back up, maybe you'd like me to repair your damaged homes as well?"

Singwit didn't hesitate. "I don't see why not, since it seems you can work great magic for a song."

"Far be it from me to play the party assassin," said Mudge as he stepped forward and put a comradely arm around the heron's shoulders, "but it might behoove you to rethink that casual permission in light o' certain experiences I've 'ad meself. You've got your bloomin' feathers back. Why not be content with that an' not press your luck?"

The tall bird wiggled free of the otter's grasp. "There is danger in continuing?"

"Mudge . . ." Jon-Tom began, but the otter ignored him.

" 'Ere now, 'tis probably none o' me business, but I ain't got nowheres to 'ide in this flat, open country an' I'm just thinkin' you might be better takin' your sorceral winnin's, as it were, an' continuin' on."

"Take the otter's advice," another of the egrets urged. "While we could not restore our bodies, we can certainly rebuild our homes."

"Daylight dissipates." Flapping experimentally, the heron Felgrin rose into the air. Like some exotic figurehead, he took up a perch on the very prow of the boat. With a wingtip he gestured toward a partly overgrown channel. "That way lies Mashupro." Teetering casually on one foot, he scratched at the side of his bill with the other.

"If you can control this demonic craft, I'll lead you straight to your destination. I've been there many times myself and know the way well."

" 'Ere then." Mudge eyed the bird suspiciously. "Wot's to prevent you runnin' us in circles an' then flyin' off whenever it suits your fancy?"

The heron looked back at him. "If I run you in circles, you might end up back here. That thought shudders my blood. I'd rather take you as far from my home as I possibly can. Mashupro will do."

The otter nudged Jon-Tom. "There be an 'onest reply. 'E'll guide us true or I ain't the Lover o' a Thousand Tearful Females."

"You ain't." Jon-Tom climbed back up into the pilot's chair. "Besides, I thought it was 'Terrified,' not 'Tearful.'"

Mudge leaned toward Pivver. "See there, Your Sleekness, 'ow too much book learnin' can ruin even a simple dumb 'uman like 'im?"

Concentrating on the swamp buggy's limited but sensitive controls, Jon-Tom made sure it was in neutral before essaying the alcohol fuel song a second time. Putting up the duar, he composed a silent prayer prior to turning the ignition. The engine roared deafeningly to life. Keeping a tight grip on the stick, he eased it gingerly forward.

In this manner they accelerated gradually. After a while the princesses soon felt confident enough to let go of seats and struts and even to stand so the wind could blow freely through their fur. Jon-Tom continued to let out the throttle until they were virtually flying across the marsh. Using the tip of his beak as a pointer, Felgrin was able to indicate the course without speaking.

Back on the partially trashed islet, its recently refeathered inhabitants assembled to evaluate the remains of several trees and homes as the noisy, smelly craft vanished into the southern reaches of the Karrakas.

"Felgrin will serve them well," one of the spoonbills avowed.

"What a strange lot!" A female egret adjusted her wispy vest. "I've never seen a group of travelers anything like them."

"That spellsinger," murmured her companion. "A human, and so tall! What marvels he must be capable of conjuring."

"And what calamities." Nearby, Singwit kicked at a clump of shattered house siding. "We'd best get to work."

"It could've been worse." A purple gallinule was turning

over fragments of ceiling with one of his oversized feet. "No one was killed, and we are only temporarily inconvenienced."

"That's right," several others readily agreed. "No serious harm done."

"I was going to remodel the old nest anyway," announced a hornbill cheerfully.

Two days later the delayed effects of Jon-Tom's spellsong began to manifest themselves.

Perching on a favorite hooknut branch that hung out over the water, Singwit courteously regurgitated the silver-sided cichlid he'd half swallowed while he addressed his friend. It wasn't polite to swallow and speak at the same time.

"Are you feeling unwell, Davil?"

The roseate spoonbill's beak clacked uncertainly. "Why wouldn't I be, Singwit?" All spoonbills had a tendency to lisp.

"Because you're on fire," the heron calmly informed him.

"Weally? I don't feel wike I'm on fire."

"Look at yourself."

Raising one wing, the spoonbill saw the unmistakable track of bright orange flames running from tip to shoulder. Flames mottled the other wing as well as most of his body.

"Funny. I don't feel even swightly overheated." One wingtip cautiously caressed the other. "It's not paint, or chalk."

"Your natural coloring has been changed." Singwit glared southward. "That damn spellsinger!"

"Oh, I don't know." Thrusting one wing skyward, the spoonbill watched as it caught and reflected the sunlight. "I kind of like it. Thpeaking of which, you ought to see yourthelf."

"Mythelf?" The heron turned wary. "What about myself?" Fearful of what he might see but incapable of not looking, he lowered his gaze.

The feathers of his wings and torso now boasted a brightly tinted, alternating pattern of emerald green and ice-blue diamonds.

The spoonbill pointed to where a pair of female egrets sat in another fishing tree. "Look at Erelmin."

Boldly streaked with black and yellow bands, the pure white feathers of the egret so singled out gave her the look of a giant streamlined hornet. Her companion flaunted pink and orange pin stripes on a background of electric crimson.

Cries and exclamations were rising all over the island now, from favorite fishing haunts to the village itself. Astonishment and shock reverberated through the trees in equal measure, though the latter faded rapidly as time passed.

While it was true that these unexpected developments left no one looking as they had previously, at the same time little despair was voiced over the alterations. The least flamboyant of the new coloring was startling and distinctive, and no one, not even the youngest fledgling, had been left out.

In fact, the only complaints came from those who thought their own magical makeovers had been slighted in favor of their neighbors. While not exactly disgruntled, these individuals could be heard to voice aloud the hope that when he'd concluded his business in distant Mashupro, the spellsinger might return by the same route to pass among them again, that they might look forward to further modifications.

In the space of a few days he had reduced them from content to miserable, only to raise them up in his absence to boastful and proud. The transformation was psychological as much as physical. The isolated, lonely fishing village had become an ever-changing parade of light and color, its inhabitants now able to challenge those of any rain forest for the title of brightest or most colorful. They were properly appreciative, if for weeks afterward still more than a little stunned.

Perhaps things would have gone differently had Jon-Tom not been forced to combine new lyrics about feathers with tried and true old ones alluding to the customization of cars.

CHAPTER 15

SEVERAL DAYS OF RUNNING THE SWAMP BUGGY AT HIGH
speed brought them, if not to civilization, at least to the occasional isolated fishing shack or houseboat. From time to time
they were forced to pause while their guide circled overhead
in search of landmarks, only to rejoin them with fresh directions.

One more day's traveling found them slowing as they
approached Mashupro Town itself.

If not a conurbation on the order of Polastrindu, Jon-Tom
had been hoping for a town at least as big as Lynchbany. In
this he was quickly disappointed.

The largest buildings boasted a maximum of three floors,
and most were single-storied. They clung to the southernmost
edge of the Karrakas where it brushed the open sea, nestled
behind a protective sandbar thick with mangrove. Cypress,
swampfilter, umber mangrove, and other dense vegetation
formed a small, isolated pocket of forest near the back of the
town.

They entered from the main channel west of the sprawling
community, Jon-Tom steering the swamp buggy in a growling arc up the narrow natural canal that formed Mashupro's
main commercial avenue. Thoughts of taking a stroll along a
cobblestone or even a dirt street vanished as soon as they
found themselves in among the buildings. Instead of proper
streets, Mashupro offered only more water.

Goggle-eyed townies hastened to pole or paddle or row
their own simple craft out of the path of the rumbling intrud-

er. Many gestures were cast in the visitors' direction, some of them other than complimentary. There was no panic: only a sort of languid curiosity. It was far too hot and humid to get intense about anything in Mashupro.

While it was not beautiful, or imposing, or even particularly clean, Mashupro Town did possess one characteristic that made it unique. The entire haphazard sprawl of houses and shacks, stores and saloons, was constructed on stilts which rose no less than ten nor more than twenty feet out of the water. A wagon would be as out of place in Mashupro as a frog on a glacier. This did not mean that the inhabitants were not mobile, however. They were more mobile, in fact, than the citizens of any settlement Jon-Tom had yet visited.

As they cruised slowly along the mossy byways the travelers observed in astonishment as one structure after another rose up on its stilts and walked to its owner's intended destination. Not every building was in motion. Without some sort of order no one would be able to find anyone else. But it was clear that every edifice was capable of and possessed a certain degree of mobility.

"Crikey," Mudge commented, " 'ow'd you like to be the local physician, wot? Give new meanin' to the idea o' 'ouse calls, it bloody would."

"I would have explained," Naike told them, "but it is a thing difficult to believe. Better to see for oneself." Jon-Tom nodded agreement, watching in fascination as two private homes presented themselves gracefully to the front of a grocery and the respective owners stepped from one porch to another to do their morning shopping. He was convinced he even saw both houses execute a slight architectural bow out of deference to the larger store.

"This is one town no one will ever map," he remarked. "Any map would be out of date by midafternoon."

They passed a chandlery as it positioned itself carefully above a damaged fishing boat and settled into place as neatly as a mother hen atop her chicks. A pair of muskrat apprentices shinnied down a rope ladder and began attaching a block

and tackle to the boat's broken mast. They paused long
enough to look up and point as the swamp buggy and its regal
cargo went humming past.

Want to visit the neighbors for a game of cards? Jon-Tom
mused. *No need to leave your house. Just find a spot conve-
nient to all, cluster together, and set up a table on the biggest
porch.* Mashupro was a mobile home park to a degree no
nomadic owners of Winnebagos and Bounders could ever
envision. If your home became immobile here, he thought, a
tire patch would do you no good. You'd need splints. At least
with a Detroit diesel you didn't have to worry about termites.

"I've 'eard o' communities with codes o' ethics," Mudge
declared as he watched two homes bow in passing, "but this
is ridiculous."

"The locals must know how to find one another."
Aleaukauna looked on longingly as they putted past a two-
story general store. "Or perhaps the buildings themselves
have learned how to recognize each other."

"I wonder what sort of consciousness they must have, if
they have any at all." Jon-Tom speculatively eyed the noisy
saloon they were passing. "Do they gossip about who needs
varnish or get embarrassed if a neighbor has a loose plank in
a sensitive spot? Do the older structures command more
respect? There may be a whole complex interedificial code
that doesn't even involve the people who live within."

"Oi, watch where you're goin'!" Mudge yelled up at a
small fishing shack. Making haste on its four tall, slim pilings
for the distant sandbar, it had nearly stepped on them. Busy
sorting out his tackle, the apologetic porcupine owner hadn't
been watching where he was going. Puffing on a curved pipe,
he leaned over and called down to them, peering through
thick bifocals.

"Sorry, friends!" He stamped one foot twice on the creaky
porch beneath him. "This place is gettin' old. Needs renova-
tion." With a wave he urged it past them. Jon-Tom watched
as the shack ambled out into deeper water.

A nice way to go fishing. Instead of a pole and tackle box,

you simply took your whole home with you. Just as the owner of the chandlery took his complete shop to each job. No need in Mashupro for children to walk to school when the school could stroll by in the morning and pick up individual students. There were, he admitted, certain advantages to such an arrangement.

As they cruised toward the harborfront he found himself wondering crazily if the smaller residences they passed were the offspring of full-sized homes. Bizarre images of copulating cottages convinced him he'd been out in the heat and humidity far too long. Did hotels give birth to motels? Could mansions sire servants' quarters? And if so, did the local hospital assist in each delivery? What would a Mashupro restaurant that offered fast food be like? His imagination threatened to run away with his common sense. Mudge would say that was his permanent state of mind anyway.

Near the harbor they began to encounter buildings that were on the whole larger and sturdier than any they had yet passed, two-story structures that hinted at a greater permanence. Among them were the warehouses which handled goods carried across the Farraglean, small hostelries catering to sailors and travelers, public houses and bars, the normal panoply of establishments which sprang up to serve any busy port. Ships tied up directly to pilings and porches, while most of the buildings were connected by a crazy-quilt network of raised plank walkways high above the water.

Not that these structures were immobile. As Jon-Tom and his companions looked for a place to dock, three warehouses raised up without so much as disengaging their respective walkways and placed themselves in position alongside a newly arrived schooner. *Can't bring your boat sufficiently inshore to unload cargo? Just wait for the harbor to come to you.*

Mashupro would be an awkward place in which to be drunk, Jon-Tom told himself. You could be staggering from one bar to another only to have them suddenly go their separate ways, taking their individual porches and walkways with them and unceremoniously dumping you in the drink.

Though he'd throttled down the swamp buggy as far as he could without bringing it to a complete stop, the whirring props still generated enough noise to draw the curious of Mashupro out of their buildings. Stares followed them until he and Mudge decided they might as well berth themselves beneath the most accessible of the waterfront structures. He found one which boasted a spiral stairway reaching down to the water, which would be far easier for the princesses to ascend than some swaying, unstable rope ladder. A curious shed sniffed at them as it ambled past.

Understandably, the majority of the population consisted of those creatures most comfortable with living in proximity to the water. The travelers saw muskrats and beavers, otters and tapirs, ocelots and primates of all kinds. There was also a large community of waterbirds. Hardly pausing long enough to bid them farewell and safe journey, Felgrin had flown off to join a trio of speckled storks. He'd fulfilled the terms of his agreement.

"i should think the locals would be more excited by our presence than they are." Quiquell eyed the spiral staircase skeptically.

"This is the principal port on the southern Karrakas," Ansibette reminded her. They must see many strange craft here, and many equally strange travelers."

"Just so long as they don't think us too strange, and get too curious." Umagi flexed rippling royal muscles. "I don't want to have to deal with unwanted suitors. I just want to get home." Jon-Tom found the notion of anyone putting a move on the intimidating scion of Exalted Tuuro highly unlikely.

"Same 'ere," barked Mudge tersely. "I don't like bein' the center o' attention in a strange place. Unless"——he winked—— "it 'appens to 'ave a light o' the red persuasion 'angin' out front."

Jon-Tom helped Karaukul secure a line. "Mudge, you're incorrigible."

"Can't be, mate. I ain't never met the lady."

"Lady? What lady?" Frustrated, he left the knot-tying to the more experienced and adept mongoose.

"Why, your theoretical Miss Corrigible, o' course."

"Commoner," sniffed Seshenshe.

"Uncommoner, I should say." No less one hundred percent otter than Jon-Tom's companion, the princess of Trenku struggled to repress a grin.

Moving to the stern, Mudge clung to the propeller cage with one paw as he studied the harborfront. "Seem to be a number o' empty boats lyin' to, mate. Burn me for a sun-struck mole if I don't think we can trade this berserk tin shingle for somethin' a tad more seaworthy."

"Why?" Aleaukauna moved to join them. "Why can we not continue on in this magical craft, which has served us so well until now?"

Jon-Tom explained. "The swamp buggy is intended for high-speed travel over flat, shallow, still water. A single modest wave would flip it, or swamp it."

The mongoose nodded understandingly. "I see. Forgive my ignorance. I am not a person of the water."

Mudge turned to call back to Naike. " 'Ere now, quick-tooth: "'Ow'd you and your mates manage your ocean crossin'?"

"Aboard an old merchant vessel, on which we had booked passage." The Lieutenant neatly whipped a line around a cleat welded to the swamp buggy's bow. "Finding one that came anywhere near this place was hard. Locating one that just happens to be going back the way we wish to return I think will prove far more difficult." He spread both paws. "Also, we are nearly broke, and now we must secure passage not merely for four soldiers but also for two fellow travelers and six princesses who would not, I think, be comfortable traveling in steerage."

"I should say not!" Umagi stuck out her lower jaw. As it already protruded a goodly distance, it was quite an impressive gesture.

"Then we'd best arrange for some sort of charter," said Jon-Tom. "At least on a boat of our own choosing we'll have some privacy."

"Ah, I like the way you think, spellsinger." Umagi ran a hand playfully along his neck caressing him with fingers that were quite capable of unscrewing his head like a cork from a perfume bottle. Her touch, however, was light. Very assiduously, he avoided her eyes.

"Wot d'you think, mate?" Mudge wondered. "Can we make a trade?"

Jon-Tom regarded the swamp buggy. "I don't know, Mudge. This is a craft of my world, inveigled here by spellsinging. For one thing, I'm sure my last fueling spell must be running low. I wouldn't want to trade with someone under false pretenses."

"That's no problem. Let me look after the details."

"Didn't you hear what I said? Mudge, you never had a pretense that wasn't false."

The otter put a hand to his chest. "Oi! Pierced through the 'eart again!" He did not seem especially offended. "If she'll run on any kind o' alcohol, mate, you needn't worry about puttin' 'er off on some local merchant. If there's one thing port towns keep in ample stock, 'tis an adequate quantity o' distillates."

"I expect you're right." They didn't have much choice. They needed an oceangoing craft and, save for the swamp buggy, had little with which to barter.

Inquiries led them to a weathered but imposing structure located midway up the harborfront. Upon presenting themselves and explaining their intent, they were shown to an inner office occupied by a typically corpulent capybara. Samples of his company's wares consisting of ship's stores from rope to brass fittings decorated the walls and hung from the ceiling. One dirty, four-paned window looked out over the water.

Just as Mudge had surmised, the capy was very interested in the swamp buggy. After several hours of intense haggling,

an exhausted Jon-Tom conceded control of the negotiations
to Mudge. Not only was the otter better suited temperamen-
tally to such commercial conflict, he positively relished the
resulting ruckus.

Only when both voices and the sun had begun to set was a
bargain finally struck. In return for the swamp buggy they
received title to a small, older, but sturdy single-masted ship.
From what little Jon-Tom knew about boats he decided it
would be slow, but would hold together in bad weather. And
it was capacious enough to accommodate all of them in some
comfort. The single belowdecks had multiple cabins and a
nice high ceiling, though the soldiers would have to sleep out
on deck. There was a galley, space for modest stores, and
even a few comfortable benches permanently affixed fore of
the mast. Naike was confident it could be handled by their
comparatively inexperienced crew.

Even the lost chords approved, the luminescent cloud of
music climbing all over the ship, ringing approvingly from
the hand-carved wheel to the tip of the bowsprit.

The capybara leaned on the walkway's railing and nodded
at the acquisition. "You won't inspire no looks of envy sailing her into distant ports, but she'll get you there. She's an old
deep-water interisland trader, built to run up on a beach or
break her way through a narrow reef. You'd have to work
hard to capsize her."

"She will do," declared Naike from nearby.

"Mudge and I have spent some time on the water," Jon-
Tom added. "We can help. Once we reach the distant coast
we'll leave you to your own devices, but by then you'll be
able to take aboard sailors from Harakun."

The capy stepped back and extended a dark-furred hand.
"No need for a solicitor to witness a straight-up trade.
Besides, it would take his office an hour to walk here from
across town. Rush-hour, you know."

Jon-Tom took the proffered paw. "I just want to make sure
that you understand what you're getting. Our craft was magicked here. I can't vouch for how long it will continue to

function, no matter what grade of alcohol you fill its tank with. Also, impurities could ruin the engine and strand you somewhere. Maybe deep in the Karrakas." Mudge was tugging hard on his sleeve. As was usual at such moments, Jon-Tom ignored the otter.

The capy looked surprised. "Oh, but I've no intention of using it for transportation." His whiskers hid much of his mouth.

Jon-Tom frowned. "Then what do you want with it?"

"As you may have noticed, our climate here is somewhat on the humid side."

" 'Umid 'ell," Mudge snorted. "There's more water in the air 'ere than lies under any boat."

Jon-Tom mopped at his face. "So you perspire. I've been perspiring for so long I'd stopped thinking about it."

"The great fan which pushes your craft? I'm going to turn the vessel on its bow and secure it beneath my building. I'll have baffles built into the floor and on the worst days run your wondrous engine." His chest expanded. "I'll have the coolest and most comfortable place of business in all of Mashupro. My friends as well as my competitors will envy me."

"Deuced clever," Mudge had to admit. Evidently just because many folk lived in Mashupro didn't mean they all found the climate equally salubrious.

"Just don't operate it at full speed," Jon-Tom warned him. "That way the engine will last longer, and you'll cool your place of business instead of blowing it away."

"We'll need supplies." Naike gazed longingly across the twilit water, past the heavily vegetated sandbar and toward the distant sea. "It's a long, long ways to Harakun, much less to the kingdoms of our other passengers."

"I've seen the elegant ladies who travel with you." The capy made too much of seeming indifferent. "They are a striking bunch."

"Simple travelers affected with pretense," Naike explained. It wouldn't do for word to get around a place like

Mashupro that their party included a number of eminently ransomable princesses.

"You could provide a minimal quantity of supplies as part of the agreement," the Lieutenant suggested. "Food, ship's stores, the basics necessary for an ocean voyage."

Mudge let out a barking hoot. The capybara glanced only briefly in the otter's direction before folding his short, thick arms across his chest.

"Aye, and I could be anointed a Prince of Benefaction, and give away all my worldly goods, and become a traveling monk, bestowing blessings upon the spiritually bereft and unfortunate. It remains, however, that I am a merchant, with staff and their own families to support." The billowing sleeves of his deeply V-cut silk shirt hung damp and limp against his fur. "I don't give anything away. Have you nothing else to barter?"

"Well, now." Mudge deliberated. "I suppose we might could do without a lady or two. That prissy lynx, for example, gets on me nerves sometimes, she does." Jon-Tom shot him an admonishing glare and the otter subsided. "Well, it were just an idea, it were."

Taking a deep breath, Jon-Tom brought the duar around in front of him. "How's this? I'll sing another spellsong and fully fill the fuel tank. It's bound to run smoother on my spell than on whatever you eventually end up using, and it'll cost you less as well."

The capy didn't hesitate. "You're a fair man, tall human. I'll see to it that you cast off decently, if not extravagantly, stocked. The Farraglean is full of islands where you'll be able to replenish your supplies."

When they had shaken hands all around, it was Mudge who indicated the darkening sky. "Now that we're all agreed, is there anyplace in this ambulatin' warren where a curious traveler might find a little excitement?"

"Mudge, aren't you exhausted? Don't you want to get a good night's sleep in a bed that doesn't rock before we head out tomorrow?"

The otter winked salaciously. "Oi, you know me, mate. A rockin' bed can be more than adequately comfortin'. And if we're goin' to be at sea for a few weeks I'd like to spend a bit o' time in the company o' those sportin' legs instead o' fins. I ain't one much for cavortin' with dolphins."

"I thought you'd put your cavorting days behind you."

Full of rising anticipations, Mudge peered hopefully down the length of the uneven raised walkway. Music and good-natured shouts in numerous dialects were beginning to issue from flickering doorways.

"See 'ere, mate, if you're so enthusiastic about relaxin', consider the good a bit o' 'armless diversion will do us. Take your mind off wot we're about, it will."

"My soldiers could do with some recreation." Naike was nodding understandingly. "For that matter, so could I. We have just completed one arduous journey across the Karrakas and are about to embark on another equally fraught with danger."

Jon-Tom weakened. Maybe it was the music, or perhaps the rich aromatic smells that were beginning to emerge from the depths of several of the ramshackle structures. "I suppose a little partying couldn't hurt, so long as we watch ourselves."

"You watch yourself, mate. I've other ocular interests in mind, don't you know." The otter looked hopefully at the knowledgeable capybara.

Formalities concluded, their host became positively fraternal. "Now that is information I'll share gladly, and at no charge."

CHAPTER 16

THE HARBORFRONT TAVERN SHIMMIED GENTLY ON ITS PIL-
ings. A number of small boats were tied up below, close to
several rope ladders which dangled conveniently from the
elevated walkway. These were used for ascent by travelers
and locals alike.

Staring out toward the vastness of the unknown Farraglean,
Jon-Tom noted how the moon cast lazy shadows on water
and marsh. As if sensing his mood, the cluster of drifting
chords muted their singing. He thought of Talea and how she
would have appreciated the view, not to mention the romantic
ambiance. Then a bottle shattered somewhere inside the tavern, someone growled a guttural curse, and the mood was
broken. Mildly depressed, he followed Mudge and the others
inside.

Though not very impressive by Jon-Tom and Mudge's
worldly standards, the tavern was spacious and packed with
patrons who gave every appearance of enjoying themselves.
Sweating profusely in the crowded, slightly swaying room,
he looked on as Naike and his companions melted into the
surging, jostling throng. Reluctant at first but with increasing
enthusiasm, the princesses allowed themselves to be whirled
about in time to the infectious music as one after another of
the eager male patrons asked them to dance.

Mudge set himself to entertain Pivver of Trenku. She
seemed to find his antics and attention amusing without taking any of it seriously. Half of Jon-Tom burned to have Ansibette take him seriously, while his other half restrained him.

The resulting internal conflict created a condition which liquor was unable to mitigate.

It didn't help that, out of breath from being swung about the floor by various enthusiastic if temporary partners, she sat down in the chair opposite him and leaned forward.

"What a grand time! Aren't you having a grand time, master spellsinger?"

"Oh yeah." Jon-Tom smiled wanly. "Grand."

"Commoners can be *so* diverting." Resting her perfect chin in one hand, she batted her eyes at him. This was a physical reaction Jon-Tom encountered infrequently at best and he had no idea how to react, though he suspected that inquiring if she was suffering from some sort of intermittent twitch would be considered improper.

"Tell me more of your wondrous adventures," she cooed, preventing Jon-Tom from pigeonholing her attitude.

Having nowhere to hide, his fingers did something inane with his glass. "I don't know that they're all that wondrous." Forcing himself to look elsewhere, he watched Umagi whirl a fairly overwhelmed orangutan dressed in sailor's garb high overhead.

The princess gestured toward the table where Pivver and Mudge were sunk in intense conversation. "I don't understand your reluctance. Your friend doesn't hesitate to speak of your travels."

"I'm sure he doesn't."

"You mustn't chide him for his zeal. We have court magicians, but they're mostly clever fakirs. I've never met a *real* spellsinger before. Were you born to the profession?"

"Yes . . . no . . . I don't really know. I haven't thought about it much. I'm as surprised by my skills as anyone." He continued fiddling with the half-empty glass. "It's what you'd call an unusual story."

"There, you see!" Sitting back, she smiled encouragingly. "I knew you had tales to tell."

"Mine's pretty hard to believe. Sometimes I don't completely believe it myself." Having deposed that caveat, he proceeded to regale her with the story of how he'd come to be in her world and make for himself a place, a respected place at that, within it.

Much impressed, Ansibette of Borobos hung intently on his every word. He was halfway through his reminiscence when he realized that the tavern band was playing the same two tunes over and over. The gibbon, weasel, serval, and wallaby struck him as too adept at their profession to be so musically constipated. To perform successfully in a venue like the tavern, a certain variety was usually demanded, lest the musicians be hooted off their small stage or become the recipients of large, disagreeable missiles.

"Have you noticed that the local band seems to know only two songs?"

"Is that so surprising?"

"What's surprising is that no one in this mob is complaining about it. It doesn't make any sense. I've been watching them, and they play well."

"Better to play two songs well than a hundred poorly," she argued, obviously bemused by his sudden obsession.

"Not in a place like this." Pushing back his chair, he started to rise.

Delicate fingers reached for his arm. "Don't go. I was just coming to know you."

Staring at the stage, he replied absently. "Sip your drink. I'll be back in a minute."

She followed him as he headed off in search of his companion. Since he did not look back, he failed to note the skill with which she tossed down the remaining contents of her glass.

He found the otter nose to nose with princess Pivver of Trenku. "Mudge?"

Favoring him with a look that promised abrupt disembowelment without anesthesia sometime in the near future, the otter growled softly, "Wot is it this time, mate?"

Jon-Tom nodded across the bobbing sea of heads. "Have you noticed the local band?"

"I am pleased to say that I 'ave not, mate. I've other matters of a rhythmic nature on me mind, I do." Turning back to the princess, he was rewarded with an enigmatic smile that, while not especially encouraging, was something other than wholly indifferent.

"They're only playing two songs," Jon-Tom informed him.

"Oi, only two? Why, I guess I'll just 'ave to drop everythin' and hie meself over there to bawl 'em out for their impertinence, won't I?"

"But it doesn't make any sense. They're good players."

The otter glared intently at his friend. "See 'ere, mate: If you're so bleedin' curious about aspects o' the local musicology, why don't you go over an' ask 'em about it yourself?"

"Yes." Pivver continued to peer deeply into Mudge's eyes. "Leave your friend and I to continue with our conversation."

"Fine! I guess I'll just have to check it out all by myself."

"Fine indeed." Mudge didn't look up.

As he pushed his way through the undulating, smelly mob, Jon-Tom saw that the musicians had broken for a rest. Glad of the opportunity, he strode right up to the gibbon, trying to wave away the aromatic smoke that tended to collect at this end of the tavern.

"You guys are pretty good."

"Thanks." The gibbon's response was neither inviting nor hostile. His long arms were crossed behind his head and he wore lacy leotards and a matching vest.

"I was just wondering if there was something wrong. I've noticed that your repertoire seems restricted to the same two tunes."

The wallaby smirked at the serval. "Observant, isn't he?"

"I've also noticed," Jon-Tom went on, "that no one's griping about it." He waved at the crowd. "I know places like this. People should be throwing things at you by now. Yet no one seems to be taking any notice."

"Why zhould they?" replied the serval. "They all live under the zame curze."

Jon-Tom frowned. "Curze? What curze?"

"You don't know?" The gibbon showed a flicker of interest. "I don't believe I've seen you in here before, and I would have remembered a human as tall as—"

Before he could finish, the weasel noted the duar strapped to Jon-Tom's back. "Hoy, are you a musician, too?"

"After a fashion." Crossing his arms, he leaned back against the wall. "I'm a spellsinger, though I can also play just for fun."

"And you don't suffer from the curse?" The wallaby's expression conveyed a mixture of hope and despair.

"I don't even know what it is." Straightening, he swung the duar around. "If you don't mind, I'd be pleased to sit in with you during your next session."

"You can play more than two zongz?" The serval was staring hard at him, showing yellow-stained teeth.

"I can play hundreds. Some of them not very well, but enough to get by. If you're having trouble with more than the two you've been playing, why don't you let me lead and you just follow along? Maybe it'll break you out of your rut. Or curse, as the case may be."

"That would be wonderful!" The gibbon eyed his companions. "I don't think it will work, but—"

"What's the harm in trying, Lesvash?" The wallaby picked up a trumpetlike instrument. "What have we got to lose?"

"I'll start with something simple." Jon-Tom strummed a few bars. "Just try to stay with me."

"Anything, anything at all." The gibbon was pitiably eager. He was holding what looked like a radically modified ukulele. The weasel hefted a double flute as long as Jon-Tom's arm, while the serval used its claws to pick at the thick strings of a cross between a cello and a drum.

They backed him perfectly, harmonizing with admirable and effortless fluidity, supporting each chord, underlining each coda. Outside, the lost chords partnered with the moonlight in a waltz of luminous intoxication.

Their efforts did not pass unnoticed by the tavern's clientele. As soon as the new music began to ring out, the dancers and drinkers and revelers responded with cheers and yells of wild approval. They sounded downright startled, Jon-Tom decided, even though he was playing only the most basic riffs and rhythms. The simplicity of the music wasn't what mattered to the enthralled, enthusiastic listeners, however.

What mattered about the music, *all* that mattered about the music, was that it was fresh.

It was a good deal later when an exhausted Jon-Tom called a halt to the session. Though his fingers hurt all the way up to his shoulders, he didn't mind the soreness. For the first time in a long while he'd been able to jam with other musicians. It was wonderful to be able to play not to cure someone of the pox or restore a dry well or demonstrate his improving sorcerous acuity to Clothahump, but simply for the sheer joy of playing. It reminded him why he'd taken up the electric guitar in the first place, all those many years ago.

Reality intruded, as it was sadly wont to do, in the form of a bright-eyed, lace-clad gibbon tugging at his arm.

"Please, stay with us! Your music is difficult and different, but exciting and new. You can't imagine how nice it is to be able to play something else besides those same two lousy, stinking songs."

Jon-Tom found an unoccupied chair and sank gratefully onto the seat. "I don't get your problem. You play well. No, you play superbly, all of you. I know clubs in L.A. that would sign you in a minute." He grinned knowingly. "Places where your appearance wouldn't even draw stares."

The weasel bent double to examine himself. "Appearance? What's wrong with our appearance?"

"If you hate those two songs, why do you keep playing them over and over? Can't you reprise some of the stuff I just showed you?"

Mournful looks were exchanged, of which the gibbon's was the most expressive. "No, we can't." He readied his ukulele. "This is a contemporary sea chantey, lively and brisk. A favorite with visiting sailors. By popular demand we used to play it half a dozen times every evening." His fingers dipped to strum the strings of the heavily varnished mellowood instrument.

No sound emerged. Not an off-key plunk, not a fragment of a melody; nothing.

Jon-Tom stared. He could see the gibbon's fingers moving, see the strings of his instrument bend and vibrate, but nothing disturbed his hearing. There was no music.

"How are you doing that?"

"I'm not doing it." The slender simian sighed soulfully as he paused. "Something's doing it to me." He indicated his companions. "Doing it to all musicians, everywhere. These past several months we've met with and shared conversation with many fellow performers. All are suffering as we are."

"You zee why we call it a curze." The serval fondly caressed his instrument. "And it zeemz to be zpreading, getting worze."

"It started quite slowly," added the wallaby. "At first you'd just lose a phrase or a chord here and there. Then whole passages would prove unplayable. Your fingers moved properly, and your lips and hands, but no music came forth. We'd play songs with unexpected, increasingly lengthy interrupts."

"Made for zome awkward movez on the dance floor," the serval recalled.

"Eventually we started losing entire arrangements, then whole songs." The weasel put his lips around the mouthpiece of his attenuated double flute and blew affectionately. A single lonely, forlorn B-sharp drifted forth like a melancholy honeybee heading hiveward at the end of a long day's work.

"That's why we're down to two songs." Like all of them, the wallaby was obviously suffering under the strain. "Soon now I expect we'll lose one of those, or so much of it that it'll become unplayable, like the others."

"Eventually we'll lose it all." The gibbon tucked his uke under one long arm. "Musicians without music. That means no music, no song for anyone. Every other group we've talked with these past months, even wandering soloists, are suffering from the same terrible, inexplicable plague."

The wallaby's eyes suddenly widened and he pointed. "What's *that*?"

Floating in from outside, the cloud of lost chords had paused to hover slightly behind and above Jon-Tom's right shoulder. Glittering like a bushel of pink diamonds suspended in a glass barrel filled with mineral oil, it chimed softly.

"Sorcery." Clearly uncomfortable, the gibbon took a step back from Jon-Tom, who hastened to reassure them.

"I told you I was a spellsinger. This is magic, yes, but not of my doing. It has nothing to do with the troubles you're having."

Taking courage and unable to restrain his curiosity, the weasel edged forward to examine the drifting mass more closely. "It doesn't sound like a very happy bit of music."

"It's not. I think it's in search of help, very anxious to get somewhere, and to have company along the way. We're letting it lead us." He smiled gently. "I've let music lead me most of my life."

"A wandering melody." Entranced, the gibbon reached tentatively for the cloud. It emitted a soft ring of suspicion as it darted back behind Jon-Tom's head. "How do you know there's no connection? We've all of us lost music, and here you are with a piece of same."

"Maybe it belongz to another unhappy, worried muzician zomewhere," the serval suggested.

Jon-Tom blinked. Here was a connection too obvious to ignore, one that at the very least deserved further consideration.

"We've no way of knowing that."

"Why not just ask it?" The gibbon continued to move closer to the cloud, which kept dodging around behind Jon-Tom.

"Ask it?

"Why not? I talk to my instrument all the time."

"Yeah, and when you've had too much happy juice, sometimes it even answers." The wallaby chuckled.

Jon-Tom glanced self-consciously back over his shoulder. "Well? *Are* you connected to the disappearance of everyone else's music. Are your condition and theirs related?" As they had been doing for weeks the chords chimed softly, with no special emphasis or force. It could hardly be considered a response.

"I suppose that's open to interpretation." The weasel looked disappointed.

"Not exactly conclusive," the wallaby added dubiously.

"A plague." The gibbon strummed his silent ukulele. "It's spreading, making musicless the whole world, and no one can do anything about it. Soon we'll be forced to consider new professions."

"I can't imagine being anything but a musician," the wallaby observed.

"Nor I," the serval admitted.

"Dammit, I *love* music!" Despite the laughter and merriment that filled the tavern, the weasel appeared on the verge of tears.

"None of these tavern trawlers you see making merry here complain because they all know about the plague." The gibbon's arm moved to encompass the swirling crowd. "They're just grateful we have as much as two songs left. How they, how everyone will react when the last of the music is gone, I don't know." He eyed the ringing cloud wistfully. "Imagine a world without music."

"But what's happened to it?" Jon-Tom eyed them each in turn. "Where's it all going?"

"Going?" The weasel shrugged helplessly. "We don't know that it's 'going' anywhere. It's simply fading away. You can't even bang out a rude tune on the underside of a metal pot. As soon as it starts to sound like music, it evaporates."

"All of it." The gibbon studied Jon-Tom's face. "All, it would seem, except yours." He indicated the duar. "Your music seems unaffected."

"I come from a far, far-off land. One untouched by this plague."

"How do you know?" The weasel sniffed. "You said that

you've been traveling for a long time, through very empty
country. How do you know what music is vanishing from
your homeland?"

Jon-Tom started to reply, stopped cold. The weasel spoke
truly. He had no idea what was happening back in the Bellwoods. For all he knew, this curse, or plague, or whatever one
chose to call the scourge, had infected the musical life of that
region as insidiously and thoroughly as it had Mashupro and
the rest of the Karrakas. He tried to envision lively Lynchbany void of music in its public places and taverns, tried to
imagine the main square without the raucous cacophony of its
amateur performers and traveling minstrels. It was a sobering
thought.

What was happening to all the music? Was every tune and
melody in the world being sucked into some sort of musical
graveyard or dumping ground?

"I can't worry about the whole world," he finally
declaimed. "Right now Mudge and I are tracking this one
group of chords. That's enough to concentrate on. We're also
trying to help half a dozen prin—persons of importance to
return to their homes. I can't worry about any music but my
own."

The gibbon wasn't buying it. "I don't believe you for a
minute, human. Spellsinger or not, you're a true *musician*.
You *must* be concerned."

"What will you do when it begins to affect you?" the
weasel pressed him. "How will you react when you start to
play that strange device you carry and no sound comes forth?
Not only will you be like us, unable to make music any
longer, you won't be able to make your magic, either."

"I don't expect to be affected," Jon-Tom replied with more
assurance than he felt. After all, why should he be exempt? A
plague was a plague, whether one was a common traveling
minstrel or an exalted spellsinger. Was there some sort of
germ that was killing off everyone's music? Some sort of
mutant hermetic virus? What reason did he have to believe he

was immune from such an infection? Germs and viruses were no respecters of reputation or position.

Could he spellsing up a musical vaccine? If so, it would be a useful concoction to carry with him on his rare transits back to his own world. He knew all too many people there who were immune to the effects of any kind of music whatsoever.

"We must be on our way," he finally informed them. "If I was traveling alone I would stay and study the trouble, but there are others depending on me. Perhaps on the return journey I can try and do something."

The gibbon and his companions looked resigned. "There is nothing we can do to persuade you to linger?" He fingered his uke longingly. "Tonight brought back many memories. Tonight we were makers and masters of music again."

"Remember some of the songs we played." Jon-Tom tried to offer some support. "Maybe they'll hang with you after I've left. For a while, anyway."

The weasel raised his instrument and blew a few cautious, experimental notes. Emerging from a double flute, "Pinball Wizard" sounded somewhat muted, but oddly appealing. It had winsome overtones Pete Townshend doubtless never envisioned.

"There!" Jon-Tom felt better, less like he was abandoning these new friends and colleagues to a despondent and uncertain fate.

The gibbon had to wipe away a tear. He was certainly the sentimental type, Jon-Tom mused.

"It's a great gift, the gift of music. We thank you for it, for as long as it will last. Though we'd rather have our own melodies restored." A murmur of agreement rose from his companions.

"String it out, be thrifty with the songs I've left you. When I've seen these ladies returned to their families, I'll come back this way and do what I can to help. That's a promise." Behind Jon-Tom the lost chords sang softly—aural perfume.

There were handshakes and back claps all around. He might differ in shape from them, Jon-Tom reflected as he

took his leave and went in search of Mudge, but what they
shared went far deeper than mere appearance. Music was the
most exclusive of all languages, and none understood it better
than those who spoke it professionally.

The otter wasn't at the table where Jon-Tom had left him.
Somewhat to his surprise, Pivver of Trenku still was.
Aleaukauna occupied Mudge's former seat. Both princesses
had decorated the tips of each whisker with silver glitter.

"Where is he?"

"I don't know." Nor did Pivver much care, Jon-Tom decided from the tone of her voice. "He was trying to demonstrate
his capacity for liquid imbibulation, but his insides betrayed
him."

"Several times." Aleaukauna took a ladylike sip from her
long-stemmed goblet.

"As you might imagine, at that point my interest in his
company began to wane." Pivver had very long eyelashes,
Jon-Tom noted, a not uncommon trait among female otters.
"There's nothing like grooming fresh vomit out of your fur to
tell you that an evening is not proceeding as hoped."

Poor Mudge, Jon-Tom thought. His appetites often got the
better of him. "Where'd he go?"

"How should I know? I don't occupy my thoughts with the
comings and goings of commoners."

Lifting his gaze, Jon-Tom resumed his search of the room.
"It's just that when he's not entirely sober he has a tendency
to get into trouble."

"I fail to see any difference. He struck me as equally
unhinged before he'd had a single drink, though a good deal
cleaner."

Further inquiries yielded the news that the otter had last
been seen wending his way outside. A worried Jon-Tom
made his way toward the entrance. If his friend took a tumble
off the raised wooden walkway, he'd float like a
cork . . . unless he struck his head on something on the way
down. Extraordinary swimmers though they were, otters were

no more immune to drowning than an unconscious bird was
to succumbing to the blandishments of gravity.

"Mudge!" The moon had crossed the noon of night and had
commenced its languid descent westward. A small fishing
boat was heading seaward, splitting the calm mirror of water
between Mashupro and its protective barrier islet. Moving to
the inadequate, rickety railing, Jon-Tom leaned over and
searched the water which lapped gently at the tavern's moss-
stained, barnacle-encrusted pilings.

"Mudge, where are you?"

The otter's voice reached him, but not from below. Turning to his left, he saw his friend clinging to a post supporting
the porch of a building south of the rowdy tavern. Despite the
racket from within and the distance between, the otter's
slurred bellowing was clearly audible. Given their present situation, his choice of words qualified as something less than
diplomatic.

"You're all a pack o' miserable stinkin' useless muckers!
Can't even walk from one place to another. Got to 'ave your
bleedin' 'ouses do it for you! This 'as got to be the crummi-
est, sorriest, filthiest, smelliest, est-est excuse for a town I've
ever seen in me 'ole bloody life, and I've seen plenty of
shit'oles in me time, I 'ave!" He lifted the bottle gripped in
his right hand, clinging to the pole with his left. " 'Ere's to
bleedin' Mashupro, the screen at the bottom o' the world's
cesspool!" Upending the bottle, he scarfed a glassful, then
blinked up at the figure that was suddenly towering over him.

"Oi. 'Ello, mate." He offered the all but empty container.
" 'Ave a nip?"

"Don't you think you've had enough for one night?"
Though he was boiling inside, Jon-Tom kept his voice calm,
reasonable.

"Enough for one night." Feathered cap askew, the otter
struggled to cerebrate this majestic aphorism, finally deliver-
ing himself of the conclusion that it was too deep for him and
besides, wasn't it a lovely evening, what with no wind and all
three moons in the sky?

"There's only one," Jon-Tom patiently corrected him. "What's got you so ticked off at Mashupro? It's no worse than many towns we've passed through. Damper, maybe, but no worse."

The otter goggled up at him. "Mate! 'Ow can you say that? Why, there's no pride o' place 'ere, none at all." He sema-phored wildly with the bottle, forcing Jon-Tom to flinch away from one wild swing. "They don't even pave their bleedin' roads!"

"There are no roads here, Mudge," Jon-Tom reminded him. "It's all water, remember? Everyone uses boats."

"Boats? Water?" Thoroughly bemused (not to mention beclouded, befogged, and blitzed), the otter turned to gawk over a railing. "Aha! See wot I've been tryin' to tell you? The bloody befouled streets 'ere don't even 'ave drains!"

Worried that the flimsy railing might snap under his friend's weight, Jon-Tom put a hand on the otter's shoulder. Mudge responded by whirling belligerently and backing away.

" 'Ere now; we'll 'ave none o' that!"

"Mudge, you need to lie down."

"Oi, is that a fact, now? When did you become my keeper, man?"

"I'm not your keeper, Mudge. I'm your friend. I've been your friend for a long time, remember?" It struck him sud-denly that something was troubling the otter, something that had nothing to do with the state or status of the local munici-pality. "What's bothering you, Mudge?"

"Nothin's botherin' me, mate. Not me! Nothin'." He hesi-tated, swaying on his short legs. " 'Tis only that . . ."

" 'Tis only what, Mudge?"

Turning away, the otter leaned heavily on the railing. It creaked alarmingly, but held. It was a good twenty feet to the water below, dangerously flecked with the stumps of old pil-ings. Small craft bobbed at their moorings. If he fell, his land-ing might not be soft.

" 'Tis that Puffer, the princess o' me very own tribe."

"Pivver," Jon-Tom corrected him softly. "What about her? You've been hitting on her ever since we got clear of that Manzai."

The otter turned uncharacteristically sad, soulful eyes on his companion. "Wot a way with words you 'umans 'ave. Jonny-Toms, she's as comely a member o' me own kind as ever I set eyes upon."

"I've seen enough of otters to know better than to disagree with you."

"Too bloody right, mate. If only it weren't for this rotten bastard excuse of a town . . ."

The walkway shimmied slightly underfoot, forcing Jon-Tom to wave his arms to keep his balance. He hadn't imagined the tremor. The planking had actually risen and dropped back several inches.

As Mudge continued his inebriated harangue, Jon-Tom risked a cautious glance over the rail. Were those pilings shifting even as he watched, stirring concentric ripples in the murky brine?

". . . and I succeeded, mate!"

Jon-Tom looked from the otter back toward the tavern. "Succeeded?"

Stumbling close, the otter grasped the lower edge of his friend's sweat-soaked shirt. "I mean she were willin', mate. Willin', 'ell! She were bloomin' ready, she were." Gently Jon-Tom disengaged from the otter's grip.

"So what happened?"

"I couldn't. For the first time in me life, I couldn't."

"I'm not sure I understand," Jon-Tom said carefully, not at all sure that he wanted to.

"I tried not to. Believe me, mate, I tried! But all I could think of when I should've been attendin' to business was those bedamned cubs and that naggin', overbearin', sharp-as-a-razor voiced female I share me burrow with."

"Weegee."

The otter fixed him with a furious stare. "Did I ask you to mention 'er name, mate? *Did I ask you?*" He tried to shove

his face right up into Jon-Tom's but was thwarted by the fact
that he was nearly two feet shorter.

"Why, Mudge! It's hard to believe, but damned if I don't
think you've acquired some morals. Must have been when I
wasn't looking," he added thoughtfully.

"Don't say that, don't say that!" The otter slapped both
hands to his ears, thereby knocking himself half silly, since
one hand still firmly gripped the sloshing bottle. "This isn't
happenin', it ain't possible!" Adopting a look of uncompro-
mising determination, he started (somewhat unevenly) past
Jon-Tom.

"I'm goin' back in, I am! I'm goin' to find that princess,
and when I do, I'm goin' to . . . I'm goin' to . . ." His voice
fell as he turned back to his friend. "If I could only get just a
wee bit loopier, mate. Just a wee bit."

"Not and remain conscious, you can't," Jon-Tom told him
firmly. "Why chastise yourself for keeping the cubs and
Weegee in your thoughts?"

"There's that bloomin' name again! I thought I told you
not to say it. I'm 'avin' enough trouble tryin' to deal with
things as it is." He straightened then, a look of dawning realization contorting his features.

" 'Tis this place, crikey! It 'as to be. Somethin' in the air
ain't right. I've been bloody polluted, I 'ave! Somethin's
infected me with a sense o' responsibility." He grew suddenly suspicious. "I know: There's got to be a potion, some kind
o' pill I can take to cleanse meself." Edgy eyes met Jon-
Tom's own. "The right proper spellsong could do it." He tried
to retrace his steps, stumbled, and avoided going over the
edge of the walkway only because his legs were too short for
him to lose his balance.

"Sing me up somethin' special, mate. For old time's sake.
Make me like the Mudge o' old. Carefree, 'appy, fun, an'
fancy-free."

"Degenerate, uncaring, thieving, and lecherous. A lying,
cheating, duplicitous sneak."

Mudge brightened immediately. "Oi, that's it, Jin-an'-

Tomic, that's me! I 'aven't changed beyond 'elp, 'ave I, mate? Tell me I 'aven't changed that much!"

Jon-Tom was not at all sure how to reply. "Well-l-l-l . . . you do occasionally still come out with an unmistakable fib."

"Yes, yes, go on, go on!"

"And you have been known, on recent occasion, to borrow that which does not belong to you. Small things, generally, but still . . ."

"Right, right; never mind the proportions. 'Tis the lack o' thought that counts. Keep goin'."

The spellsinger took a deep breath. "But in spite of all that, I'm afraid that the metamorphosis is beyond the powers of mere sorcery to reverse. It seems that you are—and I am as shocked as you by this—turning into a moral and sensitive individual."

"Moral! Sensitive! Me?" Angrily the otter slapped himself on the chest. Unfortunately, it was once again with the paw that held the bottle. The blow took some of the steam out of him. "Impossible," he mumbled. "Can't be. I'd rather be bloomin' dead. Wot about me reputation, cultivated so careful-like all these years? I've a certain status in the Thieves' Guild to maintain, a lack of standards to uphold." He looked around wildly.

" 'Tis this place for certain. I've got to get away from 'ere. 'Tis poisonin' me soul slow and sure, it 'tis." He kicked at the nearest wall, his foot scuffing the varnish. A weatherbeaten plank cracked. " 'Tis affectin' me mind. The whole 'ole should be torn down, board by board. Smashed and burned so it can be replaced with a regular, normal town, a place where a chap can 'ave a furtive assignation in peace, without bein' troubled by naggin' moral concerns." He booted the wall again, nearly putting his foot through the flaking wood.

Following the impact the walkway gave a heave and lurch, forcing Jon-Tom to grab on to a pole to keep from being thrown off his feet. It didn't help a great deal because the pole was also shaking violently. *Or was it angrily?* he wondered.

"Maybe you ought to put a damper on it, Mudge. The way this town moves around, it might be a little sensitive."

"Sensitive, 'ell! Who ever 'eard o' sensitive buildings? 'Tis a crime against nature, it 'tis!" Feeling better, he energetically resumed kicking hell out of the wall. "An' worse than that, 'tis bloody . . . bloody . . . *unaesthetic*!" he finished triumphantly.

At that point the structure apparently had had enough. The walkway beneath the otter snapped like a whip, throwing him roof-high. Landing with a thud and a grunt, Mudge rolled back onto his feet, sword in one hand, bottle in the other. From the manner in which he was waving both about, Jon-Tom wasn't at all sure his friend was aware of which was which.

Mudge hunted for his unseen antagonist, gesturing portentously with both glass and steel. Jon-Tom gave him plenty of room.

"All right, come on. Show yourself! Come out an' fight like an otter!"

Not only was the walkway twitching and heaving now, so were the attendant buildings. And not just the one Mudge had abused, but every edifice in the immediate vicinity. Windows bowed and shattered, twisting planks spat out nails as though they'd suddenly grown distasteful, screws unwound and dowels tightened in the wooden equivalent of a sudden migraine. Shutters flapped like the wings of angry birds, banging percussively against walls and doorways.

Deciding that the time for tact had passed, Jon-Tom grabbed the otter by one arm and half aimed, half thrust him forward.

"Now you've done it! Get moving. We have to find the others."

"Why, wot 'ave I done? Wot's 'appenin'?" He didn't flinch as the contorting, dancing fishing shack directly across from them fell over sideways with an impressive splash. It promptly righted itself and began shaking off water like a wet dog. Jon-Tom hoped fervently there was no one inside.

"Whoooo! Maybe I *'ave* 'ad enough tipple!" This confession notwithstanding, the otter clung firmly to the bottle as Jon-Tom hurried him along.

Screams, shrieks, shouts of fear and uncertainty were arising not only from the tavern but from the surrounding buildings. Somehow staying on his feet, Jon-Tom stumbled back inside. Passed out beyond hope of immediate revival, Mudge hung draped around his friend's neck and shoulders like the world's biggest (not to mention gamiest) otter-fur stole. Jon-Tom gladly tolerated the otter's stink in exchange for his silence.

But the damage had been done. Comprised of a line of seriously disturbed buildings, the entire agitated harborfront was jostling and heaving. Buildings banged into their neighbors or threatened to tear themselves apart. Panicky owners proved unable to calm their respective structures, while those who were merely leasing had no control at all.

A lithe, muscular shape materialized out of the chaos: Lieutenant Naike of Harakun, impressively sober. "What is it, spellsinger? What's going on?" His gaze narrowed. "What has happened to your friend?"

"No time to explain! Gather ye princesses while ye may. Get everyone together. We've got to get out of here. *Now*." Frantic yelps rose from behind the mongoose as part of the main bar—bottles, glasses, and salacious portrait of a reclining and strategically shaved nutria—all came crashing down.

"Earthquake!" Alarm was plain on Heke's face as he joined the others near the doorway.

"No earthquake." Steadying Mudge's weight with one hand, Jon-Tom beckoned anxiously with the other. "To the boat, everybody!"

As they helped the princesses descend the swaying, jerking rope ladder that led to the craft they had traded for, a large and very angry warehouse rose up on twelve pilings and strode off determinedly toward the central part of town. Lights flickered everywhere as the noncelebratory portion of the citizenry was shaken forcibly from their quiet beds. Sum-

moned by clanging alarm bells, a squadron of specially
trained house calmers was already moving into the harborfront district, reassuring nervous office buildings and soothing stressed storage sheds.

When they had succeeded in assuaging the concerns of the
stampeding structures, they would begin to ask questions. By
that time Jon-Tom hoped to be well out to sea.

As Naike and his troops fought to raise sail Jon-Tom did a
head count, repeating it to make certain everyone was aboard.
He even double-checked for the lost chords and, as he'd surmised, needn't have concerned himself. Like a frosted running light, the ever-anxious music pulsed softly from the top
of the mast.

They were on their way south again.

And not a moment too soon. Rising on their pilings, a pair
of large, well-built structures which had finally succeeded in
isolating the original source of the disturbance came splashing after them. Seeing that the fleeing craft was already out in
the deep water of the main channel, the two buildings could
only pause and fume helplessly, rattling their doors and shutters at the fugitives to the utter bafflement of their badly shak-
en inhabitants.

Frazzled and confused, Seshenshe struggled to straighten
her attire. "What happened? We were having a fine time."

"Yes," said Ansibette. "And then suddenly everything
went mad."

The silky anteater's remarkable tongue was flicking nervously about, licking not only her own snout but those close
to her. "the building went crazy," she whispered breathily.

"Ask him about it, not me." A wearied Jon-Tom jerked a
thumb to where Mudge lay snoring peacefully at the base of
the bowsprit. His cap was pulled down over his face and the
long feather fluttered each time its owner exhaled.

"Him?" Umagi's brows drew together, a movement which
half hid her eyes. "What does he know about it?"

"He instigated the trouble. Started insulting the town, the
buildings, everything. Then he tried kicking in a wall."

Seshenshe's upper lip curled back, exposing sharp teeth. "How could ssuch ssmall thingss caussse sso much trouble?"

"You don't know Mudge. He knows insults the way I know spellsinging, and he's had plenty of practice. Stimulants tend to spark his eloquence while suppressing his common sense. He kept insulting Mashupro, and I guess Mashupro finally couldn't take it anymore."

"It's my fault." Pivver stepped forward. "I should have been more understanding. But I was unsure what to do. He seemed so torn." She made a face. "Not to mention slovenly."

"Believe me, he was." Jon-Tom stretched to see behind them. In the distance the town seemed to be quieting down, the shouts and curses fading. He thanked whatever spirits had taken an interest in them for the modest breeze which filled the ship's single sail and propelled them out into the open sea. As individual features softened and merged with distance, the Karrakas was reduced to a black line demarcating the northern horizon.

In the waning moonlight they passed a number of isolated islets and sandbars, the last outposts of the great delta. With no sign of pursuit, the soldiers allowed themselves to relax. The princesses headed cautiously below the main deck, intent on sorting out permanent sleeping arrangements.

Jon-Tom turned from Naike, who had taken the wheel, to examine the sleeping otter. Mudge's sonorous snores rose even above the steady slap and slosh of water against the bow. As he listened, it struck him forcefully that he was more than fatigued enough to emulate his companion.

They'd been hounded out of other towns before, but this was the first time they'd ever been hounded out *by* one.

CHAPTER 17

THEY WERE TWO DAYS OUT, THE DELTA A HUMID MEMORY behind them, when it became apparent that where seamanship was concerned, their mongoose crew had been more hopeful than realistic.

"That doesn't look right." Pivver kept her distance as Heke and Pauko strove to set a small spinnaker. "I've spent some time on boats. I think you've got it upside down."

"We're doing the best we can, Highness." Pauko wheezed as he wrestled with the unfamiliar rigging.

"I thought you said you could sail this thing." Seated nearby, long legs crossed, the princess Ansibette was painting her nails, each a different color.

"I'm afraid I am the only one with any actual practical experience." Naike came forward to help. "Do not judge these good fellows harshly. They are more comfortable setting a tent. Never fear, we will reach the shore of beloved Harakun."

"Not at this rate." Rolling back the puffy, semitransparent sleeves of her blouse, Princess Pivver took the edge of the sheet from Heke's hands and began unfurling it properly. "Umagi, dear, can you give me a hand here?"

Rising from her seat, the gorilla added her muscle to the enterprise, and they soon had the spinnaker billowing between mast and bowsprit. The result was a notable increase in speed.

Umagi studied her palms with distaste. "These conditions are bad for one's skin."

"You should complain." Ansibette held out her own pale hands. "My skin is finer and thinner than any of yours, and I have little fur to protect it."

Jon-Tom remained resolutely behind the wheel and away from the discussion. "Listen to them gripe. You'd think they were still imprisoned back in the Karrakas."

"Don't let it trouble you, mate." Lying against the binnacle, a bleary-eyed Mudge peered out from beneath the brim of his cap and squinted briefly at the sun, which to his way of thinking had suddenly taken it upon itself to torment him without mercy. "That's wot princesses are for: to look pretty an' complain."

"Mudge, sometimes I think you don't much like people."

"On the contrary, June-Tomb, I prefer to think o' meself as an optimistic cynic."

"How's your head?"

"Still affixed to me shoulders."

"through no good sense of your own." Quiquell stood nearby, grooming the fine silky fur of her arms as she spoke. "it was your fault that we had to flee mashupro in such haste."

The otter winced. "Aye, aye, 'tis all me fault, the lot o' it."

"Then you admit to it." Seshenshe turned and called to her sisters. "Did you all hear that? The rogue confessess hiss culpability!"

"I'll admit to anythin' you want, anythin'." Mudge buried his face behind his cap. "Only please—don't shout."

"I'm not sshouting! Who iss sshouting?" roared the lynx.

"Do we have reason to shout at you?" queried Ansibette pointedly.

"Good ladies, I beg of you: a little mercy." Supporting his head in his hands as he rose, the otter stumbled to the railing.

Jon-Tom looked over from his stance behind the ship's wheel. *"Now* what are you thinking?"

"I'm wonderin' if 'tis possible to swim back to Lynchbany. Perhaps some kind soul will fish me poor body out o' the Tailaroam and return it to me kin for a proper burial. A *quiet* burial."

"Do you remember anything? We were chased out of town, by the town."

"*Oi.*" Turning from the green glass sea, the otter sat down on the deck, his back against the rail. "I ain't sure I remember this mornin'."

"Just as well. I'll spare you the pain of reminiscing. Just don't do it again."

Mudge blinked. " 'Ow can I avoid doin' it again if I can't remember wot it was I did?"

"I'll be there to let you know."

"Oh, right." The otter rose shakily. "Now if you'll excuse me a minim, I'm afraid I 'ave to do me part to contribute to the fecundity o' this particular ocean." So saying, he proceeded to toss the contents of his stomach over the stern, a process accompanied by much retching and gagging.

"Do you ssee that?" The lynx straightened an earring which had twisted around to tickle her inner ear. "What a dissgussting exhibition."

"quite," added Quiquell.

Ansibette blew on the nails of her right hand to speed the drying of the elaborately applied polish. "And to think that's what we have to depend on to return us home."

"We are not entirely dependent." They turned to see Aleaukauna neatly coiling a line around one shoulder. "We must not be afraid to rely on our own resources."

"Why? Your soldiers appear competent enough."

The mongoose princess regarded the Lieutenant and his troops fondly. "Yes, they have done well. For representatives of the lower ranks. They did find us, after all, and free us from the grasp of that unspeakable Manzai person."

"With the aid of the spellsinger," Umagi hastened to add.

"Yes, the spellsinger." Ansibette turned to gaze back at Jon-Tom, who continued to steer the boat, wholly oblivious to the attention he was receiving. "Don't you think he's sort of handsome? In a rough, unsophisticated way, of course."

Seshenshe made a face. "I'll never undersstand what you

humanss ssee in one another. All that cold, bald sskin." She shuddered slightly.

"not a decent claw on hand or foot." Quiquell flexed her own two-inch spikes.

"And those flat faces," added Aleaukauna. "Kissing must be more of a collision than a coming together."

"We manage quite well enough, thank you." Ansibette defended her tribe without a trace of self-consciousness.

"I'm just glad I'm not human." Pivver sniffed through her whiskers.

A powerful shape loomed over them. "What's all this?" Umagi of Tuuro put a heavy arm around Ansibette's shoulders. "I know humans are lacking in fur, but that should make the rest of us all the more sympathetic toward them. And they *are* simian." The heavy brow turned toward Aleaukauna. "Furthermore, I'll have you know that there are certain definite advantages to a flat face."

"Is that so? I fail to see how anyone can count the absence of a proper muzzle as a plus."

Encompassing the virtues of snouts, pelts, muzzles, and various other physical accoutrements, the argument raged—politely, of course, lest anyone forget their station. It forced Mudge, desperate for a little peace and quiet, to choose between the top of the mast or the bottom of the bilge. In the end he stayed where he was. His vaunted balance had deserted him, which ruled out sequestering himself in the crow's nest, and the condition of his stomach, which at present had elected to retreat to a locale somewhere between his esophagus and his lungs, inspired him to remain as far as possible from the undelectable aromas arising from the craft's musty interior.

Aided by a favoring (and perhaps sympathetic) breeze, they continued to make excellent progress southward.

A week had passed when the storm loomed on that chosen horizon. From his position behind the wheel, Naike beckoned Jon-Tom to join him. The sea had grown irritable and he knew from experience what the open ocean could be like on an off day.

"What do you think?" He gestured forward. The squall line extended as far as the eye could see, a threatening rampart of advancing gray-black. "We'll have to get around it somehow. Port or starboard?" His small but strong hands waited expectantly on the wheel.

"Why ask me?" Jon-Tom scrutinized the ominous clouds worriedly. A flash of lightning briefly illuminated the storm's sooty underbelly, turning one boiling Vulcansberg the color of polished antimony. "I'm no mariner. I've only traveled the seas as a passenger."

Naike nervously scratched the short beige-colored fur of his forehead. "Perhaps you could calm the storm with a spellsong, or at least conjure the most promising heading."

"It doesn't work that way. I'm much better at calling up specific objects or shapes. I've never tackled anything as substantial as the weather. I'd as like sink us as save us."

"This craft is sturdy but not large, and we are not exactly the most experienced of crews. We have some time before the weather will be upon us. Can you not think of anything?"

Jon-Tom equivocated. "No harm in thinking." Something chimed at his shoulder.

Hovering near enough to warm his face, the chord cloud was singing restively. It was astonishing, he thought, how the same melody could communicate so many different emotions merely by varying tempo and volume.

Naike looked on in wonderment. "I know nothing of matters mystic, but file my teeth if I don't think it's trying to tell you something."

"It does seem anxious, doesn't it?" The pulsating motes swirled inches from his eyes. "What are you trying to say?"

Seeming to respond, the cloud became an attenuated pink streak as it darted forward. Pausing above the rolling sea several points to starboard, it hovered there and sang out as loudly as it could. As Jon-Tom and Naike looked on, it repeated the action several times. It was a gesture the spellsinger knew well by now.

"What is it doing?" The mongoose gripped the wheel firmly, waiting.

"Suggesting a course. I suppose we might as well follow. Unless you've a better idea."

"As I have told you, spellsinger, I am no more than an amateur mariner." So saying, the Lieutenant swung the wheel hard over, bringing the bow around. "You have confidence in this heading?"

"No, but I've always had confidence in music. If we continue on the way we've been going we'll run smack into that storm for sure. If this direction's no better, we'll have done no worse. And maybe, just maybe, the music knows what it's about. *I* certainly don't."

The chords became a helix, then an ovoid. Each time it changed shape it altered tempo. In one thing only it did not vary: its chosen course.

Umagi was leaning on the portside railing, contemplating the surface of the sea, when a silvered mist crystallized in the air only a few yards from her face. Exclaiming in surprise, she stumbled back from the apparition. Jon-Tom saw that she had worked the fur on the back of her head and neck into a mass of tiny, intricate spitcurls. On the princess of Tuuro the effect was incongruously petite.

Materializing in the middle of the mist and hovering at deck level was the remarkable insectlike being they had encountered previously. He stared straight at Jon-Tom.

"Hi, you there—human! I remember what it was!"

"What what was?" Jon-Tom felt unaccountably foolish.

"What I've been searching for!" Antennae dipped forward. "Memory is such a feeble thing."

Mudge rested an arm on the rail and spoke casually. "Are you aware, guv, that at the moment there's a fair space o' nothin' but air between your sit-upon and the sea?"

"The sea? What are you talking about?" Glancing down between its forefeet, the creature emitted a high-pitched whine of surprise and promptly plummeted into the waves, landing with an impressive splash.

"It must have intended to appear on deck," observed Naike thoughtfully. "Then we made that sharp turn to starboard."

Jon-Tom wasn't paying attention to the Lieutenant. He'd rushed to the railing. Their visitor was flopping about help-lessly on the surface. Despite the presence of eight limbs, it appeared to know nothing of swimming.

"I remember!" it sputtered. "I remember!"

Cupping his hands to his mouth, Jon-Tom shouted back, "What do you remember?"

"I remember that . . . I can't swim!" It was a piteous decla-ration, voiced as the narrow head was swamped by a modest wave. Jon-Tom started to remove his cloak and shirt. When the creature bobbed back to the surface, he could see it fum-bling with the controls set into the pack on its back. Once more it was enveloped in mist, this time in the form of a sil-very lambence that was so bright he was forced to turn away, as if a hundred camera flashes had gone off in his face at the same time. Caught by surprise, the princesses cried out and rubbed at their eyes.

Peering through tears, Jon-Tom noted the presence of a neat, spherical hole in the ocean, as if someone had taken a perfect scoop out of a bowl of deep green ice cream. A couple of mackerel swam into the hole, found themselves flopping frantically as they fell, and vanished into the bottom of the aqueous excavation. Then the smooth, curving walls col-lapsed and the sea flowed on over the place as if it had never been disturbed.

"A divertin' if futile performance." Mudge had moved to join his friend. "Personal-like, I'm less than impressed by 'is flavor o' magic."

"I don't think it's magic he's employing, Mudge. I think it's science."

"Magic, science, 'tis only in the spellin' o' it. So to speak. Think 'e'll try again? 'E wants somethin' o' us, that's for sure."

"Mudge, I'm as baffled as you are."

"Now that's where you're wrong, mate. You're more baffled than me. 'Tis an inherent an' inheritable condition."

The spellsinger passed on the offer to exchange insults. "Right now all I'm interested in is outrunning or flanking this storm." He nodded toward the advancing line of threatening black clouds as Naike continued to follow the lead of the singing chords. Was that lightning off to the west, in the direction they were taking? He couldn't tell.

"How're you feeling?"

"Wot, me?" Reaching up, the otter flicked the brim of his cap. "Optimal as always, mate. I would like to know one thing, though."

"What?"

"Did I 'ave a good time?"

"Not particularly."

"Pity." The otter took a deep breath and put a paw over his chest. "Well, I feel wonderful now. So the ladies 'ave always told me." He pivoted to scrutinize the deck. The princesses were gathered around the mast, chatting and assisting each other, while the mongoose soldiers attended to the operation of the ship.

"Things'll run smooth from now on, you'll see. All we 'ave to worry about is bein' bombed by a forgetful giant bug from otherwhere. Methinks we can cope with that, don't you know." He was beaming. It was an utterly infectious and irresistible smile, one which Jon-Tom knew well. One could not help but smile back at a grinning otter.

The storm fell upon them with all the suddenness and fury of a female who'd been dieting for six months only to discover that she'd gained four pounds. It was impossible even to light the ship's lamps so they could find their way about belowdecks. Not that lamps were really necessary. The rolling barrage of lightning strobed sea and ship mercilessly, illuminating more than anyone wanted to see.

Dry as it was below, the rocking and heaving rendered the temporary haven untenable for any length of time, forcing the princesses to alternate between being soaked and queasy. A fortune in sodden silks and chiffon clung to them as they took turns traversing the single stairway.

It required the full attention of the six males aboard to keep their craft stable and upright, with Aleaukauna and Pivver assisting where they could. Unforgiving wind shredded the spinnaker before it could be furled, but they did succeed in reefing the mainsail.

Hewing close to their chosen course required all of Jon-Tom and Naike's strength, the human clinging to one side of the wheel and the mongoose to the other. At least they had no trouble seeing their guide. Glowing softly just forward of the bowsprit and apparently unaffected by the tempest, the cloud of music led them on. It might have been his imagination, spurred by lightning and clouded by driving rain, but Jon-Tom could have sworn that it was chiming in time to the thunder. He could only wonder what conditions were like at the center of the storm, whence they had originally been headed.

The waves rose so high that their crests overtopped the mast, but the sturdy little craft climbed each wall of water and slid down the opposite side like a plangent dream. Each time one of the green monsters bore down on them, Jon-Tom was certain they would be swamped. Each time the boat responded by sliding up the breaking crest as nimbly as a spider on a rock. Better in such circumstances for a ship to be buoyant, he thought grimly, than beautiful.

Her mast swayed and her timbers groaned, but she didn't crack. Seeming almost frustrated, the seas redoubled their fury. Jon-Tom worried more about the rudder than the mast. If they lost steering, the boat would swing broadside into the advancing waves and they'd capsize for sure. But the rudder, fashioned of tough swamp *surrow*, remained unsplintered on its pivot.

In the midst of lightning and thunder, screaming wind and stinging rain, Mudge could be seen strolling nonchalantly about the deck, whistling to himself and seemingly oblivious to the prospect of imminent destruction. He'd divested himself of his gear and stowed it safely below. Rain slicked his fur, imparting to his coat a natural sheen Jon-Tom could only envy.

Noticing his friend's stare, the otter put his hands to his mouth and called out, "Ain't this excitin', mate! Wot a ride!"

Jon-Tom wiped salt spray from his eyes. "Oh, it's exciting, all right. How about you share some of the excitement by coming up here and giving us a hand?"

The otter shook his head. "Wouldn't think o' spoilin' your fun, Jommy-Tin. Why don't you ask Umagi? She'd be o' more use than modest-sized me."

"She was asked," shouted Naike from alongside the spellsinger, "but while her strength is equal to the task, her constitution is not. She is unwell."

"Oi, a royal rail rider, is that it? Too bad." The otter ducked and grabbed a line as a belligerent wave crashed over the port side, soaking everything and everyone on deck. "This is the life, mate!" he yelled when the sea had drained away. "This is wot we came for, crikey but it 'tis!"

"I'm sure it's even better up in the bow!" Jon-Tom yelled back. *Besides which,* he added to himself, *we don't have to listen to you if you're up there.* "We could all drown, you know."

Instead of heading forward, the otter moved nearer. *"You* could all drown, you mean."

"Even an otter could drown in this." Naike was less than overwhelmed by Mudge's bravado. "It may be true that at swimming your tribe is the most accomplished, but I have yet to hear it told of one who could swim across an ocean."

"I'd just float," the otter replied. "Drift in the sun and eat crabs and sargassum."

"If something didn't eat you first," the mongoose shot back.

Mudge was unfazed. Very little truly upset the otter. "Then it'd be a proper end to an interestin' life, an' I'd 'ave no regrets, I wouldn't. Beats dyin' in bed o' distemper or the colic."

Naike's gaze traveled from the patient, drifting chord cloud back to Jon-Tom. "My tall friend, I begin to wonder if we were right to trust the line of this wandering music."

"If you'll recall, we didn't have a lot of choices." Salt crusted Jon-Tom's lips, leaving them wet and chapped at the same time. "If we chose wrong and we die, I'll apologize."

The mongoose grimaced. "Humans have the most peculiar sense of humor. No wonder you get along so well with the otter."

"Courage, brave Lieutenant. We still float, and we sail on."

"Toward what fate, I wonder?" The strain of wrestling with the heavy wheel was beginning to take its toll on the mongoose's smaller, lighter frame. A glance showed the top of the mast whipping like a cattail as the shrieking wind toyed with the rigging.

"What about a spellsong now? Surely our circumstances justify the taking of some risks?"

Jon-Tom blinked away rain. "I would, but there's no one else to help you hold the wheel. And I could make things worse."

"Worse? What could be worse than this?" The Lieutenant gritted his teeth as a rogue wave struck them hard aport, rocking and rolling the ship simultaneously. From belowdecks there arose a collective feminine moan.

This was followed by a dimly perceived shout from one of the soldiers, who clung grimly to the lines at the base of the bowsprit.

"Sir, master Jon-Tom: I think I see something ahead!"

Naike extended his limber body to its maximum. "Sing out! What see you, Heke?"

"Clearing! I see clearing ahead!"

Moments later Jon-Tom and the Lieutenant could see it as well—an unequivocal break in the storm, bright and beckoning. It was toward this that the music was leading them. Of course the opening could close back up at any time, but it was the first sign of hope they'd had all day.

"Steer for it!" Naike shouted superfluously. "Steer for our lives!" Jon-Tom kept his weight on the wheel and continued to pray for the integrity of the rudder.

Though the wind still howled and the rain continued to pelt

them, it was clear that the storm was moving off to the northeast. Gradually the seas decreased from the monstrous to the merely fearful, the wind became an irritant instead of a threat, and the horrible pounding they had endured came at last to an end. Heke, Pauko, and Karaukul went over every foot of the battered vessel and were able to report that the only damage it had sustained was minor. Except for a few slow leaks which the soldiers set to patching, she was in remarkably good shape.

The same could not be said for her passengers. Bruised and exhausted, they gathered on deck to try to dry out, but even this small comfort was denied them. Though the temperature had warmed considerably, the thick fog which had followed in the wake of the storm closed in smotheringly around them.

Jon-Tom had been gazing astern, studying the retreating edge of the gale. Now he turned and regripped the wheel. "I think we can resume our original course. Four points to port."

"Right." Naike put his own paws back on the wheel.

It would not turn. Not even when Pauko and Karaukul added their weight and strength to the effort.

Jon-Tom stepped back from the frozen disk. "Something has us in its grip. Has us good."

Pauko gestured forward. "The music?" Indeed, the chord cloud drifted on unconcerned, as though nothing had changed.

"I don't think so," Jon-Tom declared quietly. "It hasn't affected Mudge or me physically in any way before now. I suspect something else."

"But what?" wondered Karaukul. Jon-Tom shrugged.

"Some sorcerer," Pauko muttered under his breath.

"Let's try once more." Naike was unwilling to quietly surrender their destiny to forces unseen.

"It's no use." Mouth slightly agape and panting rhythmically, Karaukul finally stepped away from the wheel. "At least we're out of the storm. Perhaps that's a sign that the fate in store for us is a benign one."

"Or perhaps 'tis only a sign that we busted our butts to get clear." Mudge had come astern to join the others.

"We?" Naike eyed the otter sharply.

"Why, o' course, guv. Who else gave freely o' 'is emotions till nothin' were left to comfort the ladies an' see to their safety? I'm bloomin' drained, I am!"

For an instant the Lieutenant's iron self-control seemed about to snap. Eyes blazing, he took a step forward, compelling Mudge to skip back. Then, with a great effort of will, the mongoose calmed himself.

"We are in the grip of some unknown force or current, which is carrying us we know not where. We'll need all the 'comforting' you can muster, river-mouse. I suggest you ponder *that* for a while."

Mudge grinned guilefully. "I'd try, guv, but as me friend Jonny-Tom can tell you, me attention span is bleedin' brief."

The tension between the two was shattered by a frantic shout from Heke, who had stayed forward. "Lost, all is lost!"

"What?" Naike yelled back. "What are you talking about? Do you see something?"

Without waiting for a reply Mudge had raced to the mast and ascended the starboard-side ladder-rigged stay as agilely as any monkey. From the crow's nest he called down to those waiting anxiously below.

"The snake-eater's right, we're done!"

Head tilted back, Jon-Tom blinked up at his friend through the drifting fog. "What is it? What do you mean?"

"There've been plenty down through the years, mate, both friend and foe, who said I'd end up in the 'ole someday." The otter sounded unnaturally fatalistic. "But I never thought they meant it literally!"

At that moment the fog broke and they could see clearly. Several of the princesses screamed and Quiquell commenced a steady, if barely audible, sobbing. Ansibette and Seshenshe hugged each other tightly. The source of the current which had locked them in its grip and was dragging them inexorably forward was now apparent.

They were much too near the edge of the whirlpool to avoid it.

CHAPTER 18

JON-TOM HAD HEARD SAILORS' TALES OF GREAT MAELSTROMS that formed in the deep open ocean, but never of anything like this. It was perfectly circular, an inverted volcano in the sea. As they approached the rim, the spectacle acquired a voice as well as a visage: a profound, basso rumble. It was the call of the Abyss.

Even as they realized it was hopeless, Jon-Tom and Naike threw all their strength onto the wheel. It would not budge an inch. With a piercing cry from Heke, who clung desperately to the fore stays, they went over the edge. Locked in the maelstrom's inexorable grasp, they began to spin, cycling around and around the great green wall, riding the carouseling waters ever downward, accelerating as they descended.

Heeling to port, Jon-Tom was able to see all the way to the bottom. Benthic sands gleamed darkly where the whirlpool exposed the very floor of the ocean. Several of the princesses were sobbing openly as they tried to console one other, while the soldiers were exchanging solemn good-byes.

Caught as they were in the maelstrom's grip, fish and other extraordinary sea dwellers spiraled within the rotating wall of water. From time to time inorganic flotsam and jetsam appeared: the hulks of sunken ships, fragments of ruined buildings, whole chunks of polished lava like great black beads ripped from some colossus's necklace, massive tree trunks shorn of all but their heaviest branches.

Someone was pulling insistently on Jon-Tom's shirt. Looking down, he saw Naike staring up at him. The eyes of a

mongoose are particularly penetrating. "No more talk of what
'might' follow, spellsinger. If you've ever made magic, make
some now!"

"Yes. Yes, of course." He stumbled toward the stairs,
intending to remove his duar from its secure place of storage.

The boat careened sideways, heeling still farther to port,
and he was forced to grab wildly at several cross lines to keep
from being thrown over the side. Ansibette let out a shriek
and Seshenshe hissed in panic. They were spinning very fast
now indeed. Very rapidly, around and around, one revolution
after another, spinning dizzingly . . .

Jon-Tom's insides were overwhelmed. Nor was his a solitary reaction, nausea being a decidedly egalitarian condition.
Only Mudge seemed immune.

"Interestin' way to go." The otter's disarming cheerfulness
had yet to desert him. Jon-Tom wanted to strangle him but it
was all he could do to hang on, both to the lines and to his
intestines. "Smashed to bits on the bottom o' the sea with me
best friend an' 'alf a dozen noble princesses all competin' to
see who can upchuck the most. Frankly, I'd always 'oped to
depart this world in a fashion somewot flashier, I 'ad." He tilted his head back to peer philosophically at the distant sky,
now hundreds of feet overhead.

"Reminds me o' the story o' the two baker's apprentices
an' the baker's wife. You remember, mate. The one about
gettin' yeast to rise?" When a bilious, green-faced Jon-Tom
proved unable to reply, the otter proceeded to repeat the tale
anyway. It never failed to crack him up, and if he was going
to die, he was by heaven going to die laughing.

Something else, however, was paying attention.

A deep booming reverberated around them. It was akin to
the resolute roaring of the whirlpool and yet subtilely different. A variegated modulation that suggested something less
primal and more cognizant than simply a rotating hole in the
sea.

"What . . . what's that?" Jon-Tom's color was approaching
that of pea soup. His fur blocking any such subtle shifts in

epidermal hue, Naike clung weakly to the railing nearby. The state of his innards, however, was straightforwardly apparent in his voice.

"I can't . . . imagine."

"It almost sounds like . . . almost sounds . . ." Jon-Tom forced himself to turn from the railing. "Haven't we slowed down a little?"

"We must not be falling as fast," Naike suggested weakly.

"No." Jon-Tom found that concentration helped to steady his stomach. "We've definitely stopped descending. And I know that sound. It's *laughter.*"

"Laughter?" The Lieutenant's cheeks bulged. "What could be laughing here, besides an uncaring fate?"

Jon-Tom stumbled in the direction of his friend. "That . . . that was a good story, Mudge."

"Glad you liked it, mate. How are you doin'? Not that it matters, by me soul."

"You told a joke. It provoked a response." He was no longer sure if the roaring was in his ears or arose from an external source.

"Response? I were just makin' a small, final analogy between our present situation and the baker's daughters."

The booming sounded a second time. Jon-Tom whirled, anxiously searching the roiling waters. "There it was again! The maelstrom! It has to be the maelstrom."

Blimey, the otter thought, *the poor bloke's finally gone over the edge.* "Whirlpools don't laugh, mate. Gurgle, maybe, an' roar."

"Is it such a stretch from gurgling and roaring to laughing? Have you noticed that our descent has slowed? Tell another joke."

"Another joke?"

"A funny story, a dirty limerick, one of your horrible puns—anything!"

"Cor, I suppose I could think o' one or two. Right, then: 'ere goes." With evident relish, the otter proceeded to relate a famous tale involving a stallion, two ladies of the evening and a wealthy but perpetually inebriated banker. It was, on balance, considerably bluer than the waters surrounding them. It was also hysterically funny. Several of the princesses had the grace to blush through their lingering discomfort.

When with typically otterish gusto Mudge delivered the long-anticipated punch line, Pivver let out a series of startled barks, Quiquell involuntarily wrapped her remarkable tongue several times around her snout, Ansibette's face turned the most charming shade of pink, and the remaining princesses reacted similarly. Heke and Pauko would have fallen down laughing had they not already been rolling about the deck under an entirely different type of stimulus, and even the perpetually dour Karaukul cracked a broad smile.

As for the maelstrom, from its depths issued a Promethean bellow of amusement that rose clearly above the rumble of the rotating waters. Unbelievably, the tormented ship began to ascend.

"I'll be swoggled." Leaning over the side, Jon-Tom studied the sea beneath their keel. "We're rising; we're going back up." He straightened to shout the news to the others. "The whirlpool's sending us up!"

"That's nice." Mightily evacuated, Ansibette lay on her back on the saturated deck. Though not in much better shape, Umagi knelt alongside, trying to offer what comfort she could.

Jon-Tom sensed his digestive system stabilizing. All that body surfing he'd done in his youth, all those times he'd "gone over the falls" at Zuma and Santa Monica hadn't been for naught. With internal equilibrium came time for reflection.

"Keep it up," he urged the otter. "The funnier, the better."

"That's right, mate, don't put any pressure on me."

"Come on, Mudge. I know you. You must have a thousand outrageous stories and as many short gags. Tell 'em to me, one at a time. Tell 'em all!"

The otter promptly launched into another couple of his favorites, at the conclusion of which a new sound could be heard. Not the roaring of the waters or the booming of strange laughter, but something entirely different: a volatile, voluble whispering. The whirlpool was speaking to them.

It isn't enough it has to laugh, Jon-Tom reflected in astonishment. *It talks, too.* What it said was, *"That was rich, that was wonderful! Now let me tell one."*

"Why not?" The otter scampered to the railing, deftly ducking a turgid mass of kelp which came flying past. "I ain't never swapped stories with no force o' nature before."

The ship's timbers creaked dangerously as Jon-Tom waited, wondering what sort of joke something capable of sucking whole fleets down to a watery doom would tell.

He should have known.

"There were these two sperm whales, see?" rumbled the maelstrom. *"And this fishing barge."*

"Yeah, yeah, go on," Mudge urged expectantly.

At the joke's conclusion the otter guffawed uproariously. Naike grinned, but Pauko didn't get it at all and felt decidedly left out. Aleaukauna put a hand over her mouth and giggled. Jon-Tom found the tale mildly amusing, but made it a point to roar as if the ultimate gag had just been pulled on him when he wasn't looking.

Meanwhile, the boat had climbed another hundred feet and the circle of blue sky overhead had expanded perceptibly.

How long it went on like that Jon-Tom could not have said. Mudge and the maelstrom swapped jokes and jests until the witty counterpoint of watery rumble and wily otter seemed to become as one. Meanwhile, the river-rat's fellow passengers clung dismally to the ship and to their insides while the boat continued its steady ascent surfaceward. None of them had anything left to bring up, and they could only hope and pray that Mudge, in a manner of speaking, did.

Having forsaken their position just forward of the bowsprit, the glowing chords hovered close to Jon-Tom. Now and again they would ring out brightly, as if somehow sensing the essence of a joke. Not an impossibility, Jon-Tom told himself. Musical jokes were legion, if one knew how to Handel them.

God help me, he whispered to himself. *It's catching.*

Overhead, blue sky beckoned enticingly within an all-encompassing circular frame of green. They were almost back at the surface. Almost, but not quite.

"Don't quit now, Mudge," Jon-Tom exhorted the otter. "You've done a lot. Ask it to let us go."

With a nod, the otter turned to confront the swirling void. "Oi, 'ow about it, then, old funnel? 'Ow's about spittin' us out?"

"No, no," the maelstrom boomed. *"More jokes. Best jokes ever I heard!"* There was an aqueous echo to the eerie, disembodied voice which resounded all around them. *"Keep you here, tell jokes forever."*

"See 'ere, water-mate, I can tell jokes for a long time, I bloomin' can, but not quite for forever." He looked questioningly at Jon-Tom, who nodded understandingly. With a sigh, the otter resumed his licentious litany.

They neither sank nor rose, but hung suspended within the wall of the whirlpool perhaps twenty feet below its rim. The distance might as well have been twenty miles, Jon-Tom knew. With his steady stream of humorous anecdotes Mudge continued to buy them precious minutes.

It was about time, Jon-Tom thought, to put those to use.

Disappearing belowdecks, he reemerged with the duar slung over his shoulders. A couple of the soldiers raised an enfeebled cheer. Facing the awesome pit, the spellsinger deliberated how best to proceed. He knew he would have to be careful. Stop the whirlpool in its circular tracks and without its centrifugal force to press them against the watery wall, and they would probably plunge to their deaths. Collapse it, and tons of water would come crashing down atop the deck, smashing the ship and all aboard to splinters. Anger it, and there was no telling what might happen.

Could he somehow persuade the phenomenon to let them go? How did one persuade a hole in the ocean?

"Too much fun, too much fun!" the maelstrom rumbled in response to another of Mudge's tales. The otter threw his friend a warning look.

"Better think o' somethin' quick, mate."

"Running out of jokes already?" Jon-Tom inquired.

"Not jokes. Voice. Gettin' 'oarse."

Jon-Tom had to admit that his friend was beginning to sound a little raspy. He doubted that the maelstrom would either comprehend or sympathize with laryngitis. No doubt the one thing that was beyond a whirlpool's capacity to understand was excessive dryness.

That's when it came to him.

The gray mist billowed from the duar so fast and thick that for an instant he wondered if everything had gone badly wrong. In volume it exceeded anything he'd ever sung up. Even the chord cloud ducked belowdecks, peeking out uneasily from just behind the edge of the hatch. Despite their lingering nausea, the princesses, too, became aware that something extraordinary was happening.

The whirlpool began to slow, its reverberant voice to echo uncertainly. *"What is this? What is happening? This is not a joke. I can feel it."*

"Sail!" Naike sprang to the wheel. "Put on all sail!"

"Has the Lieutenant gone crazy?" Pauko struggled to comply.

"No." Karaukul fought to steady his stomach. That they had stopped spinning in circles helped a great deal. "Even though we drift on the edge of oblivion, we now have wind and still water. We sail not to port or starboard, north or south, but upward!"

Though the whirlpool had ceased revolving, because of the temperature differential between the exposed sea bottom and the surface a steady, cool breeze continued to funnel upward. It filled the ship's sails, propelling it forward.

Unsure of the effect his spellsong was having but seeing the mongooses in a frenzy of purposeful activity, Jon-Tom played and sang on. Around them the maelstrom continued to voice confusion and complaint.

Sailing at a sixty-degree angle the boat struggled to climb surfaceward, driven by gusts from the depths. Progress was slow and difficult. Their vessel stubbornly refused to ascend, preferring instead to move steadily forward. At the rate they were rising it would take a week to reach the surface, and Jon-Tom couldn't sing that long.

Then the whirlpool began to rotate once more . . . in reverse.

"This shouldn't be happening . . ." A concerned Jon-Tom gazed over the side. Their sail useless against the power of the maelstrom, they were accelerating upward. The only difference from their initial descent was that they were now traveling backward, in a counterclockwise fashion. If anything, it was even more upsetting to the equilibrium.

"What did you do, mate?" Mudge clung to a stay for support.

"I played too long, dammit! I should've stopped when the current did." Struggling to maintain his balance, he gaped at the howling, spinning wall of water. "Where I come from, playing music backward is supposed to have hermetic effects. I just wanted to make the spinning stop so we could try and sail clear, but it seems I've got it going in the opposite direction."

"Ohhhh . . . does anyone know if it's possible to throw up in reverse?" Ansibette lay on the deck, holding her stomach.

"what a charming thought, my dear." Quiquell lay alongside the human. "you have too vivid an imagination." Neither of them needed to worry, as none of them had anything left to heave.

As they continued to accelerate, Naike clung determinedly to the wheel. "Be ready, everyone! As soon as we're cast clear we need to make all possible speed away from this place!"

"Aye, sir!" came the shouts from his soldiers. Jon-Tom kept his hands on the duar's strings. There was no telling what might happen when they reached the surface. Another hasty spellsong (would he ever have the chance to sing any other kind? he wondered) might be in order.

Bereft of crew, an abandoned three-master trailing tattered sails spun past them, followed by a very disoriented school of tuna. Huge chunks of coral torn from some unknown reef threatened to smash in their hull. The sides of the whirlpool became filled with flotsam.

"What is all this?" Naike wondered aloud. It was Mudge who supplied a possible explanation.

"Since Jon-Tom's made it run backward, I expect 'tis growin' a bit queasy itself." He tightened his grip on the supporting stay. "Turnabout's fair play, I say. 'Tis the turn o' the maelstrom to upchuck!"

"Hold on, everybody!" Swinging his duar onto his back, Jon-Tom wrapped his arms around the mast and held on tight.

An incredibly violent gurgle arose from the depths of the whirlpool, followed by a maniacal lurch. Together with half a dozen sunken ships, tons of coral, whole schools of frantically flapping fish, and all manner of accompanying debris, they were flung skyward. The boat landed with a deafening *sploosh* a hundred yards from the rim of the pit. Fortune and not spellsinging saw them land upright.

The little craft bobbed several times in the calm sea before steadying as water drained from its decks and sides. Strips of seaweed streamed like attenuated green pennants from stays and rigging, railing and mast. As the soldiers dragged themselves off the deck and rushed to clear the rigging and reset the mainsail, the maelstrom continued to burble and belch prodigiously.

"Wind!" Naike gazed imploringly at the luffing sail. "Where is our wind?"

Even as he spoke, a slight breeze materialized. It filled the sail with agonizing slowness, but fill it, it did. They began to move, the cloud of music leading them south once again. An exhausted cheer rose from the princesses.

Behind them, the oceanic urpings of the distressed maelstrom gradually faded into the distance.

They sailed amid drifting debris for some time: ancient planks, the shattered keels of long-drowned ships, fragments of forest, scarred oars and binnacles. They watched in wonder as one scuttled ancient craft twenty times the size of their own drifted past. It had a single mast fixed in its center and four tiers of oar ports, from which still protruded a dozen or more oars each as big around as Clothahump's tree. What sort of crew it might have carried could only be imagined.

Glass fishing floats bumped up against their bow and went bobbing past like bubbles from a giant's pipe. Scattered rope and torn rigging were a constant threat to entangle their steering.

No one was prepared when Mudge unexpectedly flung off his clothes and dove over the side.

Jon-Tom rushed to the railing while behind him a dignified Umagi commented, "Water-rats! Always unpredictable."

"And not a little unbalanced." Seshenshe was trying to dry out her fur.

"Now just a moment—" Pivver began.

"I was referring only to commoners," the gorilla hastened to explain. Thus mollified, the princess of Trenku relented.

"Hard aport!" a disgusted Pauko barked. "Bring her around sharply, sir!"

Straining at the wheel, Jon-Tom and Naike coerced the unwieldy craft into a tight circle, bringing it back to where Mudge had entered the water. Waving cheerfully, the otter awaited them atop what appeared to be a large floating block of shining red wood.

As they drew nearer they saw that his raft had a curved top and was belted vertically with deeply patinaed bronze straps. Hollow fastenings of scored brass showed where leather carrying straps had rotted away.

"Give me a 'and 'ere, mates!" Mudge reached out to grab a trailing line.

With difficulty they succeeded in running ropes to the

vacant fastenings, Mudge diving again and again to slip the lines through the thickly encrusted openings. After the mongooses rigged a block and tackle it took the combined effort of everyone aboard, princesses included, to haul the ancient chest up over the railing and onto the deck.

"Look out!" Aleaukauna let out a yelp as the temporary tackle began to groan in protest at the weight it was being asked to carry. Everyone scattered as the lines gave way and the chest came crashing down. The deck planks held, but the corroded bronze bands belting the chest did not. As they sprang, the tough old wood finally split, spilling a shaft of light onto the deck. More light glittered within the ruptured container, hinting at clandestine wonders.

Still dripping and naked, Mudge sprang to the salvage's side and yanked hard on the sprung latch. The lid sprang back and the otter promptly jumped inside.

A contented voice reached out to the others. "Come an' 'ave a look, me friends. 'Tis a sight sure to soothe the 'eart o' the most avaricious seafarer."

They clustered around the open chest. It was filled three-quarters of the way to the top with tiny gold coins, the largest no bigger than Jon-Tom's thumbnail. Stirred in among the gold like bits of meat in a stew was a closetful of rings, necklaces, tiaras, armlets, anklets, decorative chains, and other objects of personal adornment, fashioned of platinum and gold, festooned with all manner of precious gems and enamels. As Mudge bustled about within, the crack in the side of the chest widened, spilling sunshine and rainbows onto the deck.

Selecting a golden monocle rimmed with emeralds, the otter positioned it over his right eye. The lens had been cut from a single flawless pale blue diamond.

"Wot do you think, Jonny-Tom? Do this make a fashion statement or wot?"

"Does it do anything for your vision?"

"Now that ain't the idea, mate. Wot it'll do is sharpen the sight o' any folk settin' eyes upon me."

A royal feeding frenzy set in as the princesses swarmed the chest. Not because of the riches it contained, but because of the style.

"Earrings!" Ansibette let out a triumphant shout as she held up a brace of platinum and sapphire baubles. No fisherman could have been prouder of a record catch.

Aleaukauna draped a chestpiece of pink coral and black pearls around her neck, while Seshenshe tried on armlets of solid malachite set with imperial topaz and amethyst.

"claw-tips, i see claw-tips!" Quiquell plunged her paws into the golden treasure while next to her Pivver searched anxiously for a proper tail ring.

The soldiers stood back and looked on prosaically. "I'm not greedy," remarked Heke. "A bushel or two of gold will be enough to satisfy me." Pauko nodded agreement.

" 'Ere now!" His lower torso and legs submerged in gold coins, Mudge sat erect. "Wot about me, ladies? I found the bloody chest, while you were all cursin' me for takin' me little swim. As finder I claims the major share." Exhilarated beyond hearing, the princesses ignored him. "Leave me a bloomin' armband, at least!"

Arms folded, Jon-Tom looked on diffidently as Naike came over to stand next to him.

"Your friend has an eye for treasure. I never would have identified that drifting object as a chest. I was too worn and tired, too busy thinking of flight."

"You and I aren't Mudge. You could cut off his arms and legs, blind and deafen him, and he could still sniff out a lost silver piece fallen into a crack in a tavern floor. I suppose it's a talent of sorts."

Naike looked pleased. "At least if this vessel fails us we now have the means with which to purchase alternative transportation. Nor will adequate supplies be any longer a problem."

"It's funny, you know . . ." A faraway look came into Jon-Tom's eyes.

The mongoose gazed up at the much taller human. "You find such bounty amusing?"

"No, not that. It's just that with all the adventures Mudge and I have had over the years, with all the traveling we've done and all the dangers we've survived, this is the first time we've ever run into *any* kind of treasure. I suppose that's because we've never gone looking for it. We've always been searching for other things.

"Now out here, in the middle of a strange sea, we practically run into a fortune greater than any I've ever imagined."

The Lieutenant was silent for a while before replying. "It must be, then, that your work has been rewarded on a higher plane. Yours must have been a noble career."

"Oh, I dunno. It's all very well and good to do good works and aspire to noble pursuits, but it's also nice to have a bit of treasure now and then. Talea will be pleased. So will Weegee. They like pretty things."

"I suppose I do not understand," Naike said. Before them, Mudge continued to bicker with the princesses. "Can't you just spelling up gold and jewels whenever you wish?"

"Nope. There's some sort of spectral prohibition against sorcerers using their abilities to make themselves fabulously wealthy. Otherwise none of us would have to get up and go to work in the morning. We'd all be retired and living like kings. I don't pretend to understand the rules, but Clothahump says it has something to do with the physics of ethicality. The math's too much for me. If you try it, push the limits, you end up a crotchety old dragon lording it over a useless hoard in a cave somewhere, waiting for some blond, muscular, valiant hero with an IQ the size of his biceps to show up and cut out your heart. It's not like you can stuff your pockets and hop off to Las Vegas. No, thanks. I'd rather have my family and my profession."

He nodded toward the chest and its riches. "However, there are no prohibitions against honestly *finding* treasure."

"I think I see the point of it."

A smile spread slowly across the spellsinger's face. "So

here it was up to Mudge, the old reprobate, to finally find us some treasure." He focused on the grand tiara Umagi had placed on her head. It imparted to the scion of Tuuro a regal air which had hitherto largely been absent. "I don't recognize the style or any of the engraving. Don't you want to get in on this?"

"There are ample spoils to go around. Let the ladies have their fun. Such wealth means nothing to them, whereas enhancing their appearance means everything. My soldiers and I will sate our more common appetites later."

"Take that off, pointy-ears!" Reaching for the necklace glittering on Seshenshe's neck, Mudge overbalanced and fell headlong into the gold. He came up spitting coins. " 'Tis mine by right o' discovery! I claim original rights; I claim first choice!"

Pivver inspected Ansibette's newly acquired ensemble. "The blister pearls suit you well, but I would go with rubies instead of sapphires on your ears."

"Do you think so? I was wondering." Together with their sister princesses they effortlessly ignored the violently protesting Mudge.

"*Listen to me!*" Having recovered his footing, the otter was hopping up and down atop the hoard. The princesses paid him not the slightest attention, which, Jon-Tom knew, would make his companion madder than ever.

"He'll settle down. It's not like he's going to have to make the return journey in poverty. As it is I'll have to watch to make sure he doesn't carry enough to cripple himself."

So much fabulous jewelry did the chest contain that, when every feminine limb and curvaceous body part had been appropriately adorned, the ship seemed to radiate its own light as it sailed on southward.

CHAPTER 19

RUGGED AS IT WAS, THEIR CRAFT HAD TAKEN A DREADFUL beating while trapped inside the maelstrom. Their violent ejection had put additional strains on the fastenings and timbers. Now the soldiers had to pump constantly to keep ahead of the worsening leaks. Seeping water threatened to overwhelm the single siphon, as mongoose arms and backs proved no match for the relentless pressure outside the hull.

Since the princesses steadfastly refused to have anything to do with so degrading an enterprise as operating the pump, it was imperative that a place be found where the boat could be hauled out and proper repairs made. Naike was beginning to despair even as he wondered if the tall human knew any spellsongs appropriate to boat caulking, when a line of low islands came into view on the southwest horizon.

It was decided to try to find a suitable beaching site. The princesses were elated at the prospect of taking a stroll on motionless, dry ground again and Jon-Tom had to admit he wouldn't be averse to the opportunity himself. A suitable mooring would also give them a chance to replenish their supplies. Fruits, nuts, berries, shellfish, and the like could be gathered while the otters went fishing.

It would be pleasant to stop for a while. The air was warm and not terribly humid, the sky clear, the seas cooperative. Several days ashore would serve to rehabilitate their spirits as well as their vessel.

With Heke and Karaukul riding the bow to port and starboard and acting as reef spotters, and despite the princesses

all offering suggestions simultaneously, they carefully nego-
tiated a passage into a peaceful lagoon boasting an adequate
anchorage. Unlike the surrounding islands, the one they
chose boasted a small central hill of heavily vegetated coral
rock. Rather than objecting to the delay, as was usual, the
chord chorus preceded them into the lagoon with evident
enthusiasm.

"Easy, easy," Heke shouted back. "A little to port, sir!"
Naike coaxed the wheel. "There!" With a gentle grinding
noise the boat slid up into the soft sandy beach. It heeled
slightly to starboard and stopped, comfortably aground.

It was, as they'd intended, high tide. As the morning reced-
ed, so did the water in the lagoon, leaving the vessel's underside exposed and dry. The soldiers immediately set to work
repairing the damage their craft had sustained.

Simply strolling along the unpolluted arc of beach gave a
boost to everyone's spirits. It occupied the princesses and
kept them out of the soldiers' way. Even Mudge pitched in to
help with the repairs.

"Spent me 'ole life breakin' into things," he quipped.
"Nothin' like bustin' somethin' up to learn 'ow 'tis best put
right again. 'And me that dowel, guv." Pauko passed the
requested pin across.

Jon-Tom likewise offered to assist, but on the work site his
gangly form proved more of a hindrance than a help. In no
way could he compete with the agile otter and mongooses,
who as they worked twisted and bent into various configura-
tions that would have caused permanent injury in any human
foolish enough to try to emulate them. Feeling like a loose
wheel, he decided the best thing he could do was keep out of
the way.

His services sorcerous or manual unneeded, it struck him
that for the first time in many days he could actually indulge
in a few hours of solitude without feeling guilty about it. He
resolved to explore the island, starting with the central
hillock.

The modest incline proved no obstacle and he climbed easily, making his way through scrub and palm trees. The summit afforded an excellent view of the surrounding islands as well as the lagoon and their grounded craft. The figures of the mongooses and Mudge were clearly visible as they busied themselves about the exposed hull.

Turning, he started down into the lush tropical forest that blanketed the north side of the island. Pools of rainwater gave promise of refilling the ship's casks, and numerous trees were heavy with orange and green fruit.

He was about to head back when he heard the grunting. It was a peculiar singsong that reminded him more of clamoring seals than anything else. He noted the position of the sun. It was much too early for his companions to miss him, and he knew if he wanted to check out any local life-forms he needn't worry about getting lost. The island was small enough to walk around in a few hours.

Making his way through the trees, he found himself gazing out across another part of the lagoon that encircled the island. The beach here was narrower than where they'd grounded the boat, the palms growing right down to the lagoon's edge. Transparent, waist-deep water covered sand the color of white sugar and eddied around the occasional bommie. Each of the smooth, exposed humps of blue and yellow coral was occupied, and not by seals.

Mermaids.

Looking back on the wonders he'd encountered since his original transposition it was surprising Jon-Tom hadn't chanced upon them before. Of course, he and Mudge had done the majority of their adventuring on land.

From the vicinity of the pelvis up they were exquisitely human. The precise line of demarcation between fish and human being of more than casual interest, he found himself leaning forward until he stumbled over a protruding root and tumbled out onto the sand.

Whistles and shrieks greeted his appearance, followed by a succession of splashes as the piscine lovelies vanished into the water. All save one. Hair the color of red gold covered her shoulders like rusted kelp. Narrow eyes of purest vermilion slanted upward at the outside corners. The fact that only soft, pale skin showed where a nose ought to have been was no more disconcerting than the gills that rippled along the sides of her neck. Set out from her head, her ears were large and fringed, designed to serve as small directional fins as well as organs of hearing. They fanned slowly back and forth with her breathing. Her lips . . . her lips were as boldly crimson as the folds of the nudibranch called Spanish dancer.

Slipping languidly into the water, she swam effortlessly toward the beach until she could rest her elbows on the dry sand. Propping her delicate chin on her lightly webbed hands, she stared up at him where he stood dusting off his pants. Her scaly, iridescent green tail slapped lazily back and forth.

"Hello, man."

Jon-Tom swallowed hard. "Hello," he replied, not knowing what else to say.

"Or perhaps you are more a monkey, to live in the trees?"

"Uh, no." As he stepped out onto the beach she rolled playfully onto her back and giggled up at him, a pure but far from innocent effervescence.

"How strange you look."

"Maybe it's the way you're lying."

She spun back onto her belly. "Always men run from me. Yet I am told it is the dream of many human males to make love to a mermaid."

"You're very . . . direct."

"That is the way of the sea." She arched her back and touched the tip of her remarkable tail to her forehead. "So it is not your dream?"

"It's pretty hard to dream about something you don't know exists."

Laughter bubbled from deep in the gill-lined throat and her ear-fins wiggled disconcertingly, droplets of water clinging like seed pearls to their tips.

"I heard you singing," he told her.

Her expression kinked. "Those awful noises? That wasn't singing. It is all we can do since our songs were stolen."

"Stolen?"

"Fled, vanished, disappeared, magicked away; we know not how or why. Still, we try to sing, but can only grunt in chorus like so many addled pinnipeds." For a moment he thought she was going to cry, then decided that for one who dwelt beneath the sea tears would be more than superfluous.

He raised his eyes toward the open ocean. "The curse."

"Curse?" She blinked at him and he saw that she had double eyelids, the inner pair being perfectly transparent.

"You and your sisters aren't the only ones whose music has gone missing."

"I know."

He frowned. "You know about the musicians in Mashupro?"

"What is this 'Mashupro'? I speak of the dolphins and whales, many of whom are also losing the ability to sing. For them it is more than a matter of artfulness, for if they cannot sing, they cannot find one another within the deep ocean or properly position themselves with respect to the land or the sea bottom. A songless cetacean is a half blind cetacean." She was staring at him.

"How come you to know of such matters, man? Usually land dwellers are woefully ignorant of what transpires beneath the waves."

"I'm a little different from your average land dweller." He crossed his legs and sat down in front of her. She responded by sitting up and swinging her tail around so that the tip just touched his boots. In spite of his determination he found his concentration crippled.

"I'm a spellsinger. That's a kind of sorcerer who makes magic with music."

" 'Singer.' Your songs have not been disappeared?"

"Not so far. In fact, we're traveling with a piece of music, though I don't think it belongs to you or your whales. It leads, and we follow."

"You speak of things I do not understand. But if you are a magician as well as a singer, is there nothing you can do to help return our songs to us?" Leaning forward sharply, she thrust her face close to his. She was ripe with the aroma of salt and life, kelp and crystal. "I would so do anything to make that happen."

"That's not necessary." He drew back a little, though not as much as he might have. "If I can be of any help, I'll help everyone. You, your sisters, the whales, a fresh little band in Mashupro, everyone who's lost music to this singular phenomenon."

"And what of me?" she whispered, humping forward like a seal. "Do you think of me as a singular phenomenon?" She was very near now.

"Actually—" He sneezed sharply, causing her to draw back in surprise. Her tail smacked the water, a warning reflex not unlike the lobtailing performed by her cetacean cousins.

"Sorry. It's just that I—" He sneezed again, violently, wiping at his nose with the back of his right hand.

"What is it, man? What is wrong?"

Sniffing, he managed to gasp out a reply. "I'm allergic to certain kinds of seafood."

"Seafood? You would catch and fillet me, man?"

"No, no!" he said hastily. "Not you. Tuna, mackerel, haddock, sardines—that kind of seafood."

She put her hands on her hips, just above the first iridescent scales. "I should have known. Man, some of my best friends are tuna." Her expression softened. "But you say you do not eat them."

"Can't." He sneezed again, less explosively this time now that she had moved back a little.

Both arms extended as she stretched them over her head. Her lips pursed in a fey pout. "Then it would be uncomfortable for you to make love to me."

"I don't think you'd enjoy it very much, either." The degree of disappointment in his voice surprised him.

"I will tell my sisters of your promise to help." She turned abruptly and rolled back into the water.

"Hey, wait!" He rose to his feet. "I didn't promise anything!"

Her head and shoulders reappeared, her flowing hair clinging to bare skin. "If you could hold your breath long enough, I would give you a kiss of thanks."

"I don't suppose there'd be any harm in that. Just a kiss, I mean." He moved to the water's edge and crouched.

As their lips met, a feeling coursed through him the likes of which he'd never encountered. He'd done scuba and felt the sea all around him, warm and embracing and fickle, a salty full-body caress. That was what her kiss was like—a passion that spread throughout his entire being, electric with sweet deep promises and the echoes of preternatural beauty. It was as if she were palpating his soul.

When she drew back, she left the taste of salt and sugar on his mouth. Subsequently he sneezed, causing her to laugh delightedly. Her gill slits rippled like a manta's, the upward-slanting eyes glistening wetly.

"It never works anyway," she told him. "If I come out on land I flop around like a beached flounder and love slides away. If the man enters my realm he can never hold his breath long enough or float without treading water." Tail flashing, she rolled and dove.

"That's okay," he assured her as she reappeared farther out. "I'm not much of a swimmer, and it was a wonderful kiss."

"I'm joyful you found it so. Find our music, spellsinger. Find our songs and restore them to us and you'll gain the gratitude of myself, my sisters, and all our companions in the sea." Floating on her back, she batted lazily at the water with her tail. "Practice your breath-holding skills and who knows what might become possible one day? Surely your allergy would not affect you underwater."

With that she arched her back and dove.

She was right, he realized. If he was underwater and holding his breath or breathing canned air, his allergies wouldn't be affected.

"Wait!" He waded out through the warm, clear water until it lapped at his knees. "Come back!"

No tail of shining peridot broke the surface, no eyes limpid with promise peered back at him. She had gone, leaving only the memory of that kiss lingering on his lips, rich as chocolate, pungent as dew. A kiss, and a plea.

What was happening to the world's music?

Reluctantly, he turned back toward the woods. She would have done better to encounter a human with fewer allergies and greater lung capacity.

They'd finished more than half the necessary repairs when a muting of the light announced the arrival of evening. The sun was stealing away to the west when Mudge casually accosted his friend.

"Ain't seen you all day, mate. Where'd you take yourself off to?" Though Jon-Tom didn't reply, the smile on his face was response enough to pique the otter's curiosity. Mudge didn't press the inquiry, preferring to wait until his friend looked less dazed. Or perhaps *dazzled* would have been a more accurate description.

Besides, Pivver was waiting on him. Only to talk, but otters were naturally physical creatures. A little touch here and there, he told himself. For now more here than there, but with time, who knew what marvels might transpire?

Did he want marvels to transpire? Wrestling with his damnable new conscience, he trotted off muttering to himself, leaving Jon-Tom to stare curiously at the otter's retreating back.

The following day the princesses pitched in to help with the work. Not because they were feeling particularly egalitarian but because they were already bored to tears. Though accommodating enough, the island was singularly lacking in excitement. With her natural strength, Umagi of Tuuro proved especially helpful, though everyone did their share. Watching Ansibette work, Jon-Tom reflected, was even more dangerous than watching her doing nothing. He concentrated on his own contribution, which consisted of keeping resolutely out of the way.

By the following morning they'd done all they could within the range of their limited resources. Anxious moments followed as they waited for the tide to lift them free. The boat's keel was firmly wedged in the sand, and Naike floated the possibility (as it were) of launching their single lifeboat, affixing a line to it from the ship's stern, and trying to pull the bigger vessel free. Alternatively they could haul the anchor out on the lifeboat, drop it, winch the ship backward, and in this fashion kedge their way off the beach.

Neither arduous option had to be exercised. The tide crept in just enough to float them clear. The stalwart little vessel straightened as they backed sail and drifted out into the lagoon. Under Naike's increasingly assured direction she was brought about and they made confidently for the passage through the reef.

Only when they were once more safely out on the open sea did everyone relax. Heke and Karaukul hurried belowdecks to check on the state of the repairs they'd made. There was still some seepage near the bow, but the rest of the patches were holding firm. To compensate for their lack of skill and technical knowledge, they had overcaulked and overfilled even the tiniest gap. Profligacy with time and material on land translated into safety at sea.

"She's tight below, sir," Heke reported proudly.

On the other side of the wheel Jon-Tom studied the hazy sky. "We should be okay unless we run into another storm. I don't know if she can take another pounding like that."

A small, powerful paw came to rest on his arm. "Be of good cheer, spellsinger. Do not seek storms, lest they seek you." Naike swatted absently at the string of chords swirling near his head. The music made his ears itch.

They weren't an hour out from the island, Jon-Tom regaling his companions with song, when Heke's voice reached them from the platform affixed to the top of the mast.

"Something five points to starboard, sir!"

The Lieutenant squinted at the lookout. "What is it?"

"I can't tell. But it's big, whatever it is."

Leaving the mongoose to hold the wheel, Jon-Tom rushed to the railing. So did the excited princesses.

They drew back as a titanic shape rose from the water. It was far larger than their vessel, slick of side and pale of hue. It reeked of abyssal depths. The boat rocked slightly in the waves induced by its emergence. A wary Jon-Tom readied his duar.

Weighing more than a hundred tons and stretching well over a hundred feet in length, the stupendous sulfurbottom carefully nuzzled the side of the boat. From within the forepart of that curving rampart of pale blue flesh a plate-sized eye focused firmly on Jon-Tom. The air vibrated with a voice sufficiently sonorous to set his teeth to aching.

"DON'T I KNOW YOU?"

More than a little bemused, Jon-Tom examined his reflection in the whale's eye. "Um, I don't think so. If we'd met before, I have a feeling I'd remember it."

"THAT MUSIC . . ." The leviathan effortlessly kept pace with the ship. "I COULD SWEAR I'VE HEARD ITS LIKE BEFORE. AND SEEN ITS MAKER." The eye swiveled slightly. "SURELY I KNOW YOU AS WELL."

"Me?" squeaked Mudge as the orb centered on him. "I 'ardly think so, Your Immoderateness. Not that I ain't never forgot folks I've met, but 'tis a tetch difficult to imagine forgettin' someone your size."

"I SUPPOSE SO." The eye returned to transfix Jon-Tom. "BUT I COULD SWEAR . . . NEVERTHELESS, YOU ARE THE SPELLSINGER OF WHOM THE MERMAID SPEAKS?"

"I guess so, unless she's swam into another one in the past couple of days."

As if this admission was somehow the answer to everything, the whale arched its back and sounded, leaving the boat to bob wildly for a moment in its wake.

"Well now, mate." Mudge sidled close to his friend. "Wot do you make o' that? An' wot's this about a mermaid?"

"Not much. I had a chat with one day before yesterday. She spoke of her kind losing their music, and the cetaceans likewise. I guess news travels faster underwater."

Faster than he knew, as Heke confirmed by calling out a second time from the masthead.

"There's another. And another, and another!"

The air was filled with expansive whooshing sounds as whale after whale surfaced and spouted. Soon the boat was surrounded, not by dozens of individuals but by dozens of pods. Not just blues, but all manner of tribes were represented. There were humpbacks and fins, sperms and seis, rights and orcas. Scattered among them like so many PT boats escorting a fleet of aircraft carriers and battleships were hundreds of agile, uncatchable dolphins and porpoises, leaping and darting among their more massive cousins.

"Isn't that a grand sight!" declared an awestruck Aleaukauna.

"Truly wondrous." Along with the other princesses, Pivver gazed raptly upon the cetacean flotilla.

Taking turns, the goliaths swam alongside to have a closer look at the boat and its occupants, who were delighted to return the favor. Eventually the parade made way for a patriarchal humpback whose head was as gnarly as the root ball of a sequoia.

"YOU BE THE SPELLSINGER?"

"I be," replied Jon-Tom evenly.

"YOU WERE MADE KNOWN TO US BY FRIENDS."

"The mermaids; I know." He felt a tug at his side.

" 'Tis best not to volunteer too much until we know wot they're about, mate."

"What are we going to do, Mudge? Refuse to answer their questions? In case you haven't noticed, we're a little overmatched here." He peered back over the side. "Can we do something for you? Surely this impressive gathering isn't all for my benefit."

"IT IS HOPED THAT YOUR PRESENCE WILL BE TO OUR BENEFIT." The old humpback had rolled slightly onto his right side, the better to see aboard. Thick with barnacles and whale lice, a massive pectoral fin rested on the side of the boat.

"I don't understand." Actually Jon-Tom was afraid that he did.

"WE HAVE LOST OUR MUSIC, JUST AS HAVE THE MERMAIDS. THE ONE YOU TALKED WITH SAID SHE IMPRESSED ON YOU THE DANGER THIS POSES TO US. WITHOUT SONG WE CANNOT FIND OUR WAY."

"I don't know what I can do for you. At least not right now." Jon-Tom gestured forward. "First I have to escort these six ladies homeward. After that I follow a solitary piece of music wherever it may lead." The demands on his time, he mused, were beginning to verge on the absurd. His sinuses gave a twitch, but he didn't sneeze.

"SINCE LEAVING YOUR LAST LAND WE HAVE PLOTTED YOUR DIRECTION."

"For now we go where the music leads us, but soon we'll turn east toward our passengers' kingdoms," Jon-Tom explained.

"FOR NOW." The humpback brooded. "CAN IT BE YOU DO NOT KNOW WHERE YOU ARE HEADING?"

Man and otter exchanged a look. Then they turned as one to stare at the lightly luminescent cloud of music that danced and pirouetted just forward of the bowsprit.

"How do I tell the princesses that we're not heading straight for Harakun?"

The otter shrugged. "Don't tell 'em. Say we 'ave to make a short stop on the way. Looks like we're goin' to, whether we likes it or not."

Jon-Tom nodded thoughtfully. "It was that storm that forced us to change course. You don't suppose our happy ball of harmony could have had anything to do with that little discrepancy in the weather, do you?"

"Don't very well see 'ow music can call up a storm, mate.

But then there's more than one wonder in this world that I fails to understand. Like, for example, if your spouse finds somethin' on sale for fifty coins that regular costs a 'undred, 'ow come she insists she's saved you fifty coins instead of 'avin' spent fifty?" He shook his head. "The mysteries o' the cosmos confound me continually."

"I as well." Jon-Tom looked back over the side. "I guess we'll keep on this way for a while longer, at least, and see what develops."

"WE KNEW YOU WOULD. THE MERMAID ASSURED US."

"Did she?" Apparently he'd made more of an impression on that bathyal beauty than he'd thought. *Damn allergies,* he thought to himself.

"GIVE US A SONG, SPELLSINGER. WE HAVE BEEN LONG WITHOUT SONG. THE MERMAID TELLS THAT YOU STILL CONTROL YOUR OWN MUSIC."

Jon-Tom modestly brought the duar around. "I suppose a song or two wouldn't hurt anything. Of course, I don't have your lungs. I can't sing like you."

" 'Ell, 'e can't even sing like a 'uman," Mudge informed the humpback.

"ANYTHING AT ALL WOULD BE MOST WELCOME. MUSIC IS AS LIFE TO US."

"All right. As long as you don't expect too much." His fingers rested on the duar's strings as he tried to think of something that might appeal to their escort. After several moments spent in contemplation, he began to sing.

A number of whales and dolphins crowded closer, nudging the ship and making her timbers creak. Whenever this happened the offending individual immediately moved away. The cetaceans continuously rotated places so that as many as possible would have the opportunity to hear.

When he finished the first song Jon-Tom received a kind of applause new in his experience. A hundred individuals spouted simultaneously, vitalizing the air with sound and pungent exhalation. Only the humpbacks and some of the porpoises were equipped for actual clapping. They acknowledged Jon-Tom's effort with more familiar, if decidedly damper than usual, expressions of approval.

They sailed on with Jon-Tom energetically serenading the cetacean host. Mudge and Pivver frequently joined their benthic escort in energetic swims, diving and twisting with the skill of any porpoise, though they could not match them in speed or endurance. It was something to see them clinging to the fore edge of a humpback's fin as it breached, casting themselves free, and spinning in the air with an agility the best human diver could only dream of before neatly reentering the water.

Once, a pair of pirate craft bore down on them in threatening manner. Confronted by several dozen blue and sperm whales, the oared galley and converted merchantman turned tail as fast as their crews could back sails and oars, those of the galley dipping and rising at a rate that verged on the comical.

"Per'aps if we manage to find their missin' songs," Mudge commented thoughtfully, "we can inveigle a few o' these bloated blue blokes to convoy us across to Harakun. They 'ave a way o' discouragin' unwanted visitors, they do."

"We not only have to find their music, we have to restore it to them as well." Jon-Tom idly fingered the duar's strings. "Where do you conceal missing music? In a chest, in a stoppered bottle, in an enchanted disk? As part of my education as a spellsinger I've researched such things with Clothahump. Whatever storage device can be imagined can be made. CD-ROM, for example."

"Wot's that?" The otter made a face. "Some kind o' special room?"

"A very small room. You have to know what you're doing when you access that kind of storage. It stands for 'Charged Demons—Reconstituted Out of Mayhem.' You have to handle them carefully, by their edges. There are many other kinds of containers that would hold music. Finding them's not the problem. Accessing them often is."

"You'll 'andle it, mate. I know you will."

Jon-Tom eyed his friend in surprise. "Why, Mudge. It's not like you to show such confidence in me."

"Oh, it weren't that, mate," replied the otter cheerily. "I just know you can confound any sorceral opponent because o' your unpredictability, which comes from the fact that you usually don't 'ave the foggiest notion o' wot you're about. See, if you don't know wot you're doin', ain't no way wotever you're fightin' can anticipate your next move." It was not merely a backhanded compliment, it was positively inside out.

"You know, mate, we started out on this 'ere little ramble to trail a few bars o' wanderin' music to wherever its anxiety might 'appen to take us. I don't know about you, but it strikes me as 'ow things 'ave become a bit more complicated than wot were originally intended."

Jon-Tom grinned down at his whiskery friend. "They always seem to, don't they . . . mate."

CHAPTER 20

THE ISLAND APPEARED ON THE FIFTH DAY. IT WAS DRASTI-
cally different from the inviting, sandy low isles among
which the travelers had repaired their vessel. A nightmare
sculpted from stark black basalt and decomposing schists, the
towering peaks clutched at the pallid clouds which struggled
to draw away from them.

The ancient fires which had formed the central crags had
long since been extinguished by time. Over the intervening
aeons rain and wind had gouged at the central crater and its
subsidiary pumice cones, sharpening and furrowing them.
The island was imperceptibly dissolving into the ocean.

Waves smashed into sheer black cliffs that rose precipitously a hundred feet and more from the glassy green sea. As
the whale pods led them south and then southwest the travelers came into the lee of the isolated landmass and the agitated
surface of the sea flattened out. A shattered and tumbled lava
reef further muted the force of the swells.

Once again the venerable humpback laid himself alongside
the boat. "HERE BE THE PLACE."

"HERE IS THE PLACE!" boomed the somber cetacean
chorus.

"Here it is, here it is!" sang out the smaller dolphins and
porpoises.

Mudge turned from scrutinizing the intimidating interior of
the island to confront his friend. "I could be wrong, mate, but
me unerrin' instinct tells me that we may very possibly 'ave
arrived."

Arrived where? Jon-Tom wondered. The entire aspect of the island before them was morbid and threatening.

"WE CAN GO NO FARTHER," the humpback declared. "ALREADY THE WATER GROWS TOO SHALLOW FOR COMFORT. BUT YOU MUST GO ON. FIND OUR SONGS AND RETURN THEM TO US."

"FIND OUR SONGS AND RETURN THEM TO US!" implored the vast mammalian choir.

"WE'LL BE RIGHT BEHIND YOU." The humpback rolled and pushed off toward the open sea.

"Well now, that's for sure a comfort." Mudge went to help Pivver—who had just reemerged from the water—get dressed. The fact that she required no such assistance in this task dissuaded him not in the least.

Several dolphins led them through a passage in the lava reef. Once inside, the travelers were able to drop their single anchor without fear of damaging any delicate tropical life-forms. The bottom of the lagoon was nearly devoid of life. Only a few bêche-de-mer eked out a lonely living in the sand and gravel. Of colorful corals, chromatic anemones, and tint-ed tridacna and the fish that associated with them there were none.

The dense tropical vegetation which had once covered the shore and lower slopes of the mountains lay stunted and blasted by some unknown calamity. Trees struggled to put forth the occasional wrinkled leaf, while palms drooped low, their fronds curled and crisped as if from an encounter with searing heat. Those isolated clumps of greenery which did survive huddled against the trunks of the larger growths for protection.

"Somethin' terrible 'as 'appened 'ere." Mudge peered war-ily over the bow as they swung gently at anchor.

"Lost their songs. Trees and flowers have their own music. Something's stolen it away and unlike traveling musicians or sea-spanning whales, they couldn't run from it." Jon-Tom looked to his right. The chord cloud was throbbing a deep, angry red. Its normally contented chiming had turned sharp and strident. Anyone who insisted that pure music could not convey real emotion, Jon-Tom felt, had to be either lying or tone deaf.

The princesses had gathered along the rail to point and murmur. They could afford to be indifferent: None of them would be going ashore. He walked back to join them.

"Do any of you recognize this place?"

Quiquell replied for all of them. "don't be ridiculous. this is a land to be shunned, not claimed."

"That's what I thought."

"Oi, mate!" At the otter's call Jon-Tom hurriedly raced back forward.

Still phosphorescing crimson, the cluster of chords was streaming toward the black sand beach. Jon-Tom let his gaze rise toward the topmost peak. Thunder rumbled distantly from the dark cloud which encircled the uppermost crags.

"Now that looks promisin', that do." Mudge stood at his friend's elbow. "Why do I 'ave this sinkin' feelin' that we're about to do some climbin'?" For a change Jon-Tom chose not to venture a clever, sardonic reply. He was not feeling especially witty—only apprehensive.

Flinging a few riffs off the duar made him feel a little better. Whatever was at work here still had no effect on his own music.

"I wonder what sort of phenomenon abducts music. And why? What does it do with it?"

"That rotter Manzai collected princesses," Mudge reminded him. "Maybe somethin' or someone 'ere collects music."

"Collecting is one thing. Stealing it away forever from those it belongs to is something else."

Naike had come up to join them. "If you succeed in finding this missing music, how will you know it?"

Jon-Tom regarded the mongoose. "I'll know it. If there's one thing I can recognize, it's music."

A furry paw reached up to touch his shoulder. "You have done right by us. If you wish our halberds at your sides, they will be given freely."

Emotion welled up inside the spellsinger. "Thank you, Lieutenant, but I have a feeling this is not a place where cold steel and deft soldiering will be of much use. Better you stay aboard and watch over the princesses."

"Now 'old on a minim, mate," Mudge protested. " 'Ow do you know cold steel an' wotever won't be 'elpful 'ere?"

"This isn't their quest, Mudge. We're the ones who followed the chords. It's up to us to track them to the end."

"Oh, right poetic, that is! Very noble!"

"The princesses need looking after," Jon-Tom argued.

The otter's eyes widened. "Wot, this lot? Give 'em proper weapons an' I'd wager they could make any lot o' brigands an' thieves wish they'd never 'appened across this particular bum-boat. They can bloody well look after themselves."

"Sorry, Mudge. It's going to be me and thee, as always."

Turning away, the otter voiced a succession of imprecations which struck Naike dumb with admiration.

Jon-Tom took the Lieutenant's paw. "If we're not back within a couple of days, set sail for Harakun. I'm sure the whales will guide you."

The eyes of a mongoose are extraordinarily bright and clear. Naike's were no exception, though there was presently a hint of moisture about the right one. "You will be back, spellsinger. Who else would we get to entertain and divert Their Highnesses on the long journey?" He smiled, showing small sharp teeth as his lightly furred fingers fondly squeezed Jon-Tom's naked digits.

Arms crossed over his chest, Mudge was staring at the cloud-swathed, thunder-riven central peak. "This be a good place, all right. A good place to leave one's bones."

"Be of good cheer, Mudge." Jon-Tom rejoined his friend, leaving Naike to inform the other soldiers and the princesses of the spellsinger's decision.

"Good cheer! Tell me, O cheerleadin' one, why I should come with you?"

"Because you always come with me." Jon-Tom chuckled softly. "It's inevitable. It's fate."

" 'Tis bleeding lunacy, is wot it is."

"We're simply looking for some lost music. Where's the danger in that?"

"Oi, where indeed?" The otter turned back to consider the island. "Where's the danger in wotever's laid waste to this forest? Where's the danger in sheer, naked rock an' sharp spires, or lingerin' black clouds, or thunder that breaks where there be no lightnin'? Why, only a bloomin' fool would see danger 'ere."

A delicate paw touched his arm. Turning, he found himself gazing into Pivver's admiring face. "I think it's very brave of you to accompany your friend."

"Yess." The lynx put an arm around his shoulders. "It'ss sso virtuouss and honorable of you!"

"Virtuous? 'Onorable?" The otter appeared stunned. " 'Tis true then: I'm bleedin' done for, I am. No self-respectin' thief will want to be seen in me company." Resignation underlay his response. "Might as well 'ave a go, then. Can't be nothin' worse awaitin' us up there than a kind female face wot calls me virtuous."

Jon-Tom leaned close. "Don't take it too hard, Mudge. To me you'll always be the same lying, cheating, thieving, conniving coward you've always been."

A tear welled up in the otter's eye. "Bless you, mate. 'Tis good to know that no matter 'ow I may 'ave changed, there'll always be one bloke who respects me for who I truly am."

All the princesses and soldiers had now gathered around the pair. "The embodiment of fortitude," Seshenshe avowed.

"Steadfastness personified," declared Aleaukauna.

"The essence of virility." Pivver's eyes were shining.

"Essence o' virility, eh?" The otter stood as much taller as he could manage. "Too right there, luv." He turned back to Jon-Tom. "Best we see to a boat for you, mate. O' course, I don't need one, but I wouldn't think o' askin' you to make the swim. Don't worry. I'll look after you, I will."

Jon-Tom was forced to bite down in order to maintain a straight face. Considering the number of previous times and occasions when he'd been compelled to do likewise, it was surprising his lower lip was not permanently scarred.

While he fine-tuned the duar's frets and Mudge made like a figurehead in the bow, the soldiers carefully lowered the ship's single lifeboat over the side. Admonitions to take care and not a few verbal caresses from the princesses followed them as they rowed for the shore. The agitated chord cloud danced and spun through the air just ahead of them.

Once safely aground on the fine black sand beach and out of earshot of those aboard, Mudge quickly reverted to form as they hauled the lifeboat above the water line.

"Wot the bloody 'ell am I doin' 'ere? Wot circumstances 'ave brought us to this sorrowful place, mate?"

Jon-Tom carefully shipped his oars. "Your vanity, for one thing. That's what's brought you this far, anyway. That's what propels you everywhere: vanity and greed."

The otter looked relieved. "Thank goodness! For a minim there I thought I'd really gone off the deep end." He grinned exuberantly. "Virile, she called me."

"That she did. If the appeal to one organ fails, try another." He wiped salt residue from his palms. "Let's get going."

The otter looked around. "Get goin'? Get goin' *where*?"

"Same place we've been headed all along." Jon-Tom gestured at the chord cloud. It was hovering impatiently just outside the first line of damaged brush.

"You really mean to keep followin' a lot o' mindless notes?"

"I really do."

"Why ain't I surprised?" The otter's head tilted back as he surveyed the path ahead. "Take 'er slow, mate. You know that with these legs I ain't much for climbin'. That's one spot where you 'umans 'ave it over my kind."

Jon-Tom started forward. "Don't worry. I'll help you over the rough places." When it became clear he was advancing alone, he halted and looked back. "Well, come on."

Mudge traced a thoughtful pattern in the sand with the tip

of one boot. "I could stay an' guard the lifeboat. Wouldn't want to be marooned 'ere now, would we?"

"It's a short swim. Come *on*. What about your vaunted virility?"

Reluctantly, the otter started forward. "I reckon I've still got it. I just want to make sure I 'angs on to it, is all. Some o' the situations you put us into, that ain't always so easy."

Back on the securely anchored boat the soldiers cleaned and tidied what they could while the princesses gathered to converse near the stern.

"At lasst!" Seshenshe was clearly relieved. "I thought we were never going to get that otter off."

Aleaukauna was of like mind. "Yes. Have you noticed how he looks at you? His eyes swell to the size of an owl's. Nothing subtle in his staring, either."

Quiquell was filing her claws. "subtlety is not a word in that otter's vocabulary. at least not where members of the opposite sex are concerned."

"I think you may be imagining things." Umagi lay flat on the deck, soaking up the sun. "Or overstating them. I know he doesn't look at *me* that way."

As Seshenshe and Quiquell exchanged a glance and a muffled giggle, Pivver spoke up. "Oh, I don't know. I think he's kind of cute."

"As he is of your tribe, that is understandable," remarked Aleaukauna.

"But not excussable." Seshenshe's comment was punctuated by more giggling.

"You can have him." Ansibette gave a little shudder. "Male otters are just so . . . so . . ."

"So what?" Pivver challenged her.

"So *persistent*. Don't they ever think of anything else?"

"Besides what?" Pivver wasn't about to let it go.

"Besides *fish*. That's all he ever talks about. Types of fish, cooking fish, catching fish. Furthermore, he smells of fish. He's obsessed with fish."

"Think you so?" Pivver smiled ever so wisely. "I have to

hand it to you, sister Ansibette. You humans' powers of observation never cease to astonish me."

"Well, I mean, it's just so *obvious*," Ansibette murmured.

"Oh, assuredly," Pivver agreed.

"Lieutenant?" Pauko stood in the stern, gazing out across the lagoon. Naike moved to join him.

"You see something, soldier?"

"A glow, sir. Not near us. It's a good ways out, past the reef." He strained his superb sight. "It looks almost familiar, somehow."

The chitinous, insectoid form that coalesced within the pulsing cloud had just enough time to scrutinize his surroundings and emit the equivalent in its own language of "Oh, damn!" before tumbling into the open sea. He would have blinked in surprise had he been equipped with eyelids.

Thrashing frantically as he fumbled for his instrumentation, he marveled at the ease with which he'd once again bollixed the requisite coordinates. It was entirely possible that he was being too hard on himself. Programming interdimensional transposition was rather more difficult than taking a spin around the block. Even so, he had, so to speak, missed the boat yet again.

Gasping and choking, he found himself lifted above the surface by a smooth, rubbery skull. Unceremoniously tossed through the air, he landed hard atop a similar forehead. It squeaked sonorously and chucked him to his left. In this manner he was thrown from cetacean to cetacean, each airborne interval too brief to permit him to enter the necessary retreat sequence into his gear. His yelps and hisses of distress soon faded from hearing, as did his pinwheeling form from view.

"What do you make of that?" Naike had moved to join the princesses in gazing over the stern.

"I think that was the peculiar creature that attempted to confront the spellsinger earlier." Aleaukauna rubbed the side of her muzzle. "If he, too, is some sort of sorcerer, he strikes me as a particularly inept one."

"I wonder what it wants?"

"I can't imagine." Umagi bulked large behind them. "But I'm glad he's gone again. He gives me the creep-crawlies."

"Me, too." The tufts at the tips of Seshenshe's ears twitched.

Ansibette absently brushed a few windblown strands from her forehead. "Speaking of the spellsinger, I wonder how he's doing."

Pivver sniffed and turned to stare at the brooding mountain. "I don't know, but I hope he and that filthy-minded disreputable lowlife traveling with him return soon."

Aleaukauna grinned. "Could we be worried about Mr. Feather-in-His-Cap?"

"Not at all." Pivver was properly indignant. "I'm just anxious to be on our way, is all."

"Come on. You like him, don't you?"

"Be serious! I know his type all too well."

"That doesn't answer my question." The mongoose was unrelenting.

Pivver could no longer repress a slight smile. Slight, not shy—shyness being an emotion foreign to otters. "He's quite the talker, but unlike many such, he has the experience to back it up. The trick when dealing with a male like that is to separate the fact from the friction.

"How could I not be taken with him? He's traveled far, visited extraordinary places, had remarkable adventures. Quite a contrast to the courtiers who call on me at home. Without exception they all lead lives of stultifying ennui. No, despite his lack of manners he might make an interesting companion."

"Mudge?" Umagi chuckled.

"There's something about him." Pivver was tenacious. "A certain aura, an energy."

"It'ss called lusst," Seshenshe explained helpfully.

Pivver contemplated possibilities. "Delegating any power to him would of course be out of the question. But he'd be fun to have around the palace."

Quiquell spoke quietly. "there remains the awkward fact that he is already mated."

"Awkward, perhaps, but hardly insurmountable." Pivver confronted the anteater. "Having lived and socialized with him these past many days, which do you think he'd prefer? An aimless, dead-end existence in a riverbank burrow or the life of an honored consort in a royal palace? One requiring neither work nor responsibility." A smile creased her muzzle. "Except, of course, looking after me." She turned sharply on a startled Naike.

"Which would you choose, Lieutenant?"

"I?" Naike looked blank. "Your Highness, I have never been in a position to consider such a thing." He was careful to avoid the curious, penetrating gaze of the Princess Aleaukauna.

Pivver snapped her fingers contemptuously. "Knowing Mudge's type as I do, I don't see anything as trivial as an aging relationship constraining his actions."

Quiquell was not so easily put off. "in addition to being mated, he's also a good deal older than you."

"There is that," Pivver conceded. "Youth is all very well in its way, but there is much to be said for experience." Her eyes took on a far-off look. "And that is far and away the most experienced otter I have ever encountered."

The discussion evolved into a debate on the various traits to be desired in a prospective consort. In the course of the colloquy they employed nomenclature which set the ears of the several soldiers to burning, not to mention heartily amusing the many porpoises and dolphins who clustered near the stern.

CHAPTER 21

EMERGING FROM THE LOWLAND FOREST, JON-TOM AND Mudge found themselves working their way up a brushy slope spotted with shattered boulders and tumbled volcanic columns. The vegetation was tough and dense, difficult to push through. As he battled an obstreperous bush Jon-Tom found himself looking forward to the steeper but unobstructed rocky slopes above.

An indifferent trickle of viscous, nasty-looking water meandered down the center of the shallow gully they were ascending. Catching up to his long-legged friend, Mudge put a hand on the human's arm and spoke quietly.

"We're bein' followed, mate."

"Your imagination's playing you false again, Mudge. There's nothing here. Even the bugs are hiding."

"All right, maybe not followed. But watched. I can feel the eyes."

With a sigh Jon-Tom halted and turned a slow circle. There was no wind to stir the blasted branches and browned leaves. Hopefully they would encounter more of a breeze higher up. If not, it was going to be hot climbing, the perpetual dark cloud which clung to the mountaintop nothwithstanding.

As he turned to resume the ascent, shapes burst from the brush on either side of them.

Screeching, howling, wild-eyed, they brandished imperfectly made tomahawks and spears with careless abandon. Their hair was long and unkempt and a look of madness was in their eyes. None was very big, but all were lean and muscular. Filthy rags and animal skins bounced against their otherwise naked bodies.

There was a time when Jon-Tom and Mudge would have reacted with panic and confusion to such a confrontation, but having been together for so long and dealt on numerous occasions with similar assaults they responded instinctively, as one.

Jon-Tom swung his duar around and backed quickly toward a large boulder while Mudge drew his sword and assumed a defensive stance in front of the spellsinger's legs.

" 'Old right there! I'll split the first one from knee to groin wot takes another step toward us. There's not a 'uman livin' wot's 'alf as quick as I, an' I'll take out two o' you before the first can manage a thrust." Delivered with a daunting bravado honed through long experience, the warning was enough to cause their assailants to pause and reflect. Every second they hesitated gave Jon-Tom more time to choose and perfect his lyrics.

Once his companion had begun to strum the strings of the duar, an emboldened Mudge took a step forward. "Consider this your last warnin'! Me mate 'ere is a spellsinger true, a most powerful magician. With 'is music 'e can turn the lot o' you into a tot o' tremblin' toads." The otter gestured with the point of his short sword. "Begone while you still 'ave the chance!"

Letting his tomahawk fall to his side, the nearest of their assailants used his free hand to push a handful of stringy brown hair away from his face. "No shit? Toads? Really? Wow!"

"Toadally rad, dude," exclaimed the haggard figure next to him.

Jon-Tom untensed. There were only three of them, and it was clear now they weren't about to overpower the experienced Mudge and himself. Furthermore, they were skinny and sadly undernourished.

The remaining member of the scraggly triumvirate gestured at the duar. "Hey, man, can you actually play that thing?"

"Not only can I play it"—Jon-Tom mentally downgraded their attackers from dangerous to unpredictable—"I can make magic with it."

The one who'd spoken first nodded appreciatively. "Cool. Not that we should be surprised. Why should Hinckel be the only one?"

"Uh, Hinckel?" Jon-Tom inquired.

The shortest member of the objectionable trio plopped down against a thick-boled bush. Three loop earrings dangled from one ear while a perfect cubic zirconia sparkled dully in the other.

"Don't repeat that name. One mention's more than enough." He chucked his homemade spear at an inoffensive tree. "Where you two from?"

"The Bellwoods," Jon-Tom informed him.

The youth (they all looked to be in their early twenties, Jon-Tom decided) made a face. "Never heard of it."

His lanky companion was eyeing Mudge. "Radical coat. Where'd you get it?"

" 'Tis not a coat." Mudge looked down at himself. "Possibly you mean my vest?"

"Naw. Okay, so you're a giant rat. So why should I be surprised?" A look of resignation crossed his face.

Raising his sword, Mudge replied in low, dangerous tones. "I . . . am . . . not . . . a . . . rat."

Jon-Tom restrained his friend. "He's an otter."

"Right. An otter. Cool." The nominal leader of the trio wearily set his own weapon aside. "You have to excuse us. Things have been pretty rough since we ended up here."

Ignoring a questioning look from Mudge, Jon-Tom carefully slid his duar around onto his back. Despite the hostility evinced by their initial confrontation he didn't think this grungy threesome represented much of a threat. That didn't prevent the otter from keeping a firm grip on his own sword.

Jon-Tom was gratified when the eldest of the three readily

accepted his outstretched hand. The man's grip was wiry and firm.

"Where are you guys from? I get the feeling I should know your accent."

The trio exchanged looks. The one on the ground lowered his head, shaking it slowly.

"What accent?" replied the prodigally hirsute. "We're all from Jersey."

"North Jersey," added the raggedy blonde next to him.

"Except for Hinckel." Brush-Cut put his hands behind his head and leaned back against the bush. "He's from the city. East side."

"East side?" Jon-Tom frowned.

"New York, dude, New York. Man, don't you know anything?" The leader nodded knowingly at his buddies. "He ain't from around here."

"You can always tell," agreed Brush-Cut.

Come to think of it, where was *he* "from"? Jon-Tom wondered. It had been so long, so many years. This was his home now. The land of the Bellwoods and the Tailaroam, Lynchbany and the Glittergeist Sea. To that lexicon of miraculous topography could now be added this sullen isle of devastation. Of devastation, and bedraggled visitors from Jersey.

"I'm from L.A., originally."

"All *right*." The leader looked pleased. "What was the name of your band? Who'd you play with?"

"I didn't play with anybody. Never got the chance."

"Bummer," declared the skinny figure next to the leader.

A thunderclap of prodigious proportions rattled the mountain, dislodging a few small rocks. Skipping clear, Mudge warily eyed the inconstant heights.

"There he goes again," muttered the seated member of the trio.

The leader was apologetic. "Hey, we're sorry about the salutation, but things for us lately have been like, you know, kind of weird. I'm Wolf." He proceeded to identify his companions. "This is Splitz, and the dwarf under the tree is Nuke-o."

"Outlandish namings, wot?" observed Mudge.

"Like, they ain't our given names, furry dude." Nuke-o ran a hand over his black crest. "Sarcastic otters, man. What next?"

Realization didn't so much strike Mudge as land splat in the middle of his consciousness in a wet, soggy lump. "These creatures are flotsam from your world, Jon-Tom."

"Hey, who you calling flotsam?" Splitz frowned as he turned to the one called Wolf. "Like, what's flotsam?"

Wolf ignored the query. "My real name's Jimmy Gathers. That's Felix Zimmerman on bass, Kenny Hill with his butt in the dirt. Kenny's our drummer."

"I guessed." Jon-Tom grinned. It didn't matter where you were, you could always tell a drummer. They formed a distinct subspecies with characteristics entirely their own. Jon-Tom wouldn't have been surprised to learn that there were subtle differences in their DNA.

If a chimp's DNA was ninety-nine percent that of a human, then a drummer's would be . . .

"Pancreatic Sludge," Gathers offered helpfully.

Jon-Tom blinked. "I beg your pardon?"

"The name of our group. That's it."

Mudge nodded approvingly. "The shoe fits." He sheathed his sword.

"How did you end up here, like this?" While it was nice to encounter visitors from home, Jon-Tom maintained his distance. He knew only what they'd told him and had no way of checking the truth of anything they said. Fellow musicians or not, he remained cautious.

"We're on a three-week holiday, dude," Hill grumbled. "Can't you tell?" He pulled wide the inside of his shirt. "See? Pierre Cardin rags."

Gathers's explanation was curt. "We were jerked here against our wills. What's your story?"

"Like my friend said, I'm a spellsinger. That's a kind of

sorcerer who uses music in his work. A lot of folks around here are losing their music. Even the whales are having their songs taken away. For all I know, the birds'll be next." He shrugged. "I'm trying to help. There's reason to believe something on this island is the cause of the problem." Looking around, he pointed toward a dark green copse. "It was actually some lost music that sort of led us here."

Singled out, the chord cloud drifted clear of its place of concealment. The band members regarded it laconically.

"Looks like an F-sharp," commented Zimmerman without missing a beat.

"Naw. It's a flat." Hill closed his eyes.

Gathers grinned. "The guys don't talk much, but they know their music." He lost the smile as he held up one hand, the fingers pinching half an inch of missing opportunity. "We were *this* close to signing a recording contract, man. Small label, local, but we were gonna cut a CD."

"Small, hell," groused Hill. "He had his studio in his garage."

"Yeah," Gathers conceded, "but it was, like, a *big* garage. The main thing is, he got stuff into the stores. He got airtime. Maybe only in his neighborhood, but when your neighborhood's New York, that ain't such a bad deal."

"What happened?" Jon-Tom tried to scrounge some sympathy for these obviously disoriented strangers. Had the cosmos not had a substantially different fate in store for him, his life might have taken a similar path.

"Our lead singer ups and dumps us. Just like that, man! We were doin' our first TV interview, they were gonna play the video we'd just finished, and Goldblum's like not payin' any attention. He's watchin' this pretty little techie assistant all the time.

"As soon as the interview's over, he's gone. 'Artistic differences,' was all he'd say. That techie put something in his ear and it went straight to his brain, man. What brain Goldblum had."

Hill absently peeled bark from a twig. "I mean, where are

you gonna find another Jewish-Vietnamese lead singer on short notice? Our producer was losing interest and we had to come up with somebody, anybody, fast or we'd blow the contract. This producer, he's kind of a hyper type, you know, and he, like, wanted to do everything right away or not at all."

"So you put an ad in the *Voice,* stick up want sheets in the usual places." Gathers looked unhappy. "Man, *everybody* wants in the business. There must be, like, you know, a shortage of singers. Or maybe our timing just sucked."

"Just sucked," muttered Zimmerman.

"Anyway," Gathers continued, "only this one guy shows, bright and early. He's no Jon Bon J in the looks department, but he ain't Meat Loaf, either. Kinda short, a little on the soft side, but we figured he'd work it off."

"Can't have a lead singer with a roll in a heavy metal band," Hill added. "Don't look good in an open vest."

"So he lays this long list of credits on us, real earnest-like. I mean, real impressive, you know? It sounds too good, but nobody else shows and we're, like, you know, pressed for time? We're supposed to record two tracks first thing Monday. So he says, like, no sweat, give him the lyrics and he'll be there."

"So we give him sheets and a cover tape and after the weekend we all show up at Mike's home studio."

"Oh, man." Zimmerman the one-man Greek chorus rolled his eyes.

Gathers went on. "The two techies are all ready, Mike's excited to go, we're tuned, sound's rolling, and this guy Hinckel flashes this stupid shit-eating smile and tells Kenny to start rockin'. I mean, he actually said that. I mean, you should've *heard* it."

"Lucky man he didn't." Zimmerman had now adopted the look of a stoned basset hound.

" 'Eard wot?" Mudge had finally become engrossed in the travelers' tale."

"His *voice,* dude."

Gathers was nodding vigorously. "My grandmother used

to have a saying about somebody who couldn't sing. 'He couldn't carry a tune in a bucket,' she'd say. This Hinckel guy, he couldn't lift the bucket."

"He was past awful, dude." The memory of it turned Zimmerman voluble. "He was the king of stink. Like, you know, the nadir?"

Gathers winced at the remembrance. "He couldn't lead, he couldn't follow, he couldn't phrase, he couldn't fake it. I don't know if he knew what any of the notes meant. He was so bad Mike's technicians couldn't take it. Pretty soon everybody in the studio is, like, laughing so hard they couldn't work.

"And the wonder of it is that this guy, he doesn't think anything's wrong! He doesn't understand what everyone's laughing at, or why Kenny looks like he's about to hurl. Hinckel, he wants to know why we've stopped playing 'cause he was just getting in the groove."

"That's what he said." Even now Hill couldn't believe it. " 'Getting into the groove.' "

"Nobody could look at him without cracking up," Gathers continued. "Maybe I should've been nicer to him, but shit, man, he'd wasted our time, and Mike's time, and technicians' time, and, like, those guys were getting paid, you know? We didn't have, like, the time or the money to screw around.

"So we threw him out. I mean, like in the movies, by his shirt and pants."

"Wot did you do then?" Mudge wondered.

Hill sighed. "Improvised as best we could. Jimmy and I took turns coverin' the vocals. We're no singers, but compared to Hinckel we sounded like Coverdale and Page."

"What happened to him?" Jon-Tom asked.

Hill and Gathers exchanged a glance. "Didn't see him again for a couple of months," the guitarist replied. "We had a party gig midtown. I mean, we took what we could get, the money wasn't bad, and it was worth it anyway for the exposure. There were supposed to be a lot of industry types there.

"It went pretty good. Afterward we're heading home over

the bridge in Felix's van, and, like, congratulating ourselves on maybe makin' a decent contact or two at the party, and suddenly the whole East River starts makin' like Gabriel."

"The angel?" Jon-Tom wondered.

Gathers frowned at him. "There's an angel named Gabriel? No man, *Peter* Gabriel. You know. Anyway, we're like totally freaked because we're a clean band, man, and nobody's taken anything at the party."

"Nothing." Zimmerman was emphatic.

"My first thought was that somebody slipped us something," Gathers explained. "Then we found ourselves here. Just like that. No more van, no more East River, no Jersey Turnpike, no Big Apple. No nothin'." He waved at their surroundings. "Just these rocks and these trees, which looked a lot better when we first got here."

"That's right," put in Hill. "This island didn't look like this all the time."

"One other thing." Gathers's countenance darkened. "Hinckel's waiting for us, and he's got this, like, real snotty look on his face."

"An aura of megalomania," ventured Zimmerman somberly, hinting at an education beyond the one generally available in cheap clubs and dingy venues.

"After he tells us that he's responsible for what happened," Gathers went on, "we all, like, try to rush him. You know what he does then? He sort of rises up into the air on this dark cloud of dissonance. Music to match his personality. And he just leaves, flies on up to the top of the mountain." The guitarist pointed. "Up there."

Jon-Tom and Mudge turned to follow the accusing finger, looking toward the spiraling black vortex that was slowly rotating about the uppermost crags. Sporadic thunder continued to rattle the slopes.

"Before he leaves," Gathers continued, "he tells us he's tapped into this evil force that gives him power over all music. Only in this world to start, but he's sure it won't be

long before he's master over all music everywhere." The guitarist shook his head. "What a weirdo."

"What kind of evil force?" Jon-Tom inquired.

Hill coughed. "How the hell should we know? We're just
musicians and he, like, didn't give us the details. Maybe he
found it in the phone book under 'Force, Evil.'"

Zimmerman nodded knowingly. "Like, there ain't *nothin'*
you can't find in the Manhattan Yellow Pages."

"Whatever it is"—Gathers scowled—"it was strong
enough to suck us over here. Wherever *here* is. He said he
wanted to make us pay for the way we treated him."

"Like he didn't try to screw us," Hill complained.

"You know what one of the worst things about living on
this island is?" Gathers went on. "We can't play our music.
Not a lick. We can improvise something to drum on and
something to strum, but as soon as we do, he steals the music.
I don't know how he does that, but he does."

Mudge eyed their torn, ragged attire sympathetically.
"Sounds like a real rotter, don't you know. Bastard didn't
even let you bring your clothes."

Hill drew back slightly. "What are you talkin' about,
whisker dude? These *are* our clothes."

"Oi, me apologies, guv." The otter forbore from further
comment.

"He's made himself lord of this island," Gathers informed
them, "and keeps workin' on this spell to steal all music
everywhere. With each practice he gets a little better at it, and
each time another load of music ends up on this dump."

"Even a prime doofus like Hinckel can sharpen his playing," Hill explained, "but not his singing. That's still as gross
as it gets."

"He's trapping all kinds of music," said Gathers. "I think
I've heard some of those whale songs you were talkin' about.
I recognize 'em 'cause the Exeter Whackoffs used to use
tapes of it in their act."

"Dude, the Exeter Whackoffs used *everything* in their act,"

Hill reminisced. "I remember one time they had, like, this cat—"

"The music," Jon-Tom prompted them. "Where does he keep it?"

"Inside the mountain." Zimmerman kicked at a pitted gray rock. "This whole island's built up from an old volcano, like. Plenty of lava tubes and hollows to stash stuff in."

"The stuff just lies there, sloshing back and forth inside the main crater singin' to itself, as wild and noisy a mix as you could imagine," Gathers explained. "A whole lake of ripped-off music." He indicated his tattered orange and black leather boots. "It's not an easy climb, dude. Should've had my Tevas."

"It was something to see." Hill sounded almost wistful. "Not to mention hear. I mean, you want to talk *counterpoint*, man . . ."

"Hinckel, he's storin' everything up there," Gathers continued. "Whale songs, bird songs, rock, folk, ethnic, electronic, classical, stuff like I never heard before, and all of it dumped together to get along as best it can."

"And the worst of it still sounds better than anything he can come up with," Zimmerman added emotionally.

"But why?" Jon-Tom wanted to know. "What's he after? What's his purpose in doing all this?"

Gathers's long locks shook as he replied helplessly, "How should I know? You'd have to ask him."

"At first we thought he wanted to steal it as some kind of, like, you know, revenge," Hill speculated. "Now we think there's more to it than that."

"Yeah," agreed Gathers. "Maybe he thinks that if he steals all the music everywhere, then people won't have any choice except to listen to him. And believe me, dudes, until you've heard Hieronymus Digbee Hinckel try to sing, a worse fate you can't imagine."

"Can't imagine," echoed Zimmerman.

"Righty-ho!" barked Mudge briskly. "We'll soon put a stop to this nonsense." He clapped Jon-Tom on the back. "Me mate, 'ere, 'e's not only a great spellsinger, 'e is, 'e's also a great . . . well, a bloomin' good musician."

"You're just bubbling over with compliments on this trip, aren't you?" Jon-Tom responded.

Mudge blinked innocently. "Why, mate, that's me natural nature, don't you know?"

"Won't do any good." Gathers sounded regretful. "I don't care how fine you are, man. Hinckel, he's gotten stronger every day. Go up there and he'll steal your music, too. Suck it right out of that funny-lookin' guitar you've got hanging against your back. Leave you standin' there lookin' stupid and mumbling to yourself."

"That's what he did to you?" Jon-Tom inquired.

Zimmerman nodded miserably. "Flat out. We can't even sing a cappella. It just comes out like a kind of croak, like."

Gathers tapped the blade of his homemade tomahawk in the flat of an open palm. "We've been playin' it real cool, waitin' and tryin' to bide our time so's we can get close to him. But while Hinckel can't sing worth shit, he ain't stupid, neither. He watches his ass all the time."

"We're not violent guys," Hill put in. "Offstage we're pretty laid back. But this is different. Hinckel's dangerous and he's gotta be stopped." He let his gaze rise toward the cloud-swathed crags. "Only problem is, like, he ain't alone. If he was, then the three of us would just hike up there and pound him."

"Pound him," echoed Zimmerman. "But he's got help."

" 'Elp?" Mudge was suddenly suspicious. "Wot kind o' 'elp?"

"You try to stop him and you'll see," said Gathers meaningfully. "It's worse than anything you can imagine."

"Worse than anything you've ever seen," agreed Hill "Or heard."

"I've seen and heard quite a bit." Jon-Tom remained calm. "And I've a pretty radical imagination." He nodded in the direction of the drifting, softly ringing chord cloud. "This bit of music, for example. I wonder if it's some that this Hinckel character stole but neglected to fully entrap. It's stronger music than most. I wonder if it escaped and came looking for help for its fellow notes. Chords support one another all the time."

"He ain't, like, perfect." Zimmerman chose his words carefully. "Powerful, yeah, but not like, you know, omnipotent. Not yet. But if anybody's gonna stop him, it better be soon."

"You guys look like grunge," Jon-Tom remarked, "but you don't talk like it."

"Actually, you look like 'ell," Mudge added, but under his breath.

"Hey, dude, just because we like our music heavy doesn't mean we ain't got brains, like," insisted Gathers.

"Speak for yourself." Hill was tapping out a beat on a flat rock with a couple of twigs he'd scavenged. Even this muted effort saw him eyeing the crest of the mountain nervously. "I like goin' around brainless."

"All right, some of us, then," Gathers corrected himself irritably. "What's your story, man?"

Jon-Tom remembered, "It was a long time ago. I was at college, trying to decide whether to stay with my music or finish law school."

"Tough decision, dude." Zimmerman sniggered. "Like, *not*."

"Think so? You don't know my family."

"Hey, don't whine to me about your ancestry, man," exclaimed Gathers sharply. "My family's from freakin' *Scarsdale*. I mean, it's not like they've disowned me, but when I go home and there's somebody visitin', I have to, like, use the servants' entrance, you know? My parents' friends think I'm somebody who's there to pick up the garbage."

"My family thinks I *am* the garbage," Zimmerman muttered.

"I was hoping that if the group hit big . . ." Gathers continued, "but now . . ." His voice trailed away and Jon-Tom realized that underneath the facade of cool they were really scared. Scared and lonely, not much more than a bunch of kids, all music and attitude. It was a condition he could empathize with. And now they didn't even have a tune to comfort them.

"I'll get your music back," he heard himself saying vehemently. "I'm sure it's up there with the rest of it."

"You go up there, you watch yourself, man," Hill warned him. "Hinckel may look like a nerd and sound like a toilet, but he's strong now. Real strong."

"We've 'andled worse before, ain't we, mate?" Mudge fingered the hilt of his sword. "You distract 'im with your singin' an' maybe I'll 'ave a chance to slit 'is bloomin' throat a little. Bleedin' difficult to make magic with 'alf a foot o' steel stickin' out o' your neck."

"This help he's acquired." Jon-Tom turned back to Gathers. "You can't describe it any better?"

The guitarist made a face. "Wouldn't do no good. It, like, changes according to his whim. Let's just say he ain't lonely up there. The forces he's gathered to him are, like, simpatico, you know?"

"And the worst of it is," Hill added, "he keeps singing to himself. *All the time.* If it's a real clear day and the wind is wrong, you can't not hear him." He eyed the swirling, angry clouds. "Be grateful for the thunder."

"Deuced odd sort o' thunder," Mudge observed. "Plenty o' noise, but no lightnin'."

Zimmerman speculated freely. "My own personal take on the storms is that his singing's so bad it generates an elemental migraine, and this is, like, you know, nature's way of protesting."

"To hear him is to hate him," added Hill. "That's our slogan, anyway. We're workin' on some songs about it. Maybe we can't make any music, but he can't stop us from thinking up lyrics."

Gathers nodded enthusiastically. "We've had a lot of time here. We've put together a whole double album." He looked wistful. "It'd sound great . . . if we could just get home."

Hill sat up suddenly. "Hey, dudes, your pet harmony's goin' apeshit!"

Scintillating and sparkling, ringing and chiming, the chord cloud was soaring up the slope, pausing to spin brilliantly on its axis, then returning. As they looked on, it repeated the sequence again and again.

"It gets impatient." Jon-Tom looked down at Mudge. "We've done enough talking. I guess if we're going to do this we'd better get on with it."

"Oi, for once I'm with you, mate." The otter's expression was resolute. "Imagine a world without music. Wot would a chap get drunk to? Wot would 'e dance to? Wot would 'e make . . ."

"Let's go. And no humming." Jon-Tom started after the eager, misty music. After a couple of steps he looked back. "Will you come with us? You guys have as big a stake in the outcome as anybody."

The band members exchanged a glance. Then Hill spoke for all of them. "What the hell. He can't do much more to us than he's done already."

"Damn straight," agreed Splitz Zimmerman.

Gathers advanced until he was standing alongside the spellsinger. "We'll come with you as far as we can. If we can help we will, but don't count on us. Hinckel, he knows us too well." He headed upslope. "I only hope we catch him in one of his quiet moods."

"I've heard bad singing before," Jon-Tom assured him as he stepped carefully over a fallen, rotting palm trunk.

The guitarist looked back at him. "No, you haven't, spellsinger dude. No, you haven't."

CHAPTER 22

THE TERRAIN GREW PROGRESSIVELY STEEPER AND MORE rugged. Though because of the otter's short legs there were places where they had to assist Mudge, they were never in any danger of falling. Surmounting even the most difficult rock face called only for determination, balance, and a steady hand.

Jon-Tom was grateful the ascent was not especially difficult. While he'd retained his strength, the years had wreaked havoc with his wind. Even the usually indefatigable Mudge was starting to wheeze, rapid-fire little puffs that were in keeping with his faster respiration.

As they climbed, the vegetation began to thin. All of it had been damaged to some degree. The cloud chord led them on.

"Hear that?" Jon-Tom paused both to listen and to rest. Mudge nodded.

A brilliant, pellucid susurration filled the air, intensifying as they listened. It was muddied but still euphonious.

"Not so bad," Mudge opined.

"That's not Hieronymus." Gathers pointed abruptly to his left. "Look, here it comes!"

Pouring through a saddle on the side of a mountain, a stream of music spilled toward them. It sounded strained, a reluctant clamor whose proximity caused the chord cloud to duck behind Jon-Tom and ring nervously like an agitated alarm clock.

Whole measures, ripped from their original melodic lines, clung like harmonic driftwood to the musical mass. Reverber-

ations, individual notes, plunks and whistles, echoing thren-
odies, lullabies, and martial roars, all swarmed and mixed
uncontrollably within the stream. Like a sandstorm composed
of notes instead of dust, the river of sound rushed past them,
filling their ears with a mad cacophony the likes of which no
dozen composers working in tandem could have concocted.

It pulled powerfully at the chord cloud, but that isolated
patch of harmony pressed itself against Jon-Tom's back,
using the duar as a shield. Only when the roaring had rushed
on by, leaving a few abandoned arpeggios in its wake, did the
cloud reemerge.

"Wish I could play like that." Zimmerman's ears were
ringing.

"No one plays like that." Gathers was shaking his head, as
if trying to dislodge a handful of notes that had become stuck
in his cochlea.

"It turned and went up the mountain." Hands on hips, a
grim-faced Hill was staring upward. "There's always new
music going in, but never any coming out. He keeps sucking
in more and more." The drummer caught Jon-Tom looking at
him. "Hinckel."

A few laggard streamers of sound ascended in the wake of
the main flow. Reaching out, Jon-Tom temporarily blocked
the path of what sounded like a Mozart quartet as interpreted
by John Coltrane. It was neither, of course. Except for the
sounds of Pancreatic Sludge, he knew that all the music here
had to be of this world. Dropping his hand, he let the chords
race freely on upward. It sounded to him as though they
departed reluctantly.

What if the crazed Hinckel grew powerful enough to start
stealing sounds from Jon-Tom's former world? No rock, no
metal, no rap, no grunge. No jazz or folk, no classical or
country-western, no ethnic or world music. To hear the band
members talk, Hinckel wouldn't leave so much as a nursery
rhyme. Jon-Tom didn't think he'd want to live in a world
without music. Any world.

Thunder pealed overhead. There was work to be done.

That's when the *sound* struck him.

He cringed. Though less sensitive, Mudge found himself grinding his teeth together. It was the aural equivalent of fingernails dragging across a blackboard, of a cheese grater peeling glass. It was as if someone were dragging a nail file across his nerves.

Their guides were not immune. Splitz Zimmerman shuddered visibly while Wolf Gathers squeezed his eyes shut and clapped his hands to his ears. Nuke-o Hill handled it better than any of them, but that was understandable. Hill was a drummer.

The awful din faded. Straightening, Jon-Tom took a deep breath. The sonic tremor had passed through him like a dull knife. Having shattered into a dozen individual puffs of sound, the chord cloud was only now re-forming.

"First time's the worst." Zimmerman was sympathetic.

The bass player was right. As they resumed the ascent, the sound came again. Though it continued, Jon-Tom found he was better able to tolerate the hideous voice. The guitar accompaniment, if such it could be called, was so atrocious it sounded as if the player were fingering catgut strings still attached to the original feline.

Choosing his footing carefully as he resumed the climb, Jon-Tom found that the voice was making him sweat. It didn't merely grate; it abraded, it corroded, it made one pray to be struck temporarily deaf. Jon-Tom would far rather have been subjected to a concert by a choir of tone-deaf banshees.

"Wonnnnn't you be my bayyyy-beeee!" it bawled like the voice of Hell itself. No, Jon-Tom decided. Not even Hades could tolerate such pandemonium. Compared to that voice, Jon-Tom knew he sounded like Caruso. Or at least Daltrey.

Mudge's fur had fluffed up like a spooked cat's. "Bloody 'ell but I'm grateful me ears are as small as they are! 'Tis a sound not o' this world."

"Actually, I think Hieronymus is from near Stuyvesant Town," Gathers informed them.

"Hard to believe such gibbering could come from a human throat." Jon-Tom swallowed hard.

"Can you imagine tryin' to make a recording with that as your lead?" Gathers brushed at his long locks. "I sort of think of it as the human equivalent of all those new electronic rodent repellers."

When the unearthly singing resumed it was backed by unidentifiable vocals and instrumentals only half as hideous as the lead itself. From what Jon-Tom could hear they were adequately gruesome in their own right. Though it was something of a strain just to form words while being subjected to the dissonant barrage, he forced himself to shut out much of the demonic doo-wop.

"What's all the rest of it?" he asked Gathers.

"I told you. Hieronymus isn't alone."

"Well," he muttered stubbornly, "it's only music."

"He's got to be stopped," Zimmerman exclaimed.

The band members accompanied them for another hundred feet or so before Gathers finally had to halt. He'd been slinging his head for the past several minutes, as if an angry wasp had become lodged in his ear. His expression was wretched.

"We can't go any farther, spellsinger. You've got to understand, we've had to listen to this stuff every day for weeks."

"Months." By now even the phlegmatic Hill was covering his ears.

"Eons." Zimmerman's eyes were seeping badly. "Never thought I'd hear anything that'd make industrial grunge sound sweet. Hieronymus makes a construction site sound like the Philharmonic."

Gathers nodded agreement. "Compared to him, thrash is *The Lark Ascending.*"

Jon-Tom frowned uncertainly. "I don't know that piece. Smashing Pumpkins?"

Gathers shook his head. "Vaughan Williams. I spent a year at Juilliard. Liked the music, couldn't stand the people. We're gonna have to leave you here."

Zimmerman nodded vigorously. "If I get any closer to the source, my head's gonna split."

"That's all right," Jon-Tom assured them. "We understand."

"We does?" Mudge was less forbearing.

Leaving the duo with handshakes and words of encouragement, the three band members turned and started back down. Rocks and pebbles skidded beneath their feet as they hastened to retreat.

"Not the best o' omens, mate."

"It was brave of them to accompany us this far." Turning, Jon-Tom resumed the climb. "Besides, you heard what they said before. They've tried to stop this Hinckel and failed. Now it's up to us." The black cloud and its resident thunder closed in suffocatingly around them.

Gasping for air, they eventually emerged onto a small plateau. Off in the distance a few sharp spires rose still higher. Between the edge of the stony, sheared-off platform on which they stood and the remaining crags squatted a turreted castle constructed of gray gloom that was an ill-conceived parody of every medieval fortress which had ever been built to satisfy a deranged nobleman.

It was actually fashioned of the same brooding basalt as the mountain, the building blocks torn from the ragged flanks of the great volcano. The upper levels commanded a sweeping view of the sea where it showed beyond the fringes of the all-encompassing black cloud. There was an entrance with a drawbridge and portcullis but no moat. An inner keep glistened with lingering dew.

Jon-Tom was thankful no architect was in their company, for merely gazing upon the ramshackle structure was enough to turn a professional's stomach. Walls canted crazily at impossible angles. None of the parapets was level, none of the turrets perpendicular to the ground. The central keep wasn't in much better shape. Dark banners flew from the apex of each turret as well as from the higher interior. As he studied his and Mudge's dismal destination, Jon-Tom had the feeling that the weight of the stone was all that kept the edifice from collapsing.

Of life there was no sign save for the occasional tooth-grating hubbub which emanated from somewhere within.

"The venue fits the music," Mudge commented grimly.

With an absent nod, Jon-Tom turned to take a last look behind them. Below lay the blighted rain forest. Farther on he could see the rocky shoreline with their boat and its cargo of displaced femininity. Beyond lay the ocean, clean and inviting, spacious and alive with the promise of distant welcomes. Even at their present altitude he thought he could make out the periodic spouts of the many cetaceans who had gathered around the island. Songless cetaceans, he reminded himself.

Taking a deep breath as if he could somehow inhale resolve, he brought the duar around to his front. His fingers weren't as nimble as they'd once been, his lung power not as long-lasting. He'd traded them in for experience, all of which he had the feeling he was going to need.

"Let's go."

"Right with you as always, mate." So saying, the otter accompanied his friend onward, keeping the usual couple of discreet steps behind.

Together they entered the castle.

CHAPTER 23

THE DRAWBRIDGE WAS DOWN, THE SULLEN IRON PORTCULLIS raised. As they ambled in, not even an ant appeared to challenge their advance.

"Not much security." Mudge scanned the parapets in expectation of ambush. None was forthcoming.

As they passed into the great hall of the keep, they encountered sculptures and paintings man and otter did their best to ignore. Like the heinous music, the decor grated on the senses. From what they could see, the castle's master had all the aesthetic sensibility of a banana slug. Execrably executed black velvet portraits of unrecognizable musicians lined opposing walls.

"All 'umans," Mudge observed of the pictures. "Leastwise, I think they are. The bleedin' work is so bad 'tis difficult sometimes to tell. I've eaten clams that could paint better."

"Clams have no hands," Jon-Tom pointed out.

"I rest me case, mate."

They were approaching the back of the hall. The poorly woven yellow and brown carpet across which they were striding ended at the base of a throne. Constructed of solid five-carat gold, it was embellished with musical motifs.

Seated atop a cotton cushion several days shy of a desperately needed washing and cradling an electric guitar was a skinny, chicken-pox-scarred figure. It wore artificially and imperfectly faded jeans, sneakers that looked superficially costly but were in reality rejects from a K mart blue-light special, a fraying, cut-open-to-the-lint-filled-navel sweatshirt from which the improperly appliqued cartoon characters were already peeling, and a backward-turned unauthorized navy blue L.A. Raiders baseball cap which had been produced on the cheap in Hong Kong. The pirate in the emblem had a distinctly oriental aspect.

One hand rested lazily on the guitar while the other picked at a huge rhinestone-encrusted golden bowl piled high with french fries drowning in ketchup. The body was all fish-white flesh and uncoordination, the face narrow and pinched. Brown eyes were framed by a greasy mat of black hair. It reminded Jon-Tom of a portrait he'd once seen of a sour-visaged Ichabod Crane, in the cheap edition. Try as he might, he could find nothing about the individual seated before them that was in the least appealing.

Wiping a mushy fragment of french fry from the corner of his mouth, the figure stiffened as it caught sight of them. The piece of potato tumbled to the floor, there to join a small but growing mound of deceased cousins. Hard to believe a healthy tuber had sacrificed its life for such a fate.

While noting that no cord trailed from the guitar, Jon-Tom knew from the wailing they'd heard that it had to be plugged into *something*. Sorcery could provide a suitable substitute for a socket. Professionally, he found himself wondering if it was AC or DC sorcery.

An unpleasant sound rumbled in the pit of the scrawny figure's belly. "Who the hell are you and how did you get up here?" It was the shrill voice of a dyspeptic crow, concerned but not panicky.

The weight of the duar was reassuring. Mudge stood ready at his side (well, a few paces behind). Thunder boomed outside the entrance to the castle. It had been a long time since he'd confronted a situation this intense. What if he'd lost it? This wasn't sitting around the fire, entertaining family and friends while cubs played in the background. There was much at stake here, not least perhaps their own lives.

What if this time his gift for lyrical invention failed? Or his strength, or his fingering? What if . . . ?

Don't borrow trouble, Talea was always telling him. Plenty will find you of its own accord.

"We walked," he told the skinny musician.

Hieronymus Hinckel's gaze fastened on the duar. "You a musician, too?"

No elaborate insults, no grandstanding cursing, no demonic threat could have strengthened Jon-Tom's will any better than that simple statement.

"That's right. I sing and play duar. What about you?"

"Plays with 'imself, most likely." Despite their surroundings, or perhaps because of them, Mudge managed an otterish snicker.

Hinckel's eyes flicked sideways. "I see you've got a big rat with you."

Not only did Mudge emerge from Jon-Tom's shadow, he advanced several paces forward. "I'll 'ave you know that I'm a bloomin' otter, guv. I'd also like you to know, just by way o' casual conversation, that you're the ugliest example o' your tribe 'tis ever been me misfortune to set eyes on."

"Yeah, well, lemme tell you that—" Hinckel halted in midreply. "Wait a minute. What am I arguing with you for? I'm in charge here. I command the, uh, music of the spheres."

"What kind of spheres?" Jon-Tom's fingers were ready. "Ball bearings?"

"A comedian. Where you from? Not around here."

"Originally L.A. Now . . . now I guess you'd have to say that I *am* from around here."

Hinckel nodded. "Okay. Because you're an ex-city boy I'll give you and your rat-bro one chance to get out before I lose my temper. I'm being generous. You interrupted my breakfast."

Eyeing the soggy mountain of french fries, Jon-Tom came close to losing his own latest meal. "Was everything we heard on our way up original with you?"

"Damn right. I'm workin' on a ballad."

"Ballad?" Mudge made a gagging sound. "You call those hideous sounds a ballad?"

"That's good, Mudge," Jon-Tom whispered. "Do everything you can not to incite him."

"Oi, why dance around the dickery bush, mate? You 'eard that bile clear as me."

"You must have something going for you to have made it this far." Hinckel turned thoughtful. In addition to everything else, Jon-Tom noted, their nemesis had terrible posture. "Casual travelers don't call at my island."

"A piece of music led us here," Jon-Tom told him. "A cluster of associated chords." Looking around, he wasn't surprised to see that the cloud of notes which had accompanied them all this way had chosen to remain outside the keep. He didn't blame it.

"It needs to be returned to its rightful owner. Like all the rest of the music you've appropriated."

"Rightful owner?" Hinckel was amused. "Now there's a fresh concept."

"This thieving of music has to stop." Fully committed, Jon-Tom pressed on. "You have to leave honest musicians and natural songsters like the whales alone."

"Like hell I do."

"Your former band mates say that you're doing this so that you'll be the only one left able to make music, and that because of that people will have to listen to you." The spellsinger lowered his voice. "I can tell you right now it won't make any difference. You can put every piece of music in the world under lock and key. It won't make people like you any better."

"Won't it? We'll see." A twisted grin, a sort of visual equivalent of the belch which had preceded it, creased the thin mouth. "So my ex-sidemen, my *buddies,* led you up here. I've kind of been ignoring them lately. They're overdue for a visit."

"We would've found our own way." Jon-Tom was anxious not to do anything that would contribute to the already pitiful condition of the unfortunate trio.

"Call themselves a band," Hinckel was muttering. "Bunch

of Jersey pricks. That Gathers; thought he could play guitar. And Hill. What a loser! As for Zimmerman, man, you'd think *anybody* could play bass." Their host's laugh was an unlovely screech. "Well, look at 'em now! The lost goys."

"Why don't you send them home?" Jon-Tom restrained his rising anger. "There's no need to keep them here."

"Oh, but there is! I like for them to have to listen to me. They wouldn't listen to me when they needed a new singer. Well, they can damn sure listen to me now. For eternity."

"Oi, but you are a vicious one," Mudge growled.

"Not vicious. Righteous, rat. I know what I can do, musically. I know my talent. Soon so will everyone else—they'll have no alternative. Anyone who wants to listen to music will have to listen to *mine*." Looking smug, he sat back on the throne. "Once they've acknowledged my superior talent, once they've begun to appreciate me, then maybe, *maybe,* I'll let them have some of their old music back. A trickle to a piccolo here, a silly little love song there.

"But not until I've received the acclaim my talent is due." He gestured diffidently. "Meanwhile, I give you your freedom. Go on, leave. Take a hike. I'm feeling magnanimous today."

Jon-Tom frowned. "You don't talk like your average heavy metal singer."

Hieronymus Hinckel let out a snort. "You think that schmuck Gathers is the only one with an education? I was a year short of a B.A. in economics at NYU."

Mudge leaned to whisper to his companion. " 'E's chock-full of lies, mate. Who ever 'eard o' someone goin' from studyin' economics to bein' a lead singer in a mad band?"

"We're not leaving." Jon-Tom steeled himself.

When Hinckel's brows drew together, creasing his already narrow face, he no longer looked quite so elementally nerdy. He managed to look almost threatening.

"I'm warning you. I'm only giving you a chance because you're not one of these stupid nattering animals like that rat standing next to you."

Mudge drew his sword. "Not goin' to be so easy for you to sing, guv, without any vocal cords. Or maybe we'll try permanently raisin' your voice a couple o' octaves an' see if it improves any. I guarantee your disposition will.

"As for thinkin' to insult me by callin' me an animal, why, we're all animals together 'ere, guv."

"That's so," agreed Jon-Tom proudly.

"You're right." Hinckel spun sideways and put his legs up on the side of the throne. "You *have* been here a long time. So what do you expect me to do?"

"Free the music. Remove the sorceral shackles that hobble each harmony. Let it return to the instruments and throats that wait." With a gesture Jon-Tom took in the grim battlements. "If you want to stay here and be king of the island and sing yourself silly I'll be the first to support your right to do so. But taking everyone else's music leaves you a poorer musician, not a better."

"Too bloody right," Mudge barked. "You can steal a lot o' things, guv. I should know. But you can't steal talent."

"What pretty speechifying. Are you both finished?"

Jon-Tom had been readying his lyrics. "Not quite. If you still don't get it, well, I've always been a firm believer in audiovisual aids." His hand brushed the duar and he began to sing.

An evanescence unlike any Mudge had ever seen before began to emerge from the depths of the duar's nexus. Bright as neon, the deep purple flux oozed from the impossible omphalos where the wondrous instrument's double sets of strings intersected. The otter retreated several steps. At such times there was no telling what might happen.

Jon-Tom himself was often the last to know.

"One thing 'bout the music
Most folks don't seem to know
Ain't no good to lock it up
A song needs space to grow
Doesn't matter what kind

Classical, rap, jazz, or show
Find it in your heart to find
Freedom for that rock and roll!"

Hieronymus Hinckel was less than impressed. Straightening once more, he eyed the cloud dubiously, as though it were a puff of pollution clouding the intersection of Second and Twenty-sixth.

"Hey, not bad." Rising from his erstwhile throne, he wandered over to a tall, narrow window and peered out. A rush of sound washed over the room, a vast musical sigh as of a hundred clarinets suddenly deprived of air. "Looks like you've managed to free a *small* amount of the music I've gathered here. Now I'll just have to bring it back." He turned to regard his visitors.

"Of course, I'm also going to have to make you stop. Didn't really want to take your music, but if you insist on playing hardball . . ."

Jon-Tom managed an uncharacteristic sneer even as he was concocting additional lyrics. "Hum a few bars and I'll give it a shot."

Smiling unpleasantly, from a front pocket Hinckel extracted a battered but still functional harmonica. Putting it to his lips, he blew a few simple, basic, incredibly off-key notes.

The purple haze which had begun to dominate the atmosphere of the central hall recoiled as if from a blow. It all but vanished before gathering new strength from Jon-Tom's lyrics and a shift to a major key.

Surprised, Hinckel stumbled back in the direction of the throne. The air of cockiness he'd maintained ever since their arrival vanished. As Jon-Tom continued to play and sing, the purple cloud pressed close. When Hinckel, clearly deciding that stronger methods were in order, finally began to sing, the cloud's advance was slowed but not shattered.

"That's it, mate!" Hovering close at his friend's side, Mudge was hopping about wildly, waving his sword over his head. "Give it to 'im! Show 'im wot real spellsingin's about! Fix 'im so 'e can't co-opt so much as a lazy lie-about stanza ever again!"

"I'll do just that," Jon-Tom growled, "if you don't cut my head off with that damn sword!"

"Oi, right." The otter promptly lowered his enthusiasm along with his weapon.

Unable to faze either the menacing purple cloud or Jon-Tom's music, a wide-eyed Hinckel had retreated all the way to his garish sit-upon. When Mudge seemed about to dart forward and put an end to the business with a most unmelodic thrust of his sword, the would-be singer turned and let out a cry of desperation. It was the piteous baying of a mistreated child; of the one always picked last for any game, of he who perpetually finished, not at the bottom of his class (which would have bestowed a certain perverse distinction), but simply in the lower tenth, that inchoate academic abyss from which no hint of excellence ever arises.

In response to his moan, shapes began to emerge from the insubstantiality that heretofore had held sway behind the throne. Beyond the fortress battlements lightning flared for the first time since Jon-Tom and Mudge had set foot on the island.

Black lightning.

Angry thunder rattled the ill-hewn stones of the castle, shaking them in their footings. Hinckel's lyrics were largely unintelligible, his music as excruciating as ever, but this time there was an underlying desperation to each chord, a pathetic necessity that had previously been lacking. So pitiful was it that Jon-Tom hesitated.

It was not his hesitation which cost them control. He and Mudge simply found themselves outnumbered.

Emerging from the darkness, the various specters were attired in everything from satin and silk to cotton waistcloth and breeches. Some wore Romanic togas while others showed off torn blue jeans and battered sandals. Bleached tie-dyes backgrounded chipped love beads, hairy arms bulged from too-small tuxedos, and black leather jackets glowed with lace trim.

One apparition approaching Mudge was clad in a manner so hideous that the hardened otter was forced to look away.

"Not that!" Mudge moaned. "Anythin' but . . . but *plaid*!"

Into the great hall they drifted on wings fashioned of filthy feathers and frayed membrane, each and every one of them years overdue for a bath. As they drifted, they played. And sang, and hummed, and clapped their hands to a beat no two of them seemed able to follow. In their hands they carried their instruments, from ancient lutes to not-quite-state-of-the-art synthesizers and everything in between.

Jon-Tom recognized a viola da gamba. One apparition wrestled with a mistuned gamelan. There were flutes and guitars, maracas and drums, didgereedoos and banjos. The phantasms sang as they played.

While each individually realized distinct degrees of tastelessness, not a one of them could match Hieronymus Hinckel when it came to sheer ugh. Though several did come close, Jon-Tom had to admit as his outraged ears began to ring. All poor Mudge could do to try and fend off the aural horror was hold his sword out in front of him with both hands, as if it might function as some sort of steel talisman. But while the blade could cut easily through flesh and bone, it was useless against tectonically bad music.

Once more the otter retreated behind his friend. "In the name o' the Great Odor, wot *is* this?"

"Spirits." It was becoming a real struggle to sustain any kind of musical comportment in the face of such overwhelming ghastly sonics. "The shades of dead musicians from my world." Jon-Tom winced in pain. "The worst failures and most talentless performers in the history of popular music must be in this room."

A wild-eyed Hinckel confidently slid off the throne to confront them. "Hey, they're baaaad."

"You're telling me." A particularly grating *whanggg* from

an acoustic guitar brought tears to Jon-Tom's eyes. As a riff it
was pure raff.

Hinckel continued to advance. "They're just misunder-
stood, like I am. Though none of them's as good, of course."

Mudge retreated from the hideous performance. "Do
somethin', mate! I can't stand it much longer!"

As he detected what he thought must be Gregorian chant
executed (and that was surely the right word) to a disco beat,
Jon-Tom, too, found himself having to give ground. His
retreat was cut off by the shade of a shambolic Elvis imper-
sonator from Uttar Pradesh who was essaying "Jailhouse
Rock" in a voice that verged on the Lovecraftian. His funeral
persona was complete to sequined white Vegas outfit, long
sideburns, and pompadour greased with hog lard. Worse than
a travesty, it was potentially lethal.

Hovering on slim batwings, a squat, tubby ex-accountant's
assistant from the cheaper suburbs of Osaka was fighting to
render (and that was surely the right word) a classic Bessie
Smith soliloquy. A more lyrical sound could have been produced by cutting titanium with a chain saw.

There was a would-have-been rocker from East Prussia
who added to the harmonic devastation by flagellating "Stairway to Heaven" with his accordion, a New England preppie
complete to Yale sweater, white slacks, and yachting loafers
struggling in an aching New England drawl to mimic the best
of Joe Cocker, and a humorless dyke from Des Moines out to
convince eternity she could indeed play "I Will Always Love
You" on her kazoo.

And many, all too many more.

If the threat hadn't been so real, it would have been drop-
dead funny. As it was, that was half true, and Jon-Tom was
acutely conscious of the rising danger. He had to find some
way to fight back. But it was hard to think of chords and
lyrics when your ears were screaming in pain, your teeth were
jangling, and the soul of music itself was being riven before
your very ears.

In the midst of the caterwauling, cacophonic specters he

had called forth from some unimaginable Necronomicon of Pop stood Hieronymus Hinckel and his harmonica, grinning like a malevolent troll. Beset from all sides, Jon-Tom's purple haze writhed and twisted under the dissonant assault. Just as antimatter could annihilate matter, so Hinckel's antiharmony threatened to do the same to whatever spellsong Jon-Tom tried to promulgate.

The odious vibrations threatened to shake the irreplaceable duar to splinters. If the duar failed, all was lost. Jon-Tom saw no recourse but to retreat.

"*Midi, veni, vici!*" Hinckel cackled. Beckoning his army of failures to follow, he loped off in pursuit of the intruders.

Trailed by Hinckel's wailing phantasms, Jon-Tom and Mudge fled the keep. Around them the solid rock of the mountain was exfoliating as the antimusic pulverized the gray basalt, reducing it to traumatized shards. It was not surprising that in the confusion they missed the slope by which they had ascended.

Screeching to a stop at the edge of a sheer precipice, Mudge sought frantically for an alternate route. Waves crashed against naked rock impossibly far below, their echoing boom a distant white-foam whisper. Jon-Tom slowed to a halt alongside.

Hinckel and his unholy chorus were right behind.

"Sorry, man. You had your chance. I can't let you or anyone else stand in my way." Then he did the worst thing possible.

Accompanied by his spectral attendants, he began to sing.

The open air did nothing to improve his voice, as pernicious an instrument as was ever propounded by an inimical strand of DNA.

Mudge teetered at the edge of the drop, paws clapped desperately over his ears. "Do somethin', Jon-Tom! I can't stand it!"

The spellsinger peered into the gorge. Not even an otter's agility could get them down that smooth rock face. If they could cross the chasm to the next peak lower down, they could easily negotiate a path to the shore. Since neither of them possessed wings or the immediate prospect of acquiring same, this seemed an unlikely course of action.

"I don't know . . ."

"Sing somethin' 'opeful, optimistic," Mudge urged him frantically. "Sing it loud, sing it clear."

The years had given Jon-Tom practice in composing melodies and lyrics under pressure. The song he eventually essayed was as lovely as Hinckel's was harsh. Compared to their antagonist, Jon-Tom's usually uneven tenor sounded like Nat King Cole.

Exactly how Donner's solo from the conclusion of *Das Rheingold* sprang to mind he couldn't have said, but a rock version of the heroic soliloquy turned out to be exactly what the situation called for. He didn't have a hammer with which to strike the stone underfoot, but he could call upon some seriously heavy metal.

Purple haze billowed from the duar, not as a cloud this time but in a straight, almost machined arc. It leaped from the duar's nexus across the dizzying abyss, changing color as it coalesced. Racing through all the hues of the spectrum, it solidified into a rainbow bridge that not only spanned the chasm but didn't terminate until it reached all the way to the distant shoreline.

Half mad from the pain of being subjected to Hinckel's macabre vocalizing, Mudge didn't hesitate. He jumped out onto the rainbow and started down, his boots sinking a couple of inches into soft florid evanescence with every stride.

"Come on, mate!" he called back to Jon-Tom. "She's holdin'!"

"Not fair, not fair!" Hinckel tried to follow, but his courage wasn't sufficient to let him step out onto the shimmering, translucent bridge. He didn't have to. A ketchup-stained finger pointed in Jon-Tom's direction. "Get 'em! Go for the ears. Turn up the volume!"

On tattered but all-too-functional wings, the dissonant choir soared out over the bridge in pursuit.

"Don't look down, mate!" While wide enough to accommodate them side by side, the rainbow arch was hardly expansive. On either side the earth fell away for several thousand feet.

Harmonic travesty assaulted their ears as they ran. Looking back, Jon-Tom saw that Hinckel's minions were rapidly closing the gap between them. "They're coming after us!"

Mudge tried to increase his pace. He could move much faster than Jon-Tom, but his short legs put him at a serious disadvantage.

"We'll never make it, mate!" the otter gasped. "They can fly faster than we can run."

"I know. You can't outrun bad music."

Hinckel intended to finish them, he knew. He wasn't about to let someone of Jon-Tom's ability run loose on his island, wouldn't tolerate his presence as he did that of his sorry ex-band members. Already the rainbow was beginning to vibrate uncertainly as it suffered the distorting harmonics.

Their pursuers had wings. Could he give himself wings?

Of all things, what sprang unbidden to mind was a commercial jingle for a girl's doll. A ludicrous snatch of mercantile doggerel, but it would have to serve. He didn't have time to ruminate and reflect. Providing it with a ZZ Top lilt, he gave voice to a chorus of mind-numbing mediocrity.

Silver air swirled about their feet. There were soft pinging sounds. An instant later they had resumed their downhill flight, this time accelerating without effort. Their outraged pursuers redoubled their efforts both aerial and musical, to no avail. The distance between pursuers and the pursued began to widen.

All Jon-Tom and Mudge had to do now was keep their balance.

"Bloody 'ell, mate; wot are these things?" Blessed with astonishing natural agility and a low center of gravity, Mudge had no difficulty maintaining his equilibrium. While he quickly mastered the situation, Jon-Tom was forced to work at it.

"They're called rollerblades!" Even though the otter was skating right alongside, Jon-Tom had to raise his voice to make himself heard. The wind in their ears increased along with their velocity.

"Methinks I like 'em!" So saying, the otter began to skate backward, then on alternate feet, while Jon-Tom struggled mightily just to remain vertical. He almost said something when Mudge executed a neat forward flip, landing effortlessly on both skates. *Screw him,* he thought. *If he goes sailing off the edge, it'll be his own damn fault.* He was too busy keeping upright to voice criticisms.

"Never saw the like!" As he raced along, the otter bent double to study the alien devices now attached to his boots. They weren't wings, but they enabled the two of them to rapidly outdistance the pursuing phantasms. The frightful music was now no more than a scratchy murmur in the distance.

"Left 'em starin' at themselves, we 'ave!" Gleefully, Mudge looked over at his friend. "Only one thing troubles me a mite, mate."

"What's that?" Jon-Tom didn't dare let his gaze deviate from the multihued path ahead.

" 'Ow do you stop in these things?"

"You got me." Nearly losing his balance, the spellsinger flailed madly with both arms and managed to recover. His duar bounced and bonged against his back.

Using one hand to keep his feathered cap from flying off, the otter crouched low on his blades. "Righty-ho, then. I expect we'll find out when we reach the bottom. Till then I aim to enjoy every minim o' this. 'Tis a grand way to go, in every sense o' the word!"

Moving at a velocity somewhere between twenty and two thousand miles per hour, they rocketed past the startled trio of displaced Jerseyites. As soon as they recognized the speedsters, the ragged musicians let out a cheer. Neither man nor otter could turn to acknowledge the shout of approval: They were too busy trying to keep on their feet.

Their constant companion from the time they'd left the Bell-woods, the glowing chord cloud was forced to stretch itself to keep up with them. Attenuated to a thin line of notes, it looked like a pink wire pacing them down the rainbow slope. Having less mass than your average ghost, it could do nothing to help brake them.

Having adopted an air of resigned detachment, Jon-Tom noted that the ground was coming up very fast now. He still had no idea how to stop. Nor could he utilize the duar; it was ludicrous to think of trying to play anything at the speed they were traveling. A wild light in his eyes, Mudge hung close to his side. It was a gleam Jon-Tom hadn't seen in years. His ram-bunctious, irrepressible friend had reverted to the otter of his youth. Should they fail to survive their escape, at least one of them would perish in a state of sublime contentment.

Barely able to acknowledge the enthusiastic waves and shouts, the two novice bladers shot past the assembled princesses and quartet of soldiers. Appropriately, the rainbow bridge terminated at the base of a cluster of wave-polished black boulders situated where the land met the water. There was no way anyone could possibly survive the coming impact.

Jon-Tom was about to close his eyes when a swirling, con-fused haze coalesced before them. In its midst hovered a by-now familiar shape.

"It's about time! I didn't think I'd ever—" The fixed com-pound eyes couldn't widen, but the multiple jaw sections part-ed in surprise and both antennae shot straight up as man and otter plowed into the scintillating mist.

It sucked away their inertia as efficiently as Jon-Tom would slurp chocolate milk with a straw. Throwing up his hands at the last instant to shield his face, he felt himself strike something unyielding. His stomach did a two and a half gainer with a triple twist. Nearby, Mudge let out a yelp of surprise.

Jon-Tom decided the Earth was flat, just as the ancients had insisted all along. Someone had just flipped it like a coin, and against all odds it had come down on its edge.

CHAPTER 24

WHEN HE NEXT OPENED HIS EYES, HE WAS LYING ON A PAR-
quet floor of yellow-orange wood. The individual tiles
formed interlocking hexagons. Gone were the blades on his
feet. His first thought was for the precious duar, which had
miraculously survived intact.

The floor didn't feel right. Closer inspection revealed that
it was not made of wood but some kind of clever plasticized
imitation. Feeling carefully of himself he found he was
bruised and sore but otherwise unhurt. Nothing was broken or
bleeding, everything appeared to work as nature intended.

What nature hadn't intended, he told himself, was whatever had just happened to them.

Mudge was already on his feet, sword in hand as he confronted their fellow traveler. It was, Jon-Tom had noted just
before everything had gone cockeyed, the peculiar insectoid
who had been dogging them ever since they'd left Mashupro.

It stood facing them, fiddling with the thorax controls for
the device strapped to its back. As Jon-Tom looked on, the
instrument's internal lights faded to black.

Mudge didn't take his eyes off the creature. "Jon-Tom, are
you . . . ?"

"I'm okay, I'm fine." To prove it he made himself stand.
His muscles registered a formal protest with his nervous system, but complied.

"This was not foreseen," their host was saying.

"You're not kidding." Jon-Tom towered over the insectoid,
which stood eye-level with Mudge.

The chamber in which they found themselves had a domed ceiling. Furniture designed to accommodate someone with as many limbs as Jon-Tom and Mudge put together occupied all but the far wall. This was filled to the ceiling with electronics of a type unknown to Jon-Tom. Not that this was surprising. He had never been technically adept, believing, for example, that all computers were inherently hostile toward him and that any switch on a stereo beyond the volume up/down and on/off was superfluous.

Of one thing he was certain: There was technology of a high order at work here. Or magic. It was all a matter of definition, or a definition of matter.

"What happened to us?"

"Oi, wot's goin' on 'ere?" Mudge gestured with his weapon, which in no wise seemed to intimidate their host.

The creature's voice emerged from a box hanging below its mouth. It preened its antennae with one hand while gesturing descriptively with the other three.

"I thought that I had finally managed to appropriately engage your physical presence. Indeed, in that I was successful. Unfortunately, I was unable to adjust to the condition of your motion. In fact, I barely had time to swap the field. By which time I did, you were both already impacted. I can tell you, we were most fortunate to survive."

"I can believe that," Jon-Tom declared. "I thought for sure we were people paste. Mudge, put up your sword. This . . . person . . . doesn't mean us any harm."

"I certainly don't." The insectoid spoke with feeling. "You might as well know that while the circumstances of identified retrieval were imperfect, the final result was satisfactory."

Jon-Tom blinked. "Retrieval?"

"Naturally. You don't think I've gone through all this trouble simply to talk to *you*? This time my memory held and I remembered what it was I was after in the first place. This has required a far greater effort than I originally allowed for, but I believe it has been worth it." He gestured to his left.

Confined within some kind of flickering force field was the

chord cloud. It hummed softly to itself, seeming not to mind
that its movements were constrained.

"You mean all this time that's wot you were after?" Mudge
was dubious. "That bit o' wanderin' music?"

"That's right." The creature nodded in a most humanlike
manner. "As our previous encounters have been all too brief
and my memory subject to selective transposition-imposed
blackouts, I have not had the opportunity to explain myself.
That will be rectified.

"First you should know that our more recent and altogether
too hurried meeting has resulted in your being transposed
from your world into mine. This is not a consequence of pre-
determined intent. When I planned our most recent confrontation I did not expect to find you hurtling toward me at a
dangerous rate of speed. Circumstances compelled me to act
with haste instead of forethought. Was I correct in assuming .
that you had little control over your velocity?"

"Not exactly," replied Mudge. "See, we didn't 'ave little
control. We 'ad no control wotsoever." Studying the strange
environment, he found himself speculating on the function of
various objects and devices. Also on their possible monetary
value back home.

"You're some kind of sorcerer?" Jon-Tom inquired uncertainly.

Cazpowarex tapped his translator, as if to reassure himself
that it was functioning properly. "In a manner of speaking. I
am a dimensional physicist." This time he smelled, Jon-Tom
reflected, like frangipani.

"I am also," their pleasantly aromatic host continued, "a
performing artist and musician."

"Now that's an unusual professional pairing," Jon-Tom
commented.

"In my world as well. By the way, though I am unfamiliar
with your instrument, I've observed that you play quite well."
Jon-Tom swelled with pride. "As for your singing, however, I
have to say that—"

"Don't *you* start. I have enough trouble dealing with his

comments." The spellsinger jerked a thumb in Mudge's direction.

"It would seem that your playing invokes physical properties that transcend ordinary physics. Some might think of it as magic."

"You should talk to my mentor, Clothahump. You two are sort of in the same business. How long have you been jumping between worlds, or dimensions, or whatever it is you've been doing?"

"You have been privy to my initial attempts. The instrumentation, not to mention the driving theorems, are still under development. I thought to keep things simple by searching first for something vital which had gone missing." He indicated the drifting, caged chords.

Suddenly conscious of how tired he was, Jon-Tom looked for something that might serve as a chair. Finding nothing, he remained standing.

"Seems like you've gone to an awful lot of trouble to run down a few missing bars."

"Ah, but they are critically important." Moving to a cabinet, he waved the doors aside and withdrew a device that looked enough like a gun to make Jon-Tom start. Picking up on his companion's reaction, Mudge moved closer to his friend.

"Wot is it, mate, wot's wrong? And where are we? In one of the nearer hells?"

"That's not a very nice thing to say," Caz commented. Jon-Tom stiffened slightly as their host turned to face them. "Would I go into your home and say something like that?"

"You haven't seen his home." Jon-Tom kept a wary eye on the metallic blue device in the insectoid's hand.

Placing it on a small circular table, the physicist touched something on the side. Instantly the room was filled with music. It was all around them, as if the walls themselves were functioning as speakers. Which for all Jon-Tom knew, they were.

There was visual accompaniment as well, in the form of an

oscillating mist that changed shape and color in accordance with subtle shifts in tempo and volume. Though utterly alien to Jon-Tom's ears, the waveforms were not unpleasant. A sweet, soaring melody served as the foundation for a succession of unique percussive effects. It was simultaneously uplifting and unsettling, the latter doubtless because he did not possess the cultural referents which would enable him to fully understand the music.

Having covered his ears when the first notes sounded, Mudge now relaxed and listened. While he didn't comprehend, neither was he repulsed. More musically sophisticated, Jon-Tom did a little better.

"It's very beautiful . . . I think." The notes still lingered in Jon-Tom's mind and the colors on his retinas well after Cazpowarex had shut them down. "I've never heard anything like it."

"Your reaction is understandable. It accords with that of your fellows."

Jon-Tom gaped at him. "There are humans here?"

"Oh, very definitely. I'm afraid you won't have the chance to meet any. Your presence here is an anomaly which must be redressed, and soon, or there will be consequences the seriousness of which I cannot predict."

"Right, then; suits me, guv," announced Mudge. "Ship us back."

"I hope to do just that, bearing in mind the capricious nature of my equipment."

"I still don't understand." Jon-Tom wanted to return, but not without some sort of explanation. "All this for a cluster of chords?"

The physicist tilted his head to one side, the physical equivalent of a human raising his eyebrows. "Those chords are needed to complete the final and greatest composition of the immortal J'Ameltanek, the foremost composer of visual music of my generation. No one quite understands how they happened to go missing, but music is a law unto itself. Out of my own respect and admiration for J'Ameltanek's work I decided to try and track it down. Imagine my surprise when I discovered that it had slipped through a most recent interdimensional rip."

"Not slipped. It was abducted, stolen." Jon-Tom looked at Mudge. "Remember? Hinckel spoke of taking music from other worlds. Our little cloud must have been his first bite out of this one. But he couldn't constrain it the way he has all the rest. At the same time, it couldn't find its own way back here. So it went looking for help."

Caz's gaze shifted from otter to human. "Now it is my turn to not understand."

"It's something we have to take care of," Jon-Tom told him. "When we get back. Or there'll be more incidents like this one. Not only in your world but in mine, and in every other one, assuming there are others, where music is listened to and loved." He indicated the softly ringing chord cloud.

"So it did not flee but was taken. Interesting. If what you say is true, and I have no reason to think it otherwise, this individual must be stopped." The physicist shook his head. "No species has a monopoly on evil." Four hands and sixteen digits spread wide. "How can I help?"

"I tried to fight him," Jon-Tom explained. "I'm pretty sure I could defeat him one on one, but he's called up and has some serious help on his side. Since I don't know how to do likewise, I need something to strengthen my own powers."

The insectoid considered. "Might I suggest voice lessons?"

Fate was a never-ceasing wonder, Jon-Tom decided. Of all the aliens in the universe to interact with, naturally he would end up facing a music critic.

"We don't have time for that," he replied testily.

"Yes, yes, of course you're right. Then we must think of something else. Meanwhile, you must go back." Cazpowarex indicated the bank of instruments. "Your presence is generating wave distortions which are rapidly approaching the explosive. Already, prudent chronological parameters have been exceeded. I wouldn't want you to come apart all over my floor."

"Oh, now, that sounds pleasant, that do." Mudge took up a stance in the middle of the room. "Let's get goin', then."

"Excellent idea." Moving to stand close to the otter, Cazpowarex gestured for Jon-Tom to join them.

"Stand close to me, please. Put your arms around my thorax. Mind the breathing spicules."

Jon-Tom found the chitonous exoskeleton smooth and warm under his touch. As the physicist fine-tuned controls, there was a repeat of the stomach-churning disorientation they had experienced earlier. This was accompanied by a brief moment of quasi-unconsciousness.

Then they were back, hovering just above the rocky beach. Mudge dealt with the transposition effortlessly. To his chagrin, Jon-Tom stumbled and collapsed on the narrow strip of sand.

"I'll provide whatever assistance proves feasible." Caz waved from within the supportive vapor. "Assuming anything does, of course." There was an actinic flash of light and a muffled *phut* like the sound of an imploding soap bubble. The mist and its impacted passenger promptly vanished.

Mudge gave his friend a hand up. "Wonder if 'e'll keep 'is promise."

"He's a true music lover." Jon-Tom brushed black sand from his legs. "He may not find a way to help, but I think he'll damn sure try."

Of the rainbow bridge there was no sign. It had evaporated the instant the one who had called it forth had vanished from this world. Voices hailed them and they returned the cries as best they were able.

Then the princesses and soldiers were clustered close, all talking and questioning at once.

"Easy, one at a time." Jon-Tom made quieting motions with both hands. "We were transported to another world, another dimension."

" 'Orrible place it were," Mudge added. "Fraught with unimaginable dangers every step o' the way! Fortunately I—"

"Another, uh, magician carried us through and sent us

back." Jon-Tom threw a piercing glance in the otter's direction. "It was the strange hard-bodied creature whom we've encountered several times before. He was trying to recover the music Mudge and I have been following." To his surprise, Jon-Tom found that he missed the softly luminescent chord cloud. Its familiar chiming had been good company on their long journey. Now it was only a memory.

One which he would carry with him as he strove to find a way to stop the megalomaniacal musician atop the mountain.

"Before he sent us back, he promised to try and help." He pointed to the dark clouds which hugged the topmost crags. "All the stolen music we've been hearing about is up there, and more is being wrenched from its proper place even as we stand here talking. There's a musician from my world up there whose capacity for evil far exceeds his talent. Mudge and I tried to stop him but had to retreat."

"The rainbow bridge," remarked Seshenshe.

"Yes."

"We thought you weren't coming back." The look in Ansibette's eyes hinted that this would have more than merely disappointed her.

Otters being rather more demonstrative, Pivver flung her arms around Mudge and planted a whiskery smack square on his lips. The startled otter stumbled. For one of the few times since he'd made Mudge's acquaintance, Jon-Tom saw his friend at a loss for words.

"I'm glad you're back." Lieutenant Naike shook Jon-Tom's hand, then nodded toward the mountain. "Whatever's up there is in a foul mood."

As if to emphasize his observation, an aural avalanche of thunder louder than any they'd yet heard came rattling down the mountain. Black lightning scored blue sky.

Using her long tongue instead of a hand, Quiquell pointed. "look! something's coming off the mountain!"

Figures were descending from the belly of the blackest cloud, as if the storm itself were giving birth. At this distance their outlines were still unclear, but Jon-Tom and Mudge didn't

need to be any nearer to know what they were. Having failed
to finish off the intruders atop his peak, Hieronymus Hinckel
was coming down after them.

As the winged shapes drew closer Jon-Tom recognized one
specter after another, from the would-be Elvis to the dissolute
southern belle rapper. They played and sang as they descended, their frightful music preceding them.

"What is that horrible noise?" Ansibette's pretty face was
screwed up in a rictus of distress.

For what he knew might be the last time, Jon-Tom readied
the duar. Knowing the nature of their opponent, this time he
would be better prepared. However, nothing had happened to
change the fact that he was still badly outnumbered.

The princesses had to be protected. Firmly putting the odds
out of his mind, he took up a stance between the ladies and
the mountain, instrument at the ready. He knew he was going
to have to sing like he'd never sung before in his life.

As the onrushing mass began to resolve itself into individual figures, gasps of dismay arose from the soldiers and the
princesses clustered behind them. Naike ordered his troops to
form a line behind Jon-Tom. Their halberds and courage
would be of little use against the opponent they were about to
confront, but Jon-Tom was grateful for the expression of support nonetheless.

Maybe Hinckel's powers would be reduced away from the
comfortable surroundings of his fortress, Jon-Tom rational-
ized. Maybe.

A familiar voice chirped stridently at his side. "So where's
your bleedin' sympathetic bug? I didn't think he'd be o' no
use."

"Don't go too hard on him. We've only been back a few
minutes. It's not like he's had a lot of time to analyze the situation. Besides, speed isn't a scientist's forte."

"We could use some kind of forte," the otter complained.
Despite his pessimism he held his ground, carefully notching
an arrow to his bowstring.

The chanting of Hinckel's minions started a pounding at the back of Jon-Tom's skull. If he had to listen to much more of that atrocious playing and indescribably bad singing, he was afraid the throb could develop into a migraine. He'd never tried to spellsing with a migraine and didn't know if he could.

Mudge raised his bow. "Maybe I can pick a couple of 'em off."

"Sure, if they can be affected by anything so pedestrian and mortal as a mere arrow."

The otter looked up at his companion and sniffed. "That's right, mate, go on an' encourage me."

Jon-Tom would have responded, but a wave of pseudo-rock caused him to wince in pain. A chorus of moans rose from behind him as the princesses were similarly affected. So profoundly repulsive was the music that it carried a physical punch.

Like everyone else, Jon-Tom found himself forced back toward the lagoon. Several of the princesses were soon standing ankle-deep in the tepid seawater. Beyond the reef he could hear sundry cetaceans bellowing in distress. He knew he had to do something soon: They were running out of space as well as time.

As the music momentarily subsided, a threadbare, winged drunk dressed like Liberace and a heavyset batwinged ex-headhunter from Irian Jaya who had a xylophone fashioned from human skulls hanging around his neck reverently deposited Hinckel atop the sand-and-gravel berm that marked the high-tide line. Guitar against his chest, thrashed harmonica dangling from one hand, he glared down at them like a rejected extra from the world's chintziest heavy metal video.

"You like music? I'll give you music! You'll learn to admire it, even to cherish it." His gaze rose skyward. "Everyone will listen to me! Or suffer the consequences."

"Wouldn't that be one and the same?" Jon-Tom remarked evenly.

"You have no choice." Putting the harmonica to his lips,

the deranged musician blew a single note so off-key it could have stuck honey to Teflon.

Backed by his horde of failures, he began one more time to play and sing.

Screams arose from the huddled princesses, and even the resolutely stoic Naike let out a moan. Jon-Tom struggled to come up with a suitable rejoinder, but the sheer volume and energy of the grotesque chorus threatened to addle his senses.

Taking aim, Mudge loosed his arrow. It flew straight and true toward Hinckel's neck. Lost in a reverie of his own brilliance, the singer paid it no mind. Unearthly sounds emanated from his throat, sounds reminiscent of a steam train loaded with live chickens locking up its brakes at seventy miles an hour.

So severe were the conjoined vibrations that the shaft of the arrow disintegrated in midair. The metal arrowhead spun harmlessly to the ground several feet short of Hinckel's sneakers. Behind him, Jon-Tom could hear their lifeboat shaking, the nails threatening to vibrate right out of the planks. The sand on the beach was trembling, while the water in the lagoon twitched in agitation. Even the crabs were abandoning their burrows, tripping and tumbling over their own claws as they sought the relief of deep water.

A look of hopelessness crossed the otter's face. Putting up his bow, he drew his sword preparatory to making a suicidal charge in the hopes of giving Jon-Tom enough respite to gather his thoughts and come up with some kind of musical riposte.

"Jon-Tom!" Ansibette's tormented wail rose above the din. "Make it stop!"

Having nearly exhausted his capacity for invention, Jon-Tom had a song pop unbidden into his mind. Yes, that *might* work! Modify a word here, a line there . . . With a determined expression on his face and a firm grip on the duar, he began to play and to sing.

A vast, surging, opalescent fog began to form where the sea met the sand . . . *behind* him.

Startled and surprised, the soldiers and princesses hurried to scurry clear of the dilating mist. Gigantic, blocky outlines began to coalesce within the iridescent vapor. One was a monstrous gray ovoid afire with laser-bright lights. It was flanked by two towering dark slabs that reached toward the sun. Each of the rectangular monoliths was matte black and featureless. As the mist began to evaporate and the sun struck them more forcefully, they acquired an onyxlike sheen, seeming to absorb the light as much as reflect it. So massive were they that they blocked out the cries of the despairing whales.

There was no way Hinckel could ignore them. He gawked at the mammoth apparitions but continued to sing and play, as did his revolting choir.

Temporarily forgotten, Mudge's sword hung at his side as he stared at the stupendous tripartite formation. "Bloody 'ell, mate, wot's all this?"

Pausing in his playing, Jon-Tom, too, had turned to gape at the gargantuan materialization. His long hair rippled in the ill wind generated by Hinckel and his minions. "I . . . I don't know." There was something so familiar about the arrangement . . .

A broad grin spread over his face. "I know. This is our friend's work."

"Thought you said bloomin' scientists, wherever they may be, need lots o' time to do their work."

"They do, but our friend's also a musician, and they tend to react instinctively. That's what he's done."

The otter eyed the monolithic structures. "Looks like parts o' some bleedin' alien temple, it do."

"You're not far wrong, Mudge, you're not far wrong."

"I don't see 'ow this can 'elp us, unless one o' the pieces falls on that Hinckel bloke."

"Just watch, and listen."

Stumbling through the black sand, Jon-Tom hurried past the baffled soldiers and princesses. It took only a moment to find what he was looking for. The cable was as thick around as his arm and ended in a flat, featureless terminus unlike anything he'd ever seen. But its purpose was clear enough.

"Everybody get down," he shouted, "and hold on!" Uncomprehending but responsive, his companions dropped to the sand.

Clutching the duar tightly with his right hand, he grabbed the cable with the other and jammed the terminus into the sensitive nexus where the instrument's strings intersected. Light exploded from the body of the instrument in a succession of concussive waves, while a golden nimbus expanded to engulf the immense ovoid. Though the cable writhed like a menopausal python, he held on to the duar. He wished he had some cotton for his ears, but there was no time for that now.

He'd always wondered what his music would sound like properly amped and played back through a decent pair of speakers.

CHAPTER 25

SUBTILELY MODIFIED BY JON-TOM TO RELATE TO THEIR PRESent perilous situation, the first stupendous blast of Alice Cooper's "HEY STUPID!" erupted from the monoliths. It blew a stunned Hinckel completely off his feet and sent him tumbling head over heels backward until his flight was arrested by a large, scraggly bush.

Frantically flailing their wings, his tone-deaf minions struggled to maintain their bearings. They didn't have a chance against subwoofers the size of a city bus. The overamped spellsong blew them away like leaves, overwhelming both their music and their atrophied muscles.

Somehow they held their positions. Flapping like a parody of a flock of harassed hummingbirds, they recovered, advancing to free their master from his prickly prison. Fear of failure had driven these spirits throughout eternity, and it constituted a powerful motivating force. They resumed their singing but were unable to make any headway against Jon-Tom's playing.

The result was a musical standoff of near cosmic proportions. No matter how virtuostically he played, Jon-Tom couldn't drive them off. The power of his spellsinging and that of the alien amp was matched by the sheer determination of the greatest failures in the history of music. The battle soon degenerated into a contest to see whose hands and lungs would give out first.

Hinckel took heart from his recovery and resumed his singing and playing with a will. Like many rockers, he held more strength and energy in his skinny frame than at first glance appeared likely.

There had to be a way to break the stalemate, Jon-Tom reasoned even as he sang on. Something more was needed, something else. A supplemental force not even Hinckel could counter.

A chorus of whales might have done it, but Hinckel had control of their songs, and besides, there was no way they could get close enough to shore to help. The princesses hugged the sand, too benumbed to offer assistance of any kind. If only Buncan, Nocter, and Squill had been there, he knew, thinking of the kids. They were spellsingers in their own right. But they were hundreds of leagues away. Musically, he was all alone.

That left one individual he felt he could depend on but whose musical abilities were somewhat in doubt.

Though he kept on playing, he took a break from vocalizing. "Mudge!"

From his position prone on the sand the otter twisted to look up at him. "Wot is it, mate? You're doin' great!"

"We need to do better! Mudge, I've never asked you this before even though you have two musically talented cubs. Can you play an instrument?"

"Crikey, me?" The otter blinked. His fur rippled from the force of his friend's playing, as if a strong gale were blowing across him. "I've kind o' left the playin' to me kids, mate."

"Anything!" Jon-Tom's voice barely rose above the cosmic cacophony. "Any instrument at all!"

"Well, I don't go about braggin' on it." The otter considered. "Too much else to brag about. But I always did like muckin' around with a set o' drums if one 'appened to be 'andy."

Percussive counterpoint would be just the thing, Jon-Tom decided excitedly. Unfortunately, the requisite instrument was not available, and there was no way to put such a request through to their extradimensional friend.

Which, as usual, left it up to Jon-Tom.

"A simple, straightforward rhythm," he told the otter. "Something to underlie the duar line and back me up!"

Resuming his song, he invented some hasty lyrics to fit the Coopertuned melody. Compared to some of the things he'd tried to spellsing up in the past, this seemed a comparatively simple conjuration. Though with his spellsinging, one never knew.

A purple haze tinged with blue boiled from the duar. Unexpectedly, it continued to expand and grow. Puzzled and concerned, Jon-Tom didn't know what else to do except finish the spellsong.

Higher and wider ballooned the haze. He was about to give up when it began to dissipate, revealing that in spite of his doubts he'd been successful.

Maybe a little too successful.

There was only one drum, a blue chrome-bottomed timpani, but it tended to make up in size for what it lacked in numbers, being only slightly smaller than their boat. Rising to his feet, Mudge braced himself against the thunderous musical storm that continued to blast from the monoliths.

"Now that," he exclaimed, eyes shining, "is wot I calls a *drum*!"

Clambering up the sides with unmatched otterish agility, Mudge soon found himself standing atop the taut, dance-floor-sized membrane. Removing quiver and bow, vest and pants, boots and jerkin, he stripped down to his bare fur. When Jon-Tom flashed him the go-ahead, the otter took a deep breath and began to dance. Wildly, maniacally, with the kind of energy that among all creatures only an otter could muster. It was an expression of sheer unrestrained joy and otter unadulterated delight, a 9.5 on the musical Richter scale.

It also had rhythm.

It made the difference, it carried the moment.

With the otter stepping out a berserk backbeat on the brobdignagian drum and the twin ziggurat speakers blasting Jon-Tom's inspired modifications of Cooper's classic lyrics, Hieronymus Hinckel, his morbid minions, and their ghastly concatenation were blown to bits. Feathers were blown off wings, worn leathery membranes shredded, instruments ripped apart.

Hinckel railed mercilessly at them as he clung to the ground, his fingers digging desperately into the sandy soil. There was little to differentiate his screeching from his singing, Jon-Tom decided. His demolished guitar ended up high in a tree, a clump of stringy rubble. Smashed like a tin shingle, the flattened harmonica caught a gusting chord and disappeared southward, a rectangular Frisbee caught up in the tintinabulatory tide.

The soldiers and princesses hung on as the music roared over them, shaking the very foundations of the island. It was not unlike, Jon-Tom reflected, a couple of concerts he'd attended. No wonder he was having such a good time.

"Enough, please!" The thin, reedy voice was barely audible above the reverb. Utterly exhausted, his clothes hanging in shreds, Hinckel somehow clung to a bent-over sapling. His gaunt body was stretched out parallel to the ground, fluttering in the speaker-wind like a thin, fleshy pennant as the music threatened to sweep him away.

Jon-Tom let his fingers fall from the duar's strings, stilling the thunder. Black cable trailing behind, he ascended the slight slope of the beach until he was staring down at the gasping, pummeled musician. Hinckel lay on his side, his scrawny chest rising and falling like a bellows.

"You promise? No more trouble, no more stealing of other people's music?" Hinckel nodded vigorously, despondently.

"Good." Cutting loose with a final warning riff that balled his whining antagonist into a fetal position, Jon-Tom shifted the duar to a position of rest. For the first time ever, it was actually hot to the touch.

But then it had never made use of anywhere near this degree of amplification.

Gently he tugged on the end of the cable. The flat terminus pulled free of the duar, its tip singed and blackened. A few wisps of smoke curled skyward.

All was not silence. Climbing to their feet, the princesses

chattered as they struggled to adjust their raiment. They joined
the soldiers and Jon-Tom in gathering around the base of the
colossal drum.

Tilting back his head, Jon-Tom cupped his hands to his
mouth. "That's enough, Mudge!"

"Wot's that you say, mate?" As the otter leaned over the
side, it seemed to Jon-Tom that a few curls of smoke rose from
the tips of his whiskers as well.

"I said, you can stop now!" the spellsinger screamed at the
top of his lungs.

The otter tapped the top of his head. "Can't 'ear a thing
you're sayin', mate. Got to learn to use your voice."

Clearing his throat, Jon-Tom drew a finger across it.

"Oi, 'tis like that, is it? Righty-ho." Vanishing beyond the
rim of the instrument for several moments, the otter soon reappeared fully dressed and shinnied down the side to rejoin them.

At the bottom he exchanged a congratulatory hug first with
his friend, then with the soldiers, and finally with the princesses, lingering in the grasp of several of the latter until they finally had to push him away.

"Been witness to plenty o' your spellsingin', mate, but this
be the first time I've ever 'elped you in it. Bugger me for a
goosed gopher if it weren't fun!"

"It often is." Jon-Tom was smiling broadly.

" 'Ave to speak up, mate. I can barely 'ear you. 'Tis fun, all
right, except on those all too frequent occasions when your
magic-makin' is more than a bit off." Gaze narrowing, he tried
to look behind his friend.

"Speaking o' folks wot are a bit off, where's that putrid
excuse for a warm-blooded biped?"

Jon-Tom gestured over his shoulder. "Back there, trying to
catch his breath."

They found Hinckel where Jon-Tom had left him, somewhat
recovered from the pounding he'd taken but still in no condition to offer so much as a modicum of resistance, even had he
been so inclined. Rolling over, the erstwhile master of all
music found himself staring up at an assortment of unensor-

celed but nonetheless very efficient metal blades wielded by
Mudge and the quartet of soldiers.

Pauko looked over at his friend Heke. "Why not just cut his
throat and be done with it?"

"Quick solution for a small problem." Karaukul thrust the
point of his halberd closer to Hinckel's neck.

"No, please! Don't kill me." Their former nemesis scrambled to his knees. "I just wanted people to appreciate my music,
that's all." He turned forlornly to Jon-Tom. "You're a musician; you understand."

"I understand music," the spellsinger replied quietly. "I
understand wanting to be famous and respected." He shook his
head slowly. "Swiping everyone else's music so they'd have to
listen to you I don't understand." He waxed philosophical.

"Every artist has to be able to handle criticism." A small
smile escaped his face as he caught Mudge watching. "I've had
to cope with it most of my life. For example, I'm told that my
own singing leaves something to be desired. It took a long time
and a lot of practice for me to improve it to where it is today."

"Which ain't very far," the otter added under his breath.

"I'll practice, I'll work at it." Hinckel was frantic. "I'll get
better on my own."

"What's all this talk?" Pauko jabbed with his halberd. "Kill
him."

"Or at least send him back. To his world, wot was once
yours." Mudge's voice dripped contempt. "Some'ow I don't
see 'im as bein' much o' a threat there."

Jon-Tom was uncertain. "Transposing people back and forth
between our worlds never struck me as a good idea, Mudge. I
don't want people commuting between the two. Folks from
hereabouts wouldn't understand my world, and those from
there would spoil it here."

"I don't want to go back." Hinckel was pleading.
"People . . . people laughed at me."

"They 'ave some taste, then," observed Mudge.

Hinckel sat back on his heels. "I kind of like it here."

"Easy to say when you have power." Umagi looked ready to

wring the human's neck the instant Jon-Tom gave the word. "But can you live among others as an ordinary commoner?"

"One who'll take legitimate criticism?" Jon-Tom added.

"I'll try anything. I didn't mean to hurt anybody. I just wanted . . ." he hesitated, choking up, "I just wanted an *audience*."

Heke and Karaukul looked at each other and pinched their nostrils.

"Hey, I can get better!" Hinckel climbed to his feet. "Anyone can get better." He gazed imploringly at Jon-Tom. "I'll do anything you ask." The skinny figure had been transformed from threatening to pathetic.

"All right," Jon-Tom told him evenly. "But before we part, I'm going to lay one heavy delayed-action spellsong on you. If you break your promise—"

"I won't, no way!"

"Well then, maybe we can—"

It was at that point that the three remaining active members of Pancreatic Sludge appeared, quickly appraised the situation, and fell on the hapless Hinckel with kicks and blows. Fortunately they were too tired and enfeebled to do any real damage before Jon-Tom and the soldiers could pull them off the whimpering singer.

"Hang him up by his heels!" Gathers bawled. "I'll stuff that harmonica up his—"

Jon-Tom stepped between the terrified Hinckel and his former band mates. "That's enough. You're coming with us. All four of you."

Mudge's jaw dropped. "With us? Oi, mate, wot's got into you?"

"There's room on the boat," Jon-Tom insisted.

The otter sighed heavily. "Jinny-tob, there ain't been 'room' on that bum-boat since the third princess climbed aboard. But if that's wot you want, I'd just like to bloody well know *why*."

"We can't leave them here. This island won't support them."

"You can say that again." Zimmerman patted his empty stomach meaningfully.

Jon-Tom continued. "And while I'm *sure* Mr. Hinckel here

wouldn't *think* of reneging on his promises, I'd feel better if I knew he was being watched over by some responsible authority."

"Thank you, thank you!" Nervously eyeing his former associates, Hinckel hung close to Jon-Tom. "What do you want me to do?"

"For a start, I'd recommend voice training." His attention shifted to the waiting, watching princesses. "Perhaps at some unusually tolerant royal court. I'd think twenty years or so might do it."

"Twenty years!" Hinckel blanched.

"It worked for me. Maybe by then you'll have learned how to carry a tune."

The younger man nodded reluctantly, then began searching the ground. "My harmonica. My guitar."

"Gone, finished. I'm sure suitable substitutes can be found. Personally, I'd rather see you on a lute. Not many inimical properties in a lute."

"All right." The battered musician seemed to straighten a little. "You'll see. One day . . . one day I'll be as good as you." He indicated the duar. "How do you make that kind of magic, anyway?"

Jon-Tom shrugged modestly. "Damned if I know. All I'm certain of is that the magic's in the music."

"That's good enough for me. I'll get better, I will. You'll see. Someday I'll be the best!"

"Oh yes, that's real determination! I just know it!"

A voluptuous form rushed forward to throw her arms around the startled but hardly displeased Hinckel. "*I'll* help you," Ansibette cooed, "you poor, put-upon, deprived excuse for a wandering bard. I can imagine what it's been like for you, to be denigrated in first one and now two worlds. It's not fair!"

Stunned beyond the power to respond, Jon-Tom for just an instant felt a pang of regret. Then he remembered Talea, and Buncan, and home, and was calm.

Calm, but not entirely at peace.

Mudge nudged him. "Well now, mate, explain this one to

me, if you will. Is there some mysterious form o' sorcery still at work in our midst, or wot?"

Jon-Tom looked on as Ansibette repeatedly and enthusiastically kissed and reassured the still startled but rapidly recovering Hinckel.

"Not sorcery, Mudge. The taste displayed by human females can be inexplicably perverse."

"Oi, is that all it is? Why didn't you know, mate, that the taste o' all female types is perverse? 'Tis a well-known law o' nature, it 'tis."

"I'm familiar with the corollary. The most beautiful women always gravitate to the ugliest males. There seems to be something especially alluring about emaciated, tone-deaf musicians. I think it must be one of nature's ways of limiting population growth. Hopefully one of these days it'll breed out of the species."

" 'Ere now, mate, don't act the gibberin' walrus. Maybe she's a princess an' all that rot, wot, but I don't think she 'olds a candle to Talea. Or a leg." The otter considered thoughtfully. "Other parts, now . . ."

"You're right; she doesn't," Jon-Tom declared conclusively. And he was only lying a little bit.

Her fingers locked behind his thin neck, Princess Ansibette of Borobos was beaming as she stared into Hinckel's watery eyes. "I'll see that you get the best of help. We have wonderful music teachers at court." Taking his arm in hers, she guided him gently toward the lifeboat.

Wolf Gathers's expression showed that he'd seen it all before. "That's fine for that son of a bitch, but what are we supposed to do?"

Seshenshe stepped forward and ran a thoughtful, clawed finger up and down the center of the guitarist's chest. "There'ss not a court that can't do without another mussician or two. *If* they really can play."

"Sure we can play," he shot back. "We just need a new lead singer."

"Then if you've no objection to accompanying ssome fancy

caterwauling, perhapss I can find usse for you." Opening her mouth, she demonstrated one of the sweetest, purest sopranos Jon-Tom had ever heard. At least, it was sweet and pure until it broke into a succession of growls and yowls. Raw and untutored, grating and harsh, it sounded like a dozen alley cats in heat.

"Hey, that's not bad!" An admiring Zimmerman was already humming the backbeat to the refrain. "Sounds a lot like Pearl Jam."

"Or the Chili Peppers," Hill suggested.

Gathers was nodding agreeably. "We can work with that, dudes. Does this gig, like, you know, pay?"

"Room and board," Seshenshe replied, "but on a royal sscale. Ass dessignated court mussicianss you will be well looked after."

The trio exchanged looks. Then Zimmerman spoke for all of them. "It's the best offer we've had in a while. Got to be better than playing clubs in Passaic."

Hill gave a little shudder. "Anything'd be better than that."

Bearing in mind that he was addressing a princess, Gathers inquired hesitantly, "Would there be any, like, drink to go along with the food?"

Seshenshe smiled toothily. "The finesst sspiritss my country can produce sshall be yourss to ssample. My people have a long tradition of brewing and vintnering."

"Well, all right, then!" Hill looked content. "Sounds okay to me, dudes."

"One last thing." Gathers started to say something more, looked helplessly to Jon-Tom. "Would this royal court be maybe, like, you know . . . integrated?"

Jon-Tom smiled reassuringly. "You'll find that all the warm-blooded species mix pretty freely here. I'm sure you'll encounter other humans in Paressi Glissar."

"That's the way o' things." Mudge winked. "O' course, 'tis your choice if you choose to restrict yourselves to—" Jon-Tom clamped a hand over the otter's muzzle.

"Let's let the boys find a few things out for themselves, why don't we? They don't need to be confused any more than they already are." Led by the soldiers, they started wading out to the waiting lifeboat.

"No Sixth Avenue Deli," Hill was muttering, "but I guess a royal court can't be all bad."

Mudge tugged at his friend's sleeve. "Oi then, mate. Wot about all that music wot's caught up in this place, don't you know?"

"I was getting to that." Standing on the shore, Jon-Tom turned back to face the central mountain, still shrouded in its surly cloak of dark cumulus. Unlimbering the duar, he began a last time to sing. This time his words needed no otherworldly amplification.

> "Can't bind the music
> Can't tie it down
> A song's got to be free
> To soar and bring light
> To every corner of the world
> Let the music fly
> Let there be such a sight
> Of sounds twisted and curled
> That the air itself takes flight!"

Oh, what a sound there came then! As the black clouds broke apart, all the music Hieronymus Hinckel had stealthily entrapped came rushing down the mountain in a great gal-lumphing glorious wave of pure sound, each individual note like a fragment of mother-of-pearl bathed in a hundred flood-lights.

It washed over them where they stood, a grand tsunami of melody and rhythm, harmony and tempo. It riffled their hair and teased their nerve endings, a concentration of sound the likes of which none of them had ever heard before or would ever hear again.

Quicker than a favorite memory, it was gone, dissipating out over the ocean, dispersing to the many lands from which it had

been filched. Tunes returning to their instruments, songs
reverting to their singers, eerie high-pitched wails reabsorbed
and relearned by a hundred pods of waiting whales. It left Jon-
Tom and his companions with a lingering feeling of great
warmth and contentment.

Then he heard a noise he hadn't experienced in quite some
time. One he'd nearly forgotten, so immersed had he been in
his family and spellsinging and assorted adventures. Very different from that offered by the cetaceans many days before, it
arose from the princesses and the soldiers, from the band members and even (albeit somewhat reluctantly) from a much-chas-
tened Hinckel.

They were applauding.

He did the only thing he could, of course. Sweeping his
grand purple cape behind him, he put one foot back, brought
his other arm around in front of his chest, and took a bow.

Maybe it wasn't MTV, he mused, but it wasn't so bad,
either.

"Wot about all that, mate?" As the soldiers helped the last of
the princesses to board, the otter pointed to the gargantuan
amplifier and speakers. The recklessly invoked timpani had
vanished with Jon-Tom's last song. Waves were already lapping at the base of the otherworldly electronics as the tide started to change.

"Cazpowarex sent them here. He'll have to deal with them.
Since I didn't magic them up, I don't see how I can send them
away. This is a deserted island. They won't be the source of
any distressing speculation."

"No, but I can see as 'ow they might make someone a mite
curious someday." Walking over to the nearest monolith, he
ran the tips of his fingers along the shiny black surface. There
was an imperceptible vibration. "Some folk might invent a leg-
end or two to explain 'em."

"Let them." Jon-Tom was eager to be gone from this place.

EPILOGUE

THEY TOOK THEIR LEAVE OF THE ISLAND. ATTENDED BY A thousand whales and porpoises, they safely brought the princesses to Aleaukauna's homeland of Harakun, which lay on the rich and prosperous eastern shore of the Farraglean Sea. From there it was nothing but that they had to individually escort each and every one of the rescued ladies to their respective kingdoms.

In Tuuro and Borobos, in Trenku and Paressi Glissar they were greeted and feted as heroes, much to Jon-Tom's embarrassment. Always ready to help out his reluctant companion, Mudge vowed to celebrate for the both of them, which he did to the fullest extent of his astonishing capacity.

In Trenku they parted company with a tearful Pivver, a parting far harder on Mudge than was Jon-Tom's farewell to Ansibette of Borobos, who by now had eyes only for the remarkably reformed Hinckel. After spending several weeks in her highly attentive company, he had quickly decided that twenty years of music lessons was a small price to pay to continue such a relationship indefinitely.

Wolf Gathers, Splitz Zimmerman, and Nuke-o Hill found themselves comfortably ensconced under Seshenshe's personal care at the court of Paressi Glissar. True to Jon-Tom's word, the court boasted in attendance numerous well-bred representatives of many other tribes, the human included.

Eventually man and otter managed, by means of boat and cart, foot and pack animal, to wend their way back to the familiar confines of the Bellwoods, whereupon they were

promptly confronted by a less-than-understanding Talea and
Weegee, who demanded in no uncertain terms to know precisely where the hell their wandering consorts had taken off
to for so long.

"I left you a note," Jon-Tom stammered hopefully.

"Yes, a note." Conscious of the fact that a furious Weegee
could be far more dangerous than any errant spellsong,
Mudge lingered in the spellsinger's shadow.

Knowing it was what she really wanted instead of some
half-baked male excuse, Jon-Tom took his wife in his arms.
"We were just out chasing a tune," he murmured before he
kissed her. She fully intended to formulate an angry reply, but
since that's difficult to do while in the midst of a kiss, she
decided to hold the thought until later.

Weegee stepped around the embracing humans. "And what
might be your excuse, nimble-fingers?"

"Well, you know 'ow it 'tis, luv. Where Jon-Tom goes, I
sort o' 'ave to follow." Drawing reassurance from her hesitation, he put an arm around her and drew her aside, lowering
his voice as he did so.

" 'Orrible it were, me luv, just 'orrible. Such perils, such
dangers as you can't imagine. Overcame 'em all, I did. In the
name o' music an' art. 'Tis a wonderment we survived."

"Survived, fishballs!" She jabbed him in the belly, drew
back her fist to punch him, and ended up smiling. "Flay me
for a holiday cloak if you haven't put on a hand's-breadth in
width. What sort of 'peril' caused that?"

"Now, don't fret, luv, I 'ave an explanation." Advancing,
he once again put his arms around her and affectionately
began to nuzzle her muzzle with his own until she started to
relent.

He did, of course. Have an explanation. Which only proved
that Jon-Tom wasn't the only one in the room who could
work magic.

AUTHOR'S NOTE

Off and on for nearly ten years, the rock band *BitterSweet* has been producing songs and music based on the Spellsinger stories.

Now that project has finally reached fruition and is available in the form of a <u>double album</u> on a single extended-length, high-quality tape, which I cannot recommend too highly, for $13.95 (<u>plus</u> $2.00 shipping and handling; overseas shipping slightly higher.) A <u>lot</u> of fine music for the money. It's not <u>quite</u> a rock opera, but it's mightily impressive. If you're a fan of the series, it's music I know that you'll enjoy.

ORDER FROM:

BITTERSWEET MUSIC
P.O. BOX 38811
GREENSBORO, NC 27438